May Day
Seekers: Book One

Josie Jaffrey

CONTENT WARNINGS

There is a full list of content warnings at the back of this book.

For my Patreon supporters, who have been reading along since the first draft of the first chapter of this book. Thank you.

By Josie Jaffrey

The Solis Invicti Series

A Bargain in Silver
The Price of Silver
Bound in Silver
The Silver Bullet

The Sovereign Trilogy

The Gilded King
The Silver Queen
The Blood Prince

The Seekers Series

Killian's Dead (short story prequel)
May Day

Short Stories

Living Underground
Cara Mia (available free to Josie's subscribers)
Bella Donna (available free to Josie's subscribers)

1

LET ME TELL you the problem with university students: they're stupid as fuck.

Even the most intelligent cohort will have a few members who are entirely devoid of common sense, or who are willing to gamble their safety in some extravagant stunt for the admiration of their peers. Only it's not admiration they get, it's ridicule, but they're too stupid to tell the difference.

Case in point: May Day.

This is one of Oxford's many strange traditions. Every year on the first of May at six in the morning, the junior boys from Magdalen College School troop over Magdalen Bridge and up Magdalen College tower to belt out their anthem of spring at the top of their little lungs. Their voices carry down to the crowds listening on the bridge below, clear as crystal in the dawn air. It's really rather beautiful.

Or at least, I can imagine it might once have been, before it got ruined.

Because the students have their own tradition, and it's stupid. Making it to May Morning has become a point of pride, but only if you do it by staying up drinking all night on the last day of April. The last ones standing congregate in time for the singing to start and then, for no reason at all, they hurl themselves off the side of the bridge to land in the river below.

Which is about two feet deep in hot weather, and filled with discarded bikes and glass bottles, not to mention the other students who've already had the same idea; mostly boys, because isn't it always?

Inevitably, they land on top of each other, and not gently. The rugby players in particular can pick up some decent speed on the twenty-foot drop. The result is cracked bones, lacerations, internal bleeding – you get the picture. The students apparently don't.

Stupid, like I said.

When I first came to Oxford, before I was recruited, May Day was a cavalcade of broken legs and ribs. It's different these days. Since the students wouldn't give up the lemming routine on their own, the police now erect ten-foot barriers along the edges of the bridge every year. Which the students still try to climb, making the drop on the other side even steeper, and the experience all the more Instagrammable. The bigger the audience, the bigger the stunt, and the bigger the risk, because followers are worth dying for, right?

My point is that students are fucking stupid. That's why I'm here, standing in the rain at five-thirty in the morning with an unruly crowd that exudes a fog of last night's alcohol. If it were up to me then I'd let Darwinism run its course, but apparently we have enough death to contend with in this city already. So says the captain. I didn't argue when she issued her orders, but it's an irregularity. We're not generally in the business of guarding the humans from themselves. We only exist to guard them from others like us.

The captain's not here this morning. She gets to stay in bed while rain drips down the back of my collar and under my leather jacket. It's the worst kind of English rain, the kind that falls in thick drops that soak you to the bone no matter how effective your coat, the kind that makes me wish I could put aside my vanity and pick up an anorak instead.

I smell like wet dog.

I'm not the only one, either. The crush is growing, steam rising from bodies like hot mist. I'm standing at the end of the bridge closest to the tower, a prime position, so I have to get my elbows out to avoid being shunted from my place at the barrier. On the other side of the road, Cameron is doing the same. Naia and Boyd are here somewhere too, just in case, but they're out of sight at the moment.

None of us is expecting the kind of trouble we get.

A few minutes after the boys start singing, the walkie buzzes in my ear and Naia's voice comes through.

'Idiots on your ten, Jack.'

I look across the road and, sure enough, there's a group of lads hoisting each other up the side of the barrier. It's smooth board, so they're taking their time about it, scrambling for handholds on a surface that offers none.

'I've got it,' Cam says, heading off to drag them down. There's too much attention on them for him to move at supernatural speed, but he makes it there quickly and, for the moment at least, disaster is averted.

But there's nothing we can do about what happens next.

While everyone's watching the lads at the fence, a body drops from somewhere near the top of the tower. The choristers don't see it, protected by the crenellations, but the screams from the bridge are enough to stop their singing. I turn my head quickly and just manage to spot the dark shadow as it finishes plummeting with abrupt finality, by which time the crowd is already shoving desperately in every direction.

The scent of Silver violence reaches my nostrils quickly in the damp air. We have maybe ten seconds to act.

'Cam,' Boyd says over the walkie, then they're gone in a gust of air. No one's paying attention to us anymore, so no one notices when Cam blinks out of sight.

Boyd doesn't need to say anything to me or Naia; we know what needs to be done. We can't disappear the body now – everyone's seen it – but we need to gather our evidence before the crowds or the police destroy it. We know how to do our jobs at Silver speed when the situation requires it.

I concentrate on the visual clues, while Naia collects samples. We move invisibly, shifting position so the spectators will only see a whirl of motion that they might mistake for the wind. With the rain coming down like it is, no one will ever know we were here.

The whole thing takes only a couple of seconds, start to finish. The police have barely started moving in our direction by the time we make our exit, Naia stowing her bag of swabs as I mentally catalogue what I've seen.

The captain will want to hear my account in detail, though something tells me our news won't entirely surprise her.

'You knew,' Boyd says.

The captain doesn't try to deny it.

'I suspected.'

'That's why you sent us to May Morning.'

She sighs and gestures us towards the small meeting table in her office, ignoring the muscle that's clenching in Boyd's jaw. He doesn't like to be out of the loop.

'I heard from London,' she says, claiming the biggest chair for her small frame. Captain Langford is a smartly-dressed woman, besuited today as usual, and she wears her short blonde bob brushed back from her face. She doesn't take any shit from us and her raised eyebrow is to be feared and respected, on pain of grunt duty.

'It was a hunch,' she goes on. 'They noticed some unusual activity.'

'What kind of unusual activity?' Boyd is practically vibrating with tension. He's an imposing man, over six-feet tall with dark skin and darker eyes. We don't ask about his past, but I'm pretty sure it's dark too.

'Why didn't you tell me?' he asks the captain. 'If we'd known what we were looking for, then maybe–'

'Sit down, Deputy,' the captain says, 'and we'll discuss it.'

He stays standing for a moment, but then the captain raises her eyebrow and he does as he's been told. We all know from experience that you don't want to mess with that eyebrow.

'They've had a couple of scab kills,' she says.

Scabs are what we call those of us who live outside the rules, those who murder humans instead of finding other ways – sanctioned ways – to get the blood they need to live. The restrictions aren't that rigorous. As long as the humans never work out we exist, everyone's happy.

'They've been confined to traditional events so far,' she goes on. 'The New Year's Day Parade, the Boat Race, the Palm Sunday Procession. The guys in London got close to catching the scab at the Boat Race, so they thought he might move on to a new city. We've been waiting see which one it would be.'

If Boyd was angry before, then now he's livid. 'And you didn't think you should warn me about this? If we'd known to expect something, then we might have had a chance of collaring him. As it was, he caught us off guard and got away.'

'It was a hunch, Deputy. Nothing more. Please try to control yourself.' Not Boyd's strong suit. 'I trust you learned something from your pursuit and your assessment of the scene. I suggest we concentrate on that.'

But the news from Boyd and Cam isn't good.

'We never got near him,' Cam says, taking over while Boyd tries to calm himself down. 'We were up the tower in a couple of seconds, but the room the dead guy was pushed from was already empty, and there was no trail to follow. The scab was moving at speed. He could have gone anywhere.'

'We had more luck at the scene, though,' Naia said. She's muscular, and the patterns of ink on her brown skin make her forearms look like coiled snakes. The resemblance is apt, because she can lash out like a cobra when she needs to. 'I managed to get all the usual swabs and pulled his driving licence. The name was David Grant, a property developer with a local outfit. It matches this.' She pulls a business card from her pocket and hands it to the captain. 'The swabs are already at the lab with Ed.'

'Good.'

'There was also a ticket in his pocket, stub removed. I left it there for the police. It was for a performance at the Playhouse last night, an opera.'

'That would explain why he was wearing a suit,' I say. 'Though I didn't think people bothered dressing up for the opera these days.'

'Nevertheless, he made it to the performance,' says the captain. 'We can assume that much. Now we just have to work out what happened between him arriving there last night and ending up on the pavement this morning. Do we have any further information, Deputy?'

'Jacqueline?' Boyd says to me. He's the only one who uses my full name, and he only does it because he knows how much it annoys me. He's that kind of dick.

I push away my irritation and recall the scene. It blazes to life in my mind, fully-formed and vital, almost as though I'm once again standing in the dawn rain.

This is why they made me a Seeker.

Well, sort of. I'd like to think they recruited me because I'm clever and observant, but the truth is that I got turned Silver – vampire, if you prefer – due to a colossal fuck-up. The Seekers took responsibility for me after that, but the captain didn't do it out of the goodness of her heart. It was the Seekers' fault that I got turned in the first place, so they owed me. That's what I argued, anyway. It bought me some time, during which they noticed I had a pretty decent memory, verging on photographic. That gave the captain an excuse to keep me on indefinitely, but in truth I think she did it just to stop me nagging her.

Score one for sheer bloodymindedness.

Anyway, that was twenty years ago. Back to this morning.

'It was after dawn, but the clouds were dark, so it felt earlier,' I say. 'It was tipping it down. The crowds were tight, but there was a clear space around the body where people had stepped away. I didn't see anyone suspicious.'

'And the body?' Boyd asks.

I close my eyes and let the images pour in.

'He's sprawled on his back, too far away from the tower's base to have dropped from the window. Either he jumped, or he was thrown. His suit is expensive, but it fits him badly. He's dark-haired and Caucasian. Looks about fifty, fifty-five, with lines around his eyes and mouth. Gold wedding ring. He has no coat or umbrella, so I doubt he planned to be outside.'

'Any bites?' says Boyd.

'Not that I can see. There's a puncture on the back of his right hand, surrounded by a dark bruise. Could be a needle mark. His skin is sticky there, like something's been taped to him, and beads of rain are forming on it. Bits of red lint have stuck to the stickiness.' I open my eyes. 'That's it.'

The captain turns to Naia. 'You got swabs from the puncture?'

'Yes, plus a sample of the lint.'

'And we can assume that the fall wasn't suicide?'

'Yes,' Boyd says. 'We scented Silver violence, and it was fresh.'

We're all attuned to the scent, because it's the basis of our investigations. It's a Silver thing. Whenever a Silver touches someone with violent intent – for example, by pushing them out of a window – they leave a scent mark. It's harsh and sharp, and a complete contrast with the other kind of scent mark the Silver sometimes leave behind them, which is altogether more intoxicating. But David Grant's body bore no trace of the latter.

'I'll put in a call to the theatre,' the captain says. 'Follow up with the lab this afternoon, but I don't want you to make any other enquiries until I've spoken to London. In the meantime, I suggest you all get yourselves down to the canteen to fuel up and recharge. I'll be in touch.'

We leave, though not without some obvious resentment from Boyd. I know he has his eye on the captain's job, but with his attitude and her immortality, I can't imagine how he expects to get it.

Cam fetches bottles for each of us from the fridge, lolloping across the canteen like an overgrown puppy. He has dark blond hair, skin that's so tanned it looks golden, year-round, and a personality so gentle that it's impossible not to love him. He's my closest friend and a big part of why I've stayed here for the past twenty years.

The canteen is empty apart from my team. Along with a lot of academics, there are five teams of Seekers at the college, but we're the only one in residence at the moment. The others are off around the country, chasing down leads of their own. It's unusual for the place to be this quiet, which makes it feel a little eerie.

'Well,' Cam says as he hands over the bottles. 'That was a morning.'

Boyd is glaring at the tabletop.

'Uh-huh,' Naia replies. 'Bottoms up.'

She and Cam clink their bottles together.

I drink the blood straight down and try to forget the acrid bite of violence that still lingers on my tongue.

2

I SWEAR THAT Ed's laboratory is more for show than for function. He makes his work look very serious, with his plastic goggles and white lab coat, but all his bubbling flasks and crucibles are arranged so aesthetically that they make me suspicious. There's a bright blue liquid in one and red in another, while pretty drops of something green condense onto glass beads in a distillation column. His equipment looks like a film prop, but I can't deny that he knows what he's talking about.

When Cam and I walk in, he's looking at slides through a microscope.

'Just a sec,' he says without looking up.

He shifts the slides about a bit, then packs them into a tidy pile and looks up at me.

'Right,' he says. 'The body on the bridge.'

'That's right,' I say.

But Ed freezes when he sees who's with me.

'Cam,' he says.

'Hello, Ed,' Cam replies, then immediately looks away.

'Everything all right?' I say.

'Sure,' says Ed, looking back into his microscope to avoid looking at Cam.

He's clearly lying, but neither of them is willing to explain the awkwardness.

The sudden distance between them makes no sense to me. Ed and Cam go way back. They were a couple once upon a time, and from the way they've been acting around each other recently, I thought they were getting back together. I know they still fancy each other – the physical tells are pretty obvious to the Silver – but their connection goes beyond that. It's bone deep. I've seen it with other Silver, too: there's some extra level of intimacy that accrues over hundreds of years of proximity. They're not just close, they're *that* close.

But there's been a shift in the past couple of weeks. For some reason, they're suddenly cooler to each other. I don't know why things have changed. Cam hasn't told me; he's the kind of guy who likes to know everything about other people's personal lives whilst divulging nothing about his own. Regardless, I can tell he's not happy, and from the looks of things neither is Ed. It's also clear that neither of them knows how to break the tension.

It's a shame Naia's not here, because I bet she would have a few suggestions. She likes to get to the point.

'So,' I say, trying to get us back on track, 'you got the samples?'

'Yes.' Ed clears his throat and turns back to me, an action that seems to cause him physical pain. He grabs a couple of Petri dishes and forces a smile. 'Got them right here.'

'What have we got?'

'Okay, well this one,' he says, holding up a dish, 'contains the scrapings from under his fingernails. I also have swabs from his mouth. The DNA analysis on those will take a while, so in the meantime I got going on these.' He holds up a couple of bags with cotton buds in them. 'One of these is the sticky substance from the back of his hand and the other is from the puncture itself. I'm doing chemical analysis on both, as well as the blood sample Naia took, but in the meantime I have this.'

He beckons me over to his microscope and puts a slide beneath the lens, then adjusts the focus and steps back.

'This is the contents of the other dish. Take a look.'

I do, but all I can see is some red stringy stuff. It means nothing to me.

'What is this?' I ask.

'The lint from the sticky substance,' he says. 'It's some kind of synthetic red velvet. Naia said the guy had been at the theatre the night before, right? So I'm thinking this is upholstery from the seats there. If you can get me a sample then I can compare it. If this is an IV site, like I think it is, then theatre upholstery on the glue might indicate that whatever happened to this guy happened there.'

'Might?' I ask.

'Well, it could have just stuck to his clothes during the performance, then transferred onto his hand later. But there's more. Hold on a sec.' He goes into the back room – where he keeps all the beeping electronics that do the real work – and returns a few seconds later with a printout.

'Here you go,' he says, handing it over. 'I noticed a red smear on one of the swabs Naia took from his mouth, so I tested it. It's lipstick.'

'Chanel Noir Moderne,' I read from the printout. 'This stuff's thirty quid a pop.'

'Might be his wife's,' Cam murmurs.

'Maybe. But if she was at the opera with him, then why didn't he go home with her?'

'Sounds like we need to have a conversation with Mrs Grant.'

'But we can't do anything right now,' I remind him. 'The Captain's put a moratorium on this whole investigation while she clears it with London. The evening is our own. So how about it, Ed?' I say, handing him back the printout. 'Do you fancy a drink?'

He looks at Cam before giving me his answer. 'I, er, have some work to do here. Got to get on with the samples, you know. Maybe another time, though.'

'Sure,' I say.

Cam's already halfway to the door. I say a quick goodbye to Ed and follow him out.

'What was all that about?' I ask Cam as we walk back from the lab.

'Nothing.'

'Oh, come on.'

'Drop it, Jack.'

There's no arguing with Cam when he gets like this. I've tried before, but if his face is an open book, then his heart is a steel trap.

'All right,' I say. 'Then let's just go out and get pissed. Sound good?'

'We're in the middle of an investigation.'

'An investigation that's been shelved until the captain says otherwise. Plus, it's our day off tomorrow. What could possibly go wrong?'

So out drinking we go. Now that the students are sleeping off this morning's excesses, it feels safe for the adults to cut loose. After today, we need it.

The bar we frequent is attached to the same facility in which we all have our rooms: Solomon College. It's unlike any other college in Oxford. For starters, it doesn't accept undergraduates and it's never open to the public. It was founded as a seminary back in the thirteenth century, but there was a bit of an incident shortly after it opened and now its only members are Silver. A couple of them have been here since the very beginning, though you wouldn't know that to look at them.

The Seekers have been here forever, because Oxford is a hub for our kind, but our roster changes every century or so. I'm the youngest person here. Thirty-eight years isn't much in Silver terms.

'Jack!' Naia calls, waving us over as we walk down the steps into the basement bar. 'Come and join us.'

I'm reluctant because she's sitting with Boyd, which explains why she's so enthusiastic for our company, but there's no way I can refuse. The bar is full of Silver from in and around Oxford, and if we give any hint of dissent in the ranks of the Seekers then it'll only lead to trouble. He might be a dick, but Boyd is our deputy, and we owe him our respect. Such as it is.

'Be there in a sec,' I call to Naia, then I say to Cam, 'You go and soften him up. I'll get the drinks.'

Cam's just as reluctant as I am, probably because he knows that Naia's going to ditch us the minute she has someone she can pass Boyd off to, but he sighs and goes anyway.

It's gin time for me.

Here's the thing about being supernatural: you have to approach drinking with a certain amount of determination if you want to get properly plastered. It takes time and it takes dedication, but I am nothing if not dedicated to insobriety.

Let me pass on the benefit of my knowledge.

14

My first tip for getting vampires drunk is that beer and wine are basically a waste of time. My second tip is that ordering spirits by the pint will save you from having to go back and forth to the bar every five minutes. It's expensive, but we make enough money to cover it. Just about. My third and final tip – and I really can't stress this enough – is that mixing your alcohol with blood is a Very Bad Idea. A drunk vampire is a sufficiently dangerous creature already. There's no need to go reminding them that blood is ace, particularly if you happen to be human. Also, alcohol ruins the taste.

As a veteran of the art of drinking, I get an entire bottle of gin and another of rum, then take them straight to the table where the rest of the Seekers are waiting.

'So, Jacqueline,' Boyd says, 'what do you think about this case?'

The man has no idea how to have a good time.

'Oh, come on,' says Naia. 'Does it always have to be about work? I'm trying to relax.'

He looks at her as though he can't imagine that the four of us would ever talk about anything else. We rarely do when Boyd's around.

'I just think it's interesting, don't you?' He is oblivious to Naia's eye-roll. 'The spectacle of it, I mean. This guy chooses the most dramatic and public places to reveal his kills, as though he's trying to reveal us to the humans. Doesn't that strike you as odd?'

'I guess so,' says Cam, and he does seem intrigued.

Naia groans. 'Can't we just drink?'

'I hate to say it,' I say – and I do hate it – 'but the deputy has a point there. This scab is selecting the biggest events in the local calendar and dumping the bodies where they can't be missed. Did the captain give you any more details about the London kills?'

'The first one was at the New Year's Day Parade,' Boyd says. 'The body was thrown from a nearby building directly into the parade route. The entire thing ground to a halt. The Boat Race was more of the same – the scab tied the body to a line and dragged it across the river into the path of the oncoming boats. It got stuck on a Cambridge rower's blade and nearly pulled the whole crew into the water.'

'As long as Oxford won,' says Naia, topping up her glass, 'then it's all good.'

'And the third one?' asks Cam.

'The Palm Sunday Procession. The scab dropped the body from the top of St Paul's.'

'I'm sensing a theme here,' I say. 'Climb up somewhere high, throw corpse.'

Boyd holds up a finger. 'They're not corpses, though. The three in London were still breathing when they fell, or drowned in the case of the Boat Race victim. They were missing a lot of blood, but not enough to kill them. Whoever's doing this, it matters to them that the victims don't die until the moment they're revealed to the world.'

'Assuming it's all the work of the same guy,' says Cam.

'One very sick guy.'

None of us has anything to say to that, because how can you track someone who works so far outside the realms of what we consider to be normal? We see our fair share of weird shit doing this job, but usually it's just the odd Silver who loses control because they've let themselves go too long without blood, or because they've become so addicted to it that they either don't know when to stop drinking, or don't care enough to hold back. But this kind of killer, the psychopathic serial-killing kind, is not the sort we spend much time chasing. That's not to say that the Silver aren't just as twisted as humans – honestly, we're significantly more twisted on average – but we're usually better at keeping our activities hidden.

It's a sobering thought.

'Enough work,' Naia says, slamming her empty glass down on the table. 'More booze. More fun. Why don't you come and dance with me, Deputy?' She says it with a slight leer that makes Boyd's eyes widen.

'Er, thanks, but I'm going to head back,' he says, swiftly finishing his whisky. 'I'll let you know as soon as we have our orders.'

He makes a quick exit. Smart man.

'How about you?' Naia says to Cam, taking his hand in hers and tugging. 'Fancy a dance?'

Cam just laughs and shakes his head.

'We're here to drink,' I say, 'and I'm not even seeing two of you yet. Go dance if you want, but we have some serious work to do.'

If Naia's disappointed to be going alone, then she does a good job of hiding it. Within five minutes she's hitting on half the bar, as usual. Cam gets us another round of spirits, one bottle each, and we settle in.

'You look worried,' he says.

'Aren't you? This guy's different. Calculating. He can step back from the blood, so he must be fully in control, but there's a thrill in this for him. It's like he wants to tease himself with the threat of his discovery.'

'Or the discovery of all of us,' Cam says, taking a hit from his bottle.

'Exactly. He likes the danger of it. He likes the heat of the flame, you know?'

Cam smiles. 'You get poetic when you're pissed.'

'Whatever. But consider this: I can only think of one Silver who likes to play that dangerously.'

Cam stops with his glass halfway to his mouth. 'You can't be saying what I think you're saying. If you even think of accusing–'

'I'm not accusing anyone,' I say, holding up my hands. 'But you know he's controlling. Arrogant. Entitled. Has a flair for the dramatic. You have to admit that he fits the profile.'

'I'll admit that you want him to fit it. That's clear enough.'

'All I'm saying is that this investigation might take us to some impolitic places. I'm willing to follow wherever it leads. I just want you to do the same.'

'Alright,' Cam says, lifting his bottle. 'If, and I mean only if, it's warranted.'

'Deal.'

We clink our bottles together then down the contents. The next round is mine. By the time I get back from the bar, Cam's more interested in talking about the films he's watched recently than in discussing my main suspect. I let the conversation roll and I keep drinking.

I consider resurrecting the subject of Ed, but in the end I decide not to rock the boat. Cam is restful company and I'm enjoying the peace. My eyes drift towards the group of people dancing on the far side of the bar, with Naia at its centre. I'm not sure how she does it, but she seems to have endless energy for flirting. And everything that comes afterwards.

'Does she make you uncomfortable?' Cam asks, following my line of sight. Naia's only been with us for a few months and we're still getting used to her.

I shrug. 'Nope. She's sort of voracious, though. Does she make you uncomfortable?'

'Nah. She's not my type. No penis.'

It's not very funny, but I snort gin out of my nose anyway. This is representative of my current level of inebriation.

After I've wiped my face on my sleeve, I say, 'I think *you* might be *her* type. I get the impression that pretty much everyone is.'

'Great, thanks,' Cam says. 'That's just the confidence boost I needed.'

'I didn't mean it like that. You know what I meant. I mean, you're a very attractive man.' I gulp down another half-pint of gin, aware that I'm already slurring and caring not one tiny little bit. 'Seriously. You're very hot. If you were straight and I wasn't mostly gay, I would. I mean, seriously, I would. Remind me, how old were you when you got silverified? Eighteen? Nineteen? 'Cause I was eighteen. We'd make a hot couple, don't you think?'

At least, that's what I think I say, but from the way Cam's looking at me I'm not sure it all comes out in the right order.

He says, 'I think I need to take you home.'

I blink. 'I don't really want to fuck you. You know that, right?'

'Jesus Christ, how drunk are you? I'm taking you home, not to bed. Come on.'

He tries to sling one of my arms around his neck, but I'm sliding around all over the place so in the end he just gives up and throws me over his shoulder instead.

'Come on, drunky. Wave goodbye to Naia,' he says as he carries me from the bar.

'Bye Naia!' I yell.

Naia covers her eyes. Everyone else stares. Some of the wannabe Seekers look like they might be considering speaking to the captain in the morning about job opportunities. After all, everyone knows Jack's a fuck-up, right?

Bastards.

I'm willing to admit that maybe, just maybe, getting completely smashed in the middle of an investigation wasn't the best idea I've ever had. Maybe it's not exactly responsible behaviour. Maybe they're all right about me, but you know what? Fuck them.

I'm Jack Valentine and I am fucking untouchable.

3

'JACK! OPEN UP or I'm busting in.'

Someone's pounding on the door to my rooms. They've clearly been at it for a while, because my upstairs neighbour is pounding on the floor as well. As I shiver into consciousness, I realise that my alarm is blaring and my phone has vibrated itself off my bedside table and onto the carpet.

Ugh.

'Last chance!' Naia yells.

'Fuck off,' I groan back. 'I've got a hangover.'

'You can't have a hangover. You're Silver. Open this door, you lazy cow.'

I silence my alarm and turn off my phone, then pull the duvet up over my head.

'It's my day off. Go away.'

'Not anymore, it isn't. The Secundus is here.'

That wakes me up. Naia says the word gently, but it's like a bucket of water in the face. In all the years I've been working as a Seeker, I've only met the Secundus a handful of times. If he's here, then it can't mean anything good.

'He's waiting in the conference room,' she calls. 'I'd hurry up, if I were you.'

I try to sit up, but I fall off the bed sideways instead.

'Shit, shit, shit,' I mutter to myself.

Naia's footsteps are already echoing off down the corridor. She's going to get there before me, and doubtless Boyd and Cam will too, and then I'll be walking in late for a meeting with the fucking Secundus and the captain will have my fucking head.

I scramble around in the detritus on my bedroom floor, pulling on last night's jeans and a top that smells clean enough to pass. I dig through the discarded clothes in an attempt to find my hairbrush, then give it up for a lost cause and rush towards the ensuite to brush my teeth.

'Fuck!'

There's my hairbrush.

Once I've finished hopping around the room, there's just enough time to swill some mouthwash around my mouth and tie up my hair before I have to run. A last-minute mirror check reveals crud in the corners of my eyes and spit congealed on my face from where I've drooled in my sleep.

'Shitting fuck!'

I wash my face as quickly as I can, but now I'm really cutting it fine. I look in my mini-fridge, but of course I'm out of blood, so I'm not going to be moving at Silver speed this morning. Naia could have brought me a bottle. Maybe she's trying to show me up in front of the Secundus.

Boots on feet and keys in hand, I run out of my rooms and slam the door behind me. It's only now that I notice the deodorant marks on my top, but it's too late to change. A nagging little voice at the back of my head tells me that I wouldn't have this problem if I bothered to tidy up after myself, but I shut it down before it can get into full swing. I need to focus.

'Ah,' says the captain as I screech to a halt in the doorway of the conference room. 'Here she is. You remember Jack Valentine.'

The others are here already, the bastards, and Naia is smirking. I'm going to have to give them a talking-to about what it means to be a team player.

'Secundus,' I say, hoping he can't smell the booze on me, though I'm sure he can. It got messy last night and I'm fairly certain that gin is the reason my jeans are damp. Jesus, I've only been out of bed for five minutes and I'm already in trouble.

'Valentine,' he says with a curt nod.

He can definitely smell the gin, which means I'm in the shit. The Secundus is not a cuddly guy. He can't be, not with his job, just one step away from the crown.

This is how it works: the Silver live within human society, but we have our own ruler, of sorts. His name is Solomon – hence the name of the college – but we call him the Primus, because some of the Silver are so old that, believe it or not, Latin is still their language of choice. It's almost enough to make me regret choosing the Spanish language option in school.

Anyway, the Primus has his own military – his guard, if you like – called the Solis Invicti. They deal with scab murders in London, and the Seekers deal with them everywhere else in the country. The Secundus heads up the Solis Invicti, which makes him the second-most important man in the country. After that, the hierarchy gets a bit fragmented, splitting amongst the Barons who control the various territories, and the lieutenants of the Solis Invicti.

The Secundus is responsible for keeping them all in line and is ultimately responsible for the Seekers as well.

What I'm trying to say is that he's my boss's boss and I've pissed him off.

'Well,' he says, 'now that we're all finally here.'

Earth, swallow me whole.

'I'm taking over this investigation,' he says. The captain looks unhappy, but not surprised. 'I understand that you've been told about the three scab murders we've had in London,' the Secundus says to us. 'This latest one of yours seems to be the work of the same individual, so I'm bringing in my people. I'd like to introduce Thomas Meyer of the Solis Invicti and Dr Ross, from our medical team.'

We all say our hellos, exchanging backgrounds, insights and expertise.

Meyer is composed in a way that some people might find intimidating: still and self-contained, assessing everything around him with efficient skill. I bet he didn't spend last night drinking his bodyweight in gin.

But it's the doctor who draws my attention. She is gorgeous. She has a round little body and a round little face, with bright blue eyes and a pile of reddish-brown curls secured to the top of her head with a pencil. And her accent. Dear god, her accent. She's Scottish, from Glasgow, I think, and every time she opens her mouth I find myself watching her lips as though I'm hypnotised.

Which is fucking embarrassing, because the thing about the Silver is that we're perceptive. Supernatural senses means supernatural sight, supernatural hearing and, worst of all, supernatural smell. Everyone around me can hear my heartbeat ratcheting up a notch or two whenever I look at her. They can smell the heat coming off me. Everyone in this room, including the gorgeous doctor, knows exactly what I'm feeling, even if they're all too polite to say anything.

All of them except Naia, that is. She looks over at me and raises her eyebrows suggestively.

I am never going to live this down.

We sit around the conference table and wait for the Londoners to lay out the situation for us. I fix my attention on the Secundus and pray for this meeting to end quickly so I can get out of here and away from the curvy temptation of Dr Ross.

'I managed to get a quick look at the body,' she's saying. 'I know some people in the mortuary service and they're not all as stiff as you'd expect.' She smiles, her eyes twinkling. She has to be messing with us, but she doesn't try to explain away the uncomfortable silence that has descended on the group. She seems to enjoy it.

If I had to describe her in three words, those words would be: Weird. Unapologetic. Vixen.

That's when I know that I am utterly fucked.

'Completely drained?' Boyd asks.

I've lost track of the conversation.

'Not completely,' says Dr Ross. 'There was enough left in him to send for testing, but not much more. He was already dead when he hit the ground. Someone made a meal of him, I'd guess, but then there's the mark on the back of his hand.'

'We noticed that,' Naia says. 'Are you thinking he was drained that way?'

'Either that, or it was an IV. We'll have to wait for the blood tests to come back to be sure, but it seems like a good bet that the blood came out through that puncture. We didn't find any other marks on him.'

'And the London victims?' I ask the Secundus, because I can't look at the doctor. 'Were they the same?'

'No,' he says. 'They were different.' He exchanges a glance with Meyer and I know they're holding something back.

The captain raises her eyebrow at him. It turns out that even the Secundus can't deny its power. He nods to Meyer, giving him permission to spill the beans.

'They were all bitten,' Meyer says, 'but we can't take that as conclusive at this stage. There are some key similarities in all three of the London cases: the dumping of the body at a public event, the draining of the blood, and the high social status of the individual targeted. The victims are always in formal wear, always pillars of the community, always politically influential, always male and always wealthy. This latest one fits, even if the details are different. This scab is trying to cause a stir. He wants to be caught.'

'Why haven't you caught him, then?' Naia asks. It's the obvious question, but it's not one a sensible person would ask. I notice the captain's tiny wince, though I think I'm the only one.

Surprisingly, the Secundus doesn't seem offended by Naia's directness.

'It's a fair question,' he says.

'There's never any hard evidence,' says Meyer. 'He always moves in crowded places, so we struggle to get a clear enough personal scent to track it. He seems to be masking it somehow, so all we pick up is the scent of the violence, as though he's angry enough that it's all there is.'

'Is that possible?' the captain asks Dr Ross.

'Sure,' she replies. 'It's not something I've come across before – most scab killings aren't as emotional as that – but it's possible.'

'These don't sound like emotional killings,' Cam says. 'They're planned and executed meticulously. I mean, to have set up the rig for the boat race so the body would be drawn across the water at exactly the moment when the rowers were reaching that part of the course…'

'It doesn't seem like an act of rage,' says Boyd.

'No, but it's also possible that our scab is using humans to dump the bodies,' Meyer says. 'That would explain why we pick up the scent of Silver violence, which would be on the body itself, but not the personal scent of the Silver, because he wouldn't have touched it recently enough to have left any trace. At least, we've never found any.'

Everyone is quiet for a moment, reflecting on where this all leaves us. The truth is that there's very little to go on. We're used to relying on our Silver senses, but we can't do that here.

'So you have no idea who's behind this?' I say.

'No,' the Secundus replies. To his credit, he doesn't waver as he admits this. He knows they have nothing, and he owns it. 'Our people are following up on some leads back in the City' – I can hear the capital letter as he says it, as though London is the only city in the world and we're all provincial bumpkins – 'and I'll let you know if anything relevant comes to light. Until then, we need to find out everything we can about this latest incident.'

'Then I guess we'd better get to work,' says Cam, clapping his hands together. I can only think about my duvet, either with or without Dr Ross in it, but he seems genuinely enthusiastic. It makes me hate him just a tiny bit.

'Good,' says the Secundus. 'Current avenues of enquiry are: the opera, the police, forensics, the body, and we'd better check out the latest victim's work and family life as well. Anything I've missed?'

'Witnesses?' suggests Naia.

'I doubt the humans will have anything to tell us, but go over to Magdalen College and ask some questions anyway. My team will follow up with the police. Sawyer, you go to see the wife. I've heard good things about your work.' He looks at Cam with interest. Then he looks at me in a way that suggests he's heard nothing good about me at all.

Meanwhile, Boyd has gone very still. I know that means trouble for later, but Cam is smiling at the Secundus's praise. If he had a tail, it would be wagging. The boy is basically a big golden Labrador. He's still grinning to himself as we leave the others behind and walk out to the car.

'Oh, stop it,' I say to him. 'Your cheerfulness is giving me a headache.'

'I think we both know the headache has more to do with last night's gin.'

'Silver don't get hangovers.'

Cam laughs. 'With the amount you put away last night, even the Secundus would be struggling.'

I groan. 'Worst. Timing. Ever. Did you see the size of the stick up his arse?'

I'm speaking more aggressively than I mean to, because I'm hoping to steer the conversation away from my raging hormones, and the words come out too harsh.

'Jack...' Cam squirms, uncomfortable with my insubordination. He really isn't cut out to be friends with me, but he tries all the same.

'Have you worked with him before?' I ask, trying to soften my tone. 'Do you know much about him?' I'm only interested because I want to know how many corners I can cut, and how much the Primus's guard will let me push. I know who deserves to go down for this and I don't want the Londoners getting in my way.

'He's got a reputation. He's tough, but he's a good guy from what I've heard and people respect him. Don't mess with him.'

'Who says I was going to?'

'Your face. And you'd mess with the Primus himself if you thought you could get away with it. For both our sakes, I'm begging you, just do the job. All right?'

He pulls a set of keys from his pocket and beeps one of the Seeker cars open, a boring hatchback in boring blue.

'Fine,' I say, getting in the driver's side.

'Are you sure you should be driving?'

'I'm fine. I'll behave myself, I promise.'

He stares at me like he doesn't believe it, so I drive under the speed limit the whole way just to prove my point.

4

I DON'T SEE my family anymore. It's too complicated.

I tried to stay in touch for a couple of years after I turned, but it just didn't work out. I thought the problems would come later, when I'd have to put distance between us so they didn't notice that I wasn't aging like they were, but it all came to a head much earlier than that. It turns out that it's difficult to find common ground with people who think the type of person you are doesn't even exist.

Come to think of it, being Silver is kind of like being bisexual. I came out to them when I was sixteen and they never believed that was real, either.

In the end, we grew apart. My parents retired to Spain and my brother took a job at an investment bank in London. I went to his wedding, but I've never met his kids. I guess I probably never will. I accept that, because the Seekers are my family now, but it makes encountering other people's relatives a bit of a strange experience.

David Grant's wife is no exception. She is not pleased to see us.

'I spent the whole of yesterday talking to your detectives.' She thinks we're the police. 'I've just found out my husband's dead. Can't you leave me alone to grieve?'

'I'm sorry, Mrs Grant,' says Cam, all soft voice and puppy-dog eyes. 'I know how difficult this must be for you and I know it's not fair of me to ask for more of your time, but it could be vital to discovering your husband's killer.'

'You think he was murdered?' she says. She obviously thought it was suicide, something we'd ruled out from the beginning.

'I do,' Cam says. 'I think your husband is one of at least four innocent people who have been killed by the same individual over the past few months. With your help, I think we have a good chance of finding the person responsible and bringing them to justice.'

I can see her barriers coming down. It isn't just Cam's gentle approach, it's the implication that the attack was random.

Strange, isn't it? You'd think that the existence of a serial killer would cause more panic, not less, but it's different for those close to the victims. They get anxious when their loved ones are murdered because they think they might be next, or that they might be suspects. In those circumstances, the anonymity of serial killers is a comfort: they follow patterns. Their victims are selected not because of who they are but because of what they are. Those kinds of killers are forces of nature, as uncontrollable as fire or flood, and – crucially – they are no one's fault. The victims' families can chalk it all up to bad luck.

Shit happens, life goes on.

'You'd better come in,' she says, then she stands aside and lets us into her home.

We're not in Oxford anymore, with its Victorian terraces and Georgian townhouses. Instead, we're in a new-build monstrosity that casts an ugly shadow on the village in which it squats. It's exactly what I'd expect a property developer's home to look like: glass and white paint and not a single feature older than my latest phone upgrade.

'David had such a good eye,' she says, seeing our attention trail up the glass to the concrete mezzanine.

She's magicked a tissue from somewhere and she's dabbing at her face with it. It comes away clean; she's not wearing any make up. She doesn't strike me as the kind of woman who would go in for Noir Moderne. She's more interested in pearls and cashmere than satin and lace, elegant even in her grief. If I had the energy for it, I might feel scruffy next to her in my deodorant-stained top and gin-soaked jeans. Fortunately, I have run out of my daily quota of fucks to give.

'He had so many ideas,' Mrs Grant goes on. 'Always up late, meeting with investors or scribbling in that notebook of his.'

Cam and I exchange a glance. *What notebook?*

She leads us to a seating area with a glass table and white sofas. I don't have to ask whether the Grants have any children still living at home, or pets for that matter. As soon as I see the decor, I know that they don't.

'Please,' she says, indicating one of the sofas while she sits on the one opposite. I feel like I'm going to get the fabric dirty just by looking at it.

'And what about the night of the opera?' Cam says once we're settled. 'Was your husband meeting investors then?'

'No,' she says, crossing her legs and sitting back in her chair, putting space between us.

There's something she hasn't told the police.

Cam doesn't go right for it. He's not the type to go for the jugular; that's more my style. Instead, he asks about her family, their routine, her husband's habits. He makes her comfortable by asking questions about their grown-up children, makes her feel as though we haven't noticed the slip. By the time he circles back around to it, she's smiling at Cam as though he's one of her son's friends, just another gangly kid, fresh out of university.

He asks the question softly. 'Who was he meeting that night, Mrs Grant?'

She looks down at her hands for a moment before answering, but she does answer eventually.

'I don't know.'

'You don't know?'

'There was a woman,' she says, then she's on her feet, moving towards the window. She doesn't want us to see her face, either because she's angry or because she's crying, but I'm not sure which. Her heartbeat would be racing like it is either way.

'He told you?' I ask.

'No. I just knew. The way that you know.'

'I'm not sure I understand,' Cam says, feigning ignorance like the clueless rookie he's pretending to be. People discount him because he looks young and innocent and that's what makes him such a brutal interviewer. He doesn't go for the throat; he goes for the heart.

'We've always been open with each other.' She turns back to look at Cam, wiping her cheeks. 'He invited me to events with his work friends, he told me about his day, he made plans for us to spend time together. If his phone rang when he was in the shower, I'd answer it for him and take a message. That's the kind of relationship we had. Until January.'

It doesn't escape my notice that January was when the first of the murders took place in London. I can tell from the uptick in Cam's respiration that he's marked it too, but he gives no outward sign of its significance. He's good at this.

'Then things changed,' she goes on. 'Suddenly, he was busy all the time. Every conversation we had was excuses – work was busy, he had a big deal on, he had to stay late at the office – but then he'd come back in the early hours reeking of alcohol. And if I touched his phone, suddenly I was crossing a line that had never been there before. I didn't think we had those kinds of secrets. I guess I was wrong.'

'Did you ask him about it?' I say.

'Why on earth would I do that?' she says, looking at me as though I've just sprouted a third arm.

'Didn't you want to know?' I ask.

'You're young,' she says, joining us back on the sofas. 'I suppose I can't explain to you what it's like. I had the children to think of, and…' She looks around at her empty modern palace, glass and metal and concrete, as though she is displaying it for us. 'You compromise. You decide what you want from life and then you decide what price you're willing to pay for it. None of this is mine.' She smiles, tight-lipped and grim. 'Well, I suppose it is now. But before this week, I was only renting it from my husband. Compliance pays the rent. Do you understand?'

I nod, but I don't understand at all. I don't understand how someone could sell so much of their freedom and self-respect for something so hollow.

'I didn't want to know,' she says. 'It wouldn't have made any difference anyway. I loved my husband, I did, but in the same way you love a familiar routine or an annoying pet that you're used to having around. I think we stopped caring about each other a long time ago.'

'So you're not sad he's dead?' I ask.

'I am,' she says, dabbing at her eyes again. 'I'm just not entirely sure why.'

'Well, that was bleak,' I say as we walk back to the car.

'Tell me about it.'

Cam asked Mrs Grant a few more questions – did her husband have any enemies, were there any problems at work, how did he get on with the children – but she had nothing of note to add. That doesn't bother us. The truth is that the Grants' personal circumstances are irrelevant, because we're fairly certain that David Grant's death is the work of a scab serial killer. Now I'm wishing we hadn't bothered speaking to Mrs Grant at all. It was just depressing.

'If I ever let myself get that ground down,' I say, 'please shoot me in the head.'

'It wouldn't kill you,' Cam says.

'No, but it might make me think twice about my choices. Imagine thinking so little of yourself that you'd happily bargain away your free will and independence for a shiny glass house and a philandering husband.'

'I don't think you have to worry about that.' Cam says as we get into the car. 'You're too proud to compromise and I'd be surprised if you ever settled down, particularly with a man.'

'I could settle down,' I say and just like that, I'm thinking about the doctor again.

'Your longest relationship was with a bottle of gin,' Cam says.

I smile, but I'm thinking of Winta, the one who got away.

Which brings me back to my own prime suspect. I can't stop thinking about it on the drive home.

'If one of the Barons goes to London,' I say when we arrive back at Solomon College, 'the Solis Invicti would have a record of that, right?'

'If the Baron had a business meeting with the Primus or someone else in the hierarchy, then yes, I guess so. Otherwise, maybe not. Why are you asking?'

'No reason,' I say, but Cam isn't convinced. He's right to be suspicious. I'm trying to work out if there's a way to prove that a certain Baron was in London at the time of the three scab murders there.

'You're up to something,' Cam says.

'I resent your insinuation, sir,' I say haughtily, walking through the college lodge with my head held high. Cam is close behind.

'Jack…'

The college porter stands up from his seat as he sees us coming. 'Captain wants to see you, Mr Sawyer,' he says. 'She asked you and Ms Valentine to report back on your return.'

So we do. When we get to her office, half of it has been taken over by the Secundus. The captain is working on her laptop at the table she uses for meetings while the Secundus sits at her desk. I think less of him for it.

'Sawyer, Valentine,' he says as we walk in. 'Any news?'

Cam takes the lead.

'Not much, sir. Just two interesting bits: the wife suspects that Grant was having an affair, and she mentioned a notebook that he used to scribble in a lot. I don't remember hearing about that before, so maybe the fact that it's missing is significant.'

'Good work, Sawyer,' says the Secundus, as though I wasn't involved at all. 'Captain Langford has heard back from the theatre,' the Secundus says, ignoring the fact that she's right there in the room with us, 'and they'll make themselves available this afternoon. Go and speak to their director. Her name's De Palma.'

'Yes, sir.'

'The police have spoken to witnesses who were at the opera the same night as Grant and apparently he disappeared with a short, dark-haired woman just after the performance. Find out if De Palma knows anything else. In the meantime, we'll try to track down that notebook. Report back here afterwards and we'll see where we've all got to.'

'Yes, sir.'

I have to stifle my irritation. Suddenly it's like we're in the bloody military. If I'd wanted five o'clock starts, invisible women, fierce supervision and *yes sir, no sir*, then I would have joined the army at eighteen instead of applying to study an arts subject at university. I take a leisurely approach towards punctuality and standards of attire. I like a lie in. I'm not used to dealing with a boss who's so concerned with discipline and who is, frankly, just a bit of a dickhead.

Cam, on the other hand, is fitting right in. The Secundus even shakes his hand as he sends us on our way.

'Suck-up,' I say to him once we've been dismissed.

'I'm not sucking up, Jack, I'm just not being overtly hostile. I mean, what did you expect me to say?'

I grumble under my breath, because he's right and I know it.

'But I'm not going to take your grumpiness personally,' he goes on, 'because I can hear your stomach rumbling and I know how you get when you skip meals.'

'I think you'll find that I am a fucking delight, as usual,' I lie.

'If you say so.' He grins. 'I guess we'll just go straight to the theatre, then?'

I punch him in the arm, which is how I tell him that I love him even though he's annoying me. He's right. I need lunch. Two or three bottles of it probably, given the amount of alcohol-induced brain damage my body has had to repair this morning.

I trip over my own feet on the way to the canteen. I only avoid cracking my head open on the wall because Cam is there to catch me.

Better make that four bottles. Maybe five and a filthy burger as well.

5

CAM AND I rock up at the Playhouse early in the afternoon. I'm expecting it to be a ghost town because the opera isn't due to start for another five hours, but the place writhes with activity. People are sawing at bits of scenery upstage, trying on costumes in the stalls and practicing choreography in the aisles. Meanwhile, a couple of women in athleisure gear are on the stage, projecting their voices up to the gods, while others sit in the front row and watch everything. I assume they're the directors. One of them, a woman, has a heartbeat too slow to be human.

She turns as we enter, then whispers something to her colleagues and stands from her seat. We wait at the back of the theatre for her to join us. When she does, her forehead creases in concern as she puts the pieces together.

'Seekers?' she asks.

'That's right. Is there somewhere we can talk?' says Cam.

Ten minutes later, we're sitting in her suite at the nearby Randolph Hotel while room service waiters wheel in afternoon tea.

'This really isn't necessary,' I say.

'It's no trouble at all.'

The inconvenience isn't what bothers me, it's more that the proffered snacks have been so over-gilded that I no longer recognise them as food. Instead of sandwiches, we have anaemic slices of bread stuck together with something that might once have been cucumber before it was peeled and covered in cream cheese. Instead of cake, which I enjoy only when it comes in wedges of fruit-filled or icing-covered stodge, we have dainty little layers of gunge topped with colourful froufrou. They can only be consumed with a fork. Even the scones look sad. They're a quarter of the size of normal scones and they come with a pitiful amount of clotted cream.

I eschew the food and take a tiny cup of tea instead.

'Ms De Palma–' says Cam.

'Gabriella, please.'

She gives him her most seductive smile. I'd tell her that she was wasting her time, but she's so beautiful that I wouldn't blame Cam if he made an exception. She's the perfect stereotype of a glamorous Italian woman: slim and stylish, with delicately tanned skin and hair that's been highlighted to a natural-looking gold. If I tried to walk two steps in her Louboutin heels then I'd end up on my arse in the deep-pile carpet. I have no idea what her outfit cost, but I'm willing to bet it's more than one of our cars. Which isn't saying much.

'Gabriella,' Cam smiles at her. 'Did you know David Grant?'

'Of course! Dear David. He was one of our most generous benefactors. He *loved* the opera. It was in his soul. He was a very artistic man, so accomplished. What a loss his death is to us all.'

I bring David Grant to mind – a boring, middle-aged property developer – and try to imagine him and Gabriella

De Palma being friends. It's incongruous. I can barely even imagine them being in the same room together.

'You were close?' I ask.

'Yes. Professionally, of course. He was a patron of the arts. He looked after our little company, but not just for the look of it. He had a real passion for what we do. David followed us all around the country on tour when he could, bringing guests and introducing new supporters. We owe him a great debt of gratitude.'

I might be imagining it, and I know Gabriella is far too slick for me to take anything she says at face value, but I think I detect a little resentment. There's a hint of it in the emphasis she puts on the word *debt*, in the staccato bite of that final consonant.

'Was that uncomfortable for you?' I ask. 'Being indebted to a human, I mean?'

She smiles. It's a tolerant smile, the forbearing sort of expression you might present to a toddler whom you love, but who is being a right pain in the arse just at the moment.

I realise then that she is very old indeed.

'Ms Valentine,' she says. 'You must understand our position. Like most Silver of my age I am, of course, very wealthy. I have enough money to fund a different opera each night, every night, for millennia. That is how compound interest works, yes? But as far as the human world is concerned, I am an artistic eccentric with a driving vision, excellent taste and only a few pennies to my name. These humans are used to subsidising the arts, because that is what their rich people have done with their money for centuries. It's a way for talentless money-dealers to feel that they are something more than heartless ghouls, you understand? We serve them. They pay for us, and so our art belongs to them and they can take credit for it. It is distasteful, but that is how patronage works. For me, if I want to do the thing that makes my life worth living, I must play the part. I must bring glamour and spectacle and, above all, gratitude. Anything else would be unbelievable and I cannot take that risk. This is what our Primus demands of us, that we live below the waterline.

'So no, Ms Valentine, it was not uncomfortable. I could subsidise the opera myself and exclude patrons like David Grant, but I choose not to because my calling demands it. Because my Primus demands it. And I am nothing if not loyal to my Primus.'

'And I'm sure your loyalty is appreciated,' Cam says, smoothing ruffled feathers.

'Oh, I know it is, Mr Sawyer. I am sure of that. Solomon and I are very close, you see.'

Gabriella's expression is benign, but the threat is there nonetheless. I wonder how many centuries of acquaintance she shares with our Primus and exactly how well they know each other. Intimately, I would guess. From what I know of him, I'd think her over-groomed look would appeal to him. He has that same manicured aloofness.

'Is there anything you can tell us about the night Mr Grant went missing?' Cam says, steering us back to the point.

'Well, let me see. It was a good performance, one of our best, I would say. Mr Grant was in the front row of the circle with a few associates.'

'Associates?' I interrupt.

'Business associates, I assume. He often comes with clients and friends of his from work.'

'Could you describe them?'

'Two men about his age. I've met them before at our performances. David introduced us, but I neglected to remember their names.' She says this in a throwaway manner, as though they were of no consequence. 'Then there was the woman.'

'Oh?' Cam says.

'Yes. Her, I hadn't seen before. She was in her forties, I'd guess. A brunette, petite, but fierce. I don't think she smiled all night. She wasn't putting up with any of David's nonsense.' Gabriella smiles. 'I liked her.'

'David's nonsense?' I ask.

She waves a hand dismissively. 'Oh, you know men. Always taking up too much space and putting their hands where they don't belong.'

'Did he try that with you?'

Her eyes twinkle. 'Not more than once.'

To my surprise, I find that I like Gabriella. For all her polish and stupid micro-cakes, she is a woman who speaks my language.

'Did Captain Langford tell you that it was a Silver who killed Mr Grant?' Cam asks.

'She did.'

'Then I hope you'll understand that we have to ask where you were when Mr Grant disappeared, shortly after the opera finished.'

'Of course. I was backstage for some time, making sure that everyone was happy, encouraging them. You know how it is with performers. Some of them are so insecure. Brilliant, but insecure. Then afterwards, I had plans for a midnight dinner.'

'Were you with anyone who can confirm that?'

'I was supposed to be,' she says. 'My date stood me up.' She waves it away as though it's nothing, but she's clearly uncomfortable with the admission. 'He was supposed to meet me backstage and then we were going on to dinner together, but he never appeared. I suppose something must have come up.'

I'm getting a tingling feeling in my stomach. This is it.

'You can probably confirm my whereabouts with the staff here at the Randolph,' she goes on. 'I took my dinner in the dining room, alone. They were very accommodating, despite the hour.'

I imagine they would be, for her.

It's not a perfect alibi. Grant probably wasn't killed until the early hours of the morning, but De Palma doesn't know that. His killer would.

'This man you were supposed to meet, was he Silver?' I ask.

'Yes.'

I can't imagine many people who would pass up the chance for a date with Gabriella. It's suspicious in and of itself. More suspicious still is the timing, coupled with the fact that her date was Silver. Maybe he was just busy, or maybe he changed his mind, but maybe the urgent matter detaining him was the draining and disposal of David Grant.

I lean towards her, resting my elbows on my knees.

'What was his name?'

I know what I want to hear. I want to hear the words so badly that when they finally come, I have to rerun them mentally to make sure that I'm not just imagining it.

'Killian Drake,' she says.

'The Baron of Oxford?' Cam asks, surprised.

'The very same.'

Gotcha.

I'm so delighted that I can't suppress my grin.

'Thank you, Ms De Palma,' I say. 'You have been so helpful. So very helpful.'

She looks surprised. 'Don't you have any more questions for me?'

Cam does, boring ones about the production and David Grant's financial contributions. He also asks about his alleged affair, but Gabriella knows nothing about that. I let the conversation wash over me, irrelevant now that I have found what I was looking for.

I've got you now, you bastard.

It's mid-afternoon by the time we leave the Randolph. The sun has come out, making the afternoon surprisingly pleasant. I yearn for a little hair of the dog. This is the perfect weather to grab a bottle of gin and go lie in the quad to drink it. Or it would be, if there wasn't more urgent business requiring my attention.

We walk De Palma back to the Playhouse. She takes a moment to introduce us to a few of her principal singers and crew members. They are all polite, but too busy to pay much attention to us. I try to pay attention to them, despite my distraction.

The stage manager gives off the air of being the person who's really in charge here, a man by the name of Iain Halberd. He's in his forties and balding, with a bearing of quiet efficiency. Several people come up to him with questions in the brief minutes during which we speak with him and he answers them briskly but kindly. No one challenges his authority. He is the first person I notice.

The second is introduced as the lead soprano. She is the most beautiful woman I've ever seen. Cold and distant in person, with a dead-fish handshake and minimal eye contact, but her standoffishness suits her hard-edged features. She looks as though she could kill without remorse.

And yet even considering her is pointless, because not one member of the company is Silver. The only immortal here is Gabriella De Palma and she doesn't strike me as a serial killer.

We're looking in the wrong place.

'Thank you so much for your time, Gabriella,' Cam says, shaking her hand.

'You are so welcome, darling boy.' She pulls him close and kisses each of his cheeks in turn. I back off a little, so she won't try to do the same with me.

'Here,' she says, pulling a couple of tickets from her bag and putting them into Cam's hands. 'Come tonight. You'll enjoy it, I promise.'

'The opera?' Cam says.

'Of course, the opera! What else is there but opera? You must. I shall be distraught if you refuse. You wouldn't want to upset an old woman, would you?' she adds, lowering her voice with a wink.

Cam smiles back, noncommittal. We take our leave.

On our way out, we collect a sample of the upholstery for Ed to test against the lint we found on the body. De Palma is already back into the swing of her rehearsal by the time we're done, so we don't hang around. We have what we need.

'So,' Cam says to me as we exit onto Beaumont Street. 'David Grant goes missing right after the opera and his notebook goes missing with him. He leaves with a petite, dark-haired woman who hasn't yet surfaced. His wife suspects he was having an affair, so maybe she's our mystery woman. Then his body is dumped eight hours later, killed by a Silver, drained of blood and with a smear of Noir Moderne lipstick on his mouth. It sounds to me like our next move is tracking down the mystery woman.'

I stop in the middle of the pavement, because I'm not going any further until we've got one very important thing straight.

'Are you kidding me?' I say.

'What?' he asks, but Cam knows exactly what I mean. He just doesn't want me to say the words.

'You know where we're going next.'

He sighs. 'Killian Drake?'

'Killian Drake.'

I can feel my grin turning feral, because if there's one man in the world that I want to collar then it's him. I've been waiting two decades for the day that I can pay him back and I'm not about to waste this opportunity. I'm not beyond framing him either. You can judge me all you like for my lack of morals, but I'm happy to give David Grant's killer a free pass if it means taking down my nemesis. It'll be worth it.

Cam's looking at me as though he can read my mind.

'He's the Baron of Oxford,' he says. 'You do remember that, right? You can't go around accusing him of murder without any physical evidence whatsoever. Please tell me you're not going to turn this into some mindless vendetta.'

'We agreed, Cam. We follow this investigation wherever it leads.'

'Come off it. You can't hold me accountable for things I said when I was that drunk.'

'But you heard De Palma. This investigation is leading straight to him. I'm not bending it that way. It just is. It would be negligent of me as an investigator not to follow up on this lead.'

Cam gives me a frank look. 'You're not the officious type, Jack. Stop pretending.'

'Fine,' I huff, 'but I'm going after him anyway. I can handle him on my own if you don't want to be involved.'

'Shouldn't we report to the Secundus first?'

'Sure. You go and do that. I'll question Drake and meet you back at the college.'

'Jack.' He looks me dead in the eye. 'Are you sure you should be the one to question him? Alone?'

'Trust me,' I say, 'I'm the only one who can.'

48

6

KILLIAN DRAKE IS an unmitigated bastard.

He's rich and powerful, which is a bad place for any man to start, but he's also arrogant and elitist, which makes him a particularly wanky breed of wanker.

You might call me prejudiced, because it's true that I blame him for the disappearance of the first and sole love of my life, but that's only because he was the one responsible for it. So yes, we have history, but trust me when I say that he deserves every drop of my vitriol.

'Jack Valentine,' he says as his goon leads me into the study of his Summertown mansion. 'It's been a while.'

'And I'm sure we're both very grateful for that.' I flop into one of his leather armchairs without waiting to be offered a seat. 'What can you tell me about David Grant?'

Drake pauses for a moment, smiles to himself, then comes around his desk to take the chair opposite me. 'Straight to business, then?'

'Why else would I be here?'

'Why, indeed?'

We stare at each other for a good few seconds. His eyes are a shade of brown so dark it's almost black. They're bottomless, like shark's eyes, predatory and vicious. There's a twinkle in them that I assume is for my benefit, an amused condescension that riles me up. He's trying to bait me.

The goon takes the opportunity to excuse himself.

'David Grant,' I say once he's gone.

'And who is David Grant?'

'Middle-aged white guy, dark hair, property developer – a business acquaintance of yours, I gather – and now as flat as a pancake. Ring any bells?'

'Ah,' Drake says. 'The May Day jumper.'

'The May Day pushee,' I correct him.

A muscle in his jaw twitches.

'I see.'

'I'm not sure you do. David Grant was thrown from Magdalen College tower yesterday morning. He was missing a lot of blood and there was a scent mark on the body. Obviously, we're thinking Silver. Gabriella De Palma said you were supposed to meet her for dinner the night he disappeared, but you never showed. So where were you?'

'You think I did this?' He seems genuinely affronted, as though he can't understand why I would think him capable of such a thing. He's either an excellent actor or he has a very short memory.

'David Grant was a fancy guy,' I say. 'He went to the opera that night. Still had the ticket in his pocket. You're pretty fancy yourself.'

'Why, thank you.'

I glare at him before continuing. It wasn't a compliment. 'You can see how I might think the two of you would move in the same circles. Maybe you met him at the opera. Maybe you got hungry. Then maybe you needed to get rid of the body.'

'And you think I'd be stupid enough to chuck his body off Magdalen tower instead of disposing of it quietly? I thought you knew me better than that. You're fishing, Jack. I'm not that crude.'

It's a good point. Drake isn't the kind of man to create a spectacle when it would be more convenient and more profitable to arrange everything behind the scenes. But I also notice that he's avoided my question.

'Then why did you stand up your date?'

He pushes his dark hair back from his face and leans towards me, resting his elbows on his knees. He's a handsome man and he knows it, but he's not turning on the charm for me. He just never bothers to turn it off.

'Have you met Gabriella?' he asks, his voice low and confidential. It rumbles in a way I'm sure most women find sexy, but it just makes me feel like there's a fly in my ear. 'She doesn't take no for an answer, even when you insist. She might have believed we had a social engagement. She pushed me to meet with her, as she does every time her company comes to Oxford, and I declined. Apparently she didn't take my refusal to heart.' He sits back in his chair and tugs at his shirt cuffs. 'As for the opera, I never acquired a taste for it. I was in London at the time of the man's death and I only returned this afternoon.'

'I don't suppose anyone except your employees will be able to vouch for that.'

'Actually, there is someone else who can confirm my whereabouts,' he says, and he's really smiling now. His lips part over perfect white teeth in a wolfish grin.

'And who would that be?'

'The Primus.'

Fuck.

Of all the alibis he could have provided, that one is the least assailable. If the Primus says Drake was with him at the time of the murder, then Drake was with him at the time of the murder. Even if it's a lie, there's nothing I can do about it, and Drake knows that.

'Do you ever wonder about this fixation of yours?' he says, leaning forward again. He's trying to crowd me out, but I stay exactly where I am. 'Winta's gone, Jack. She's been gone for twenty years and you know I don't have her. You also know that I'd never turn scab, at least not in a way that would ever trace back to me. I'm smarter than that. So why are you back here, haunting my doorstep?'

I don't like what he's implying.

'Because one day, I'm going to take you down,' I say. 'You're careful, but you're not perfect. I'll pin something on you eventually. I'm in no rush.'

'You know, there's a thin line between vendetta and obsession. The longer you walk it, the more likely it becomes that you'll end up crossing it, one way or another. So which side are you on?'

I laugh, a bitter noise that catches in my throat, then I lean in closer, getting right up in his face.

'I'm going to end you,' I growl. 'I don't care how close you are to the Primus. I don't care that you're the Baron. I don't care if you never kill another human in your miserable, empty life. All that matters to me is what you did to Winta and for that, I'm going to make you pay.'

I surge out of my chair and stalk from the room without a backward glance.

'Better luck next time, Jack,' he calls after me.

I almost turn around, because I feel so impotent that I want to wrap my fingers around his throat and squeeze, but instead I clench my hands into fists and speed out of the house before I can change my mind.

'You're back,' Cam says when he answers the door to my knock. He's in his rooms back at the college. 'How did it go?'

'I don't want to talk about it.'

'You missed the meeting with the Secundus.'

'Yeah, well I'm sure you managed without me. Why are you all dressed up?'

He's wearing a suit. I can't remember the last time I saw Cam in a suit. It's a brighter blue than is common and his tie is outlandish, but he looks sharp as hell.

'The opera, remember? The tickets from De Palma?'

'Oh, shit. Are you seriously going to that? You don't strike me as the opera type.'

'I'm going, and so are you.'

I groan and turn back down the corridor to my own rooms. 'Bye, Cam.'

'Come on, Jack,' he says, catching up with me. 'Give it a try. You might like it.'

'I doubt that. Why don't you take Ed instead?'

'Why don't you leave it alone?'

'I will not,' I say, stopping outside my own door. 'You're unhappy. I don't like it when you're unhappy.'

'Then take me to the opera and cheer me up.' He looks at me hopefully, flashing his baby browns, and I fold like wet paper.

'Fine. Just let me get changed.'

There's nothing appropriate in my wardrobe. I have one dress and, although it's a modest length, the neckline is lower than I'd like. It's not so much fancy as it is mildly trashy, but Cam's already banging on my door and I have no other options.

'Wowsers,' he says when I open up. 'Your tits are really right there, aren't they?'

'Where else would they be?' I grab a coat and throw it on, covering up the worst excesses of my cleavage. 'Are we going, or what?'

We bump into De Palma in the foyer of the Playhouse. Cam chats to her while I head to the bar for gin. After today's encounter with the bastard who shall not be named, I really need it.

I'm paying for our drinks when a familiar voice distracts me, I turn towards it without thinking and, although I turn away quickly, it's too late to pretend I haven't seen him. He's already coming this way.

'Jack Valentine,' he says.

Fuck.

'Twice in one day. What are the chances?'

I down my gin and wave to the bartender for another. 'I thought you didn't like the opera.'

'I made an exception for a friend,' Drake says, resting against the bar next to me.

'I really hope you're not talking about me.'

'Do you?' he says, leaning in closer. 'Because I can hear your heart racing.'

He's right; it is. Damn him and his Silver hearing.

I grit my teeth. 'That's because I'm trying to stop myself from decking you in front of all these nice people. Why don't you do us both a favour and remove the temptation. Go away.'

He pushes back from the bar. 'Well, you know where to find me. I'm sure we'll be seeing each other again soon.'

'I seriously hope not.'

Thankfully, Cam joins us at then. He nods to Drake and says, 'Sir,' because I suppose technically the bastard is our superior. The captain's superior, too. Still, I can't suppress my derisive snort.

'Don't mind Jack,' Cam says.

'Oh, I don't mind her at all,' Drake says, smiling at Cam. 'Enjoy the opera.'

I'm spitting tacks by the time he's out of earshot.

'The utter bastard. Did you hear that?'

'What? One of the most important men in the country being extremely tolerant and forgiving in the face of you being, well, you? Yes, I heard it.'

'Hey. You're supposed to be on my side.'

'I am, Jack. That's why I'm telling you to cool it. Can't you at least try to be nice? For my sake, please. I know you've got this weird obsession with him–'

'I am *not* obsessed with Killian bloody Drake. I have a grudge against him. The two things are startlingly different.'

'Okay, okay. You have a grudge. Sure. That's why you're looking at his arse.'

'I am *not*–'

Our conversation is cut short by the ten-minute bell.

'Come on,' says Cam. 'Let's find our seats.'

De Palma has set us up nicely. Our tickets are for the front row of the circle, bang in the centre, the best in the house.

Unfortunately, Cam and I aren't the only ones with comped seats.

'Mr Sawyer, Ms Valentine,' Drake says, getting to his feet.

He and his date are in the seats next to ours. She's stunning: dark hair, pale skin and legs for days. And she's human. I've gone into the row first, so if I don't act quickly then I'm going to be stuck next to Drake for the whole performance. I try to back out, to let Cam go in front of me, but he pushes me forwards.

'May I introduce Veronica Astley?' Drake says. 'She's a visiting professor from Cambridge. Veronica, these are my colleagues Cameron Sawyer and Jacqueline Valentine.'

We go through the usual pleased-to-meet-yous, then Drake turns back to me.

'May I help you with your coat?'

He's being so chivalrous that I can't refuse without upsetting Cam, so I unbutton it and let him draw it from my shoulders. I kept it on in the bar, because I'm not at all comfortable with how much of me the dress shows, but there's no hiding now.

I can hear the uptick in his pulse as he notices the low neckline. I wish I hated his reaction, but I don't entirely. It makes me feel powerful.

His eyes lock with mine.

The orchestra strikes up a few tuning notes and I use the distraction as an excuse to look away. We all sit. My worst nightmare has come true: I'm inches away from Killian Drake, in the dark, for the next four hours.

'You scrub up nicely, Jack,' he whispers, deliberately eyeing my dress rather than my cleavage.

I smile prettily for Cam's sake, but whisper, 'Fuck you, Drake.'

He smiles back.

By the time the lights go down, I'm praying for a fire, or a flood, or an asteroid strike, anything to get me out of this seat and away from the man beside me.

We're staring at each other in the dark when everyone comes on stage and starts belting out the first number. It's some sort of party scene, the men in tailcoats and the ladies in big floofy dresses.

Cam nudges me and draws my attention to the singers.

'What?' I whisper.

'Look.' He points.

And then I see it. Every single one of the women is wearing dark red lipstick, exactly the same shade as Noir Moderne.

7

THERE'S A SPECIAL allure to exclusive places. Members-only clubs, gated gardens, private parties. Backstage at the Playhouse is no exception. It's dirty and reeks of mothballs, but it's still exclusive.

Unfortunately, Cam and I have company.

'Baron, darling!'

'Gabriella,' he says, letting her kiss him loudly on both cheeks.

He made the sensible decision to send Veronica home when the opera finished, so it's just the three of us visiting with Gabriella De Palma after the show. I tried to protest against Drake tagging along, but he pointed out that we'd never get backstage without his help. To every human here we're just regular theatre-goers, whereas Killian Drake, billionaire bachelor, is a big fucking deal.

'I didn't know you'd be coming tonight,' De Palma says, tapping his arm. 'Naughty man. You should have told me.'

'My sincerest apologies.' He lifts her hand to his lips, a gesture as ancient as it is corny, but De Palma laps it up. 'I came with Veronica.'

'Oh, darling Veronica! And how is she? I meant to say hello, but I didn't get a chance to slip away during the interval.'

They embark upon a labyrinthine name-dropping session that seems to encompass every well-to-do person in England, with more Cholmondeleys and Featherstonhaughs than I care to count. Or spell.

After a few minutes have passed, I've had enough. I clear my throat.

'Oh, Ms Valentine,' Gabriella says, apparently seeing us for the first time. She balks a little at the low cut of my dress, but I'm not sure I can blame her for that. I feel like it's only wishful thinking that's keeping it up at this point. 'And Mr Sawyer.' She takes Cam's hand. 'Delighted to see that you both made it. And what did you think of our little opera? Be honest, now. I'm not too delicate to stand a little criticism.'

I nod along as Cam says nice things about the singers, the set, the direction, and a lot of other details I hadn't noticed. He's better at this part of the job than I am, so I just sit back and let him do his thing. Once I can see that Gabriella is distracted chatting to him, I take the opportunity to have a look around.

I was expecting it to be more glamorous, but the floor is concrete and cold. Exposed pipes line the corridor, which must once have been painted white but is now marked with scuffs and smudges. There aren't many dressing rooms, so everyone is crammed in together, leaning towards lines of mirrors as they rub the make up from their faces. There's a lot of it, caked on dark and deep. The bin is filled with discarded balls of cotton wool, stained with black mascara and burgundy Noir Moderne.

The female singers smile when they see me at the door to their dressing room. At least, I think they're smiling at me, until I turn around to see Drake standing at my shoulder.

'Brava,' he says to them. 'Brava, ladies.'

Most of them just smile or giggle, depending on their natures, but one comes right up to him. I have no idea what character she was playing in the opera because I barely followed it, but she had a few solos so I guess she must be someone special. Her looks are striking – she has beautiful features and very dark skin – but she isn't one of the women Cam and I met on our first visit the Playhouse. In fact, I can't see the standoffish lead soprano anywhere.

'You came,' the woman says, leaning past me to kiss Drake on the cheek. She leaves a smudge of Noir Moderne in her wake. 'Thank you. You heard about Mr Grant, I suppose?' The tone of her voice suggests that she was not one of his fans.

'That's why we're here,' Drake says, turning to me. 'Ms Valentine is investigating. Jack, this is Fabiana. She sang the part of Violetta tonight, quite beautifully, I might add. She's the lead soprano.'

This confuses me, because the lead soprano I met the other day was definitely not Fabiana.

'You knew David Grant?' I ask her, more out of curiosity than suspicion. She's human, so there's no way she was the one who tossed his body from the tower, but her distaste for him is evident.

'Yes, I did,' she says. 'He was around a lot, always backstage getting in the way while he took his notes. He made me uncomfortable.'

'Taking notes? Of what?' I say, hoping I might be able to cross the mystery of the missing notebook off our list, but I'm destined to be disappointed.

'I don't know. He was very secretive about it, but he scribbled away like a reporter without a recorder. It felt like we were under surveillance.'

I'm about to press her further, but then Halberd – the stage manager – bustles in and hurries the singers along. He's the only one who doesn't pander to Drake, pushing past him as though he's not a famous entrepreneur, but an irritation who's in his way. Maybe Halberd doesn't realise who he is, or maybe he just doesn't care. Either way, it makes me warm to the efficient little man.

'Ten minutes, girls!' he shouts. 'The taxis are waiting!'

'Taxis?' I ask him. 'Is there an afterparty?' But Halberd ignores me, moving on to the next dressing room.

'No party,' says Fabiana. 'He's just making sure we all get home safely. He worries.' She turns back to Drake. 'Forgive me for hurrying off. Another time?'

'Of course.' He smiles at her, then puts his hand on the small of my back to usher me out. It doesn't improve my mood that, after an evening sitting right next to him, I've grown accustomed so to his proximity that I almost leaned into his touch. I elbow him away then increase my pace to escape his grasp.

I can't work out whether I'm more angry at him or myself.

'Well,' De Palma is saying to Cam when we rejoin them, 'it was so lovely to see you, but I really should be getting back to my company.'

'There's actually something we needed to speak to you about, Ms De Palma,' Cam says. 'If you could spare us a couple more minutes?'

'Gabriella, darling,' she reminds him. 'Please. And of course. Anything I can do to help the Seekers.'

'Perhaps we should go somewhere a little more private?' says Drake.

The way he's taking over our investigation irritates me further, but he's right. We're standing at the side of the stage, gathered in a group by the edge of the curtain, and it's far from discreet. I can see the theatre staff moving between the tiers of seats out in the auditorium, picking up rubbish and checking for lost belongings. Behind us, performers and crew are talking loudly as they make their way to the exits, following Halberd's directions to hurry out to the waiting cars. I don't want to have this discussion somewhere so exposed.

'Of course,' De Palma says, putting her hand on Drake's chest in a way that is strangely proprietorial. 'Come this way, darling.' The way she says it makes her words sound more like an invitation to bed than an invitation to discuss a murder.

She leads the three of us to a cupboard-sized room that has been taken over by the costume department. There's a sewing machine on a tiny table and two chairs are crammed in around racks of dresses and suits. I'm not sure we're all going to fit at first, but De Palma shoves one of the rolling rails into a corner to make room before taking one of the chairs. Drake offers me the other, but I shake my head. I'd prefer to look down on him than have him tower over me.

'There,' De Palma says, turning to Cam, 'isn't this cosy? Now, darling, what did you want to ask me about?'

'It's about the lipstick, Ms De Palma,' I say, cutting in. I notice that she doesn't tell me to call her Gabriella. 'Noir Moderne?'

'Lipstick?' she says, sounding worried now. She's looking at Cam as though he can help. 'You mean the lipstick the girls wear?'

'That's right,' I say. 'We found a smear of it on David Grant's face.'

Her expression transforms instantly. She laughs, relieved. 'Oh, well, that's no surprise, is it? He popped backstage after every performance to congratulate the girls, just like you did tonight.'

'He did that the night he disappeared?' Cam asks.

'Of course.'

He clears his throat. 'You didn't mention that when we last spoke.'

'Well, darling, you didn't ask. He wasn't here for long, and he left a long while before I did. I was here until quite late.' She turns to Drake and adds softly, 'I don't want you to think I was just sitting and waiting for you. I have more pride than that. I was busy with the production.'

'Of course,' he says, even though it's clear from her demeanour that she was doing nothing but waiting. Drake is acting the gentleman while De Palma looks at him like he's the one who got away. She tries to hide it, but she's not fooling anyone. There's heartbreak in her eyes.

I feel bad for her, bad enough to intervene, to say anything to stop her from looking at Drake like that. The crumbling of her polish is devastating to watch. She is made of gold and sunshine and he's not worth her misery. I wish I could tell her that.

'The lipstick was on his mouth, Ms De Palma,' I say.

She blinks a few times, quickly, then looks at me.

'The lipstick?' she says. She waves away the words. 'That means nothing. They're affectionate, my singers. They appreciate a man who appreciates the arts.'

'So he wasn't having an affair with one of them?'

'An affair?' She laughs, though the sound is a little forced. She's recovering her composure well, but it can't be easy to go from disappointment to amusement so quickly. 'Of course not. Look,' she says, leaning forward to wipe lipstick from the side of Drake's mouth. 'Even the Baron has Noir Moderne on his mouth and he certainly hasn't been having an affair with any of my singers. Have you, darling?'

Her tone is light, but there is grit behind the question. The words are a challenge to which she clearly expects a response.

'You know that I would never,' Drake says quietly.

'See?' she says, all smiles and levity once more. She rubs the lipstick between her fingers for a moment, then takes a scrap of fabric from the table and uses it to wipe them clean. She turns back to Cam with a smile. 'I hope that answers your questions?'

'You really are a bastard,' I say to Drake as we leave De Palma backstage and make our way to the foyer. Cam, walking ahead, pretends he hasn't heard.

'Am I?' Drake says. 'Wouldn't it be crueller to pretend feelings I don't have? To draw things out? I made my refusal polite, but clear. If Gabriella convinced herself otherwise, then it's not because of anything I said or did.'

'Bastard,' I mutter, fastening my coat around me.

'Jack, wait,' he says. He puts his hand on my shoulder, holding me back. He doesn't speak until Cam has gone ahead into the foyer.

'How long are we going to carry on like this?' he asks.

'What are you talking about?'

'You know exactly what I'm talking about. How long are you going to keep attacking me? We could work together. Maybe even find Winta. But making an enemy of me isn't going to help you.'

'Is that a threat?'

He shakes his head, bewildered. 'Why are you like this? How long are you going to keep hiding behind a twenty-year-old fling?'

'You think I'm hiding?'

'Of course you are,' he says, leaning in closer. 'But I see you.'

He's backing me up against the wall of the corridor, and I'm letting him because my pulse is roaring in my ears and I'm starting to feel dizzy. I probably have low blood sugar.

'There's been no one since her, has there?' he says. 'Not a single person.'

'I'm not a fucking nun,' I say, but the words come out too defensive.

'That's not what I mean. I mean the rush of it. You know, when it gets you right here.' He puts his fist to his sternum, grinding it into the bone. 'Like a lightning bolt. The excitement.'

His eyes are bright. Maybe I should feel threatened by him, but I don't. Instead, I feel like we're sharing a secret. I can feel his mood infecting me, shaking me up until my skin feels like it's fizzing.

But I can't tell him that, so instead I say, 'I don't know what you mean.'

'Yes, you do.' He backs off a little and I have to resist the urge to move with him. I resent it, but he has that magnetic quality. 'That's why I turned down De Palma. Without the thrill, what's the point? And that's why you're still searching for her. You want to feel it again. You want it to hit you, here.' He pushes his fist against my chest. 'I could help you.'

The offer sounds genuine, but I know there would be a price. There's always a price.

'I don't want your help,' I say, brushing his hand away.

'Then what do you want?'

'I want you to stay away from me and my business.'

'I can't do that, Jack,' he says, colder now. 'Or have you forgotten? I'm the Baron of this city.'

He looks at me for a long moment, but I can't decipher his expression. He seems suddenly tired. Then he walks away, leaving me to follow along behind. Cam is waiting for us in the foyer.

'I'll bid you both a good night,' Drake says abruptly, shaking Cam's hand. 'Mr Sawyer. Always a pleasure.'

'Goodnight, Baron Drake,' he replies.

'Goodnight, Ms Valentine,' Drake says, then he walks out of the front door without looking back.

I have no idea what just happened, but I'm not happy about it. I feel like I've done something wrong, or that I should be angry with Drake for something he did wrong, but I can't work out which.

'Shit,' I say, kicking the wall. 'Fucking shit. Fucking *wanking* shit.'

The front-of-house staff are still here, tidying the desk and the bar. They tell us they need to lock up now and ask if we wouldn't mind vacating the premises. Quickly.

They probably think I'm drunk.

Cam apologises on my behalf, then turns to me and says, 'What the hell was that about?'

'Who the fuck knows? I think I really pissed him off this time.'

'I don't know why he lets you get away with so much.' Cam shakes his head. 'You're playing with fire, Jack.'

'Maybe, but then so is he.'

Cam looks worried as he holds the doors open for me. I'm worried too, and I hate it.

Time to change the subject.

'Did you notice that the stage manager is a bit on-edge about security, or is that just me?' I ask him as we step out into the night. It's drizzling, the moisture settling on my coat like tiny pearls that glint in the light leaking out from the foyer.

'They weren't very keen on letting the singers hang around, that's for sure,' he says. 'But maybe that's not surprising, so soon after the murder. You can understand why they'd be protective of their performers, especially given that Grant went missing right after he left the opera. He could have been abducted from the doorstep.'

'Maybe,' I concede. 'Did you notice the new soprano?'

We start to walk back to the college.

'Probably an understudy,' Cam says.

'She said Grant brought his notebook backstage, that he was always writing in it. She didn't like it. Made her uncomfortable.'

'Well, Grant's wife said he never put it down, that he was always busy working. It doesn't seem like much to go on.'

I sigh and wipe the rain from my cheeks, wishing I'd brought an umbrella. My hair is going to be a soaked, frizzy mess.

'So you're telling me I just sat through an entire opera for nothing?' I say. 'Worse, I had to spend the whole evening in the company of Killian fucking Drake, and we've made zero progress.'

'That's about the size of it.'

'Fuck. Well, now that we're out in the rain, we may as well make the most of it. Chips?'

He grins at me. 'I'll race you to the kebab van.'

8

THE NEXT MORNING, Cam and I decide to split our tasks between us. While he goes to report to the captain on last night's adventures at the Playhouse, I go to the lab to drop off the upholstery sample with Ed. That way, not only do we save time, but Cam doesn't have to see Ed – I'm still not sure what's going on with them – and I don't have to confess to the captain that I went to the Baron of Oxford's mansion to harass him. With any luck, that incident can be gently brushed under the carpet and never brought up again.

When I get to the lab, Ed is looking into his microscope, his glasses pushed onto the top of his head.

'Do you have a time of death yet?' I ask him.

'You'll have to wait for the post mortem for that,' he says without looking up. 'I did find something interesting in the blood, though.'

'Oh?'

'Oh, yes. You're going to like this.'

When he looks up, his eyes are glittering. He pulls his glasses down over them, which is a redundant gesture as far as I can tell, since all the Silver have twenty-twenty vision. They must be an affectation, completing the hipster look his beard has started. It's a strangely self-conscious fashion choice for someone who must be three hundred years old, at least.

'So,' he says, 'this took a while because it's so obscure, but it's really cool.'

'Okay…'

'I started out doing the usual toxicology stuff, because there was a weird kind of smell to the sample you brought in.'

'There was?'

'Oh yeah. Like burning rubber and bleach. At least, that's what it smelled like to me. It's not very pleasant. Here,' he says, picking up the blood sample tube with gloved hands and popping it open.

I doubt that a human nose would be sensitive enough to pick up the smell, but to my Silver senses it is indescribably awful. Blood generally smells wonderful; rich, spicy and tangy. It's perfectly delicious. But the smell of this sample curdles in my nostrils, turning every pleasant note into something acrid and sharp.

'Ugh,' I say, covering my nose with my sleeve. 'That's revolting.'

'I know,' he says, resealing the sample. 'So I took a closer look, and guess what I found?'

He looks at me expectantly, as though he's waiting for me to play along. He does this a lot. However bored we look when we visit him in the lab, he can't seem to understand that no one else gets excited about Petri dishes and test tubes. He always seems convinced that if he explains a little more of the science, we'll suddenly all catch on. Now he's looking at me with his eyebrows raised, his face a picture of childlike delight.

'I have no idea,' I say, trying to muster up some enthusiasm. 'Tell me.'

'No, go on,' he insists. 'Guess.'

'I don't know, Ed.' My patience is running out. 'That's why we asked you to look at it.'

The disappointment that crosses his face is short-lived, erased by his fascination with his discovery.

'Rohypnol,' he says.

'Rohypnol?' I no longer have to pretend that I'm interested. 'The date-rape drug?'

'That's right. Enough of it to incapacitate a small elephant, if I'm any judge. Or a large horse.'

'You're a large horse?' I ask, deadpan, because I can't resist.

'What? No. Never mind.' The man has no sense of humour. 'What I'm saying is that whoever dosed him wanted to be sure that he'd stay under. They used far more than they needed to. That's why his blood reeks. I can't imagine it would have been very appetising to whichever Silver drugged him.'

'But Dr Ross said the body was nearly drained.'

It makes no sense. Why drug someone you're intending to drain if the drug will make the blood unpalatable? It's like deliberately over-seasoning your food.

'Do you think the blood could have been dumped rather than drunk?' I ask. 'There was the needle mark on his hand.'

Ed takes off his glasses and wipes the lenses clean. The useless, non-prescription lenses. 'I don't know. The injection site could have been used to drain him, or it could just as easily have been used to get the drug into his system in the first place.'

'So maybe he was injected after he was already drained,' I suggest.

That must be the answer. No Silver would drink that putrid muck, so Grant must have been drained before he was drugged.

But my theory gets a definite nope from Ed. He doesn't even have to say the word, because his expression is eloquent enough, one eyebrow raised scornfully as he settles his glasses back on his nose. He obviously thinks I'm an idiot for even suggesting it.

Scientists, I tell you. They're just a bunch of superior know-it-alls.

'There's two reasons why it must have been drug first, draining after,' he says. 'One: why bother drugging someone once they're already drained? The sedative would have been pointless since the blood loss would have been enough to sedate the victim on its own. Two: once he was drained, the blood would have stopped pumping around him pretty quickly. Dr Ross found high levels of the drug in his organs, and there's no way that could have happened if he hadn't been full of blood when the rohypnol was introduced.'

The brief mention of her name is enough to bring the image of her back into my head, eyes smiling and curls tumbling. They'd look good on my pillow.

'She's working on the post mortem?' I ask, clearing my throat.

'Not yet, but she's managed to get some samples to work with in the meantime.'

'I see.' Stupid crush. I need to stop picturing the doctor in my bed and concentrate on this case. 'So what do you think happened? Why would a Silver have drugged our victim before draining him?'

Ed shrugs. 'That's your department. I'm sure you and... erm, the other Seekers can manage it.'

I'm doing some eyebrow-raising of my own now.

'The other Seekers, eh? Let me ask you something, Ed. What's going on with you and Cam?'

He takes off his glasses and tucks them into the pocket of his lab coat, then crosses his arms over his chest. He's obviously as reluctant to talk about it as Cam is.

'Fine,' I say, throwing up my hands. 'I guess I'll just be getting back to work then. With my partner. You know, Cam. Good-looking guy, dark blond hair, normally bounces around like a happy golden retriever. By the way, I've been meaning to ask: do you like puppies?'

He sighs derisively and goes back to his microscope.

I'm holding in a sigh of my own. I can do without a cranky partner. I'll get to the bottom of this tiff one day soon – I promise myself that – but it won't be today.

'You look like you have good news,' Cam says as I join him in our office.

All the Seekers have offices here, sharing two desks to a room, but there isn't a lot of paperwork in this job. The nice thing about operating outside of the human law is that we don't have to deal with their bureaucracy. The captain handles that, spending most of her time chained to her desk answering calls and letters, which leaves us free to do the work on the ground. It beats wasting every day writing reports that no one will ever read.

But we do write down the important stuff. Cam likes to make lists and spider graphs as a case develops, because he says it helps him piece things together. I usually do a bit of doodling, mapping out crime scenes and other locations, because that's just the way my brain works. I like visual cues. We all have our own ways of remembering the details.

'I wouldn't call it good news,' I say as I flop down into my desk chair. 'It's just news. There was rohypnol in David Grant's blood sample.'

Cam sits up taller in his seat. 'He was drugged?'

'Yeah, and get this: the rohypnol made his blood smell revolting. As in, Cowley Road on a Friday night in freshers' week revolting. Piss and vomit. That kind of revolting. But Grant was drained after he was drugged, so either the Silver who killed him had the constitution of an iron bucket, or they didn't even drink the blood.'

'Then why would they drain it?'

'No idea.'

We sit in silence for a few minutes while Cam thinks this over and I check my emails. Two, both junk.

'Did you speak to the captain?' I ask him, but he knows that isn't my real question.

'Yes,' he says, 'but don't worry, I didn't mention that you'd paid a visit to the Baron. Because I'm the best partner in the world.'

'Thank you, Cam.'

He smiles and looks back at his computer screen. 'You owe me a drink.'

'I'll get you five,' I say in a fit of generosity. 'Any other news?'

'The police tracked down the woman, the one Grant was with on the night he went missing.'

'Really?' I say, leaning around my computer monitor. I remember De Palma's description of her: *brunette, petite, fierce.* 'Who is she?'

'She's a lawyer. She specialises in insolvency.'

That stops me dead. I gesture impatiently at Cam, because he's got that look on his face that tells me he's about to say something scandalous. He's dragging it out just to annoy me.

Finally he says, 'David Grant was flat broke.'

'You're kidding. With the massive house, the Mercedes, and the equity he owned in the business?'

'Mortgaged for their entire value and beyond. The business has been losing money for years. They overextended, due to Grant's mismanagement apparently, and they're on the verge of going into administration. There was talk of embezzlement. His partners are not happy.'

'Are any of them Silver? That would be an easy solve.'

'Sadly not, and neither is the lawyer. Grant was trying to keep her sweet with the corporate hospitality routine, but apparently it backfired. She left in a snit as soon as the opera finished, along with Grant's other business associates. Last they saw him, he was standing in the foyer of the Playhouse, waiting for a taxi.'

'Did the police find out why the lawyer was so upset?'

'Yup. He tried to cop a feel when the lights went down.'

I roll my eyes. 'Ugh. What a creep.'

'Creep is right. I'm starting to think that whoever killed David Grant did womankind a favour.'

I mull that over for a while, tapping my fingers on the table.

After a few seconds, Cam says, 'What are you thinking?'

'Well, the business partners are more than a little annoyed with Grant, right? Have we looked into their backgrounds? Do they have any Silver friends? I can see them moving in rarified circles.'

'You mean rarified like those of a certain Baron we know?'

Dammit. He always sees right through me.

'Maybe,' I say. 'It's worth a look, isn't it?'

Cam leans back in his chair and looks at the ceiling, letting out a world-weary sigh.

'The man has an alibi, Jack,' he says. 'A really good alibi. Give it up already.'

'That doesn't mean one of his goons didn't do it for him. I mean, doesn't it seem a little too convenient to you that on the night of the murder he just happened to be in London visiting the Primus? Why not a hired gun?'

'It's a stretch and you know it,' Cam says.

He's right, but it's not just my vendetta that's pushing me in this direction. There was something about the way Drake behaved yesterday, something that's making me uneasy. I can't shake the feeling that there's something he's not telling me.

'I don't trust him,' I say.

'That's not news.'

'I just don't, Cam. He's connected to this somehow. I can feel it in my gut. And this case just gets weirder and weirder. First the affair that doesn't seem to be an affair at all, then the embezzlement, and now blood that's been drugged into inedibility. None of it makes any sense.'

'I know,' Cam says. He looks as miserable as I feel, which isn't normal for him. He's usually sunshine to my grouchy clouds. With both of us in a bad mood, it throws off our whole dynamic.

'Ed doesn't seem happy,' I say, hedging. 'Are you ready to talk about it?'

He looks back at his screen and says, 'Not yet.'

It's not much, but it's more than I got from him last time, which gives me hope that he might open up soon. I'm counting that as a win.

When the college bells chime one o'clock we make our way to the canteen, where Boyd and Naia are already eating and drinking their lunch. It might seem like overkill to have a proper canteen in a college with only a few hundred members, of whom only a fraction are in residence at any one time, but it's more a necessity than a luxury. The difference between a hungry Silver and a well-fed one is startling in terms of strength.

Also, I get hangry, and I'm not the only one.

'Any news from the opera?' Naia asks us when we join them with our lunch trays.

'A little,' Cam replies, 'though I'm not sure how much of it is relevant.' He looks at me with an odd expression when he says this. He's hinting that we should tell them about my visit to Drake. It makes me want to kick him because I don't want to, and if Cam keeps mugging like this then they'll guess something's up.

'Any news from Magdalen College?' I ask, to distract them.

'No one saw anything,' Naia says, stabbing her fork into her pad thai and twirling it around. 'No one knows anything. No one seems to have any idea what happened. They all just kept going on about the poor school kids and how traumatised they're going to be. I mean, come on. I'd seen loads of people murdered by the time I was their age and I turned out okay.'

The rest of us exchange glances, but no one's going to touch that one. Naia doesn't look up from her food.

'Besides,' she goes on, 'they didn't even see anything. Not the fall, not the blood. No one did.' She forks more noodles into her mouth than will reasonably fit in it, which is her usual method of eating. I turn away before she starts chewing, because I'd definitely rather witness a murder than watch Naia butchering her lunch.

'We do have some other news to report,' I say.

I tell them about the blood results and Cam rattles off the details of conversations with Gabriella. Boyd already knows the news from the police, having spoken to the captain himself this morning. We impart the information efficiently and concisely, but we still don't manage to finish our reports before Naia finishes her lunch. I swear, sometimes I wonder if she can unhinge her jaw like a snake, because I can't understand how else she manages to shove her food in so quickly.

'You know what it sounds like to me?' she says, wiping her mouth with a napkin, which isn't necessary because she's a very neat eater. Not a single crumb is wasted.

'What?' I say, starting on my own lunch.

'It sounds like a fetish. You know, someone who loves the taste of foetid blood. Like a kink.'

'A weird kink,' Cam says.

Naia laughs. 'You're so vanilla. Bless your little cotton socks. When was the last time you dated?'

'Shut up,' Cam mumbles, but there's no sting in it. Naia knows even less about Ed than I do. She didn't mean anything by it.

Now that the conversation has descended into our usual banter, Boyd makes his excuses and leaves us to it. He's not very good in social situations, I think because he just doesn't understand people. It doesn't help that his deputy rank brings the hierarchy into play as well, which makes it even messier. He's as relieved to leave as we are to see him go.

'You know what we should do?' says Naia.

'Make you eat behind a screen?' I suggest, watching her inhale the chocolate brownie she's chosen for pudding.

'Ha ha,' she says, licking her fingers clean. 'No. We should check the files. If there's a Silver in Britain who likes the taste of rohypnol, we'll have a record of it, right?'

'Maybe,' I say. 'It's definitely worth a look.'

Naia gets to her feet. 'Come on, then.'

I'm only halfway through my lunch, but I drop my cutlery and abandon it. I've lost my appetite anyway. Cam looks at me, fork halfway to his mouth.

'Don't worry,' I say, 'I'll go. You finish your lunch.'

I go after Naia. 'All right, then,' I say. 'Let's bust out the Creep Box.'

It's less an actual box than an external hard drive containing records of all our usual suspects. I follow Naia back to her office so we can start searching through it.

The heart of our data is stored on the Dead Box, which contains brief notes of all of our closed and ongoing cases. Each unit has its own Dead Box, and they're all backed up individually to a master copy that the captain holds. The back-up process is laborious without automation, but you can imagine why we prefer to keep that information off the network and out of the cloud. We work hard to make our files un-hackable.

The Creep Box is a little different. Instead of case details, it contains information we've picked up on the job, or outside of it. Sometimes it's fairly innocuous, like which Silver have been known to liberate blood donations from the John Radcliffe Hospital, and sometimes it's less pleasant. Right now, we're looking for details of Silver who have been known to drug humans.

After just a few minutes' searching, Naia pushes back from her computer and says, 'Bingo.'

I look at the screen.

Matthew Felton. He's a fairly new Silver, just forty years post-human, and he likes to play with drugs. All kinds of drugs. The notes on the Creep Box say he abducts humans, drugs them, then dresses them up and poses them before he drinks their blood.

'Jesus Christ,' I say.

'I know, right?'

Felton's on the Creep Box rather than the Dead Box because nothing he does is actually against the rules. The Seekers are only interested in punishing Silver who risk exposing our existence to the humans. Since Felton returns his victims to their own homes after he's done with them, leaving them feeling hungover but otherwise unaware of their experiences, officially we have no problem with him. As long as he keeps them alive and doesn't raise suspicions, we're not supposed to care.

But his victims are mostly university-aged girls and there are photographs of his activities attached to his file. They're not pretty.

Naia finishes reading the entry, then looks at me.

'How about we leave the boys at home for this one?' she suggests. 'Girls' trip. Just you and me.'

'Why not?' I smile, mirroring Naia's expression as I coat my anger in sweetness. 'Let's go pay him a visit.'

9

NO ONE SMOKES anymore. If you so much as pull out a cigarette in public these days, people look at you as though you've just suggested torturing children for fun. I used to smoke myself, but then, well. Love can make you do crazy things.

This all goes to say that it's a warning sign when the overgrown front garden of Felton's Iffley Road home is thick with fag ends. Some of the houses in this area are four storeys tall, with loft and basement conversions that make them larger still. They're grand, owned by old money or split into multiple-person dwellings by rich landlords and colleges. This isn't somewhere you'd expect to find such antisocial behaviour. At least, not during exam season.

'Nice place,' Naia says, kicking through the rubbish that has accumulated by the doorstep. 'How the fuck can this creep afford it?'

'Not honestly, I'll bet.'

I press the doorbell, but nothing happens. Even to my sensitive ears, the bell is silent. When I knock against the door instead, it swings open a few ominous inches.

'Fucksake,' says Naia. 'If there's someone dead in there, then you're dealing with it. My lunch was great on the way down, but I'd rather not see it again so soon, if you know what I mean.'

'Oh, stop whining.' We both know Naia would be the last person in the world to get sick at a crime scene. 'Come on.'

The door swings into a drift of unopened post that has accumulated behind it. We're clearly not the first people to come tromping in over it, because the envelopes are stained with bootprints. And blood.

Then we hear the noise. It's faint, just on the edge of Silver hearing, and yet it is distinctive: the soft moan of a woman in pain.

There's no keeping us back now. Naia pushes ahead, ignoring the stairs down to the basement and rushing straight up to the attic. It makes sense that he would build his nest up there between the rafters. It's a good vantage point, with plenty of sturdy beams for securing ligatures. After four flights of stairs, I can't help but reflect on the parallels with Magdalen tower. Felton is a crow who likes to perch up high.

When we barrel through the door into the large attic, I am relieved and disgusted in equal measure. I was prepared for it after reading Felton's details on the Creep Box, but none of the photos could do justice to the horror of standing six feet away from his work.

'Shit,' Naia says, taking in the scene.

No one is dead or dying, but it's not pleasant. There are four people in the room: Felton and three women. I say women, but honestly they're more like girls. None of them can be older than twenty and I wouldn't be surprised to learn that they're underage. They are costumed as characters – a princess, a fairy, a ballerina – and suspended from the ceiling beams in poses, secured by silks tied around their limbs.

They have to be tied that way, because they're all fast asleep, drugged out of their minds. It's probably for the best, because the tableau is creepy as hell. The ballerina is mid-jeté, the princess mid-curtsey, while the fairy is bent at the waist with a wand raised in her hand, as though in the process of granting a wish. They're like frozen puppets, with Felton as the puppet master.

He must have been asleep when we arrived, because he's only now pushing himself upright from a double mattress that's been shoved up against the wall. The roof starts slanting inwards just a few feet above his head, making a foetid, blanket-filled nook under the skylight. The window pane is covered with tin foil. This room could be a weed farm – warm and secretive – but Felton has made it into a blood bank instead.

'What the fuck,' I say, 'is this?'

The ballerina murmurs and I realise that's the noise we heard from downstairs. She's not in pain, not exactly. It's just the drugs wearing off.

'This is my little theatre,' Felton says, finally staggering to his feet. 'Do you like it?' He smiles and raises an eyebrow, as though he's flirting. He expects us to be impressed. Worse than that, he expects us to enjoy it, to be excited by what he has done.

That's what pushes Naia over the edge. She's been quiet up until now, watching the marionettes as they spin gently on their silks, but his attitude cracks her composure. Before he's taken more than a step towards us, she darts forward and snaps his arm across her knee.

His scream is loud enough that the ballerina startles in her slumber, her limbs stretching their restraints tight for a moment before she settles back down into unconsciousness.

'What was that for?' Felton yells, dropping onto the mattress with all the grace of a drunken hedgehog.

'You'll heal,' Naia says dismissively. 'Don't be such a wuss about it.'

With the amount of blood Felton has likely been drinking, he'll be fine in an hour or so, but the arm will hurt like hell until then. We might be quick healers, but we're not immune to pain. I'm exceedingly glad of that in this moment. If anyone deserves pain, it's this sorry excuse for a Silver.

'Who turned you?' I ask, unable to keep the disgust from my voice. 'Who would be stupid enough to make a twisted fucker like you immortal?'

'Who knows?' Felton replies, apparently untouched by my insults. 'Dead of night, drunk on my way back from the pub, all that clichéd stuff. Fuck, this really hurts.' He's cradling his arm like a baby. I think we have him subdued until Naia steps over to his little freak show.

'Hey!' he says, getting to his feet again. 'Don't touch those! Do you have any idea how long it took me to get them looking like that? They're perfect. You'll ruin them.'

'If you don't want me to break your other arm,' Naia says, starting to untie the fairy, 'then sit down and shut up.'

He does as he's told, reluctantly. I join Naia in releasing the girls: untying the silks, checking their vitals and then laying them gently on the floor. They're still out for the count, which is a mercy in the circumstances. All the while, Felton is chain-smoking while he runs his hands through his hair, pouting, distraught that we are dismantling his art.

'You've got no right,' he says once the girls are safely released. 'You've got no right at all.'

'And you think you do?' Naia says, turning to face him. 'You think you're entitled to use these girls as your playthings?'

'I've done nothing wrong!' he yells, gesturing with such force that ash flies from the end of his cigarette. 'I can take anyone I like and do whatever I want to them, as long as they don't remember me afterwards. I'm doing nothing that risks revealing our existence to the humans, so what's the big fucking deal?'

Naia's brown skin flushes darker. Felton notices her reaction and makes some placating gestures.

'Okay, okay,' he says. 'Look, I give them drugs. Sedatives, so I can take the blood. They're totally safe. It's the most humane way of doing it. They never feel a thing, and they remember nothing. I swear, it's the best way.' While he talks, he pulls a tin out of his pocket and starts cutting up a line on the shiny inside of its lid.

'You give them cocaine?' I ask, wondering what he could hope to achieve with that strategy.

'A little, sometimes. Just as an ice-breaker.' He wipes his nose on the back of his hand as he sniffs through powder-filled sinuses. I wonder how many times he's lost his septum, only to have it grow back the next day. The man is a mess. 'Then I dose them up with the other stuff. Knocks them out completely. They never know about any of this,' he says, waving towards his little stage. 'I put them back where I found them afterwards, none the wiser. As far as they're concerned, nothing happened, so what does it matter what I do with them while they're out? It's all above board. I'm not doing anything wrong.'

'It's illegal,' says Naia. 'Really fucking illegal.' Her voice comes out as a growl and I know she's as disgusted as I am. Neither of us has been Silver very long. We both could have been one of those girls in another life.

'Yeah, so what?' Felton says. 'It's no threat to the Silver. You don't care about illegal. Who the fuck cares about illegal?' He wipes at his nose again, sniffing. 'I'm being discreet. I've done nothing wrong.'

He's blinking up at us, bewildered, as though he genuinely can't understand what the problem is. Morality doesn't exist for him. There is no right and wrong, just can and cannot. The Seekers exist in order to preserve our secrecy, nothing more. He's protesting that he's done nothing wrong because he truly believes that and it's difficult to disagree when that accords with the official line.

Naia's fists are clenched by her sides. She's silent, her jaw tight, her weight balanced on the balls of her feet, as though she's about to take a step forward.

'Look,' I say, 'we're not here about the girls.'

It's not that I don't feel exactly the same way as Naia, but I need to diffuse the situation before she flies into a proper rage. If I let her get going, then she'll beat him so badly that we'll have to let him heal before we can get any answers.

'We're here about the May Day murder,' I go on. 'You've heard about it, I guess?'

Felton shrugs, relaxing a little, puts his tin away, then lights another cigarette off the one he's been smoking.

'A man named David Grant was drained, then thrown off Magdalen College tower by a Silver.'

'And why would I know anything about that?' Felton says, defiant now that he has nothing left to lose. He's grumpy because we've taken away his toys.

'Grant had drugs in his system,' I say. 'Rohypnol.'

From the way Felton's face contorts at the mention of the date-rape drug, I know he's familiar with it.

'That stuff?' he says. 'Jesus, have you ever smelled that stuff? Ever tasted it?'

'Unlike you,' Naia says in a tone that cuts like ice, 'we don't drug our dates.'

Felton looks us both up and down in a way that makes me feel like I need five consecutive showers.

'No,' he says eventually. 'I guess you don't have to. Well, it stinks. Reeks, really. I never use the stuff. I have my own formula, carefully constructed over years and years of study. It's perfect: odourless, colourless, and mostly importantly it tastes of absolutely nothing. It knocks people out like that–' He clicks his fingers. '–and can keep them out as long as you like with extra doses, with no side effects at all. I have my lab set up downstairs. I am a master chemist.'

Naia grunts derisively at his arrogance. I should have guessed he was a chemist, given the number of substances he's smoked and snorted since we arrived. I'm half-surprised he hasn't already rolled up his sleeve and started tapping up a vein.

'Show me,' I say.

He points to a curtain on the other side of the room, pulled across the far corner. I go to investigate.

There are a few IV stands behind the curtain, doubtless what he uses to keep the girls healthy and subdued during their stay in his attic. Next to them is a fridge. It contains bags of fluids, together with vials of things I'd rather not touch. If these are Felton's experiments, who knows what they'll do?

'Test them,' he says. 'Test the dead guy. The chemicals won't be the same, I promise you. I had nothing to do with his death. I didn't drink from him.'

'Then prove it,' Naia says. She hasn't moved from her position next to Felton. She's just standing there, watching him. 'Volunteer some samples for us to test. Blood. That sort of thing.'

She's not genuinely expecting the samples to help. She just wants an excuse to hurt Felton.

DNA doesn't often work in scab cases. Our lives would be a whole lot easier if it did, but the problem is that the Silver are constantly drinking other people's blood, imbibing other people's DNA. That blood doesn't get processed and discarded by our digestive systems with our food. Instead, it filters out into our own blood, spreading through our bodies to be used in repairing damaged cells, then it stays there until it's replaced again. In our long lives we become chimeras several thousand times over, comprised of little pieces of everyone whose blood we have ever drunk. We are a patchwork of DNA.

But sometimes, if we get to a scab suspect soon after the victim has been drained, we get lucky. If we hit while the human's blood is still rushing around in the Silver's veins, we might get a sample large enough to find a match.

That's why Naia has the bundle of syringes strapped to her belt.

'Alright,' he says, offering her his arm.

But Naia doesn't get out the little needle. She gets out the big one, the one for extracting bone marrow.

'We need to get the whole spectrum of samples,' she says, malice glinting in her eyes. 'I'm sure you understand.' She stabs the needle into his femur until he screams. Then she does it again, into his hip this time, then a rib, then his humerus, all while he continues to scream. 'Have to get multiple sample sites,' she says with entirely too much glee. 'Protocol.'

'You're a fucking lunatic,' he says, rubbing at the various places she has stabbed. Between that and the broken arm, he's starting to look like a broken puppet himself.

Naia takes one final sample from him, his blood, but it's probably too late by now. Even if he was the one who drank from Grant, his body will have distributed and modified all that blood already. We won't find any trace of Grant's DNA.

Still, I can't say I don't enjoy watching Felton squirm.

Meanwhile, I call in our clean-up team, who arrive within minutes to take the girls away. They'll get them washed up, check there's nothing wrong with them, then sneak them home or, if appropriate, into A&E at the John Radcliffe. The team is brisk and efficient, and they don't stop to question what's going on.

Felton is apoplectic.

'You have no idea what you've just done,' he says, lighting another cigarette with shaking fingers. 'I've got friends you can't even imagine. You have no idea who you're dealing with.'

'No,' Naia says, safely stowing her samples in the bundle on her belt. 'I know exactly who I'm dealing with.'

He laughs, a gloating chuckle that promises vengeance. 'You're going to regret this. You can't just come into my home, take away my donors and assault me without the slightest shred of evidence that I had anything to do with that guy's death.'

That's where he's wrong.

'Your donors?' Naia says, striding closer. 'Your prisoners, you mean.'

She swings her boot back – steel toe-capped, I'll bet – and kicks it straight into his face. The cigarette falls from his mouth and onto the mattress, smouldering.

He's right: we don't have any proof. I'm pretty sure he isn't our guy, but the reality is that it doesn't matter. We don't *need* proof. We don't need to bring evidence in front of a jury of Felton's peers and convince them beyond a reasonable doubt that he's guilty. If we believe that he's the one responsible, then we can take any action we deem appropriate in bringing him in. It's only afterwards that any explanation is necessary, and that's only for the purpose of securing longterm punishment. At this stage, we don't have to explain ourselves to anyone except the captain and if she were here, then odds are she'd be getting her boots wet too.

Moral: don't piss off the Seekers.

Felton has been doing this for decades and frankly he should know better, but some of these aging Silver still haven't got it through their heads that the patriarchy is crumbling. Felton looks at me and Naia and sees a couple of girls, when what he should be seeing is two highly-trained, highly dangerous Seekers who are now highly-motivated to beat him to a bloody pulp.

'Hey!' he says, sputtering through the blood. 'What the fuck are you doing? You can't just beat me up.'

'Why not?' Naia says to him. 'It's no threat to the secrecy of the Silver. That's the only thing that matters, right?' She kicks him again. 'Illegal is irrelevant,' she says with another kick to his face. 'Isn't that what you said?' Kick. '*Who the fuck cares about illegal?*' Kick. 'I'm doing nothing wrong.' Kick.

At first he was too shocked to fight back, but now he couldn't manage it even if he tried. He's unconscious and his face is a mess. If he were human then he'd be dead, but even as a Silver it will take him a good day or so to heal himself from those injuries.

'Naia,' I say eventually, once she seems to have worked out most of her anger. 'The mattress is on fire.'

She uses one of the blankets to wipe her bloody boot clean, then chucks it into the small fire, feeding the flames.

'Should we put it out, do you think?' I ask her.

'Nah,' she says. 'I'm doing an experiment. Let's see how long it takes him to reconstitute himself from ash.'

Before we leave, I grab a plastic bag from downstairs and use it like a glove to extract all the vials from the fridge, wrapping them into a bundle. It's a long shot, but I'll have Ed test them against the drug he found in David Grant's blood. Even if he finds nothing, at least I've made it a little harder for Felton to snatch any more girls.

For the moment.

'It wasn't him, was it?' Naia asks me as we leave the burning building behind us and head back to the college.

'Nope.'

She didn't need to ask the question. We both want Felton to be responsible for Grant's murder, not only because it would mean the end of this investigation, but because he's an opportunistic pervert who deserves the worst punishment the Baron can hand down to him. If we don't intervene, then we know there will be more girls, more marionettes, and more ruined lives.

But the humans Felton kidnaps are girls and only girls. The sole Y chromosome in the room belonged to Felton. I can't see any reason why he'd suddenly start targeting men. Plus, everything Felton does is done in private, for his own entertainment. He likes the intimacy of his display, and there was nothing intimate about David Grant's death. It was meant to be a spectacle. Felton has been operating under the radar for long enough to know that if he wants to carry on with his perversions, he needs to do it quietly. Even putting aside the fact that the drug is wrong, David Grant's murder doesn't fit his pattern at all.

I'm surprised by how much that frustrates me. It won't be long before Felton is back on his feet and back to his old tricks.

'Maybe…' Naia says. Even though she doesn't finish the thought, I can tell that she's thinking the same as me.

'After all this is over,' I say.
'Yes,' she replies. 'When it's over. We'll make it right.'
That's our pact.

10

ED'S INITIAL TESTS confirm what we already knew: none of the substances in Felton's fridge matches the drug found in David Grant's system. We're just getting the bad news when the delectable Dr Ross bustles in, lab coat on, pencils in hair and attention fixed on a file she's holding in her hands.

'Nothing on sample G28,' she says without looking up. 'Was that the IV bag or–'

'Hello,' Naia says, smiling like a fox.

Dr Ross looks up, obviously surprised to see anyone here but Ed. After a moment's confusion, she smiles so widely that she might have mistaken us for long-lost family rather than a couple of random colleagues she's only just met.

'Naia,' she says. 'Jack.'

She remembers my name. I want her to say it again. I want her to whisper it. I want her to yell it. Most of all, I want her to moan it.

Naia sniggers, which tells me that everyone in the room is perfectly aware of what I want. This is why Silver romance is such a fucking nightmare.

'Hi,' I say to Dr Ross, because it's better than just standing here like a lemon. 'What are you working on?'

'I was looking at some samples from the post mortem,' she says, returning the vials she's holding to the fridge, 'but I'm afraid I got a wee bit distracted helping Ed identify the substances you brought in. I thought it was worth having another keek, just to see if there was anything here we should be worried about, or something we could use.'

'And?' asks Naia.

'No, nothing.'

'We'll keep looking,' says Ed, then goes back to his microscope. The man loves his microscope.

'Well,' says Dr Ross, 'I should be off. I need to report back to Meyer.'

The Secundus has gone off chasing leads in London and in the meantime he's left Thomas Meyer – the composed Solis Invicti – behind in his stead. Meyer's running this investigation now, from a makeshift office in our conference room.

'We need to do the same,' says Naia. 'We'll walk you there.'

I give her a look, because she's clearly up to something and I don't appreciate her interference. I can mess up my love life all by myself. But I can hardly retract the offer now that it's been made and the truth is that I don't want to. I'd relish the chance to spend a few more minutes with the fair doctor, even with Naia eavesdropping.

We all say goodbye to Ed, who gives us a vague wave in return. He's not chatty at the best of times, unless science is involved, but today he was particularly taciturn. He's anxious and unhappy, just like someone else I know.

He and Cam really need to talk.

When we get out into the corridor, a wide glassed-in colonnade that skirts the edge of the quad, Dr Ross gets a cheeky smile on her face.

'I heard you two burned down a house today,' she says. 'Is it true?'

'More or less,' says Naia.

'Less,' I correct her. 'We just singed the top floor. The fire brigade got there before there was any structural damage.'

'The bastard got lucky,' Naia growls.

'There was someone in there?' asks Dr Ross.

Naia opens her mouth to reply, but I get in there first, diverting the conversation by asking about her laboratory tests. I don't want Naia to tell her how we left Felton to burn. I'd rather hide the dark parts of myself that enjoyed his pain. I might not have participated as fully as Naia did, but I didn't stop her either. I didn't even want to. The truth is, she was right to do what she did. If anything, she didn't go far enough. Justice demands that we exact more from Felton than we did today.

I'm comfortable with that. I'm not sure the doctor would be, so I make small talk instead.

All too soon, we reach the conference room. We each speak to Meyer to update him on our progress, then we're back out in the corridor.

This is the parting of the ways.

I look at Dr Ross.

She smiles at me.

I think of all the ways this could go. I could ask her out. We'd have a drink, maybe have a nice time, but I'd have nothing interesting to say. She's clever, really clever, and I'm a complete dunce when it comes to science. The only thing we have in common is murder. Maybe we'd push on regardless of that, maybe even go so far as dating, but sooner or later my questionable moral compass would force us apart. Despite her wicked sense of humour, she's a good person. I can tell by the way she smiles at the world, expecting it to welcome her rather than hurt her. I, on the other hand, expect nothing but pain.

We are too different. It would never work.

'Goodbye, Dr Ross,' I say, with regret.

'Goodbye,' she says, apparently with no regret at all.

Who am I kidding? She would never have gone out with me, even if I'd asked. She's too professional for that. She's probably not even interested. Why would she be? She's got her shit together, whereas it's a good day if I can turn up for work showered, fed and dressed in clothes that aren't covered in gin.

'We're all going out for a drink tonight,' Naia says quickly. 'Maybe you'd like to join us?'

Dr Ross looks surprised at the invitation, but not unhappy. I, on the other hand, am glaring daggers at Naia. I know this is her idea of helpful assistance, because she can never understand why people don't just jump into bed with each other all the time – it's what she does – but I don't appreciate the strong-arming. She waggles her eyebrows at me.

Then the doctor turns to me and smiles. She's still looking at me when she says, 'I'd love to. See you at eight?'

Maybe Naia has the right idea after all.

The first thing I do when I arrive is order some blood from the bar. It'll help me feel more controlled and make me less liable to start salivating the moment Dr Gorgeous arrives. I settle myself onto a barstool with my bottle and think about Matthew Felton while I wait.

Blood is available from several vendors within the city, so there's really no need for anyone to go taking humans off the streets. The problem is that it's expensive, which is a reflection of how much effort goes into obtaining it.

It works like this: the academics of Solomon College focus on the sciences, with a particular emphasis on producing spin-out companies that run various and numerous drug trials. Those trials always involve taking large amounts of blood from the volunteer participants – for which they are financially incentivised – but very few of the drugs ever make it to market. That's not because the drugs the college produces aren't effective, but because the drugs never exist in the first place. The sole objective of the enterprise is to obtain the participants' blood.

You can see how that rigmarole might rack up the costs. Some Silver aren't able to pay for it and some just aren't willing. I put Felton in the latter category. For him, it's clearly about more than sustenance.

Thankfully, there aren't that many Silver like him. It's usually the older ones who cause the most problems, the ones who've grown old through centuries of stalking and taking what they want from whomever they want. They don't see why they should have to give up the thrill of the hunt. But occasionally someone like Felton comes along, someone for whom the world is a playground of epic proportions, in which every other living thing is just their toy. You won't be surprised to learn that they're usually men.

And men like Felton never stop.

I've just finished my drink when the door to the bar swings open. It's a good thing I've already put the bottle down, because I might have dropped it otherwise.

Dr Ross has arrived and my god does she know how to make an entrance.

It's raining outside, but she must have forgotten to bring an umbrella because soggy little curls have plastered themselves to the sides of her face. She's pink in the cheeks from the spring chill, which isn't surprising, because she's just wearing a skirt with a shirt and cardigan; no coat. A few of the top buttons of her shirt are undone, revealing a modest amount of delicate skin that's decorated with the trails of descending raindrops.

How I envy them.

I don't realise I've zoned out until Cam yells my name. He's standing behind the doctor, waving me towards a table Naia has secured in the corner. Dr Ross takes off her cardigan to sit down and with it comes a waft of scent that is precisely hers: jasmine and gunpowder, a floral explosion of mystery and mischief. I'm instantly captivated.

'Hello,' she says, lashes dipped. Her voice is pitched softly, for me alone.

I murmur something back. She smiles.

I am so far gone. No amount of blood can help me now.

'So,' she says once we're all settled at the table. 'Good day?'

'Crappy day,' says Naia. 'I'm going to the bar.'

She takes our orders and is back in record time, carrying a handful of glasses and an armful of gin bottles.

'I see,' says Dr Ross. 'That kind of day, huh?'

'Yup,' says Naia, biting the cork out of the first bottle and swigging straight from the neck. 'That kind of day. Though I did get to kick a pervert's head in. The same one we burned. That was kind of satisfying.'

'Okay.' Dr Ross nods, looking a little terrified. 'And what about you?' she says, turning to me.

'Um.' I'm not sure how to answer. 'I helped.'

She laughs. She laughs and it's a beautiful sound, not because it's melodious or sweet or any of the things that a delicate woman's laugh is supposed to be, but because it's raucous and real and so loud that Cam jumps a little in his seat. For such a petite person, Dr Ross has a cracking set of lungs.

'Sorry,' she says, calming down after a few seconds. 'I'm not sure why that was so funny.'

Then she lets out a final honking snort that sounds like a cross between a goose and a pig, and suddenly we're all laughing. Tears are streaming down Naia's face as she struggles to breathe through the hysteria.

'My god,' she gasps. 'What was that? Did someone let a stray goat in here?'

Then we're off again. It's amazing how funny mundane things can become with a little alcoholic lubrication. We're all enjoying ourselves so much that when Cam stops laughing, his silence is glaringly obvious. I turn to follow his gaze.

Ed has just walked into the bar, and he's not alone. There's a woman on his arm, a brunette with a kind face and the sort of self-assurance that tells me she's been Silver for at least a century. I don't recognise her from around here, but she's comfortable in Ed's company and comfortable to claim him. Her grip on his arm is proprietorial.

She's steering Ed to the bar, but then he freezes, catching sight of Cam. He pushes the useless glasses up his nose, apparently unsure what to do. The woman on his arm notices his attention and a brief whispered conversation follows. It's too loud in here for me to make out their words. After a moment, they make a beeline in our direction.

Oh no.

Cam sits up straighter in his seat, as though he's gearing up for battle. His expression is grim, but resigned.

'Ed,' he says.

'Cam,' Ed replies, hesitantly. 'Everyone, this is Carrie. Carrie, these are some of the people I work with.'

I see the barb landing in Cam's heart. He is just someone Ed works with. Not a friend, not a confidante of several centuries. Not a lover, once. Just someone he works with.

Ed introduces us one by one, but the joy has been sucked out of our corner of the bar by his intrusion and he knows it. He seems embarrassed, but I can't tell whether it's because of us or because of the awkwardness of the situation. I hope it's the latter. I want him to feel bad for doing this to Cam. Carrie seems nice enough, but I still want Ed to regret this decision every day for the rest of his life.

Worse, I want to do to him what we did to Felton earlier today. Naia catches my eye and I know she's thinking the same thing.

No one hurts Cam.

Carrie's friends arrive then. She and Ed follow them over to the other side of the bar. It's probably for the best. Naia and I have a lot of impotent rage left to spend today and Cam would be upset if we took it out on Ed. He isn't angry. He's just devastated.

'Are you okay?' I whisper to him once Ed is out of earshot.

'I'm fine,' he says. His head is bowed, staring down into his glass. 'I knew. He told me. It was just a shock, you know? Seeing them. Together.'

'I'm so sorry, Cam.'

I kiss his cheek and he nods his thanks, but he doesn't look up.

I hate seeing him like this. Cam isn't this introverted creature, turned in on himself and avoiding the real world. Cam is a smiling, bouncy riot of happiness. He's eager and hopeful and never, ever says a bad word against anyone unless they truly deserve it.

If Cam is my sunshine, then Ed is his cloud. I need to get him out from behind it.

Fuck it. There's only one solution.

Here's the thing about my three rules for getting vampires drunk: there's a fourth one. It's strictly for non-human company, and if you do it regularly then your brain cells might never grow back properly, but it is technically possible to create a Silver super-beverage by combining certain specialist ingredients.

Step one: select a spirit of your choice. My preference is for gin, but vodka works well too. Whisky is a fucking travesty and should be avoided in this drink, because it's so strongly flavoured that it wipes out everything else. Also, it tastes like mud.

Step two: add human blood. Look, I know I said that mixing blood with alcohol was a Very Bad Idea and I stand by that advice, but frankly if you've got to the point where you need this drink then you have bigger things to worry about than developing a ravening thirst. Just make sure there are no humans nearby and everything will be hunky-dory.

Step three: find a compliant vampire to give up half a pint of blood. I'll be honest, this is the hard bit. This is why you never see humans drinking this stuff. Not only would it likely kill them, but getting a vampire to give up their blood is about as easy as getting Boyd to take the stick out of his arse. It only works tonight because I make everyone chip in, all four of us donating to the pot.

Step four: mix well, and make sure there's someone sober on stand-by to carry you home afterwards.

I call this the Valentine's Massacre. It lives up to its name.

The fact that Dr Ross is up for drinking it makes me think I may have misjudged her. No, I've definitely misjudged her. Right now, she's halfway through her first Massacre, her shoes are off and she only has one pencil left in her hair. She's using the other to stir her drink.

Her first name is Tabitha.

Tabs. Tabby. I wonder if she'd purr like a cat if I stroked her.

'My turn,' says Cam, licking the back of a playing card and using his spit to stick it to his head. It's an eight. 'Okay, I'm going with... five.'

'Nope. Three fingers!' Naia shouts joyously.

This is our favourite drinking game. You guess the number on your card, then drink as many fingers as you are wrong by. The major drawback of the game is that it involves maths, which is tough when you're already halfway down the glass, and even tougher when that glass contains my patented brew. The major benefit is that as our maths gets worse, it tends to err towards more generous calculations, meaning that everyone gets drunker that much more quickly.

It was probably a bad idea to play the game with Massacres.

'You know what?' Cam says, his chin propped up in his hand. He's looking across the bar to where Ed is having a very civilised drink with Carrie. 'I never understood him. The tube tests and the forming... formulae and the–' He waves his hand, looking for the word. '–science. All the science.'

'Science is a bitch,' Tabitha says, emphatically.

I snort into my drink.

Cam points at her. 'Exactly. You know. And you know what he said to me? You know what he said?'

'What?' Tabitha mirrors his pose, propping her chin in her hand and leaning towards him.

'He said he wanted to try polymer... poly... polyamory. Worse, he said he was *going to*. I had no choice. Wouldn't talk about it.' He makes a cutting motion with his hand and hits an empty bottle of gin. It smashes on the floor. Ed looks over to see what the noise is about and their eyes lock for a long, painful moment before Cam puts his head in his hands.

'No choice,' he says again.

'Fuck, Cam.' I put my arms around him and hold him close. 'I'm sorry.'

'I'm just not built that way,' he mumbles. 'I only want him.'

'Well, fuck him,' Naia says loudly. She has a problem with volume control at the best of times, but it goes completely out of the window when she's drunk. 'Giving polyamory a bad name. He's just a dick.'

'He just met someone else,' Cam says, without any rancour. 'S'not his fault.'

'Well, then you should too. You can do whatever you like.' Naia downs the last of her drink – which is ill-advised – then stands up unsteadily, offering Cam her hand. 'We'll show him.'

'Naia,' he says seriously. 'I am gay.'

She rolls her eyes. 'Just come on.'

Naia gets the bar to play some salsa, and it's not long before she and Cam are whirling around each other on the dance floor, throwing crazy moves, laughing in each other's faces and apparently having the time of their lives. Cam isn't the most graceful dancer. In fact, he looks a bit like a baby giraffe finding its feet for the first time, but it doesn't matter. Naia has done what she set out to do. There's so much joy in them that they are captivating. I can't stop watching.

'Do you want to join them?' Tabitha asks me.

I finally look away from Cam and Naia to see that the doctor is watching me, her drink finished, her eyes big and dark.

'I can't dance,' I say.

She laughs that big rolling laugh of hers. 'Neither can I, hen. It's not stopping them though, is it? Why should it stop us?'

I think for a reason to say no, but find none. Why the hell not?

'All right, then,' I say. 'Let's give it a try.'

11

I WAKE UP to a persistent buzzing. This time, I manage to catch my phone before it vibrates itself off the bedside table. I check my alarm clock, but it hasn't rung. I forgot to set it.

'Fuuuuuck.' I answer the phone. 'Yeah?'

It's Boyd. 'Conference room, ten minutes.'

Shit, not again.

'Yes, Deputy,' I say, ending the call before he can hear me groan. My head feels like something's trying to escape from it.

I look down at myself, counting appendages. By some small miracle they are not only all present, but also still clothed from the night before. That'll make getting ready easier, which is a relief because right now I'm not sure I can even sit up.

The mattress moves behind me.

'Whatimesit?' someone mumbles.

I roll over to find the delectable Dr Ross curled up beside me, also fully-clothed. I'm almost certain nothing happened between us last night, but her hair has tumbled free from its topknot and the sleepy look in her eyes makes her seem downright dissolute. I stifle another groan. Getting out of this bed while she's still in it might kill me, but I have no choice. Duty calls.

'It's just before nine,' I say.

'Oh.' There's a pause. 'What day is it?'

I smile, because I feel her pain. 'Friday. I've got to work.'

'Oh god,' she groans. 'Work.'

College quarters are not generous with the sizing. My entire living space is twenty by twenty feet, including the bathroom and kitchen/sitting room, and my bed is a single. We're crammed in tight, her body pressed between mine and the wall, but I'm so out of it that it wasn't until she spoke that I realised I wasn't alone. My limbs feel heavy and numb and I still can't remember how we got back here.

This is why Valentine's Massacres are drinks for special occasions only. This is also why my first attempt to get out of bed is less than successful. Dr Ross ends up pushing me from behind to stop me from falling back down on top of her. This means that her hands are now cupping my bum. When I finally get upright and look back at her, I catch a sly little grin on her face.

I can't believe it. Does she actually like me?

I was ready to assume that we'd only staggered back here because it was the nearest room, or because she couldn't remember where she lived – it wouldn't be the first time that had happened to a Massacre victim – but I'm starting to think she might have come here by choice.

'About last night,' I say.

'Ugh.' She sits up and tries to push her hair away from her face. It's proving tricky, because she's drooled in her sleep and the dried spit has stuck some of her hair to her cheek. She's batting at it like a snoozy kitten.

She is fucking adorable.

'How much do you remember?' I ask her.

'I remember dancing,' she says, wrangling her hair up into a bun. She looks around for something to pin it with, but she seems to have lost both of her pencils. 'I remember going back for more drinks. Then I remember falling over on the dance floor. It wasn't graceful. I think I flashed my knickers.'

I hand her some chopsticks I haven't used; the sushi place always gives me them, but I'd rather eat with my fingers.

'Thanks,' she says, using them to secure her bun. 'Then I think I passed out, though obviously I can't remember that part.'

I'm half disappointed that nothing happened between us, and half relieved that I haven't missed it. It would be a tragedy if that experience had been consigned to the black-out bin.

'Those drinks of yours are killer,' she goes on. 'I've not felt this rough since I was human.'

I want to tell her that she doesn't look rough. She looks beautiful. Her accent does amazing things to her sleepy voice, making it deep and gravelly. It's a resonant form of seduction.

But it's already been five minutes at least since Boyd called and I have to get going.

'Be right back.'

I race through the bathroom, quickly brushing my teeth and hair, and by the time I get back out she's looking a little more awake.

'I've got to go,' I say. 'Help yourself to whatever. There's a clean towel in the cupboard if you want a shower.' The idea seems to challenge her. 'Or you could go back to sleep if you want,' I add.

'Thank god,' she says, flopping back down onto the bed. 'I am dead.' She groans as she pulls the duvet back over herself, burrowing into it like a mole.

I laugh and say, 'I'll come back later with coffee.'

'You are a goddess,' she mumbles from her nest.

Despite the hangover, I'm glowing when I leave my rooms. It's a great start to what turns out to be a thoroughly shit day.

When I get to the conference room, the Secundus is waiting. He's obviously finished doing whatever he was doing in London, but it's not just him and the rest of the team who are waiting. Killian Drake is there too.

'Jack Valentine,' Drake says as I walk in, announcing me in the same self-satisfied tone he always uses. I hate the sound of my name in his mouth, the way he rolls it around his tongue. 'I see you had a good night.'

His nose is twitching. I've just rolled out of bed with a woman I have a serious crush on and I must stink of pheromones.

I don't bother to reply.

'I hope Dr Ross will be able to give us the results of the post mortem later today,' the Secundus says. The words are pointed, and not a person in the room misses his meaning. 'In the meantime, Baron Drake has kindly offered to assist with our investigation.'

I'm sure there's nothing kind about it. I mean to keep my derision to myself, but last night's drinking has done something to my already limited self-control and I can't stop my disbelief from showing.

That earns me a glare from the Secundus. 'Something to add, Valentine?'

'No, sir,' I say.

'Good. Then let's get started.'

We all sit down at the table, the Secundus at one end and the captain at the other. It's a visual representation of our division and without exactly meaning to, we all take our sides. The Seekers congregate around the captain, while Drake and Meyer sit to either side of the Secundus. I sit as far away from Drake as possible, which puts me between Boyd and the captain.

'So,' the Secundus says. 'This is what we have so far. David Grant went to the opera with some business associates on the night of his murder. He was a regular patron, so his attendance was expected. If his murder was premeditated, then the opera was a predictable place to find him. Agreed?'

We all nod.

The Secundus continues. 'After going backstage to see the performers, he was last seen waiting outside for a taxi at about half eleven. By six the next morning, his body had been drained of blood and dumped off Magdalen tower. No one at the college saw anything.'

'Which can't be right,' Naia mumbles. 'Someone had to have seen something.'

'So that's loose thread number one,' the Secundus says, nodding to Meyer. In response, Meyer gets up from his seat and makes a note on the whiteboard behind him.

'Then there's the body,' he goes on. 'Grant's body was almost completely drained, and he was dead when he hit the ground. He has what looks like a needle mark on the back of his hand, and red lint was found in the glue surrounding the mark. Do we have any news on that?'

'We took a sample of the theatre's upholstery,' Cam says. 'It's with the lab.'

'Loose thread number two,' the Secundus says. Meyer adds it to the board.

If it were me talking, then I would have made a joke about this loose thread being literally a loose thread, but the opportunity sails right over the Secundus's head.

'He also had a smear of Noir Moderne lipstick on his mouth,' he says. 'Is that right?'

'Yes,' I say, playing along, 'but we've already discounted it. The opera uses that shade. There was a lot of it at the Playhouse and apparently Grant was friendly enough with the singers that it probably transferred when he was kissing cheeks backstage on the night he died. It smudges easily. The Baron can attest to that.' I look pointedly at Drake. 'You're an avid supporter of the arts too, right?'

Eyebrows raise around the table. I smile innocently, but I'm fooling no one. The truth is that my head is killing me and I couldn't resist taking some of my pain out on Drake.

The Secundus does not look pleased.

'The Baron is not under investigation,' he says, in a tone that does not invite argument. I'm about to argue nonetheless, but Drake gets there first.

'It's all right, Drew,' he says, smiling at me. 'Ms Valentine is right on both counts. Yes, I'm a supporter of the arts and yes, Noir Moderne has a habit of transferring to the cheeks of the opera's benefactors. It can be discounted.'

'Very well,' the Secundus says, but the look he gives me is a warning. He fences me in with his gaze and I can't look away until he does. When he finally dismisses me, it's such a relief that I look at Drake without thinking. He winks at me.

Arrogant bastard.

'Back to the body,' the Secundus goes on. 'We're waiting on the post mortem, but initial tests have shown rohypnol in his blood.'

'We had a look in the Creep Box,' Naia says. 'There was one suspect who seemed like he might fit the M.O., but Ed tested the substances he uses against the sample of Grant's blood and there's no match, so either he changed up his method or he's not our guy.'

'He's not our guy,' I say, wishing Naia had said nothing. We're going to be the ones to deal with Felton. I don't want to say too much to the Invicti, because once they're involved we'll never get away clean. 'The only common element was the use of sedatives. Nothing else matches. It's a dead end.'

Naia cottons on quickly. She says, 'I agree. Dead end.'

'All right, then,' says the Secundus. 'Then there's the wife. She thinks he might have been having an affair, because something changed a few months ago.'

'I don't think that's it,' says Meyer from his position by the board. 'She only thinks he was having an affair because he was out a lot of evenings and started behaving differently, right?'

'That's what she said,' Cam confirms.

'Right,' says Meyer. 'But we know that he was practically bankrupt. He was working overtime to try to cover his tracks before his partners noticed the embezzlement–'

'We're not sure that it's embezzlement yet,' the captain interrupts.

'Sure, but it was at least mismanagement. Either way, he's been spending all his time smoothing things over, trying to climb out of the hole. That could just as easily explain his absences and his strange behaviour. There's no reason to think it's an affair.'

'Then that's number three,' says the Secundus. 'We need to speak to the business partners and their associates.' Meyer adds it to the board. 'That's why Baron Drake is here today. Baron, if you wouldn't mind laying it out for us?'

His title doesn't suit him. Barons are long-haired, mediæval weirdos in tights and codpieces, or they're the dashing, ripped-shirt heroes of romance novels. Drake is neither. His dark hair is too short to be mediæval, and his brown-black eyes lack the gold flecking that is required of romance heartthrobs. In his black jeans and blue shirt, he's a disappointment.

'Cope, Grant and Carding Limited is a property investment company,' he says. 'The three directors are right there in the name, and they're big business. You might never have heard of them, but every Silver with money to spare has. CGC has made us some serious profits with their investment portfolios. The way I see it, that's the strongest link between the Silver and David Grant.'

'You think this is about money?' Meyer asks.

'Maybe,' Drake says. 'It wouldn't hurt to have a look at CGC's records to see whose money they've lost recently.'

The Secundus nods to Meyer, and it goes on the board.

'Will you be on the list?' I ask Drake, prodding to see if he'll bite.

'Valentine,' the Secundus warns, but Drake is already answering me.

'I will be,' he says, his dark eyes burning into mine. 'But you don't need to worry about my finances. I assure you, I have more than enough to get by on. I've already given you my alibi, but perhaps you'd like me to show you exactly what kind of resources I have at my disposal?'

'You're not under investigation,' the Secundus says again, glaring at me before turning back to Drake. 'We're grateful for your time, Baron. You know the local Silver dignitaries better than I do. Is there anyone you think we should check out?'

Drake drags his gaze away from me and focuses on the Secundus. 'You might take a look at Percival Windsor. He's been around these parts for centuries, but he has far less money than he should, because he also has a bit of a gambling habit. If any Silver would have overstretched himself on speculative investments, it would be Percy. And then there's Lydia Gainsborough. She's relatively new, only fifty or so years turned, but she's rising quickly and likely to take big risks.'

Their names go on the board.

'Have we missed anything?' the Secundus asks the table.

'The notebook,' says Cam. 'The wife said Grant had a notebook he was always scribbling in. She couldn't find it at the house and it wasn't on his body.'

It goes on the board.

'Okay then,' the Secundus says. 'Let's divide up the—'

'We're ignoring the obvious,' Boyd interrupts. His tone is one of contained frustration. He's trying to play the part of the dutiful foot soldier, but he's doing it badly. He hates being just another subordinate, instead of the deputy. The Secundus must realise that, because when he answers his tone is gentle.

'Go on,' he says.

'There are two options here. Option one is that the murder of David Grant is about him personally. In that case, I'd agree that this is all relevant. We need to gather as much information as possible about who he was, what he was doing the night he died and who might have wanted him dead, because if it's about him then the motive will lead us to the killer. But option two is that the murder is related to the London scab killings. If that's the case, then we're wasting our time because all indications are that the scab chose the London victims randomly – who they were was irrelevant as long as they fit the profile. Correct me if I'm wrong, but the only reason you're here is that you believe they *are* connected, so why are we bothering with any of this? We should be concentrating on profiling the rogue Silver, not examining the ins and outs of Grant's life.'

Boyd has his elbows on the table now, leaning forward. The Secundus mirrors his posture as he replies.

'We can't rule out anything right now. The methods aren't a perfect match. The London victims were bitten, not drained.'

'Serial killers evolve,' says Boyd.

'*Human* serials, yes. Silver serials? Not so much. In my experience, they like to be recognised, so they don't change their signatures. Either way, we have to investigate every avenue.'

'But your working theory is that they're connected?' Boyd presses.

'Yes,' he says. 'That's the theory. Now we just have to prove it and hope that it will lead us to our man.'

The captain holds me and Naia back while the others leave the conference room.

'Before you go,' she says, 'we've had a complaint from a Matthew Felton. Said a couple of Seekers broke into his place, removed three donors and stole his property, all without cause. He described them as two women, one white with dark hair, the other brown-skinned with lots of tattoos. Ring any bells?'

'He complained?' Naia says in disbelief. 'That pervert? He deserved everything he got, and more.'

'And to be fair,' I add, 'the door was open. We didn't actually break in.'

The captain stares at us both for a long moment.

'Just be careful with that one,' she says eventually. 'He has influential friends.'

One name leaps to mind.

Killian fucking Drake.

But Captain Langford follows my train of thought and promptly derails it.

'There's more than one influential Silver in this country, Valentine,' she says. 'Stop fixating on the Baron. It's becoming petty. Don't forget that if it wasn't for him, you wouldn't even have this job.'

I blink.

'What?'

'You didn't know?' The captain seems genuinely surprised. 'I thought you'd have worked it out by now. He insisted that you join the Seekers. You've certainly earned your place over the last couple of decades, but back then? If he hadn't pushed for it, it would never have happened. You owe him, Valentine, whether you like it or not. You might want to start acting like it.'

I stare at her, retrofitting the pieces of my history and finding that they suddenly make a very different picture from the one I had imagined.

Eighteen-year-old me was convinced she had the gift of the gab, that she could talk her way into anything and then out of trouble just as easily. When Winta – one-night stand and love of my short life – went missing, I swore I would find her and eventually I did. She was trapped in Drake's basement, caged up and blood-starved. Of course, back then I didn't know that vampires were real. I looked at her and saw a helpless girl enslaved, when in reality I was looking at a rogue vampire who had been contained for the good of humanity.

I had no idea what I was walking into. I thought I was going to save her, if you can believe that. What a joke. I got too close to the bars and suddenly she wasn't blood-starved anymore. She was strong enough to free herself and run. She was long gone before the Seekers had a chance to find her trail.

This is the truth I can't voice: it was my fault she went missing.

I can blame Drake for not containing Winta and blame the Seekers for not coming soon enough, but it was my blood that set her free. Without me, she would never have got loose.

Drake knows what I did. He knows that I was a naïve little girl who thought she was in love and let Winta take advantage of that, and I hate him for it. I blame him because I can't blame her, because despite what she'd done, for a long time I missed her so much that it hurt. I blamed him because I was sure that he blamed me.

But now that certainty is gone.

I look out through the window of the conference room and into the quad, where Drake is standing with Meyer and the Secundus. He nods at Meyer, then looks back in our direction and catches my eye through the glass. He smiles, the same sly smile he always gives me, the one that says he knows more than I do. I've always assumed that he was threatening me with that hidden knowledge.

I don't know whether to resent him or thank him. All I know is that I feel impotent and empty, because I no longer have a target on which to spend my rage.

A distraction is in order, and thankfully there's one waiting for me in my bed.

I swing by the canteen to grab a couple of coffees to take back to my rooms. Naia and Cam are already there, fuelling up for this morning's outings.

'You're a mess, Jack,' Naia says to me.

She's not wrong, but I'm riled up after the captain's big revelation and her scathing tone rubs me up the wrong way.

'You're the one who wanted me to let my hair down,' I say.

'I didn't tell you to get Massacre-drunk while the Invicti are visiting. I just wanted you to get laid. Which I'm guessing you didn't, because you couldn't even walk by the time I left last night.'

I cannot believe what I'm hearing. The way the judgement rolls off her, you'd think she was tucked up in bed by ten with a hot cocoa instead of dancing the night away with Cam.

'You're such a hypocrite,' I say. 'You were right there with us last night.'

'I had one of those drinks. One. Then I switched back to the straight stuff, because I knew I had to work today and I knew I'd be worthless if I drank more than that. Did you even count how many you necked?'

I cross my arms, sulking because I don't have an answer for her. I remember the first three Massacres, but after that my mind is a blank.

'What's with the attitude?' she says. 'I get it: you don't like people telling you what to do. You think you're a free spirit and a rebel and that you're standing up to the man, but you're really just being a dick, and you're fucking up any chance you ever have of joining the Solis Invicti. The *Invicti*, Jack.'

'You think I want to be part of their club?'

'Yes, however much you deny it. Of course you do. Everyone does, because they're the *fucking Invicti*. The most elite Silver guard in the country, with all the perks and power that come with being so close to the Primus. So stop acting like a twat and listen to what they have to say. Who knows? You might even learn something.'

'Learn something?' I say, getting angry now. 'Who was it who caught the Sunday Serial? Who was it who worked out that the Norwich murders were about trafficking people and not drugs? And when everyone else had given up on ever finding the Cheltenham strangler, who stayed awake for five days in a row to track the money back to Russia? My record speaks for itself.'

'Yeah, but so does the blood on your jeans.' She sneers and looks down at my legs.

Fuck.

I must have spilled a Massacre last night. It's not just that I can smell it, I can also see the darker spots on the black denim where it's sunk into the weave. By the time I look up again, Naia is already walking away.

'Shit,' I say, dropping down into the seat next to Cam.

'Are you okay?' he asks.

'Sure. What does she know?' I force a laugh, taking down my ponytail then putting it up again, just to give me something to do with my hands.

He raises his eyebrows at me.

'What?'

'You're a crap liar, Jack.'

'Well, that's insulting on several levels.'

'I mean it. You're doing what you always do. You had a bit of a shaky start with the Secundus, so instead of trying to redeem yourself, to show him how good you really are, you've just given up. You're sabotaging yourself, so when you fail you can tell yourself it doesn't matter, that no one is judging your actual worth, because you weren't even trying.' He points a finger at me. 'Classic self-saboteur.'

'Oh, fuck off.' I bat his finger away, trying to laugh it off, but it won't work because I know he's right. Damn him, he always is.

'You're going up against the Baron of Oxford,' he says, 'who's cosying up to the Primus, and here you are pissing off him and the Secundus. It's like you're deliberately screwing yourself over, and I'm not going to sit here and watch it. If you're going to keep up this vendetta, whether or not the Baron had anything to do with the May Day murder, then you need to play the game. Besides which, Drew is actually an okay guy.'

'So it's Drew now, is it? You're on nickname terms?'

He smiles, then chucks me under the chin. 'Give him a chance, Jack. He might surprise you.'

'I doubt that,' I mutter, but not with any conviction.

'Then give yourself the chance to surprise him. What have you got to lose?'

'My self respect?'

He laughs. 'As though you ever had any. You were asleep under the table last night. I had to carry you half the way home.'

'Thanks, Cam,' I say, pulling his arms around me. 'And hey, I'm sorry about Ed.'

'Thanks, but it's okay. I'm all right, really.' He holds me close, squeezing me tight.

'So,' he says after a moment. 'Did your Tabby purr?'

'Don't you start.'

'Go on,' he says, releasing me with one final squeeze. 'Get cleaned up. I'll see you out front in an hour.'

I'm pissed off and nervous when I leave the canteen, a coffee cup in each hand. I'm pissed off because I know that Naia and Cam are both right and I'm nervous because bringing coffee for the doctor feels worryingly domestic. Sure, nothing's happened between us yet, but I want it to. As I walk, I'm thinking my way through every direction this conversation could take, good and bad.

Maybe she's waiting for me, naked.

Maybe she's straight and just really friendly.

Or maybe this could be something special. I can feel the potential in it. It makes my stomach flip as I remember her smile. It's been a long time since I felt this way about anyone and I'm scared I'm going to mess it up.

But all my speculation is irrelevant, because when I get back to my rooms Dr Ross is no longer there. Instead, there's just a note. She's placed it carefully on the pillow of my neatly-made bed.

Got called into work. Sorry about last night. Thank you for letting me stay. Tabitha

Sorry? She's *sorry* about last night? What is that supposed to mean?

I want to send her a text to ask, but I was so drunk that I never thought to exchange numbers with her and this morning I was in such a rush that the future got lost in the sheer joy of seeing her wake up in my bed.

All trace of that feeling has gone now. The hangover regrets are hitting and they're hitting hard. I'm second-guessing everything, because I'm sure I must have done something to drive her away.

Somehow, this is my fault.

12

WE ALL MEET in the quad at half past ten: Boyd, Cam, Naia, Meyer, the Secundus and me.

'Jacqueline,' Boyd says. He's standing with Meyer. 'You're with us.'

I've clearly missed a conversation while I was showering and changing. The split must have been pre-arranged, because no one objects.

'Just like we discussed,' says the Secundus. Like *they* discussed. 'We'll meet back here afterwards. Stay in touch.'

'Yes, sir,' we all chorus. I join in even though I have no idea what's going on, because I figure I've damaged my reputation enough for the day. Naia's right: I need to start mending fences, or building bridges, or some other kind of construction metaphor.

The Secundus marches off with Cam and Naia, while I follow Boyd and Meyer over to one of the Seeker cars. It's a three-door Fiat 500, great for city driving, but not so great when there are three of you and two of them are men over six feet tall. Without any kind of discussion, it is accepted that I will be sitting in the back seat. Normally I might object, but I'm playing the contrite subordinate, so I just fold the seat forwards and clamber in without complaint.

I feel like I deserve a pat on the head from Boyd for my compliance, but he's giving me nothing.

'So,' I say as he reverses out onto the road. 'Where are we going?'

'First out to the business park, then on to a village called Aston,' says Meyer from the front passenger seat. He's had to push it all the way back to make room for his knees. 'We're visiting the offices of Cope, Grant and Carding to speak to Mr Cope, then we're speaking to Percival Windsor. The others are interviewing Carding and Gainsborough at their homes.'

'Haven't the police already interviewed the business partners?'

'You trust the plods?' Meyer says. 'We'll do our own interviews.'

I raise my eyebrows at Boyd in the rear-view mirror. The Seekers have a decent working relationship with the police, but the Solis Invicti clearly feel no need to get along with the locals. This is a worry, since the Secundus has been the one liaising with the police since he arrived. I can only hope that he hasn't trashed the rapport we've spent the past couple of decades building.

We get stuck in traffic on the Cowley Road, so it takes forty-five minutes to get to the business park. When we arrive, it takes another quarter of an hour to navigate the roundabouts and find the building we're looking for. The offices of Cope, Grant and Carding Limited are not signposted. We finally track them down on the north side of the park, where they occupy the top two floors of a five-storey block of managed office space. We only discover this by driving up to every building one by one and having

Meyer get out of the car to look at the names on the doorbells for each floor.

CGC obviously doesn't get many visitors, or at least none that have not been given detailed instructions.

Once we've parked the car and Boyd has hauled me out of the back seat, we all walk up to the door together. Meyer presses the appropriate buzzer. There's no response. He tries the door, but it's locked tight.

After a few seconds, he tries the buzzer again.

When that fails, he leans on the buzzers for all five floors and we hear the door click open like magic. We're in and apparently we're not expected.

This is a fancy building, but there's no music in the lift, nor is there a mirror. I feel sold short by every television show I've ever watched.

'Is that what you always wear?' Meyer says to me as we ascend.

'Yeah,' I reply, not sure what he's getting at. 'It's practical. Jeans, boots, leather jacket. What's wrong with that?' Boyd is wearing a similar outfit, although his jacket is canvas and somehow makes him look altogether smarter.

'You look like a biker,' Meyer says to me.

I eye his cargos. 'Well, you look like a soldier.' It's not as cutting as I had hoped, but it's accurate.

'Most days,' he says, 'I am.' When he smiles at me, there's a hint of humour in his eyes. He's just testing the water.

I'm reserving my judgement about the Secundus, but maybe Meyer's not so bad.

The lift doors ping open and disgorge us into a marble-floored waiting room with leather sofas and a wide marble reception desk. It's empty. To either side of the desk, doorways lead to open-plan office space that is filled with desks and computers, and yet everything is utterly silent.

There's not one keyboard clacking, not one pair of heels tapping, and not one single telephone ringing.

'It's Friday, right?' I say, worried that the Massacres have affected my perception of time.

'It's definitely Friday,' Meyer confirms.

'Four-day week?' Boyd suggests. 'Grief counselling for Grant? Or maybe compassionate leave?'

Then we hear a noise from the far end of the building.

The three of us exchange glances. If we were human and in America, this is the point at which we'd draw our guns, but we're vampires in England, so we swallow blood tablets from our belts instead. Our Silver abilities are our best offensive weapons.

Boyd goes in first, staying close to the wall. I follow on behind, with Meyer guarding our backs. We're not usually so cautious when dealing with humans, but the noise from the closed office we're heading towards sounded a lot like the ratchet of a shotgun. A shot from one of those might not be fatal to the Silver, but it could blow a big enough hole to take us out for a day or two. Plus, it would hurt like hell. I'm not volunteering as cannon fodder.

When we're only a few metres away from the closed door, we hear voices on the other side. They're low and urgent.

A man says, 'Just hand them over. No one has to get hurt.'

Then a woman's voice, her words eclipsed by her distress. Her breath is hitching in panic.

Meyer nods and Boyd takes it as his signal to kick in the door.

For a moment, I'm confused.

I was expecting a hostage situation. I thought maybe one of CGC's investors had lost big and turned up here with a gun to try to recoup his losses. It wouldn't be the first time white-collar crime inspired that sort of rage. Instead, the door opens to reveal a man and woman wrestling over a handful of papers. They each have hold of one edge and neither is letting go. On the desk in front of them, there's a large hole punch sitting next to an open lever-arch file.

Boyd walks over to the desk and tests the hole punch.

Meyer groans.

The noise we heard from outside wasn't a shotgun ratcheting. It was just the sound of paper being hole-punched.

What a waste of blood tablets.

'Who are you?' the man says to us, still not letting go of the papers. The woman is equally tenacious, so they're in a stalemate.

'We're working with the police to investigate the death of Mr Grant,' says Meyer, then he steps forward and takes the papers easily from their combined grip. 'Are you Mr Cope?'

The man nods, rubbing his hands together as though he's itching to snatch back the documents. 'Those are confidential papers,' he says, but Meyer is already leafing through them. 'They're not subject to disclosure—'

'A man is dead, Mr Cope,' says Boyd, then he turns to the woman. 'And you are?'

'Sarah Jenkins,' the woman says. She's in her early forties, with brown skin, a dark bob and a generous figure. She wears a dark blue skirt-suit that looks as though it was tailored for her. 'I was Mr Grant's associate. I was about to become partner, actually, before…' She gestures vaguely, not needing to finish the sentence. It's clear from the way she's looking at Cope that her prospects of partnership are now rather diminished.

'What's this all about, Ms Jenkins?' Meyer says, waving the papers.

She sighs. 'Embezzlement.'

'That is a slander,' says Cope, indignant. He must be in his sixties, with a belly that attests to too many boozy lunches and a bald spot he's trying to hide under a wispy combover. 'There is no proof that—'

'That's the proof,' says Jenkins, pointing at the papers. 'You can't just shred it all and expect it to go away. It's filed electronically, backed-up and duplicated.' She shakes her head in exasperation, then looks at us and mutters, 'Bloody dinosaur.'

If only she knew who she was talking to. I'm willing to put money on the fact that Meyer is on his third century at least. He conveys his age in the way he behaves with these two, treating them as though they are misbehaving children rather than the executives of a multi-million pound enterprise, but he still retains an appropriate level of civility. He's obviously done this thousands of times before, not just recently, but in times when social classes were more clearly defined, when proper manners were essential.

He has a talent for it.

'Sit down, please,' Meyer says to the humans. 'Both of you.'

There's a small meeting table to one side of the room. Jenkins takes a seat there, while Cope sits down in his desk chair. Meyer and I join Jenkins at the table, but Boyd hovers in the doorway, making sure everyone is aware of who's controlling this meeting. Meyer hands the papers to Boyd, getting them out of reach of the humans.

'Start at the beginning, please,' Meyer says.

Jenkins is the one who replies. 'Money is missing from some of our customers' accounts.'

'There is no proof—'

'We will get to you in a moment, Mr Cope,' says Meyer. 'Please continue, Ms Jenkins.'

'I've been looking at the accounts closely for the past couple of months. I was deciding whether it would be worth putting myself forward for the board when Carding retires at the end of the year. But I found that there were inconsistencies.'

'What kind of inconsistencies?'

'Well,' she says, sitting back in her seat, 'the fact that we kept losing money, for one. We were taking on more properties every year, advertising better returns on investment, and we were working hard to make sure they paid off. But still, the company and its investors weren't making the kinds of gains they should have been. So I checked the portfolios one by one and found that some of the entries had been faked. Grant was picking the investors whose portfolios were performing well, then adding non-existent investments to offset their gains. He made it look as though the value of the portfolios had increased only slightly, then skimmed the balance of the profits for himself. It's amazingly complicated and he hid the trail well, but it's there if you look for it. I've highlighted the relevant funds.'

Boyd glances at the papers in his hands. Meyer has his back to him so he misses it, but I see the moment when Boyd's eyes go wide. I'm about to ask what he's found, but he gives me a tiny shake of the head and looks pointedly at Meyer. Whatever Boyd's looking at, it is not for the ears of the Invicti.

I'm impatient to speak to Boyd alone, so I don't pay much attention to the rest of the discussion. There's no love lost between Cope and Jenkins, but Cope eventually has to admit that there is something suspicious in CGC's accounts. He's worried about his liability as a director – that much is clear – but once Meyer has assured him that we're only interested in his business dealings to the extent that they pertain to Grant's murder, he relaxes visibly.

'Where's everyone else?' Meyer asks.

Jenkins gives him a resigned look. 'How were we supposed to pay them? We had to let them all go. We're shutting down. The creditors will get everything that's left.'

'And what about your clients? Do you think the embezzlement could have been a motive for Grant's murder?'

'How? No one knew,' Cope says. 'We only found out a couple of days before he died, and that was only because Sarah spoke to the lawyer about it. We didn't have a clue until then.'

'You told no one else?'

'No,' says Cope and Jenkins repeats the same. 'We were all sworn to secrecy,' Cope goes on, 'and it was in our interests to keep it all under wraps. You must see that. Making some kind of an insolvency arrangement was our only chance of getting out of this with our reputations and fortunes intact. No chance of that now, is there? This whole business has just shone a light on things we'd rather not have examined. Why would we want that?'

'And the opera trip with the lawyer?' I ask.

Cope shakes his head. 'David's stupid idea to get her on side. It didn't work anyway, not that I ever thought it would. He was always trying to manipulate his way out of holes he'd dug for himself, stupid boy. I knew it would be the death of this company when we took him on.'

While Cope speaks, Jenkins purses her lips. She's holding something back.

'Ms Jenkins?' I ask.

She looks at Cope for a second before turning to me and saying, 'If you want the truth, he was a social-climbing sleaze.'

'Sarah!' Cope says.

'What does it matter?' she replies. 'He's dead and gone and everyone knew it anyway. The only reason he was prepared to put me forward for the board was that he fancied me. Don't get me wrong, I'm damn good at this job and I deserved it, but he wouldn't have stuck his neck out for me if he wasn't hoping for a payoff later. That's the kind of man he was, always trying to buy you with money or favours.'

I look at Cope, who has deflated like a sad soufflé.

'You shouldn't speak ill of the dead,' he says. 'But she's not wrong.'

'If it were me,' says Jenkins, 'I'd go looking for the pissed-off husbands. I bet you anything, that's what got him killed.'

'So we're back to the affair theory?' Boyd asks as we leave the building. He's trying to distract attention from the papers Meyer handed him, which have magically disappeared somewhere about his person.

'I don't know,' I reply. 'Plenty of letches out there, but I can't imagine one of the Silver getting that worked up over a human.'

Cross-race romantic relationships aren't completely unknown, but the occurrences are rare enough to be remarkable. My only personal experience of them was with Winta when I was still human, and we all know how well that worked out.

'We can be just as possessive as they are,' Meyer says. 'More so, sometimes. We can't rule it out completely, but I agree that it seems unlikely. The embezzlement angle seems like the stronger lead. Let's see what the next interview brings, then we can check in with the others and see what Carding had to say for himself.'

I crawl into the back seat of the Fiat again. It's lucky I have so little dignity left to lose, because the process is not graceful.

'I'll drive,' Meyer says to Boyd. 'We've got GPS, right?'

Boyd hands over the keys because he has no other choice, but he looks helpless and uncomfortable as he cedes control, as though something is itching under his skin.

This is why he'll never make the cut for the Solis Invicti. Boyd is bad at hierarchy. He likes to be in charge when we're out in the field. Actually, he doesn't just like it, he needs it. If he's not in control then he gets antsy and nervous, which is when he makes mistakes. When he's our leader, calling the shots and supporting us all, then he is an excellent investigator, despite the stick up his arse. When he's not, he's so busy trying to take back control that he misses the big picture. He can be petty like that.

I'm tempted to think that his pettiness is the reason he's concealed the papers as well, but he's not that insubordinate. If he's keeping them from Meyer, then there must be a good reason for it.

I just wish I knew what it was.

13

ASTON MANOR HOUSE is the centrepiece of the most beautiful Cotswolds village I've ever seen. Everything is pale stone and tumbling ivy. Farrow and Ball paint colours abound, with names like *bone*, *lichen* and *pigeon*. Boyd rattles them all off for us as we crawl down the narrow country lanes.

'How do you know this shit?' I ask, peering over his shoulder from the back seat. He's taking photos of every house we pass, then cataloguing them in an app on his phone.

'I like design,' he replies, as though it's the most natural thing in the world. You'd think you'd know everything there was to know about someone after working with them for twenty years, but apparently I'm still capable of being surprised.

The gravelled driveway crunches under the tyres as we turn past the sign for the house. It's a long drive, lined with trees and those big stone mushrooms that seem to have no purpose whatsoever.

'Staddle stones,' Boyd says as we pass a whole line of them. He takes more photos. 'They used to be the supports for granaries, to keep water and vermin out.'

'How do you *know* this shit?' I say again.

'I used to build them.'

That shuts me up. We don't talk much about our former lives, or how we were turned, not with people who aren't our closest friends. I don't even know all the details of Cam's past lives. It's a bit taboo in Silver circles.

But I'm still surprised to learn that Boyd is so old. It makes sense, because he's the deputy after all and the Silver are gerontocratic by nature, but he's just so modern that it's difficult to imagine him living in any other century. I can't see him as a farmer, busily building granaries. The only way Boyd makes sense is as a slightly awkward investigator, gadget-mad, wearing clothes that make him look like a geriatric trying to dress cool. I'm guessing that he's always been a little out of step with the rest of the world.

When we finally reach the house, we're faced with a Georgian mansion that wouldn't be out of place in a BBC period drama. The building is enormous and it's covered with sags of wisteria in full bloom. I'm not much of a homes and gardens connoisseur – unlike Boyd, apparently – but even I'm impressed.

'I've heard about this place,' Meyer says as he parks the car. There's a football field's worth of gravel, so it's not so much about finding a space as it is about working out where we're least likely to be sullying the view. A stagecoach and four horses would have been more appropriate, if impractical.

'There are gatherings here,' he goes on. 'Parties. People come out from London for them. Windsor's a popular guy.'

'Windsor,' Boyd says as he helps me out of the back seat. 'Any relation to the royal family?'

'Not that he lets on,' says Meyer. 'I wouldn't be surprised, though. He has old money, and even older secrets. His associates are as close-lipped as he is.'

Meyer rings the doorbell under the ornate porch, which is held up by actual columns. We can hear the bell ringing from this side of the door, and it sounds like an actual bell. I wonder whether they have them in every room, to summon servants bringing lemon tea and scones. That's the impression the place gives off. That's why I'm expecting a butler to open the door, or maybe a housekeeper wearing a neat apron and a stern expression. What I get is a louche Silver aristocrat whose generous, hairless body is barely covered by a silk dressing gown. He looks like an overgrown baby with a mop of blond hair, and his eyes have such dark shadows underneath them that for a moment I think he has twin shiners. The odour coming off him makes it clear that what he actually has is a killer hangover and the aftereffects of a sleepless night spent with two – no, three – women. Either they must be extremely indiscriminate, or he must be paying them extravagantly.

'Who are you? What do you want?' He sounds as though he's speaking whilst chewing a toffee. It might be the hangover, or maybe he's just so posh that all of his words run into each other.

The upwardly-mobile enunciate, but the truly privileged have no use for consonants.

'Percival Windsor?' Meyer asks.

'Answer the damn question, man.'

'My name is Thomas Meyer. This is Deputy Boyd and Ms Valentine of the Seekers.'

Windsor is not impressed.

There's a barking noise coming from somewhere inside the house, which surprises me since the Silver aren't generally fond of canines. There's a lot of bollocks talked about the difference between cat people and dog people – how cat people are independent and difficult, whereas dog people are needy and easy-going – but since I turned Silver the real difference has become obvious: dog people have practically zero sense of smell.

Dogs smell revolting. I'll grant you that there are some exceptions, but for the most part they have a potent aroma of dirty puddle mixed with effluent. Cats, on the other hand, smell much more tolerable. It's something about the type of bacteria they have in their mouths. Ed tried to explain it to me once, but then he started getting out slides and showing me cultures, so I had to make up an excuse to get out of the lab sharpish, but the point is that this is a documented phenomenon amongst the Silver. Our sense of smell is so acute that even being in the same room as a dog can be grating, so the fact that Windsor chooses to own one is remarkable. And worrying. I can think of only two reasons for it: either he's frequently out of it and needs a dog to fetch help when he takes his indulgences too far – which I wouldn't put past him, given his dishevelled appearance – or something makes him feel like he needs a guard dog.

But what could he want to protect so fiercely that it would be worth the reek?

He turns into the house and shouts, 'Caldwell! Check on the dog!' Then he pauses, waiting to hear that his order is obeyed before turning back to us.

'Seekers, hmm?' he says, looking unimpressed. 'And what do you want?'

'We're investigating a murder,' Meyer says.

'Oh?'

This is where a normal person would invite us in, maybe offer us some tea and a biscuit. From the way he's blocking the door, it's clear that Windsor doesn't have the slightest intention of doing so.

Maybe Windsor has something in the house he doesn't want us to see.

Or maybe he's just rude.

'David Grant,' Meyer perseveres. 'Did you know him?'

'Silver?' Windsor asks.

'Human.'

'Then of course I didn't bloody well know him. Don't you know who I am? You think I'd bother with humans? They only live for five minutes.'

'He was a partner in Cope, Grant and Carding. You've heard of them?'

'Rings a bell. Investments, that sort of thing. I've heard people mention them.'

'At your parties?'

'Gatherings,' Windsor corrects, but he doesn't respond to the question.

'Perhaps we could attend one of them,' Boyd suggests, putting on his most deferential tone. 'Speak to the guests?'

'Out of the question,' Windsor says with a dismissive wave of the hand. 'My gatherings are absolutely exclusive and your sort would only lower the tone.'

'*My* sort?' Boyd says.

Uh oh.

I suspect that Boyd and Windsor experienced the transatlantic slave trade rather differently. One wrong word now and Windsor is mincemeat, no matter what his pedigree.

'Seekers,' he hisses, as though he can think of nothing more repugnant. 'You think you have the right to police us, we who've been vested in the glorious state of eternity for centuries? It is our inheritance, our birthright.' He eyes me and Boyd with a sneer. 'New blood.'

I've had enough.

'Okay, Mr Windsor–'

'It's Sir Percival, to you.'

Of course he has a knighthood. All the toffs probably come to his parties to get their upper-class rocks off.

'Sir Percival,' says Meyer, sensibly taking control again. 'I am one of the Solis Invicti.' That gets his attention.

'Are you?' Windsor says. 'Well, I'll have you know that the Tertius is a close personal friend of mine.'

'That's as may be, but I am here under the authority of the Secundus, who is here in Oxfordshire to run this investigation. He would appreciate your cooperation.'

Windsor eyes Boyd and me once more, but he bites his tongue.

Crisis averted. Boyd simmers down, though if I were him then I probably would have punched Windsor anyway. I'm sure he's done more than enough to deserve it.

'I'm sorry,' Windsor says to Meyer, though he's obviously not the least bit sorry, 'but it's quite impossible. I cannot compromise the confidentiality of my guests. In any case, your Seekers would stick out like a sore thumb. Quite impossible.'

'Sir Perci–'

But Windsor has already turned back into the house, yelling, 'Caldwell!'

He leaves the door open by just a few inches. We can hear footsteps approaching fast, but we can't see who's coming.

'Where the hell were you, man?' Windsor says.

The voice that answers is too quiet for me to make out.

'Deal with this rabble,' says Windsor. 'I'm going back to bed.'

We stand on the doorstep and wait as the footsteps approach. I'm expecting another Silver when the door swings open once more, perhaps another partygoer who can help us with our investigation, but instead we are greeted by a human. He's maybe forty years old, with greying hair and a dark suit. He's a bit young for it, but my brain immediately fills in the gaps: butler.

'Good day to you, sirs, madam,' he says.

Then he slams the door in our faces.

When we get back to the college, we meet with the others in the conference room to exchange news. We've fared better than they have. Carding refused to say anything at all without his lawyer present and Lydia Gainsborough never invested with CGC, although when they turned up she was in the middle of a drunken orgy that required significant clean-up from the Seekers.

'It was like the last days of Rome,' Cam says, his eyes wide. The poor boy looks as though he's been scarred for life. 'Humans and Silver everywhere, running around with no clothes on.' He shudders. Sometimes Cam can be positively Victorian in his attitudes.

'No leads though?' Boyd asks.

'Nothing,' says the Secundus. 'After that day's work, it looks like the only useful thing we've gained is the paperwork from CGC.'

'I'm on it, sir,' Boyd says, before anyone can suggest an alternative. 'I'll comb through the documents and let you know what I find.'

'Very well. Keep me informed, but I think it's time that we divide our efforts. As you pointed out, Deputy, we're working on the assumption that this case is connected to the London murders, so for now the Invicti will concentrate on the commonalities and put together a profile. In the meantime, the Seekers will concentrate on chasing down the leads on the Grant case alone.'

The captain says, 'I agree,' as though the Secundus has asked for her input. In reality, it's clear that she has no say in the matter.

'We'll be in touch,' says the Secundus.

He and Meyer don't waste any time leaving.

'He's handsome all right,' Naia says when they've gone, 'but he's bloody bossy.'

'They have bigger things to worry about than one human death,' says Captain Langford. 'I'm surprised they stayed as long as they did.'

'Back to London then?' I say.

'Not for long, I'm sure,' says Langford. 'They'll be back on Monday. They can't leave this one unsolved. It's bad enough that we have a serial-killing Silver on our hands, but to have it all displayed so publicly? It's bad news.' Langford looks more serious than I've ever seen her before, but she also seems vulnerable, unbuttoning her suit jacket as she slumps back into her chair. It makes me uneasy. 'If this goes on too long, we might have to take drastic action.'

'What do you mean?' Cam asks.

'They're not saying it, but they're worried.' She pushes her hand back through her short hair, sending it into disarray. 'We have to think about the end game. What happens if there are so many murders that the population starts panicking? Worse, what if these public displays start to incorporate the killings themselves? What if whoever is behind them decides to show himself to the world? What do we do then?'

We're all silent for a moment as we process the implications.

'I guess we come out,' says Naia, then she looks at Cam. 'It wouldn't be the first time, for some of us.'

'Very funny,' he mutters with a wry smile.

But the captain isn't laughing.

'This is not a joke,' she says. 'You don't realise how much is at stake here.' Naia opens her mouth, doubtless going for the obvious pun, but Langford cuts her off. 'Don't. Just think about it. If we have to go public, then there'll be all-out war. Life as we know it will turn on its head, and that's not good for us or the humans. People will die, people whose blood we depend on to survive. I don't mean to be bleak, but that's what we're facing here. You know why the Seekers exist, but I'm not sure any of you appreciates how vital our work is. Our Primus is principled, I believe, but in the face of human panic he'd have no choice but to rise up. I know what the world looks like with him in charge and I don't want to see it again in my lifetime. Trust me, you don't either. It's not a kind world, or one that appreciates individuality and compromise. I need you all to understand the situation as it is.'

All of us nod solemnly, except Boyd. He just looks worried.

'I think the situation might be worse than you think,' he says, pulling the papers from CGC out of his jacket. 'I don't think it's the humans we have to worry about.'

He slides the papers onto the tabletop then fans them out so we can all see. They contain densely-packed lines of text detailing the values of various funds. I guess they must represent different portfolios of investments. Some are highlighted, I assume by Ms Jenkins.

The name of one catches my eye: *Silver Services Ltd.* Then another: *Solomon Enterprises Limited.* And most worryingly of all: *Solis Invicti Holdings Ltd.*

'Holy shit,' Naia breathes.

'What does this mean?' Cam asks, flipping through the pages. 'Are you suggesting that the Primus is caught up in all this? That he's involved in the embezzlement at CGC? The murders?'

'If he is, then the Secundus and Meyer don't know it,' says Boyd. 'Meyer's the one who gave me the papers back at CGC and the Secundus didn't have any problem with me being the one to sift through these records. Why would they have let me do that if they knew this was what I'd find?'

'Have you pulled up details on the companies?' I ask.

'Not yet, but I will.'

'Holy shit,' Naia says again. 'What do we do now?'

'Well,' I say, 'we obviously can't trust the Invicti right now. Maybe Meyer and the Secundus aren't involved, but there's clearly something going on.'

'We need to dig into the embezzlement,' Boyd says. 'We need to go through the paperwork and we need to talk to Sir Percival's friends.'

The captain clears her throat. Up until now, she has been conspicuously silent.

'You didn't show this to me,' she says, pushing the papers back over the table towards Boyd. 'I never saw it.'

She looks at each of us, making sure we've got the message.

'Now,' she goes on, 'I'm going home for the weekend. I suggest you all do the same, because on Monday the remaining test results will be in and then you won't get a break until we've wrapped this case. Understood?'

'Yes, Captain,' we chorus, because we understand perfectly: we have two days to get to the bottom of this mess while she maintains deniability.

'Good. You might want to consider taking your paperwork home with you,' she says to Boyd, then she leaves the four of us alone in the conference room, shutting the door firmly behind her.

Cam and I take our homework into our office. The whole college is a ghost town on Friday nights, because people either go out drinking or go back to their country homes for the weekend. We're the only ones still here.

We're supposed to be skimming through the CGC investor records, trying to pick out those who were Silver, but I'm finding it hard to concentrate on my task. I know there are bigger things going on right now, but I can't stop thinking about the doctor's hair on my pillow, the rumbling Scots lilt to her voice, and those horrible words: *Sorry about last night.*

I'm obviously not hiding my distraction very well, because Cam notices.

'What's up?' he asks me.

So I tell him about the doctor.

'I didn't get her number,' I say despondently. 'Didn't give her mine either.'

'Rookie mistake.'

'I was – and I'm not sure if you noticed this – *extremely* inebriated.'

He smiles. 'The weight of your drunken carcass over my shoulder did give me a clue.'

Naia comes in to join us then, carrying a handful of papers.

'This is fucking hopeless,' she says. 'Any one of these rich old bastards could be investing with CGC. There's nothing to choose between them.'

'We're not doing any better,' Cam says, pushing back from his screen.

We're stuck. I can only hope that Boyd is getting on better with CGC's records.

'Hey,' I say to Naia. 'Sorry for being a bitch this morning. You were right. I'll try to get my act together.'

'No worries,' she says, and she means it. This is why Naia and I work well together: she speaks her mind, and she doesn't hold a grudge.

Unlike me. A twisted part of my psyche feels like my hatred brings me power, that the more I rage the stronger and more fearsome I become. It's bollocks, of course. I'm not some avenging demon, I'm just behaving like a five-year old, and it's getting in the way of this investigation.

The realisation is revelatory, and it means I have to do something extremely distasteful.

14

FIRST THING ON Saturday morning, I drag myself up to Summertown to apologise to Drake.

I know. I never thought I'd be saying those words either, but I need his help.

Ugh.

This time, we meet in a seating area in his conservatory. It's a huge room filled with exotic plants, so densely packed that it's like walking into a rainforest.

It's also weird, because it doesn't fit him well. Killian Drake is a man who haunts dark, shadowy places. He's the archetypal modern vampire, a denizen of lairs filled with glass, black wood and chrome. He is not the kind of person I expect to meet in a bright, sunny room filled with plants. I can't see him with a trowel in his hand, potting out seedlings. I associate him with vodka and cigars, not watering cans and secateurs.

Well, maybe the secateurs, but strictly for the purpose of torturing information out of reluctant business associates. Not for pruning the roses.

He grins when he sees me approaching.

'What?' I say, scowling.

I admit it: I'm bad at apologies.

'You found the thrill,' he says. 'The lightning bolt. Makes life worth living, doesn't it?'

'I don't know what you're talking about.'

'Really,' he says as I help myself to a seat next to his. It's one of four arranged around a small table, and they're placed so close together that my knee is practically touching Drake's. The chair is covered with decorative cushions, and it's made of wicker. *Wicker.* I feel like I've walked into a parallel universe.

'Drew says she's a doctor,' he goes on. 'A pathologist. Clever and creepy. Perfect for you.'

But there's something off in his tone. He's too chirpy. His words are forced in a way that makes me feel as though he's trying too hard.

'Oh my god,' I say as it dawns on me. 'Are you jealous?'

At that moment, a woman walks into the conservatory carrying a breakfast tray. She's Drake's date from the opera, the beautiful long-legged one with the doctorate or whatever, and she's only wearing a bathrobe. On her, it looks like couture.

She puts the tray down on the table, kisses the top of his head, then takes a seat next to him and starts buttering a slice of toast.

'Thanks, Veronica,' he says. 'You remember Jack? From the opera?'

She smiles at me with perfect self-assurance.

'Of course,' she says. 'Good morning.'

I try to smile back, but I'm not entirely successful.

You know those TV adverts for fancy kitchens, where the beautiful couple shares a meal together, laughing at salad and drinking black coffee from extravagant cafetières? I'm stuck in the middle of one of those right now, a captive viewer, unable to change the channel.

Drake's not jealous. What does he have to be jealous about? He's just spent the night with a super-brained super-model who serves him wholemeal toast and egg-white omelettes the next morning. She's cultured, clever and kind, and not the least bit threatened by me.

She finishes composing her plate of food from the tray, then says amiably, 'I'll leave you two to talk. Nice to see you again, Jack.'

'You too,' I say, because I'm too embarrassed to come up with anything else.

She leaves as gracefully as she arrived, bare feet padding away on the tiled conservatory floor. As she reaches the door, she turns to look back over her shoulder and Drake smiles at her in a way I've never seen him smile before. It's not a mocking grin or a sly smile. It's almost as though he's happy.

'Are *you* jealous?' he asks me when Veronica has closed the door behind her.

'A little,' I admit. 'But I'm guessing she's probably straight.'

He laughs and suddenly this doesn't seem so difficult. I've told myself so many times that I hate him, that I blame him for what happened with Winta, but the truth is that he's right: my anger has mutated. I spent less than twelve hours with Winta before she was out of my life forever and I claimed to love her, but I've spent twenty years chasing this man. It's brought us closer together, despite the antagonism.

I can work with this.

'So,' I say.

'So,' he replies.

'I wanted to apologise.'

'Okay,' he says, pouring us both a coffee. 'What for?'

'I don't know. For being a dick? For always thinking the worst of you? For trying to pin David Grant's murder on you?'

'I thought you'd given up on that.'

'Not until yesterday.'

He looks at me for a long moment, as though he can read my thoughts in my expression. I think I'm giving nothing away, but apparently I'm wrong.

'Fuck,' he says eventually. 'She told you.'

I don't reply, because I don't want to drop the captain in it for revealing Drake's part in my admission to the Seekers, but he doesn't need me to say anything. He's worked it out for himself. If only he were as thick as he is annoying.

'I knew she would eventually,' he says. 'What did you do to make her crack?'

'She thought I was holding a grudge.'

'And? You can't go forgiving me now, Jack. It'll fuck up the whole dynamic of our relationship.'

'What are you talking about?'

'I mean, look at you,' he says, gesturing irritably. 'You have no idea how to behave around me now you've decided to be friendly. It's unsettling. All I wanted was for you to stop being hyper aggressive all the time. I just wanted you to ditch the vendetta. I didn't want you to stop being yourself.'

'Well, fuck you, then. I was only trying to say sorry.'

'Well, don't.'

'Fine,' I say, getting to my feet. 'I won't.'

Then I remember why I'm here and sit back down abruptly.

'What?' he says.

'I, um… I need a–'

Drake leans forward and says, 'I can't hear you.'

'I need a favour,' I say, too loudly.

He looks at me for a second, blinks, then laughs.

'Oh, I'm going to enjoy this, aren't I? Is it my birthday?'

'Can't you remember? I knew you were old, but I didn't know vampires got Alzheimer's.' I shouldn't be baiting him, not when I'm about to ask him to put his reputation on the line for me, but his glee is irritating me into retaliation.

'Jack,' he says, lowering his voice to a soft rumble. 'You might think you're being vicious, but you're actually just flirting.'

'You might think you're being clever,' I say, leaning forward and matching his tone, 'but actually you're just an arrogant wanker.'

'Guilty as charged,' he whispers, then he reaches out and twirls a piece of my hair that has come loose from my ponytail. I bat his hand away.

'Easy, killer,' he says, smiling as he leans back in his seat.

I'm not sure why he's trying to rile me, but he has been entirely successful. Every time he invades my personal space, it spins me off balance. I'm so used to seeing him as a threat that his proximity sets off blaring alarms throughout my body.

I hate that something so small can make me feel so vulnerable.

'What's this favour you want to ask me?' he says, getting back to business.

'I met Percival Windsor yesterday,' I say, trying to ease into it in the hopes that he'll guess what I'm asking and I won't actually have to say the words.

'Oh? And how is old Percy?' he asks, taking a sip of his coffee.

'Close-lipped,' I say frankly. 'But he has access to people we need to speak to. Word is that his social circle is filled with exactly the sort of Silver who are most likely to have been the victims of Grant's embezzlement. If any Silver has a motive to kill him, it would be one of them.'

'And you want me to put you in touch with them?'

'Sort of. He has parties.'

Drake raises an eyebrow. 'Oh, I'm well aware. I've heard about Percy's parties. Apparently they can become rather... debauched. And you want me to secure a ticket for you?'

'Not exactly,' I wince. 'You see, it needs to be covert, which means sneaking in with someone who's important enough not to be questioned.'

'You want *me* to take you to one of Percy's parties?'

'He actually prefers to call them gatherings–'

'As my date.'

I press my lips closed. I can't do it.

'Don't go shy on me,' Drake says. 'You want me to help, don't you?' He's having the time of his life.

I can hear my teeth grinding together. 'Yes.'

'Then say it.' He grins.

'I would like you to take me to one of Percy's parties,' I say.

'As my date.'

'As your date.' I bite out the words.

'See?' He smiles. 'That wasn't so hard, was it? But I'd better send you a new dress, because if you go in the one you wore to the opera then I'm not sure I can guarantee your safety.'

'Let's get something straight right now, Drake,' I say, letting all my irritation fill my voice. 'You are not some Romeo who's going to be sending me dresses and pinning corsages and acting out your bullshit macho ideal of romance by protecting my honour and virtue. The only reason we're doing this is that I need someone to get me into

Windsor's party. Once we're there, you will smile and laugh and generally be a useless ornament while I do my work. If there's any fighting to be done, I'll be the one doing it. Is that understood?'

He raises his eyebrows, which is the least I expect given the tone I've taken, but he also agrees, much to my surprise.

'Yes, Ma'am. Shall I have a car pick us up, or will you be driving too?'

'A car will be fine,' I say graciously, because the alternative is driving in heels.

'All right, then. I'll be in touch when I have the details.'

He's being so accommodating that I really have only two options: climb off my high horse, or ride it straight out of here. I choose the latter, because it's a long way down.

I get to my feet with the hauteur of a duchess, nodding imperiously at him as I take my leave. He nods back deferentially, which is ominous, but he says nothing. I think I've got away clean, but when I'm halfway to the conservatory door he clears his throat and calls my name.

I turn.

'Admit it,' he says with a twinkle in his eye. 'You were just a tiny bit jealous.'

I storm off without saying goodbye.

When I get back to the college, Cam is waiting for me in the corridor outside my rooms with a pile of papers. More homework.

'Did you apologise?' he asks.

'Yes,' I say, fumbling with my keys.

'So everything's sorted? You're dropping this crazy vendetta?'

'Nope.'

'But he's taking you to the party.'

'Yep.'

'Well, thank fuck for that.'

I let us both inside and we cram into my sitting room. It's sectioned off from the bedroom, and has a small sofa and TV at one end and a makeshift kitchen at the other. I say kitchen, but it's really just a table with a mini-fridge and a microwave on top. I don't do much entertaining.

Cam dumps the pile of papers down onto the coffee table. There's about a ream of it, thickly inked and double-sided.

'Well?' he asks.

'Well... What?'

'What happened?'

'I've realised that he's not entirely to blame for Winta,' I say, sitting down on the sofa. 'I've also realised that he's done some things for me in the past that weren't entirely evil. I accept both of these things to be true.'

'But?'

'But that doesn't mean he's not also a complete and utter wanker. The two are not mutually exclusive.'

Cam groans and flops down next to me.

'I swear,' he says, 'one day the two of you have to deal with each other. If you just had one night of seriously depraved sex, you could get it out of your systems and we could all move on. But no, you have to be adults about it.'

I make a face at him. The thought of being yet another notch on Drake's bedpost makes me shudder. 'You're revolting.'

'You're impossible,' he replies.

'But you love me anyway.' I grin.

He sighs. 'I do.'

We get to work. Cam's managed to get copies of Windsor's bank records from somewhere and we're looking at rows and rows of transactions, trying to find something, anything, to tie him to CGC. When that brings us no joy, we move on to Grant's phone records, tracing every number on his call list until we have just a few unidentified: a local Oxford number that seems to have no record in the directory, a London number likewise, and finally a mobile number that called Grant fifteen times in the month before he died.

We manage to identify the Oxford and London numbers eventually – neither is suspicious – but the mobile number is more elusive. We try calling it, but no one answers. We work late into the night cross-referencing and searching databases, but it gets us precisely nowhere.

'We need to get our hands on his mobile,' Cam says. 'Check out his messages.' All we have here are his call records.

'Good luck getting that from the police,' I say.

'We'll just have to hope they're still talking to us.'

As though on cue, my own phone buzzes. It's on the coffee table, somewhere under the drifts of paper, and I have to scrabble around to dig it out.

'Fuck,' I say as I read the message.

This is bad news. This is very bad news.

'What?' Cam asks.

'Tomorrow. Windsor's next party is tomorrow.'

I thought I would have time to prepare. I thought we would have found something that could direct me towards the right targets. And honestly, I didn't think I would have to see Drake again so soon.

'What are you talking about?' Cam says. 'It's great news.'

'I mean, who the fuck has a party on a Sunday night? What's that about?'

'There's no accounting for rich old Silver. But listen, Jack: we've got nothing here.' He gestures at the papers. 'The important thing is that the party gives us a way in, and before the captain comes back. This is great news.'

'Sure,' I say morosely. 'It's great news.'

'Come on, let's pack it in for the night. We can carry on tomorrow.'

I need no convincing.

We argue over the remote for a couple of minutes, finally settling on a series to binge-watch, then we order pizza and ice-cream. It's actually enjoyable to have a sober night for once. We both need it. When we've eaten all the food, I grab the duvet from my bed. We both fall asleep under it with the TV still on.

Cam's right: we can worry about murder again tomorrow.

15

MY PHONE RINGS early the next morning. Not just early for a Sunday, but early for any day. I try to ignore it, but it's no use. Cam groans incoherently from beside me. We're still on the sofa and I have a killer crick in my neck.

'What?' I mumble into the phone, answering it blindly.

'The doctor's finished the post mortem,' Naia says.

'What?'

'The doctor,' Naia says, her words heavily enunciated, as though she's speaking to someone who's just learning English. 'Short, cute, Scottish. The one you fancy. She was doing the post mortem, remember? Well, she's done.'

'And she called you?' I resent that, even though I know she doesn't have my number. It begs the question: why does she have Naia's?

'No, you dimwit,' Naia says. 'She called the lodge and asked for the captain. The captain's off maintaining her plausible deniability, so the call came through to me instead. Jesus, are you jealous?'

'No,' I grumble. I wish people would stop asking me that.

'Then are you coming?'

'We'll see you in the canteen in fifteen.'

152

'We?' Naia asks. 'Who's with you?'

'Just Cam. We were working late.'

'Hurry up, then,' she says and hangs up.

Cam groans again.

'I think I have a sugar hangover from all the ice cream,' he says.

'No, you don't. You're just making up an excuse because you hate morgues.'

'That too.'

I can't blame him. The smell might be bad for humans, but for the Silver it's overpowering. It's not so much the smell of rot and decay – we drink blood, so we're used to that – it's more the smell of wrongness that comes with the clinical environment. It feels like a contaminant to the Silver nose, and ironically we'd be more comfortable without all the detergents and deodorisers that are supposed to cover up the natural smell of death.

I'd be reluctant to go myself, but then there's Dr Ross. I like her more than I dislike the smell of the morgue.

'Fine,' I say. 'I'll go with Naia. You can go back to your own room, though, and stop cluttering up mine.'

But he's already asleep. I leave him to it, have a quick shower, then go downstairs to meet Naia.

When I arrive, she looks me up and down with approval.

'Clean clothes and you've showered,' she says. 'It must be a special occasion.'

'Shut up. What's the plan?'

'Where's Cam?'

'He ditched me and went back to sleep. It's just the two of us.'

She shakes her head at me. 'I know he's sad, but you've got to stop letting that lost puppy sleep on your sofa. You'll never get laid with him hanging around all the time.'

'Naia…' I warn her.

'Fine. Whatever. We're meeting out at her lab.'

'Dr Ross has her own lab?'

Naia smirks at me. 'Impressed?'

'Shut up,' I say again, punching her in the arm. It's like punching a brick wall.

She laughs. 'Come on. I'll drive.'

Dr Ross's lab doesn't look like much from the outside. It's in a sleepy little village halfway to London, and it's thatched.

'Does she live here?' I ask Naia as we park up next to the ivy-strewn wall that edges the drive. There are well-tended flowerbeds along the sides of the half-timbered house. They're liberally crammed with herbs, lavender and spring bulbs, and there are even a couple of hanging baskets attached to either side of the front door.

'Maybe,' Naia says. 'But don't get any ideas. This isn't a social call. If you want to make small talk, or sex talk, then you can find your own way back to Oxford.'

Dr Ross chooses that moment to open the door to greet us.

'Sorry to call so early,' she says, smiling at me. She looks outrageously sexy in her lab coat. 'I was working all night and I lost track of time. Come on out to the lab. See what's on the slab.'

She chuckles to herself as she closes the front door behind her, then she leads us along a path that skirts around the house. We emerge into a neat little garden with a flat-roofed outbuilding at its far end.

'This is where you work?' I ask.

'Most of the time.'

'And you have… bodies in here?'

'Oh, no,' she says, looking at me over her shoulder. 'Bless you, no. The bodies stay in the morgue. I bring the samples and photographs back here to work on them, and to write my reports.'

Which sounds reassuring, but I keep tripping over that word: *samples*. It feels unsettling here, in a place that's so perfectly quaint. It occurs to me that Dr Ross is the archetypal witch: she lives in a thatched cottage in a quiet village, smiling happily to all the local children, probably putting a pumpkin out at Halloween, and all the while she's busy making up potions in her back garden, some of which involve *samples*.

I should be creeped out, but I kind of love it.

'Here we are,' she says as she unlocks the door and invites us in.

It's sterile inside, which I suppose is only natural, but part of me was expecting to see pot plants on the windowsills and herbs hanging from the ceiling. Instead, the lab is white-walled and lino-floored, with lab benches on three sides of the room. One holds a desktop computer, while the other two are covered with papers, Petri dishes, test tubes, swabs, and all manner of complicated machinery. The only thing I recognise is the microscope, perching on the edge of the worktop like a bird of prey. The whole place is like a less-pretentious version of Ed's lab.

'I knew he didn't need all the bubbling cauldrons,' I murmur under my breath.

'What was that, hen?' says Dr Ross.

Every time she calls me that my knees go a bit wobbly. Her accent is unbearable.

'Nothing,' I say. 'Just talking to myself.'

Oh, great. That makes me sound perfectly healthy and stable. Good one, Jack.

But she just laughs and says, 'I do it all the time. Working on your own, you know. Sometimes you just need to hear a voice.'

If I were her, I'd talk to myself too. I could listen to her voice all day.

'So,' she says, 'first things first: I guess you want to know cause of death?'

'I thought it was draining?' Naia says. 'You said he was dead when he hit the ground?'

'He was, and yes, he was missing a lot of blood. But that's not all he was missing.'

'Excuse me?' Naia's eyes are wide.

'You're going to like this,' she says, logging in to her computer. Her smile has a gruesomely gleeful edge to it and I know I'm sunk. She's not only a witch, she's an *evil* witch when she wants to be. Of course she's a pathologist.

'Let me show you what we've got.' She has two screens and she swivels one so we can see it. 'These are the crime scene photos. Nothing new here.' She scrolls through the photos as she narrates their content. 'A close-up of the sticky patch on the back of his hand, the red threads, the theatre ticket in his pocket – I have that, by the way, and I've tested it – then here are the post mortem photos. This is the injection site pre- and post-cleaning, the lipstick on his mouth–'

'Wait a minute,' I interrupt. 'Go back to that last photo of his face.'

She flicks back quickly through a couple of body shots – a relief, because I definitely didn't need to see David Grant's goolies – and there's the photo that caught my eye. It's a close-up of Grant's face, but it's been photographed in a way that makes every tiny detail and discolouration clear. For the first time, I can see things that weren't apparent to me on May Morning in the rainy dawn light.

'That's not just a smear of lipstick,' I say.

'And there's more than a bit of it,' says Naia.

'Shit.'

'Looks like Grant was a little more intimate with the singers than the Baron was.'

There are faint traces of the lipstick all over his mouth, gathered in the creases of his lips and even staining one front tooth. This wasn't an accidental transfer.

'He was definitely smooching someone,' Dr Ross says. 'Either that or he was wearing the lipstick himself, but he doesn't seem like the type, does he? A little too buttoned up for that.' She winks at me and I can't resist inferring that she's more of the unbuttoned persuasion. It makes me wish Naia wasn't here, because I'd be more than happy to oblige.

'With that shade, it has to be one of the opera singers,' I say, trying to concentrate on the matter at hand.

'Back to the Playhouse, then?' Naia asks.

'No point. All the singers are human. Even if he was having an affair with one of them, then so what? His wife is human too. It's not as though she could have killed him out of revenge, is it?'

Naia nods. 'The finances do seem like the stronger motive right now. We have a lot to investigate there.' She gives me a meaningful look. I know she's thinking about the CGC portfolios and their damning names. If any thread in Grant's life leads straight to the Silver, it's that one.

Dr Ross waits until we've finished conferring, then that grin is back on her face again. She wants to tell us what else Mr Grant was missing.

'So, are you ready for the big reveal?' she asks.

'Uh-huh.' Naia's expression walks the line between intrigued and wary as Dr Ross clicks to the next photograph. I'm not exactly sure what it shows, but I guess we're looking at the inside of Grant's body cavity.

'We didn't notice the incisions until we'd got him stripped,' says Dr Ross. 'He was so drained that the wounds were practically dry. But when we'd finished the external examination and got him down to the skin, we found the cuts. When we opened him up, well, see for yourselves.'

I can see lungs and intestines, but there's a mess where his heart should be.

'His *heart's* missing?'

'Yes, and some of his liver. About two hundred grams, I estimate.'

She looks expectantly between me and Naia, waiting for the penny to drop. Unfortunately, whatever connection she wants us to make is beyond us both.

'A human heart weighs about three hundred grams,' she says, 'so he lost about half a kilo of organ tissue.'

She looks at us again, but we've still got nothing. I hate that I'm disappointing her, but she doesn't seem to mind. She grins when she gives us her final prompt.

'Or, in old money...'

And there it is.

'A pound of flesh,' I say, remembering my Shakespeare from school. It's from the Merchant of Venice. A moneylender demands a pound of flesh from a debtor when he fails to repay a loan.

'Are you serious?' says Naia.

'I'd guess that this is definitely about the money,' the doctor concludes.

After that bombshell, there's not much else to learn.

'There were fingerprints on the opera ticket,' Dr Ross says as she shuts down her computer. 'Grant's and a couple more that haven't been matched. Not unexpected. We've pinned time of death to the early hours of the morning, some time between midnight and 2am. Here's the report.' She hands the pages to me. 'No usable DNA, again not unexpected. Then there's this.'

The second report that she presents is complete gibberish to me. There are a lot of numbers and some diagrams, but I can't decipher it.

'What am I looking at?' I ask.

'I've spoken to Ed in your lab and he's looking at the DNA under the victim's fingernails. This is DNA taken from the site of the injection. I've sent him the details so he can run both together and see if he can find a match. This is the paper copy.'

'Okay,' I say, not sure what I'm supposed to do with it. Her fingers brush mine as she hands it over. It's just a fleeting contact, but it's so sensual that it feels like an assault. My mind goes blank.

'We'll give them to Ed,' Naia says, taking them from me. 'Thanks. We'd better get going now. Time's a-wasting.'

We both know the Invicti will be back tomorrow, and when they are we'll lose any chance of directing this investigation on our own terms. Boyd's working hard on the financial documents, but we need to push forwards with the rest of the case.

'Can I tempt you to a cup of tea?' Dr Ross asks as she follows us out of the lab, locking it behind us. 'Or maybe a bottle of blood? I just got a new batch this morning. I could warm it up, maybe put a wee dram of rum in it too, to keep out the chill.'

'Thank you,' Naia says, 'but we have to be getting back.'

'Oh,' says the doctor, disappointed. 'Of course.'

I know we're under pressure, but I can't bear this. Naia has a twisted sense of humour: one minute encouraging me to get laid and the next minute blocking any chance I have of getting closer to that goal. I suppose she doesn't want to be a third wheel.

'It was good to see you,' I say to Dr Ross. 'Maybe we could get together another time. The next time you're in Oxford, I mean. For a coffee, or a drink, or whatever. To, you know, chat?'

Naia rolls her eyes and gives me a look that says, *You suck at this.*

But it doesn't seem to bother Dr Ross. She grins from ear to ear.

'I'd like that,' she says. 'How about tonight?'

I'm about to say yes when I remember that I'm already busy tonight, going to Sir Percival Wanker's party.

Of all the lousy timing.

'I can't,' I say to her. 'Not tonight.'

Don't ask why. Don't ask why.

'Oh,' she says, her smile dimming.

She looks so bleak that now I wish she had asked. I want to elaborate, but I have no idea how to explain what I'm doing tonight and besides, the whole point is that it's supposed to be covert. I hope to god that it will be, because the last thing I want is to be recognised in public with Killian fucking Drake.

'Maybe another time?' I say, desperately.

'Of course,' she says, smiling as though she's holding something back. 'Another time.'

We stand there looking at each other as the seconds pass, neither of us sure what to do next. I can smell the pheromones in the air and I'm sure they're not just coming from me. We like each other, I'm almost certain of it. So what the hell am I supposed to do next?

'Okay,' I say after a few more seconds of awkward silence. 'Good to see you.'

'Good to see you too,' she replies, but she looks faintly miserable. She flashes me another uncertain smile, then she turns and starts walking back to the house.

I am so hopelessly bad at this that I have no idea whether I should stop her or not.

'For chrissakes,' Naia says. 'Dr Ross, wait!'

She turns back. 'Yes?'

'Jack has something she'd like to ask you.'

Naia nudges me, but I'm drawing a blank.

'I do?' I whisper to her.

'Her number, you idiot,' Naia whispers back.

'Oh, shit, yes. Dr Ross–'

'Tabitha,' she corrects me. She's smiling now. I hope it's because she's heard my exchange with Naia and already knows what I'm going to ask.

'Tabitha.' Her name is a pitter-patter of joy on my lips. 'Could I have your number? Please?'

'Of course, hen.' Now she's smiling. 'You'd better come in.'

Two minutes later, I'm back in the car with the delectable doctor's number in my phone and an irrepressible grin on my face.

'What would you do without me?' Naia asks as she puts the car into gear. Right then I'm too happy to snark back.

Dr Ross – Tabitha – likes me.

She actually likes me.

There was never any hope that the afternoon would hold a candle to this morning, but it ends up being even duller than

I had hoped. First there's more research and then, with Drake's threats of dressing me ringing in my ears, I accept the fact that I have to go shopping.

Some of the old-school Silver – the ones who've been around for centuries – are rich. Some of them are really, really rich. But we young ones – the ones who've lived our immortal lives through recession after recession – are pretty much dead broke. The only reason I'm not is that I have this job. The Seekers give me somewhere to live, food to eat, blood to drink, and a modest salary by way of per diem. It just about covers alcohol and the odd luxury.

Which means that I don't have the cash to go splashy shopping, but I can scrape together a hundred quid from savings for a fancy dress. I suppose I could expense it, but for some reason I need this dressy armour to be mine and mine alone, so it retains the thrill of a special object. I don't want to interrogate that decision too closely, so I tell myself that buying it outright is the quickest way to do it. I can always save the receipt and claim the cost back later, right?

I stride into town like a warrior laying siege to the high street, because this feels like a battle. Rails of brightly-coloured cloth assault me. Shop assistants assail me with can-I-help-yous, offered kindly but not without a silent, scathing assessment of the outfit I'm already wearing. I ignore them, pillaging handfuls of hangers before making a break for a changing room. I will not be conquered by this mundane task. I will emerge triumphant.

Except I can't. Maybe I'm distracted by the events of this morning and the thought of Tabitha's number burning a hole in my phone, but I just can't shop right. Everything I try on looks strange, as though I'm pretending to be someone I'm not. That's the point, I suppose, but I can't tell whether frills are good, whether diamanté looks tacky, or whether bodycon is a bridge too far for an event like this. I can't dress for my shape, either, so at least half of the dresses I've selected look awful, clinging to my narrow hips and making me look like a man in drag. And I don't mean good drag, I mean bad drag, like a drag virgin who has no idea how to balance the width of his shoulders with hip padding. I am completely lost in a world of satins and synthetics in which I have absolutely zero expertise.

Eventually, I surrender and throw myself on the mercy of the shop assistants, who take me in their capable hands. An hour later, I'm on my way home with a reasonably-priced dress that will go with some heels I already own. I am the queen of economy.

By then I can't resist the allure of my phone any longer. But I'm a coward, so I text instead of calling.

Hey, it's Jack. It was good to see you today. When are you next going to be in Oxford?

No reply.

I finish my walk back to the college, promising myself that I can check my phone again the moment I get back to my rooms. As soon as I've chucked my shopping bag on the bed, I do just that.

Still no reply.

I can see she's received my message. I can see she's read it. But she's not replying.

Why isn't she replying?

I hang up the dress, removing the tags with abandon. Now I've finally found a dress that suits me, I'm never letting it go.

My phone buzzes.

How about tomorrow night? ;)

16

AT EIGHT O'CLOCK, I'm wrapped up in my coat outside the lodge, waiting for my ride. It's unseasonably cold for May, with a chilly breeze biting at my bare ankles, but at least it's not raining.

I'm expecting Drake to do that annoying thing rich wankers think will sweep girls off their feet. You know, he turns up wearing a tux in the back of a huge limo stocked with champagne and blaring *Careless Whisper*. Instead, he pulls into the college in a black Volkswagen Polo, which looks a lot like the car I took my driving lessons in. He's wearing a simple black suit and tie, and he's driving.

He loops around the car park to turn around, then pulls up in front of me and rolls down the passenger side window.

'Well?' he says. 'Are you getting in?'

'Er, sure. Hi.'

'Hi.' He smiles as I angle myself into the car.

I get my seatbelt on and face forward, ready to go, but the car isn't moving. For a moment, he just looks at me.

'I like your hair,' he says, reaching out to touch one of the curling tendrils that frames my face.

I'm not sure why he keeps doing this, or why he thinks he has the right to touch my hair. It feels intimate and intimidating all at once, as though it's a calculated ploy to get in my space under the pretence of flattery.

I slap his hand away, again.

'No touching. Do you know how much hairspray it takes to get this shit to stay like this?'

'No touching? That wasn't part of the deal. If I'm escorting you to this party then I'm going to have to touch you, at least a bit.'

'How much is a bit?'

'Let me put it like this,' he says. 'You're a good-looking woman who's about to walk into a house filled with the type of Silver men who don't have a reputation for gallantry. If you're going as my date then you'll be fine, but you'll have to make them believe that you are, in fact, my date.'

It takes me a moment to understand what he's suggesting. When the realisation hits, I'm tempted to climb out of his car, go straight back to my room and call the whole thing off. Who cares about David Grant anyway?

But this is my job. My life.

Still, I say, 'No.'

He raises his eyebrow at me. 'No?'

'I said no. No way. You're not marking me. End of discussion.'

'Okay,' he says, putting the car into gear and pulling away. 'If you don't want anyone to believe you. At a party like this, it'll be like throwing chum into a shark tank. You'll be lucky to get out of there fully-dressed.'

'I'm more than capable of looking after myself.'

'I don't doubt that, but can you do it while keeping your cover?'

'I'm sure I'll find a way,' I say, because I can't stomach the alternative.

I've mentioned Silver scent marks before. There was one on David Grant's body, a mark of violence that gave us irrefutable evidence that a Silver killed him. But there's another kind of scent mark too, one of possession. Unlike the violent version, this one leaves behind the individual scent of the Silver who made it, identifying the person they've scent-marked as theirs. It's archaic and unpleasantly animalistic, but that's how the Silver are. A lot of humans are the same anyway, all wedding rings and dick swinging, so it's not much of a culture shock. It actually prevents more arguments than it causes, because if you can smell a scent mark on someone, you know you're asking for trouble if you try it on with them.

If I walk into Windsor's party with Drake's scent mark on me, I couldn't be more off-limits. It will achieve the deception I want, but I can't imagine going through with the marking process, not with him.

'It's just a kiss,' he says as we leave the city for the countryside.

I laugh scathingly in reply.

The Silver can kiss without leaving a scent mark. The mark is much more meaningful. I've kissed plenty, but I've never marked or been marked.

In any case, we both know it wouldn't be *just* anything. How could it be, after twenty years of cat and mouse?

The thought of it makes me feel sick, but – and I hate to admit this – not because I'm entirely disgusted by it. The truth is that for all that I object to the little intimacies he foists upon me, they aren't entirely uninvited. His senses are just as attuned as those of any other Silver, probably even more so, and he knows I like it when he touches me. I can deny it all I want, but it won't change the fact that there is something between us, however unwelcome.

Still, I won't let him mark me, because there are a million reasons why it's a horrible idea. Firstly, there's Tabitha to consider. Even though I can see the logic behind Drake's suggestion, I'd feel like a dick for going so quickly from arranging a date with her to whatever this is with Drake. Even if it really was just a kiss, it would feel uncomfortable.

Secondly, I know he's a dangerous man. Yes, I'm a Seeker, and yes, we are dangerous ourselves, but Drake is dangerous on a different scale. He's insidious and clever, careful and devious. He knows how to play the long game and I have a suspicion this is part of it. Getting involved with him in any way would be ill-advised.

And finally, the very thought of it makes me nervous, and I can't afford to be nervous around him. He'll see it and he won't hesitate to use it against me.

Drake stays quiet, his eyes on the road, while my thoughts go around in circles. I'm expecting him to push, to force me to see the sense in his plan, but that's not how he works. He gives me space to come up with my own solution.

But as we get closer to Windsor's gathering, with its ancient Silver and their wandering hands, I realise that there is only one.

It's dark in Aston.

When we pull up to the house, the driveway is already filled with fancy cars. I can see a gaggle of chauffeurs gathered under the eaves of the building, smoking and chatting as they pass the time. Drake's Polo matches the other cars only in colour – they're all black – but otherwise it's a fraction of the cost of any other car here. It strikes me as strange that the Baron of Oxford, the most important

Silver in the county, should turn up driving his own cheap car while everyone else comes driven in luxury. I guess he feels like he doesn't have much to prove.

He turns off the engine.

We unbuckle our seatbelts.

Silence descends.

He's waiting.

'All right,' I say into the darkness. It's so tree-shaded in this corner of the driveway that we might as well be in the middle of nowhere.

'All right, what?'

He knows, but he wants me to say it anyway.

'You are a manipulative, self-centred bastard and I will make you pay for this one day, I swear, but I need this to be convincing. So fine, yes, all right, we can mark each other.'

'Well, if that's your attitude, then it won't work.'

I groan, because I can feel him trying to squeeze every drop of dignity from me. This is the thing about possessive scent marks: they only work if they're freely given and freely accepted. Basically, you have to be into the person you're kissing for the mark to stick. We both know that.

'I'll imagine you're someone else,' I say.

'Your Dr Ross?' He leans in close, his fingers flirting with my hair again. 'Will you close your eyes and wish me away? Do you think you'll be able to banish me, Valentine?'

I want to say yes. I want to say that I'll banish him to the ends of the earth, but while I'm sitting in this tiny space so close to him, with his fingertips kissing my skin, it's impossible to imagine that he's anyone else.

I won't close my eyes. I tell myself it's because I don't want to be that vulnerable to him, but in truth I keep them open because there is no point in trying to pretend him away. This close, his eyes are black, black, black, and they pull me in. I can feel the gravity of him. It's an undertow that's trying to pull me out to sea and I have nothing to hold on to but him.

'Tell me that you hate me now,' he whispers. He's so close that I can feel the warmth of his breath on my lips.

'I have always hated you,' I whisper back.

His fingertips are moving along my cheek, under my ear, until they come to rest in the fine hairs at the back of my neck. It's the most sensitive place on my body and I love being touched there. He can tell. He exploits it. His touch sends warm ripples through me that I can't deny. My body betrays me, shivering me further towards him.

But it's not enough for him. He wants my lips to confess it.

'Tell me how you hate me. Tell me to stop.'

'I do hate you.'

'But you don't want me to stop.'

I don't and I hate it. I shouldn't want his fingers to press into my skin.

I want his hands to grab at me as though he were taking me against my will, because then I could fight back. When he offers himself like this, there's nothing for me to fight except myself, and I've always had crummy willpower.

He leans in closer, his lips hovering just a fraction of an inch away from mine, and then he waits.

'Tell me to stop,' he says again.

I refuse to surrender to him, so I conquer instead.

I kiss him.

His lips are warm against mine. This close, his skin smells like cinnamon and something darker: wet stone, iron, blood.

It's so intoxicating that I'm losing myself in it, in the darkness and the warmth and the dizziness that comes with the taste of his breath. My brain tells me to stop now before it's too late, to pull back before he opens his mouth to mine, but every other part of me insists that kissing him is something I should never, ever stop.

Then he pulls away.

'You're sure?' he asks.

I am incredulous. 'You're arguing, now? This was your stupid idea, Drake.'

He looks at me, the darkness of his eyes reflecting the ambient light. When he inhales, I know what he's scenting. It flickers through him, the knowledge that I wish he didn't have. His fingers go still at the back of my neck.

'You want this,' he says, surprised. It's not a question.

'Shut up.'

When I lean in to kiss him again, he pulls me to him, wrapping a hand around my waist to crush my chest to his. There is no hesitation this time, no coaxing. There is violence in the way our lips meet.

I can taste his desire on my tongue. It's aggravating and enticing and it makes me *want*. I want to kiss him and wrap my fingers into his hair, but at the same time I want to rip the tie from his neck and bite him, for pain or pleasure, I'm not sure which. I want him with such aggression that I don't know how much of the wanting is about my lips and how much is about my teeth. I simply want.

I'm not trying to mark him, not yet, but apparently my body doesn't know that, because I can already smell my scent in the air. It's not the only one, either. Another scent joins it so quickly that I can't tell which came first. It's Drake concentrated: spice and copper, with the edge of something that feels dangerous enough to raise the hairs on the back of my neck.

It frightens me. Even though every instinct in my body is telling me to own him and use him, to pull him to me and never let go, I push him away instead.

He groans and tightens his grip on my waist.

'Don't run off,' he says, pressing his cheek against mine.

I am surrounded by the scent of what we've done. I can smell myself on his skin, can smell him on mine, and the marks are trying to drag me back to him. I feel sick with the sensation, like I'm falling and rising at the same time. My palms are against his chest and I can feel his heartbeat through my fingers, the slow pulse of immortal life beneath his skin. I have to fist my hands to stop myself from running them up into his hair, or slipping them under his shirt, or worse.

'Valentine,' he whispers, brushing his lips over my cheek.

When I push him away this time, it is firm and final.

I sit back in my seat.

'Enough,' I say.

He looks at me for a moment through the darkness. Light touches his face here and there: the curve of his brow, his bottomless eyes, the soft edge of his mouth darkened by my lipstick. I have to resist the urge to reach out to wipe it away, because I know if I touch him again then we might never leave the car.

Stupid Silver pheromones.

'Job done,' I say. 'Are you happy?'

'Not particularly,' he says, straightening his tie. He wipes my lipstick off onto the back of his hand. 'I don't really feel like I got my money's worth. Isn't it supposed to take longer?'

'Don't you know?' After his centuries of existence, I'm sure this isn't Drake's first marking.

'Don't *you*?'

I clear my throat and pull down the passenger sun visor so I can touch up my make up in the mirror.

'Is there something you want to tell me?' he asks.

'Should there be?' I ignore him, fiddling with the hair around my face until it sits neatly.

'That didn't feel like work. That felt like more than a ruse for your mission. Which means something, wouldn't you say?'

'That,' I reply, snapping the sun visor shut, 'meant nothing at all. Shall we go inside?'

17

THE BUTLER MEETS us at the door. If he recognises me from the other day, then he doesn't let on.

'Can I take your coat, Miss?' he asks.

I let him help me out of it, revealing this afternoon's purchase. It's a floor-length bias-cut dress in emerald velvet with delicate, jewelled straps, and it is beautiful.

Drake raises his eyebrows, but he doesn't comment. At least, not until he puts his hand on the small of my back to guide me into the house. Then he makes a strangled little noise as his palm meets my skin. There are a few velvet swags from my shoulders down to the base of my spine, but otherwise the dress is entirely backless.

'You're half naked,' he whispers.

I shrug. 'It seemed like that kind of party.'

He looks down at me, then looks back up again quickly when he realises I'm not wearing a bra.

'You'll be the death of me, Valentine,' he says. 'I shudder to think what might have happened if you hadn't let me mark you.'

The reminder makes me uncomfortable, but thankfully there's no more time to chat. We've reached what appears to be a ballroom, bustling with Silver laughing, drinking and generally having a raucously good time. There are gilded high ceilings, floor-length curtains, and walls adorned with ancient family portraits. One long side is edged with tables set for a buffet and although the food is not yet in attendance, its audience certainly is. There must be a hundred people in this room alone.

'Baron!' Windsor says, opening his arms wide in an expansive gesture of welcome. 'How long has it been?'

'Percy,' Drake replies, letting Windsor shake his hand. 'It's been a while.'

Windsor's nostrils twitch, scenting the mark as he looks between me and Drake, but his eyes pass over me as though I am irrelevant. He clearly doesn't recognise me from our visit here in daylight hours, nor is he surprised to see Drake here with a marked Silver. Looking around the room, I can see why. There are dozens of old Silver men here – old not in appearance but in years of immortality – and a lot of them have Silver women on their arms, a few of whom I recognise as being of a newer vintage than me. There's even the odd human girl too, all young. I'm probably the oldest woman here.

It's true that the passage of time makes age gaps less taboo for the Silver, but it's creepy when it only goes one way. In human terms, this is a room full of octogenarian men dating teenaged girls.

Ick.

Drake and I fit right in.

'You never come to my gatherings,' Windsor is saying. 'I was gratified to hear from you.'

'Always busy,' Drake replies. 'You know how it is. I'm happy that I finally had the opportunity to visit.'

'As am I. As am I. Well, dinner will be served in a few hours, and there's dancing later if that's your fancy. The bar and smoking room are next door. Everything's on offer: champagne, whisky, blood, whatever you prefer. In terms of entertainment, if you head towards the back of the house you'll find the library and games room, and the bedrooms upstairs are yours for the asking. Just speak to the staff and they'll oblige.' As he speaks, he looks pointedly at me and I have to suppress a curl of disgust. 'Enjoy your evening.'

'Thank you, Percy,' Drake replies. 'Ever the gracious host.'

I watch Windsor go, making sure he's far away on the other side of the ballroom before I retch.

'Lovely friends you have,' I say.

'I'm here at your request, if you recall. You're the one who wanted a date.' His fingers are moving on my skin, stroking along my spine. I can't slap him away without arousing suspicion.

'No, I *needed* a date,' I say. 'There's a difference. Now, stop that.'

'Stop what?' He slides his hand up to tease the hairs at the back of my neck, pressing my buttons because he knows I can't stop him here. The shivers are back.

'Drake,' I warn him.

'You want it to be convincing. They're watching.'

He's right. I can see heads lifting from conversations, can hear the spattering doppler of chatter throwing out his name. We are arousing more interest than I expected.

'Go on, Valentine.' He pulls me in close with one hand and strokes my cheek with the other. 'Pretend that you want me.'

I wish I had to pretend harder.

When he lowers his face to mine, I turn at the last moment to put our cheeks together instead of our lips. I don't want to kiss him again, not with an audience.

Not at all.

But then his hand is at the back of my neck again and I feel my body arching against his.

'Jesus,' he mutters. 'I don't suppose I could persuade you that we need to get a room?'

I'm tempted. After all, it would mean less than nothing. Just a quick lay. Part of me thinks: what's the harm? But the rest of me knows that this is just the bloody Silver pheromones, robbing me of control.

This was a mistake.

But when his lips find mine, I don't fight it. I let him turn my back against the wall, giving us a modicum of privacy from the gaping hordes. His fingers slip over the velvet at my thighs, at my hips, at my waist, and from there to my exposed back. My hands are on his hips without any conscious decision on my part. All I want is to pull him up against me.

'Fuck,' I say, breaking the kiss by tipping my head back against the wall. 'I didn't realise it would be this bad.'

'What?'

'The mark.'

He looks at me for a long moment.

'The mark,' he says. 'Right.' Then he pushes away from the wall.

He's not smiling. He seems to find this just as disturbing as I do. I should probably be insulted.

'I guess that's enough convincing,' he says, nodding towards the centre of the party. A number of heads have only just turned away from us. 'Shall we?'

This time, instead of settling his hand on my back, he offers me his arm. I take it, but part of me regrets the change. The part of me that I am trying very hard to crush beneath my stylish stilettos.

We walk straight through the ballroom and into the bar, where most people seem to be congregating this early in the evening. It's a large room, as large as an actual bar, but instead of side benches and bar stools this room is liberally filled with leather armchairs. Most of them are already occupied, but I can see more in the next room.

'So,' Drake breathes, 'what are we looking for?'

'*You're* not looking for anything.' The less Drake knows, the better. 'Let's split up. You go schmooze and circulate or whatever the hell you're supposed to do at a gathering like this and I'll go and do my job.'

'Jack, look where we are. As much as I hate to ruin your plans, no one's going to talk to you.'

I look around the room. I have the sinking feeling that he's probably right. Men are clustered in groups, conversing seriously whilst their young women stand bored beside them. When I do hear female voices, they're raised in the kind of vacuous tittering that I'm sure is more for the benefit of the men than for each other. It says: *I'm purely incidental and only here for your enjoyment. Go back to your serious male matters of business.*

Apparently, Windsor's social circle is comprised of like-minded men and absolutely no one else. It's as though I've just stepped back in time two hundred years.

'Shit,' I say.

'But they'll talk to me. I suggest we start with a drink and go from there.'

'All right.'

'Baron Drake!' a man yells as we approach the bar, waving us over. 'It's been a dog's age.' Going by his accent he's American, but he looks like the Monopoly man.

'Harrison,' Drake replies. He makes no attempt to introduce me, nor does Harrison seem interested in being introduced. I might as well be invisible.

'Did you hear about Grant?' Harrison asks.

My ears prick up.

'Messy business,' Drake replies. 'Did you invest?'

'With him? Good god, no. Do I look crazy?' Harrison has a whisky in his hand and he swirls the tumbler as he talks. 'He was selling, no doubt, but none of us were buying. He saved his scams for the humans, and just as well. You think he wanted to jerk us around? He knew what we'd do to him.' He laughs, and there's an edge of glee to it.

But that's not the thing that catches my attention.

He knew what we'd do.

Is Harrison implying that Grant knew about the Silver? The portfolio names have already hinted at that, but this could be the confirmation I need. I squeeze Drake's arm and hope he gets the message.

'You knew him well, then?' he asks.

I smile.

Good boy.

'I wouldn't say that,' Harrison replies. 'I saw him when he came here, of course. The man could talk the hind leg off a donkey. Always pushing, trying to get what he wanted. Weaselly little asshole. Anyway, what are you drinking? Bourbon? Scotch?' He clicks his fingers to summon the barman. I've worked behind a bar before and I know what it's like to serve people like him. I hope the barman spits in his drink.

'Gin for the lady,' Drake says. 'Vodka for me.'

Aha! I knew he'd be a vodka man. I'm slightly disturbed that he knows my own drink, but then I was covered in it that day he came to the college to meet with the Secundus.

The barman does the honours while Harrison taps the shoulder of the man next to him and presents him to Drake.

'You remember Mainwaring,' Harrison says. The man looks young, maybe late twenties in human terms, with light brown hair and tiny eyes that are set too far apart. He gives off a sleazy air, but I can't pinpoint why. It makes my gaze slide away from his face, unwilling to meet his eyes.

'Baron,' Mainwaring says, shaking Drake's hand too slowly. I bet his palm is sticky. 'It's been too long. I hoped we might see you at one of these gatherings. I think you'll find that we have similar tastes.'

He grins, all teeth. It's then that I realise he smells of fear, but it's not his own. He's wearing someone else's terror like perfume.

'I suspect you might be right,' Drake says, smiling back.

'We were just discussing Grant,' says Harrison.

'Oh, that idiot,' says Mainwaring. 'I don't care how much Percy liked him. He was allied with our values, yes, but he was too stupid to earn his admission fee and too flagrant to live as a Silver. Good riddance, I say.'

'Admission fee?' Drake asks.

'To the fraternity of the Silver,' says Harrison. 'They're all expected to buy their entrance. Can't let just anyone become immortal. I'm sure you sympathise.'

'And Grant decided embezzlement was the way to raise it,' says Mainwaring, shaking his head. 'Idiot.'

My grip on Drake's arm has tightened so much that he takes my hand to loosen it.

It's forbidden to make more Silver without the approval of the Primus. It's not something that people just go around doing whenever they feel like it, so either Harrison and Mainwaring are comfortable enough here to let loose their secrets, or this club of Percy's is operating under the authority of the Primus. That is a terrifying thought.

The barman hands over our drinks and I gulp mine down.

If the people in this room are the future of the Silver, then I despair for us all.

An hour later, we've somehow become attached to a large group of these bores. Or, more accurately, they've attached themselves to us. Apparently Drake is a bit of a draw.

They've arranged the armchairs so ten of them now sit in a circle, each occupied by a whisky-swilling, cigar-smoking dullard. The women don't get seats of their own. They're expected to perch on the edge of their gentlemen's chairs, adorning them like birds of paradise. It makes me wonder how many of them are hired escorts, because I can't imagine why else they'd put up with this shit. My feet hurt, my arse has gone numb, and I'm so bored that I've started counting the seconds on the long-case clock just to pass the time.

'I've come out of oil entirely,' one of them is saying. 'The place to invest is gold. It's timeless, stable–'

'And so boring,' another interrupts. 'Commodities, Randall? *Gold?* Really? Can you think of anything more crass? It's bonds or nothing.'

'And you say *commodities* are crass? If you're not buying into securities already then you're going to get a shock come the next recession.'

On and on and on until my brain feels like it's going to start running out of my ears. I was hoping this conversation would steer back around to CGC at some point, but no one seems interested in talking about David Grant, his embezzlement, or his pending Silver-dom.

Then, one by one, the women start to disappear. I don't notice the first leaving and I pay no attention when the second slips away, but the third catches my eye. She doesn't look as though she's moving just to escape the boredom. There's purpose in her eyes, in her walk, in the way she nods to one of the other women before leaving the room. The one she gives the nod is the next one to leave, and so on, until I'm the last woman sitting, as it were.

No one ever gave me the nod.

I follow them anyway. Every one of them is Silver, so I fit right in as I follow them back through the house to a grand staircase leading up to the first floor. It's everything you'd expect from a mansion like this: wide and sweeping, with two arms that split off to different wings of the house. The women go left, into a long corridor with rooms on one side and a gallery of windows on the other. The carpet is so thick that I have to be careful not to catch my heels in it. I almost trip, then spend the next few steps watching my feet, but when I look up again I'm the only one left in the hallway.

Where did they go?

'Ladies. Thank you for coming.' The voice is raised as though to address an audience and it's coming from a room at the end of the corridor.

I creep in that direction, hanging back to peek through the half-open door.

The room is arrayed like an auditorium, with lines of chairs packed in tightly. The women are standing at the far side, facing a room full of seated men who have their backs to me, about twenty of them in total. The majority of the men are human, but there are a few Silver scattered here and there, mostly around the periphery. One of them looks familiar, but I can't place him. Brown hair, brown eyes, muscular build. I can feel the threat rolling off him from the far side of the room. He's the one speaking. He seems to be in charge.

'Gentlemen, this is how it works. First, we need your buy-in. You know the price, and we expect it to be deposited into our account before things go any further. If you haven't already, then I suggest you start saving.'

There's some nervous laughter.

'But some of you are now ready to join us, so here's the list: Carlyle, Fontaine, Jones, Wright, Gosford and Sanderson.' There's a round of applause from the audience. 'Let's start with Carlyle.'

A man gets up from the audience and makes his way to the front. Once he gets there, he walks along the row of women, sizing them up as though they're livestock. After a minute or so, he makes his selection, taking a red-haired woman by her hand and leading her out of the room through a door at the far end. Initially I think this is some kind of fucked up prostitution ring – the women all have that dead look in their eyes that tells me they're wishing themselves away from here – but then a couple of Silver men follow them out.

A few minutes pass, then there's a scream. I'm pretty sure it's not coming from the woman.

When the three Silver come back into the room – the two men and the woman – the human isn't with them, but there's a lot of blood on the woman's dress. On all of them, actually.

'Well?' says the guy in charge.

One of the men shakes his head in reply.

'That's how it goes,' says the speaker, turning back to the audience. 'There's no great reward without great risk. So, who's next?'

Despite the grim demonstration, the eagerness of the selected men is undiminished. They get up one after another, each picking a new woman and avoiding the ones that have failed, then dying in their turn until the final candidate rises from the crowd.

Except he's not human.

'Mr Sanderson,' says the speaker. 'Step right up.'

Just like the humans who came before him, he takes his time choosing one of the women. Just like the humans before him, he takes her into the back room. But unlike them, he comes back out again, to rapturous applause. He's showing off his 'new' powers, running at speed from one end of the room to the other, and the crowd is loving it.

'Yeah!' he yells, punching the air. 'I'm a winner, baby!'

The crowd yells back, congratulating him on his transformation. But he was Silver long before he walked into that back room.

It's a racket. They're taking the humans' money and killing them.

They never had any intention of turning them Silver.

18

I'M ON MY way back through the bar to find Drake when the consequences of my last excursion catch up with me.

'What the fuck are you doing here?'

Shit.

It's Felton, and he's not happy. I obviously made a bigger impression on him than I did on Windsor, because he has no trouble remembering my face.

'How did you get in here, and what were you doing upstairs?'

'I was invited, actually,' I say.

Felton laughs. 'Not likely. Percy would never let a Seeker in the door.' He grabs my wrist, squeezing tightly enough to bruise. I try to shake him free, but he pushes me into a corner, putting the wall at my back.

'The Solis Invicti are going to come for you. Your life is over, girl.' He's in my face, pointing and looming in a way that makes me think it won't be long before he starts swinging.

'Look, Felton–'

'No, you look. I've got friends, bitch. They know how to put people like you in their place.'

I've had enough. I'm about to put Felton in *his* place, but someone catches my fist as I draw it back. My arm is abruptly pinned to my side.

'Are you all right, pumpkin?' Drake says, putting his arm around my shoulders.

Pumpkin? I'm going to kill him. First Felton, then Drake.

'What are you doing?' I ask him through gritted teeth.

'What are *you* doing, honeybun? Aren't we supposed to be keeping a low profile?'

Felton has been thrown by our conversation, but now he focuses his attention on Drake and says, 'Who the fuck are you?' Which is implausible, since he's lived in Oxford all of his immortal life and should be well aware of who Drake is.

'Don't go out much?' I ask him. 'Prefer to stay at home and practice your perversions alone?'

'I'm never alone for long,' he says with a smirk. 'There's nothing you can do to change that.'

'Want to bet?'

I surge towards Felton, but Drake tightens his arm around me, pulling me away. I give him a look, trying to get him to back off because I'd really like to punch Felton in the face. I know it's a bad idea, but it feels like it would be worth it.

'Don't look at him,' Felton says. 'He can't help you. I've got friends in places you can't even imagine. You'll be dead before the end of the month.'

'Matthew,' Windsor says to him in a sharp stage-whisper. Neither Felton nor I noticed that our host had joined us. We were too busy glaring at each other. We barely break eye-contact now. 'Matthew, what the bloody hell are you doing?'

'This bitch–'

Shit.

If Felton mentions that I'm a Seeker, then Windsor will remember who I am and that will be the end of my undercover career. I'll never find out what's going on here, never find Grant's killer and, most importantly, I'll never hear the end of it from Drake.

But Windsor gives Felton a quick punch in the nose before he can say anything else.

'Please accept my apologies, Baron,' Windsor says as he shoves Felton away from us. 'I'm sure he meant no disrespect.'

'That bitch stole from me!' Felton yells. Windsor clamps a hand over Felton's mouth, then uses the grip to steer him towards the other end of the corridor and away from us.

I'm tempted to make a break for it then and there, but Drake's arm is tight around my shoulders, holding me in place.

'Easy,' he says under his breath. 'You'd be better off playing the part of the distraught little floozie you're supposed to be.'

I roll my eyes, then let out a sob and bury my face in Drake's shoulder. The scent of the two of us is mingled together on his clothing, on his skin. It hits me soul-deep, to smell my scent mixed with his own. I hate the lie.

Windsor has Felton off in the corner now, but they're not whispering softly enough to escape being overheard. I realise that this is a show of loyalty from Windsor, that he wants to prove to Drake that he's sound.

'That is the Baron of Oxford,' Windsor says.

'That bitch–'

'Is the guest of the Baron of Oxford. Do you understand what I'm saying at all? Can your brain process language into comprehension?'

'But she–'

Windsor hits Felton around the face, hard. Hard enough that I hear his skull cracking, but not hard enough to put him down. A servant is summoned to take Felton away while Windsor wipes Felton's blood from his hand with a clean white handkerchief. There's an insult in that: Felton is sullied enough that Windsor would rather waste his blood than lick it from his fingers. Maybe it's for Drake's benefit, or maybe Felton turns Windsor's stomach as much as he turns mine, but either way the point is made.

Drake nods at Windsor.

'About time we got out of here,' I whisper to him. 'Let's get my coat and get the hell out of dodge.'

We slip out of the bar and across the ballroom, hoping to make a quiet exit, but no such luck.

'Surely you're not leaving just yet,' Windsor says, intercepting us on the way to the door. He must have moved at Silver speed to beat us here. 'It's barely nine o'clock. I hope that toe-rag Felton didn't offend you, Baron. Please, let me entertain you. The dancing is just about to start.'

Drake looks at me. I realise we're going to have to relent if we don't want to raise suspicions. If we run off now, everyone will wonder why we came in the first place, and they might make some connections I'd rather they didn't.

'We may as well have some fun while we're here, right?' I say.

'Good!' Windsor says. 'Let me freshen your drinks.'

He escorts us back into the ballroom and beckons over a waitress, who hands us each a flute of champagne.

'Please,' Windsor says, 'enjoy yourselves.' Then he takes his leave.

There's a swing band playing. I'm not much of a dancer, but a few of the other attendees are and they're whirling each other around as though this is some kind of contest.

Drake knocks back his drink then offers me his hand. 'Would you like to dance?'

'You're kidding, right? I have two left feet.'

'Well, I have two right feet, so I imagine we'll muddle along.'

'Drake...'

'Come on,' he says, putting our champagne flutes on a table nearby. 'How bad can it be?'

Not that bad, as it turns out. My dress isn't made for swing, but Drake guides my feet and lets me ride out the twirls slowly. We laugh and spin and his hand fits at the small of my back like it's made to rest there.

Then, inevitably, the music slows.

'Do you want to stop?' he asks, but Felton is watching from the other side of the room, so I pull Drake closer and let him take me in his arms.

'I've changed my mind about the dress,' he says as the lights dim.

'Oh?'

'I like it. I like it a lot.' His fingertips play down my naked spine like whispers on the breeze, there and yet not, tickling my skin. We are cheek to cheek, until he lowers his head to kiss my bare shoulder.

'This isn't real, Drake,' I whisper. I'm surprised that I sound a little sad about it. That's the mark talking.

'Let me dream.' He kisses my neck. 'Just for a few hours.'

This is what it's like to be wrapped in the scent of the mark, with every pheromone telling us that we belong to each other. It's exactly like a dream, as though we've stepped beyond the world and are swaying in a space carved outside it just for us. The low lights don't help.

'This isn't me,' I say, more to myself than to him.

'Is that what you think?' He lifts his head to look into my eyes. 'You think you have to be just one person? With all due respect, that's bollocks. You can be as many different versions of yourself as you like. The tenacious one who solves every case, the fucked-up one who turns up for meetings covered in blood and alcohol, and the aggressive one who barges into my own home to yell at me.'

I smile despite myself.

'Then there's the one in my arms right now,' he whispers, swaying me gently, 'all soft velvet and skin. You can be whoever you want to be, Valentine. They're all you.'

'And how many versions of Killian Drake are there in your head?' I ask, trying to brush away the intimacy of his words.

'More than you'll ever know.' His eyes are fixed on mine, dark and unreadable. 'Some versions of me get washed away with the years and some embed like bullets then fragment until they're too small to pull back out again.'

'Sounds painful.'

'The pieces I can't shake aren't always the ones I'd choose to keep.' He's still now, his hand at my cheek, his thumb stroking my skin. 'It's the broken parts that get lodged in your bones.'

He's going to kiss me. I can see it in the slight tilt of his head, in his hooded eyes and parted lips, and I can't bear it. It doesn't feel like we're pretending anymore.

I step out of his arms and smile.

'Shall we do something else?' I say brightly. 'Maybe a game? Didn't Windsor say there was a games room?'

Then I catch sight of the buffet being set up behind him.

This is why Felton is here. There are at least ten women and men, all unconscious, arrayed in various positions amongst the food. Their bodies are gilded and painted, with pulse-points left clear and angled invitingly towards the diners.

'Jesus,' I hiss. I can feel the anger burning through my muscles, urging me to intervene.

Drake follows my gaze. 'Jack... Maybe you should–'

'These fucking people,' I say, clenching my fists impotently, because I know there's nothing I can do for these humans without blowing our cover. I need to protect the knowledge I've gathered tonight.

'I know it's distasteful, but they'll be fine,' Drake says, taking my fists in his hands. 'They'll be back in their beds by morning, none the wiser.'

He's probably right, because this is Felton we're talking about, but there's no accounting for the occasional bastard who gets carried away. With this crowd, no human is safe.

'You don't know that,' I say, watching as a lecherous old Silver lifts one of the girls' wrists to his mouth. 'You can't promise me that.'

'I'll make sure of it,' he says, then kisses me on the forehead and walks off through the crowd. He isn't gone more than a couple of minutes.

'Now I can promise you,' he says on his return.

I look across the ballroom in the direction from which he came and see Windsor, looking as though he's just won the lottery.

'What did you do?'

'I gave him a reason to want to keep me happy, then I told him what that would take. People like Percy are pitifully easy to manipulate. Power, money, fame. So dull.'

'Isn't that exactly what you want?'

The corner of his mouth twitches into the ghost of a smile. 'My appetites run in other directions.'

He leans in, moving to pull me close again, but before he can do so I take his hand and lead him straight across the dance floor.

'Let's see about that game, shall we?'

He sighs, but lets me drag him along behind me.

There aren't many people in the games room, but most of them are quietly shuffling cards across the tables or prodding snooker balls across green baize. The cigar smoke hangs heavily in the air. It feels more like a mausoleum than a place where people are supposed to be having fun.

'Poker?' I say, sidling up to the nearest table. 'That's dull. I was expecting something a little more scandalous from a party like this. Can't we play a real game?'

A moustachioed player raises an imperious eyebrow at me. I wonder if he learned that trick from the captain.

'What did you have in mind?' he asks.

I grab the deck from the centre of the table and take a seat as I start shuffling.

'Have you guys ever played Ring of Fire?'

'Suck it, Geoff!' I say, slamming my card down onto the table. 'I am the thumb master! Drink!'

Geoff, if that's actually his name – I'm having trouble remembering things at this point in the game – is already halfway under the table. I've introduced Windsor's guests to my signature cocktail and they're serving it by the jug. I have no idea how much we've all consumed, but since we're nearly out of cards it must be a lot.

'Noooo,' maybe-Geoff moans. 'Not again.'

Then he slides off his chair.

'One down,' I say, looking around the table. 'Six to go. Your turn, Randy.'

It turns out that Randall the bore is hilarious once you get a Massacre in him. Actually, pretty much everyone is hilarious when they're that inebriated. They haven't had the practice I have, and it turns out they're all lightweights.

By the time we leave the table, Geoff is sobbing into the carpet.

'Come on, you,' Drake says, helping me to my feet. 'Time to go home.'

Sensibly, he declined to join the game and chose to watch instead. He drank a couple of Massacres of his own, though, and it's showing. I'm not sure how we manage to get out of the building still upright, but somehow we stumble into a car that Drake has summoned to take us home. It's exactly what I was expecting for the journey out: tinted windows, leather seats and a screen separating us from our chauffeur.

'In for a penny, Valentine,' Drake says, pulling me into his arms as he slides onto the seat beside me. Some unseen attendant closes the door behind him, shutting us into the darkness of the back seat together.

'Fuck off,' I laugh.

'You're already marked,' Drake whispers. 'So what's the harm?'

'I might be drunk, but I'm not a complete idiot.'

'You'd have to be an idiot to kiss me?'

'You said it,' I shrug. 'Not me.'

'Then how are we going to pass the time while we drive back to Oxford?'

It's the last thing I hear before I pass out. When I finally come back around, we're already inside the ring road that surrounds the city.

I sit up in my seat – Drake must have strapped me in, because I don't remember doing it myself – and fumble in the pocket of my coat for my phone so I can check the time.

There's a text message from Tabitha:

Looking forward to tomorrow. Sleep well ;)

Oh, god. I'm supposed to be on a date with her tomorrow night and I'm wearing Drake's fucking scent mark. I groan and drop my head into my hands.

'Something wrong?' Drake asks. He doesn't sound any the worse for wear after his Massacre experience, and for that I'd happily lamp him right now. Well, part of me would. The other part is all wrapped up in the romance of his perfume and wants to do something entirely different.

'It's fine,' I say.

We don't speak for a few minutes. He waits until we're pulling up at the college to break his silence.

'Is it about your date?'

I turn in my seat to face him. 'Excuse me?'

'With Dr Ross. Tomorrow night, isn't it?'

His expression is all innocence, but there's triumph in his eyes. He knew about my date with Tabitha. He knew I would be seeing her in less than twenty-four hours, and he was relishing the fact that I would be doing so wearing his mark. Had he planned this?

'You knew,' I say, prodding him in the chest. 'You *bastard*.'

He takes my chin in his hand and smiles, then he whispers, 'You knew, too. But it was necessary, so you did what had to be done. I was only doing the same.'

'No,' I say, pulling away from him and removing my seatbelt. We've pulled up at the college now and I'm already halfway out of the car. 'This wasn't your mission. You couldn't care less whether or not it succeeded. So why? Were you just messing with me, or what?'

He laughs then, and the sound of it sends a shiver down my spine.

'Oh, Jack,' he says, leaning back into the shadows. 'I'm not a good man. I never pretended that I was.'

I leave him in the darkness and slam the door behind me, but the promise of his return is written in the air. He has marked me and I have marked him. The scent might have disappeared by this time tomorrow, but the repercussions will be harder to wash away.

The shiver follows me back to my rooms. I kick off my heels and strip off the dress without ceremony, leaving it in a pile on the floor. It doesn't deserve to be hung up. All I can think about is Drake's hands on it, on my skin, and the way I didn't hate how it felt. I think about his fingers stroking the shimmering velvet, the same fingers stroking through my hair, and I feel the awful shame crowding my throat in the same way that his mark crowds my senses.

It was supposed to be Tabitha. It's not a betrayal exactly, because we've made no promises. We haven't even kissed. Yet it feels as though I've taken the delicate creature that could have been us and crushed it in my hands.

If nothing else, I'm going to have to break our date.

Something's come up, I text her. *I'm really sorry, but I can't do tomorrow night. Are you free Tuesday?*

It's late, so it's no wonder that she doesn't reply immediately, but I fall asleep with the phone on my pillow, waiting for her to message me back.

19

THERE ARE A lot of things about the Silver mark that are undeniably amazing, and that I hadn't fully appreciated before experiencing it myself. When I wake up the next morning, I practically spring out of bed, hours before my alarm. I feel like I'm walking on air, like the whole world is glittering, like my heart could burst with the simple joy of existing.

But every part of that feeling is tied to him. It wants to pull us back together.

The mark is designed this way. It makes you want to renew it, to get marked again and again, to perpetuate it until you're so addicted to the scent that you will never let yourself be without it again. But the addiction only lasts for twenty-four hours. I only have to make it to this evening and then I'll be in the clear.

Until then, I have to suppress the scent and ignore the memories that keep flitting unwanted into my mind: Drake's lips, the rumble of his voice, his fingers in my hair, and the knowledge that every touch carried with it the promise of something more.

Until then, I have to work.

I'm dreading facing the others, but there's no escape. I can't just disappear for a day, not when we're in the middle of this investigation. Not with the Invicti back this morning, expecting us to report progress on the case. Not with a conspiracy to uncover, a conspiracy that might lead to the most powerful Silver in the country.

So I get up, shower – which does nothing to mitigate the dark scent of Drake threaded under my skin – and head for the canteen. I'm the first one there, but Cam arrives when I've barely made a start on my breakfast.

'You're up early,' he says, grinning as he ambles towards my table. 'I heard you come in late and wasn't expecting you to– Oh my god.' He pulls up short, his expression horrified. 'What did you do?'

Naia prowls in next, looking curiously between us. Boyd is right behind her.

'What's up?' Naia says to Cam. 'You look like you've just seen a– Holy fucking shit!'

They're both staring at me now, wide-eyed.

Behind her, Boyd says, 'Uh-oh,' just before all hell breaks loose.

'The Baron?' Naia splutters. 'You fucked the Baron? When I said you needed to get laid, that was categorically not what I had in mind.'

'You actually took my advice?' Cam says, looking confused. 'Seriously? You... You made love?'

'Are you fucking crazy?' Naia says. 'He's the fucking *Baron*. I mean, what the hell does this mean? I thought you hated him?'

'Methinks the lady doth protest too much,' Boyd chimes in.

'Shut up, Deputy,' Naia says, absentmindedly. 'Are you, like, a couple now? Are you leaving the Seekers? Are you going to be Mrs Baron?'

'It would be Baroness Drake, actually.'

'Shut *up*, Boyd.'

'How about *everybody* shuts up,' I say, standing from my chair. 'I did not have sex with Killian Drake. I didn't even want to kiss the bastard, but I needed him to mark me so I could get into Windsor's party.'

'Mm-hmm,' Naia says. 'Sure. You know he wouldn't have been able to mark you unless you had the hots for him. Ergo—'

'I was thinking of someone else! The someone, in fact, with whom I have a date tomorrow night.' I hope. I'm still waiting for her to reply to my text. 'Can we just drop it, please? It's done, it happened, and it won't happen again. So if you've finished making shit up, then perhaps we could put it behind us so I can brief you on what *actually* happened at last night's party. Is that okay with everyone?'

'Fine by me,' says Boyd.

Naia holds up her hands in surrender, then goes with the others to fetch her breakfast from the servers. I can hear Naia and Cam gossiping behind me, but I ignore them and concentrate on finishing my eggs.

'Right,' I say when they return to the table. 'Have we got any news?'

'You mean other than the obvious?' Naia says, looking me up and down.

'It turns out that these portfolios are for genuine, registered companies,' Boyd says, ignoring Naia. He's not one for gossip. 'They seem like shells owned by shells, because I can't track down any directors who haven't just been paid fifty quid to have their names on the documents, but they're doing well. Really well. Millions and millions of pounds are floating around in their accounts.'

'I might have an explanation for that.' I lower my voice as I tell them about the scam I uncovered last night, the humans who think they're buying their way into the fraternity of the Silver.

'And this is sanctioned?' Boyd asks, looking horrified. 'An actual Casting ceremony?'

It's the official term for the ceremony at which humans are turned Silver, but what I saw last night didn't look anything like I imagined it would. I've never been to a Casting myself, but they're supposed to be solemn and dark with candles and Latin and all that jazz. I hadn't imagined that such a revered ceremony would take place at a seedy house party in the Cotswolds.

'I don't know,' I say. 'They weren't exactly trying to hide it. The way everyone was speaking made me think they believed it was above board. I'd guess either it's sanctioned, or they've been told it is.'

'It must be. You can't just go around making more Silver without the approval of the Primus,' says Cam.

'Maybe not, but then they're not actually *making* any more Silver, are they?' I say. 'They're just murdering them.'

'So this is Seeker business,' says Boyd.

'Hang on, now,' Naia interrupts, leaning over the table and looking between the three of us confidentially. 'Let's not get carried away, here. It sounds like these scummy humans got what was coming to them.'

'And when it all comes out?' Boyd says. 'When someone wonders what's happening to these men? When someone finds a body? And what about the other humans who were in the room, who didn't get turned? They know about the Silver. We need to take this to the captain. Now.'

There goes her plausible deniability.

As we make our way to the captain's office, we're arguing about the motive for Grant's murder.

'It has to be the money,' Boyd says. 'Why take a pound of flesh otherwise? Doesn't that seem strangely deliberate to you? If he was embezzling from the clients of CGC, maybe he embezzled from one of the Silver too. All those company names—'

'But we know he was trying to buy his way into getting turned,' Naia interrupts. 'That's his main point of contact with the Silver. Maybe he thought he was getting turned the night he died. That would make more sense in the circumstances, otherwise it's just too much of a coincidence.'

'But he didn't have the money to buy in,' I point out. 'He was flat broke.'

We've already been over this more than once. The Silver I saw last night wouldn't even have pretended to turn Grant without being paid for it, not unless something went wrong. That was my theory: something went wrong.

'Maybe he was only broke because he'd paid his buy-in already,' Naia says. 'Otherwise, where did all his money go? He was rich, right?'

'Okay, then why throw him off the tower? Why the pageantry?'

'Maybe it really was a coincidence,' Cam says. 'Maybe the Secundus is right, and it's connected to the murders in London.'

I groan and push my hair back from my face with both hands. I can't remember the last time we had a case this convoluted.

'Let's see what the captain thinks,' says Cam, knocking on her door.

'Come in.'

The captain double-takes when we gather inside. She's looking at me. Three guesses as to why.

'Jack?' she says.

'Captain.'

'I…' She looks puzzled. 'Well. That's a surprise.'

'I went undercover last night, Captain. We had to be creative to get me into Windsor's party.'

'Oh. I see.' She doesn't look any less puzzled. 'Perhaps you'd better sit down and explain.'

We gather around the table in her room and take it in turns to give our updates: the financial records, the phone records, the party. It's a frustrating exercise, because I've been over this time and time again in my head and still can't work out how it adds up to a murder. We have a lot more information, but we're still no closer to finding out what happened to David Grant.

The captain steeples her fingers and presses them to her lips.

'So,' she says, 'we have a leak. Someone is telling these humans about the Silver.'

'It seems that way,' says Boyd.

'Then our priority is containment. Are you proposing to take this to the Solis Invicti?'

'They might be in on it, Captain,' I say. 'In which case, we're screwed.'

'We can't be sure of that,' says Boyd.

'I'm pretty damn sure.'

'Enough,' says the captain. 'I'll deal with the containment of the individuals at Sir Percival's party. Leave it with me. In the meantime, we keep this to ourselves. I'll talk to the police and try to get my hands on David Grant's phone. Jack and Cam, go back to Magdalen – the clandestine route, this time –and see if you can find a Silver who saw something. If that fails, try charming the porters. Boyd and Naia, keep working on the CGC records. In the meantime, no mention of any of this new information to the Invicti, and *particularly* no mention of the party. They'd have a field day with that. I mean, Christ, Valentine, what were you thinking?'

'It seemed like a good idea at the time.'

'It got us new information, sir,' Boyd says. 'It could be valuable.' I'm surprised to hear him coming to my defence, but I'm not going to complain.

The captain looks sceptical about how valuable that information might be, but she drops it.

'Well, we'd better get to the conference room,' she says. 'The Invicti are back, and they want to hear from Ed.'

At that point, my day goes sharply downhill.

'Baron Drake,' the captain says as she walks into the conference room in front of me. 'Good of you to come.'

No. Please, no.

I stop walking. The only thing that gets me into the room is that Cam is walking right behind me, pushing.

'Jack,' Drake says as I stumble in. The room is filled with Invicti, not just the Secundus and Meyer, but a load of other faces I don't recognise, and they're all staring at me and Drake.

Kill me now.

'I was hoping I might see you,' he says, getting to his feet. He crosses the room towards me, then ushers me to a seat next to his. He holds it out for me while I sit and all the time he's smiling at me. It's not his normal smile, either; the one that says *I know something you don't and I'm going to use it to screw you over*. Instead, it seems almost genuine. He's behaving as though this thing between us is real and I don't know how to react.

Apparently the Invicti do. If the Secundus is still unimpressed with me, there's no trace of it on his face now. He nods a formal greeting, as do the other Invicti. They're treating me like I'm suddenly worthy of respect. It's the most uncomfortable feeling I've ever experienced, as though an attachment to Drake makes me an entirely different person. I'm no longer myself, I'm just a shadow of him.

He reaches over to take my hand in his and I realise that I can't deny him. After what we discovered last night, how can I trust the Invicti? I wouldn't be surprised if they know that I was at Windsor's party with Drake. They need to believe this is real, otherwise they'll know why I was really there last night. They'll know that we're on to them.

Drake smiles as he wraps his fingers around mine.

'Some of us had a good weekend, then,' Meyer says, laughing.

When Drake looks at me, I make myself smile back at him.

'Oh-kay,' Ed says. I didn't notice him until he got to his feet. 'Who wants to hear the DNA results?'

'Please go ahead,' says the Secundus.

'Right, well, as you know, DNA is kind of crappy in these cases, but this time we got lucky. We took DNA from under David Grant's nails and from the injection site on his hand, and managed to isolate several different DNA profiles. I've compared them to the profiles from the London murders and there are two common donors.'

Ed pauses, looking around the room as his words hit home.

'You're saying they match?' Meyer probes. 'So it's the same killer?'

'Not exactly. I'm saying that of the samples we recovered, two of them were matches to profiles obtained from the two latest London murders.'

'Which means?'

'That the London killer and whoever killed David Grant are likely feeding from the same people.'

The Secundus and Meyer share a look.

'What are the odds of two Silver sharing the same food source?' Cam asks.

'In London?' the Secundus says. 'There are blood bars with regular donors. It's not impossible for it to happen. But for two Silver to share the same food source when one's in London and the other's in Oxford?' He shakes his head. 'It's got to be the same killer. It's just too much of a coincidence.'

There's that word again. *Coincidence*. The coincidences are just piling up in this case. It makes me uncomfortable. It feels forced, perhaps even deliberate, but I can't put my finger on why. There's the trailing end of a thought I can't catch; I'm too distracted by the effort of ignoring Drake's thumb, which is stroking gently across the back of my hand. It's rhythmic, soothing, and I wish he would stop.

'I've also finished comparing the thread samples,' Ed goes on. 'I can confirm that the red fibres found on Grant's hand came from the seats at the Playhouse.'

'So, nothing useful there,' says the Secundus.

'Nothing surprising, at least,' says Boyd.

'That's all from my lab,' Ed says. 'Then there's the post mortem.'

Drake squeezes my hand and flashes his silver at me. It's something we all have, the little threads of silver in the whites of our eyes. It's why we're called the Silver, in fact.

All except the very youngest of us can hide the threads when we want to, and we do that almost permanently because otherwise the humans would work out that we aren't like them. But there are times when we reveal the silver for a moment to another of our kind, flashing it like Drake has just done to me. Sometimes it's aggressive, sometimes provocative, and sometimes it means nothing more than *hello*.

In these circumstances, I can't tell whether it's a threat or a flirtation.

'Okay,' says the Secundus. 'Let's bring in the doctor.'

The doctor?

Meyer pops outside for a moment, and when he comes back in he has Tabitha with him.

Oh no.

She's wearing my crappy takeaway chopsticks in her hair. When she sees me sitting at the table she beams at me, as though she's been looking forward to this very moment, but then she scents the air and her expression falls little by little until it sinks with disappointment. I drop Drake's hand, but not quickly enough to stop her from seeing it.

If we were alone, this is where she would say, *Oh*. But we're not alone, so she cranks her smile back up and turns to the Secundus.

'Good to see you,' she says, shaking his hand. She stumbles over her words a little as she turns her attention to Drake, but she recovers well. 'Hello, Baron Drake.'

'Dr Ross.'

I want to punch him. He's sitting there all haughty with his suit and his ego and he's not telling her that she has the wrong idea. He's letting her believe that the scent marks are real. He's letting everyone believe it and he's acting like he's enjoying it.

I clench my fists under the table.

Tabitha takes a deep breath and says, 'Right, then. The post mortem results.'

She tells the room everything she told me and Naia yesterday, clearly and efficiently. I want her to look at me so I can give her some kind of signal, some kind of clue that this isn't what it seems, but she never even glances my way.

When Tabitha leaves, I follow her out into the quad.

'Tabitha, wait. I can explain.'

'No need,' she says, hurrying on.

'It's not what it looks like. Please, just talk to me.'

She stops and waits for me to catch up, but she's uncomfortable, looking from side to side. She doesn't want to be seen talking to me. She doesn't want to be anywhere near me while I'm wearing Drake's mark, because she can't risk the repercussions if someone decides she's challenging Drake's claim. He's powerful enough that the mark matters.

Before I can get within six feet of her, she holds out a hand to ward me off.

'That's close enough.'

'But–'

'They're watching.' She's right. The conference room window looks out onto the quad and the Invicti are still in there, wrapping up the briefing whilst surreptitiously glancing our way.

'Maybe we could go somewhere more private? To discuss it?'

She laughs, bitterly.

'I like you, hen,' she says, 'but I'm not going to fight the Baron for you.'

'I'm not asking you to.'

'With that kind of talk? Yes, you are.'

'Then tomorrow,' I say as she turns to walk away. 'The mark will be gone and I'll tell you all about it. Please, Tabitha.'

'All right,' she whispers, but she doesn't turn back to me. She just keeps on walking until she's out of the quad, out of the college, and out of sight.

When I get back to the conference room, the Invicti are already on their way out.

'Jack, you're with Cam,' the captain reminds me. 'The rest of you have your assignments.'

'We'll, er...' Cam says, looking between me and Drake. I'm glaring daggers at Drake, while he lounges back in his chair as though he hasn't a care in the world. 'We'll let you two chat.'

They leave me and Drake together, closing the door behind them. The moment it shuts, I'm marching towards him, powered entirely by rage.

'Why didn't you say something?' I ask.

He raises his eyebrows. 'What exactly did you want me to say?'

'Oh, I don't know, maybe something about the mark not meaning anything. Maybe that it wasn't real?'

'In front of all the Invicti? I thought you didn't want them to know that you crashed Percy's party for investigative purposes. Wasn't that the whole point of your duplicity in there? I was just playing along.'

I want to scream, because he's right. If I can't even blame him for this, then I might self-combust.

'You are the most irritating, infuriating—'

'You had a good time last night,' he says, rising to his feet. 'Admit it.'

'I did not,' I reply, but then I remember the intrigue, the bickering, the games, the dancing, the *kissing*, and I feel a smile tugging at the edge of my mouth.

'I never thought I'd see a grown man cry like that,' he says.

'He couldn't handle his drink.'

'I'm not sure anyone can handle more than two of those concoctions of yours.' He smiles and that look is back in his eye again, the one that makes it seem as though this could actually be real. But this time we have no audience, and there's no point to it. I wish he'd stop pretending.

'Cut it out.'

But he just keeps on smiling.

'You're a fun date, Jack. We should do it again sometime.'

'Well, that's never going to happen. It was just the mark doing its magic. You know that.'

'If you say so.' He's close now, not moving in, but hovering there like an invitation.

'Stop messing around.'

'I'm not messing around.'

I can't tell whether or not he's serious, but despite the mark urging me towards him, I decide I don't want to find out. I take a step backwards.

'Goodbye, Drake.'

He laughs at me, as though this is all a game to him.

'Goodbye, Jack.'

20

CAM IS WAITING for me outside my rooms.

'So,' he says.

'So?'

'You and the Baron—'

'Let's just focus on the case, shall we?' I unlock my door and let us both inside. 'We need to get over to Magdalen College to see if we can track down a Silver informant.'

'Okay,' Cam says, following me in, 'but we're going to have to talk about this sometime.'

'As long as it's not this decade, that's fine with me.'

He raises his eyebrows, but lets the subject drop.

I sit on the sofa to switch my boots for shoes and Cam flops down next to me like the big puppy he is.

'Okay,' I say. 'The DNA results. Are you thinking this is all the same killer?'

'I don't know. It's what the Solis Invicti seem to think.'

'Yeah, well, I might agree with them,' I say. 'The killer came from London to Oxford. Who do we know from London who's in Oxford now?'

We exchange a glance. *The Solis Invicti.*

Cam chews on his lower lip.

'I don't like this, Jack. I don't like it one bit.'

'Me neither, but what can we do? If the Solis Invicti are behind this, then all we can do is keep investigating and pretend we don't suspect anything until we find proof. Right?'

'Right,' Cam says. 'But I'm not sure what you're expecting us to do with the proof if we do find it.'

He has a point there. I might have been able to report Drake to the Invicti if he'd done this, but I can't exactly arrest the Solis Invicti and drag them to Drake for punishment. A good number of them outrank him.

'Look,' Cam says after a moment, 'they're not the only suspects here. Even if you're already convinced, we still need to investigate the other options, or at least pretend to. We've got more to go on now. The DNA match is a lucky break, because it means we know that whoever killed Grant also killed the three London victims. That gives us four dates to check. The Secundus has already started gathering the alibis of the Silver we've encountered so far.'

'Oh, he has, has he?'

I know it's illogical, but I'm possessive of this case. I don't want the Secundus coming in and solving it for us. Quite apart from my suspicions about the Invicti, which give me a very good reason not to trust any conclusion they reach, their involvement feels like a criticism. It's demeaning to have them swoop in here and take the case from us, as though we're not competent enough to handle it ourselves, as though we haven't handled hundreds of cases like this over the years. It's like your parents correcting your homework for you, then tattling to your teacher.

'Come on, Jack,' Cam says me. 'You hate that kind of grunt work. He's done you a favour. You would have had to round up all the Silver and sift through their diaries to work out exactly where they were at the time of each murder. Does that sound like fun?'

'Yes,' I grumble.

'You're impossible. And anyway, it's done. The main players have all given alibis for at least one of the dates, except Baron Drake. The Secundus is interviewing him this evening, but I imagine you wouldn't want to see the Baron right now anyway. Or maybe you would. I don't know, since you won't talk to me about it.'

'Forget it,' I say. 'Let's just do as the captain said.'

'I never thought I'd hear those words coming out of your mouth.'

I thump him on the arm and say, 'Head in the game. How do we approach Magdalen College?'

'Well, Naia went right after it happened and the place was bustling with humans wanting to be interviewed by the "police".' He marks the inverted commas with his fingers. 'Now that it's calmed down a bit, we might have more luck tracking down a resident Silver, but we'll need to be sneaky.'

'So we go in from the river, after dark.'

'Agreed,' says Cam. 'Should we go and help the deputy with the financial records until then?'

I laugh. I can imagine exactly how that would go. I'd highlight the wrong thing, or put a piece of paper in the wrong place, or mess up his filing system by ordering the records alphabetically or chronologically instead of in some labyrinthine Boyd-approved order that only he can navigate.

Hard pass.

'Screw Boyd,' I say, picking up the TV remote and switching on the flatscreen. 'He can manage on his own.'

We wait until ten o'clock before making our way east to the river, where Magdalen College crouches at the foot of the bridge like a gateway to the wild beyonds of East Oxford. When we arrive, we slip down the side of the bridge to the boathouse, then scale the building to the roof.

That sounds dramatic and exciting, and I bet you're imagining one of those nineties heist films where everyone's swinging around on wires in black catsuits. In fact, I'm wearing jeans, and the whole thing is kind of pedestrian to the Silver. You'd think you'd never get bored of jumping three storeys in a single bound, or crawling up the side of a building like Spiderman, but the truth is that big leaps burn a lot of blood, the exertion makes me all sweaty, and the outside of these old college buildings is not as clean as I'd like it to be. By the time we reach the roof overlooking the quad, I'm covered in pigeon shit and my hair is sticking to my forehead.

'Anything?' Cam asks me.

'Give me a minute, will you?'

I scrape my hair back from my face and try to concentrate on what's going on around us. It's Monday night on the run-up to Finals, so the college isn't exactly party central. I can hear laughter coming from the direction of the bar, but most of the voices I pick up on are originating from individual rooms where people are studying late into the night, or trying to relax by binging Netflix.

I zero in on every heartbeat I can find, narrowing the scope of my hearing just long enough to determine that each one is the fast pulse of a human rather than the slow one of a Silver, then I move on to the next. Beside me, Cam is doing the same, only much more efficiently. He's been doing this for centuries longer than I have, and he's good at it.

'Got one,' he says after a minute or so.

'Where?'

'Follow me.'

We run the roofs for a few seconds, then Cam is clambering down a wall in the shaded corner between the north and east cloisters. I follow him, then wait as he knocks on a nearby window.

'Heavens,' says a woman's voice from inside. A couple of seconds later, the window opens. 'Yes?'

'Seekers,' Cam says, just as though we were standing on her doorstep instead of hanging off a wall outside her bedroom window. 'Can we have a word?'

She looks reluctant, but she moves her pot plants from the windowsill and invites us inside. I'd feel bad about leaving bird crap all over her floor, but she's in college accommodation, which means she won't be the one who'll have to clean it up. I'm sure she'll get the scouts – the college cleaners – as soon as we've left.

'You heard about the May Morning murder?' Cam asks as she ushers us onto her sofa.

'Yes,' she murmurs. She takes a seat on the edge of her bed, opposite the sofa. She's a small woman, slight in a way that suggests frailty, with pale blond hair and skin so white it's practically blue. I wouldn't have pegged her for a Silver if I couldn't hear and smell the evidence for myself.

'And were you here at the time, Ms...?'

'Thompson. Mary Thompson.'

Even her name makes me want to yawn.

'I don't get out much,' she says, smiling apologetically. 'I'm a visiting professor. When I'm not in tutorials or lectures, I spend most of my time in the library.'

'Was that where you were on May Morning?' I ask.

Thompson looks down at her hands.

'Ms Thompson?' Cam says.

'Look,' she says, 'I don't want any trouble. I've had enough of that and I've paid for it. I don't want to get wrapped up in this, whatever it is.'

'Just answer the question, Ms Thompson,' I say. 'If you weren't involved, there'll be no trouble.'

She looks up and her gaze drifts sideways, out of the window and across the quad. 'There's always trouble,' she says, but she goes on nonetheless. 'I was here when it happened. I heard the screams, so I looked down into the quadrangle to see what was going on. I saw someone running, a Silver, moving so fast that I doubt anyone else saw them.'

'Can you describe them?' Cam asks.

She bites the inside of her cheek. 'It was still mostly dark and they were moving so quickly. There was just a flash of colour, purple and green, from underneath a dark coat. That's all I saw.'

'Purple and green,' Cam repeats.

Thompson nods to herself. 'Purple and green.'

'Thank you, Ms Thompson,' Cam says, getting to his feet. He offers her his hand, and when she takes it I see the scar on the inside of her wrist: a black mark that follows the path of the veins. Something about it is familiar.

I nod my farewell. We take the stairs this time; we've found our quarry, so there's no further need for secrecy. Or so I think. Cam waits until we're outside the college before he speaks.

'Do you know who that was?' he asks.

'What?' I'm distracted, running through all the information we have in this case and trying to make the pieces fit together. They won't.

'Thompson. Do you know who she is?'

I raise my eyebrows at him as we start walking back up the High Street.

'Black Mary,' he says. 'You saw the veins in her wrist, right? That was Black Mary! I thought she was a fairy tale. They used to sing songs about her when I was freshly made: *Black Mary in the dairy, cutting lengths of cloth to bury, wrap them tight around the vein, and soon they'll never scream again.* You don't remember that one?'

I do. I remember the rhyme from when I was a kid, a human kid. Black Mary was a horror story, a woman who drained the blood from the children she was supposed to be nursing and then buried them under the dirt floor of the barn. As the story went, she came back as a ghost to haunt the farm, with black veins patterning every inch of her skin.

'She's *real*? I though she was just a ghost story.'

'Ed always said she was real. I never believed him, but he said the black veins thing was a punishment, a black spot given by the Seekers to mark her out. I can't believe Ed was right.'

His expression shutters a little at the mention of Ed's name. I can only imagine that he's remembering happier times and trying not to find them painful in retrospect.

'Were you okay today?' I ask him. 'Seeing Ed, I mean.'

He pulls up his collar; it's starting to drizzle. We walk along in silence for a few seconds before he answers.

'It'll be a long time before it's easy, I think, but it's not as bad.'

'I'm sorry it didn't work out.'

Cam shrugs. 'Maybe it's for the best. Maybe he was right about that, too.'

'I'm sorry anyway.'

'Don't be,' Cam says, pasting a smile onto his face, even though it looks like it costs him to do it. 'We should be talking about you and your own burgeoning romance.'

'Ugh,' I groan. 'Which one?'

'That was pretty dramatic this morning. You know how to put on a show, I'll give you that.'

'Well, I couldn't exactly disown Drake in a room full of Invicti, could I? God, I hate this case. There are too many clues, it's impossible to fit them all together, and now the investigation is sabotaging my love life. I had to *mark* Killian Drake.'

'Yeah,' Cam says, side-eyeing me, 'I'm sure you hated that.'

'I hated what it did to Tabitha,' I say quietly.

Cam wraps his arm around my shoulders and pulls me close as we walk into Solomon College.

'Hey, it's okay. You've got a date tomorrow, remember?'

'I hope it's a date,' I say, remembering Tabitha's reaction this morning.

'Of course it's a date. She likes you, Jack, and you like her. Forget everything else and just try to concentrate on that.'

I smile a little. 'Yeah. Fuck Killian Drake.'

'Not literally, I hope.'

'Definitely not literally.'

But by midnight, I'm burning up. I can scent Drake's mark all over my skin, dark and rich. I can feel its hunger. There are only a couple of hours left before it wears off, and it wants to be renewed.

I just have to get through the next couple of hours. Once I've done that, I can forget about him and his bloody mark. But his words stay with me.

I am not a good man.

21

THE NEXT DAY passes in a mess of meetings and internet searches, and then it's suddenly Tuesday night.

Finally, Tabitha and I are going out on a date.

I think.

We meet at a little after seven at a candlelit Italian place in town. It's cheesy to bring her here, I know, but after everything that's happened I feel like I owe it to her to play it by the book. I don't want her to doubt my intentions.

'Hi,' I say, rising from the table by the window to greet her. I've been sitting here for half an hour, because I was too nervous to sit at home and wait until it was time to go out. I've already had two beers and I've been twisting my white-linen napkin so vigorously that when I put it down on my empty plate, it looks like it's been turned into a rope.

'Hi,' Tabitha says as she takes her own seat. She smiles, but it's not her usual beaming grin. I wonder how much damage I've caused by postponing on her. I wonder how much damage Drake has caused by claiming me so publicly.

'Are you hungry?' I ask.

Inane. Vacuous. Stupid question.

'Sure,' she says, picking up her menu. 'What are you having?'

We talk about the menu. We make chit chat. When the waiter arrives, we order a bottle of red wine. Not the house red, because I'm not that cheap, but not from the bottom of the menu either. My bank account is still sore from Sunday's shopping trip.

Which I'm trying not to think about, because when I think of the dress I think of everything that happened while I was wearing it.

Our food arrives. We eat. We smile politely. I ask about her work, she asks about mine, and underneath it all there is an undercurrent of grim misery, because we both know how much we've left unsaid. It hangs between us like a bubble that neither of us wants to pop for fear that it'll expand and eat us whole, consuming whatever hope we have of making this work.

Eventually, she's the one who brings it up.

'All right, then,' she says once our plates have been cleared and the wine bottle emptied. She takes a deep breath and says, 'I think we need to talk about the Baron of Oxford.'

My stomach is spinning.

'I can explain,' I say.

'You're bi,' she says. 'I get it.'

'No, not that.'

'You're not bi?'

'No, I mean yes, I am bi. But me and Killian—'

'Killian?' She raises an eyebrow.

Shit. No one calls him that. It betrays a shocking lack of decorum. Or a shocking abundance of intimacy.

I feel like I've just knocked into a pyramid of glasses, and I'm trying to stop it from falling, but every glass I catch and return to the stack just knocks off three more. The final collapse is inexorable.

'Look,' I say, 'the Baron and I are nothing. We're not even friends. He helped me for a mission and that mission required scent-marking. I was undercover. It was just work. That's all.'

'Oh,' she says, looking down at the tablecloth.

I hate the way she says that word. *Oh*. It's a sad little noise acknowledging that the world is not the way she wants it to be. I want to rearrange it for her, but I don't know how.

'I didn't want to do it,' I say. 'I didn't want to mark him.'

She looks up at me and says, 'But you were able to. That has to mean something, doesn't it, hen?'

She's being *kind*. We're sitting here talking about how I broke a date with her because I was marked by someone else, and she's looking at me with compassion. She's looking at me like she wants to understand. It's heart-breaking.

'I hate the man,' I say.

She laughs softly, incredulously.

I press on regardless. 'He doesn't matter to me. And just because I'm bi... I mean, that's not how it works. I don't need one of each, you know? It's not like I'm missing out. That's not the way I am.'

She holds up a hand to stop me rambling.

'Hen,' she says, leaning forward, 'you may think he doesn't matter to you, but the key thing here is that *you* matter to *him*. Do you really think you can get out from under that? That *I* can?'

I reach for her hand across the table. 'Tabitha–'

'He was the one who called me in, Jack.'

I stop dead, my hand inches away from hers. 'What?'

'The Baron was the one who called me. I didn't need to be at that meeting. Ed has my report and he could have presented it himself. Baron Drake asked me to come, told me it would be *illuminating*. He was clearly trying to make a point, wouldn't you say?'

That bastard. That *utter* bastard.

I want to scream. I want to stomp up to his fancy mansion right now and punch him in his lying, cheating, *evil* face, but instead I just gape at Tabitha and say, 'I didn't know.'

'I know you didn't, pet,' she says, patting my hand. 'I could tell when I walked in there yesterday. But I'd say he's made his intentions clear.'

I wave the suggestion away. 'He's a bored old bastard who likes messing with other people's lives. He's not serious. He just wants another notch on his bedpost and it irritates him that I won't swoon on command. I'm nothing but a challenge to him, particularly now you're in the picture. Whatever his intentions are, I've made mine clear to him. He's nothing to me.'

'He's the Baron of Oxford.'

'All right, yes, I know, but look, can we just ignore him? Please? I don't want him to ruin this.' I squeeze her hand lightly in mine. 'I like you, Tabitha. I like you a lot. I know we haven't known each other that long and it's a lot to ask, but could we just try? Please? Just give me a chance to get to know you.'

She's still worried, but her gaze softens as she looks at me across the table. She'll let me have my chance.

We go on to a pub and, after a few drinks, everything seems much simpler.

I like Tabitha. She likes me. We're well fed and slightly tipsy, and it's only a few minutes' walk back to the college.

I snag a couple of blood bottles from the canteen then creep through the corridors, leading her behind me, her hand in mine. The moment I shut the door to my rooms behind us, she grabs my waist and pulls me to her. I chuck the blood bottles onto a pile of clothes in the corner, where they stay for the rest of the night, forgotten.

Her hair is pinned up with a pencil and a spoon, which I think she might have stolen from the restaurant. My little thief. I pull out first one, then the other, letting her hair slide loose over my hands, then I lean down and kiss her cheek.

Her skin smells like nectarines and honey, sweet and light and perfectly Tabitha. She's not wearing perfume – it's too pungent for most Silver – so there's no brashness to her scent. It's a persuasion of an aroma, an encouragement to drag her into my arms, not an assault like–

Well, someone I definitely shouldn't be thinking about right now. I push the thought away.

Her mouth is at my neck, kissing her way gently up my jawline. Her kisses are like butterfly wings on my skin, all tentative and gentle, but our hands are anything but. One of hers is pulling me closer by my belt loops while the other slips up beneath my T-shirt, and mine are in her hair, at her waist, shoving her cardigan to the ground and sliding the straps of her top from her shoulders. When my lips find hers, finally, it feels like I've been waiting for this moment my whole life.

'Jack,' she whispers, and the name shivers down my spine.

I move backwards, coaxing her along with me, until the back of my calves hit the bed. When I lay her down and stroke her hair, she moans.

'You really do purr,' I whisper, kissing her shoulder.

'Huh?'

'Like a tabby cat.'

She looks at me and laughs, warm and generous, then I'm kissing her again, because I can't help myself. I'd never have thought that laughing in bed was a good thing, but here she is in my arms, and I'm so happy that I can feel the joy bubbling up into my throat, so happy that the force of my kisses is shaped by my smile.

And it's good. I mean, it's great. She's great. She's beautiful and funny and she makes me feel like someone who could actually have a proper life, maybe a family one day, instead of this liminal existence on the edge of other people's tragedies. She makes me feel almost normal.

But part of me – a very small part of me that I shout down into silence – misses the darkness.

I slip my hands under her top, but she softly catches my wrist.

'Hey,' she whispers. 'Do you mind if we take things slowly, hen? It's just, you know, with everything...'

'Sure,' I say, snatching my hand away. 'Of course. I understand. Whatever you want.'

There's an awkward pause, because I'm being weird. I'm so desperate not to chase her away that I freeze.

'Did you want me to go?' she asks.

My other arm tightens around her waist. I don't mean to do it, because maybe she's right, maybe she should go so I can sort out the mess in my head, but I want her here to chase away the shadows. Being with Tabitha is simple. Straightforward. It makes me happy. *She* makes me happy, I think.

'No,' I say. 'Stay. Please?'

She smiles at me in the moonlight – I haven't bothered to turn on the lights or draw the curtains – and says, 'Of course,' then she kisses my forehead and pulls me into her arms.

It isn't like last time.

Last time Tabitha was in my bed, I was mostly unconscious. When I woke up I was incredulous. Hopeful. And, let's be honest, more than a little hungover.

Everything has changed since then. Now, when she snuggles her cheek against my shoulder and curls into my side, I feel guilty. I'm taking comfort from her because I need it, selfishly, but it's not enough to distract me from the hollow feeling that's growing in my belly.

Something's missing, and I think I know what it is.

Nothing about being with Tabitha hurts. That should be a good thing, but maybe I've just become accustomed to the pain. I'm lying in bed with this gorgeous, kind, genius of a woman, and I'm thinking about Killian's fingers wrapped around mine, his touch at the back of my neck, his mark on my lips.

Now that the mark has worn off, all I can feel is anger. Anger that things aren't how I want them to be with Tabitha. Anger that I let myself get into this situation. And most of all, anger at Killian for manoeuvring me into it.

It's not long before Tabitha is snoring softly beside me, but I don't sleep.

22

WHEN TABITHA LEAVES the next morning, I stomp up to Summertown without stopping to think it through.

'How dare you,' I say as I barge my way past Killian's guards and into his office.

He's in the middle of a meeting. There are two business people sitting in the chairs opposite his desk, a man and a woman, but they may as well be invisible for all I care.

'Ah, Jack,' he says with a smile. 'I thought I might be seeing you today.'

'You utter bastard.'

'Perhaps we should reconvene this afternoon?' he says to the business people. 'Say, three o'clock?'

They hurry out and shut the door behind them, but I'm not done yet.

'You indescribable, unbelievable, inexcusable bastard.'

'I don't know what you mean.'

'You called that meeting,' I say, digging my fingers into the back of one of his leather chairs to stop myself from digging them into his neck. 'You called Dr Ross in. So tell me, what exactly were you trying to prove? Was it some kind of territorial pissing, or were you just trying to fuck with me?'

He leans forward in his chair, resting his elbows on his desk.

'Drew wanted to meet with her to discuss the post mortem, which I believe you'd already done without the involvement of the Invicti. Did you expect me to refuse the Secundus?'

'Yes!' I say as my fingernails punch through the leather. 'Of course you were supposed to say no!'

He looks at me for a long moment, holding my gaze across the desk, then he stands and comes around it to face me.

'You expected this to be our little secret?' he asks, his voice low. 'You expected that you'd just wear my mark and then, what, walk away?'

'In case you didn't notice, that's exactly what I did.'

'Oh, Jack,' he says softly. 'That's not how it works. You can still taste it, can't you? Still catch the edge of the scent at the back of your throat, like a memory you're desperate to recapture. You might have made it through the first twenty-four hours, but it's burned into you now. You can't cut it out, or cover it up, however hard you try.'

He takes a step towards me and I realise that he's right, because the scent of him calls to me. I can feel the promise of the mark in its gentle notes. I remember the way it overwhelmed me in a wash of him and I want it again.

'And from the scent of your skin,' he goes on, leaning towards me, 'you're obviously not trying too hard to erase me. Did you not kiss your doctor, or did you just not want to keep her enough to mark her?'

'She has nothing to do with you.'

'You wouldn't be here right now if you believed that.'

We stare at each other. I unclench my hands, releasing the now-battered chair from my grip, and raise them to push him away, but he catches my wrists against his chest.

'You can't push me away,' he whispers, leaning in until he's only a breath away. His dark hair tumbles from his forehead as the tendrils of his scent find their way onto my tongue, and from there they deliver an electric shock to the rest of my body.

It remembers him.

He wraps his hands around mine and clutches them to his shirt, pressing them into the muscle over his heart.

'You'd miss the lightning bolt,' he whispers, his eyes dark as jet and just as hard.

'I hate you,' I say.

'Maybe you need to hate me. Maybe that's what makes it thrilling.'

I want to tell him he's wrong, to shove him on his arse and leave this place, maybe get in a car and drive out to Tabitha's cottage, go after her, but I don't even pull away. Instead, I stand there and let myself fall into the darkness of his eyes.

'I shouldn't have come,' I breathe.

'But you did.'

He raises one hand to my face, letting the back of his fingers trail down my cheek with the softest of touches.

'Why are you doing this?' I whisper.

'Why am *I* doing this? None of this is my doing, Jack. You kissed me at Windsor's party.' He runs his fingertips over my hair. 'You came here today.' He brushes his thumb against my cheek. 'And you're the one who's going to kiss me again now.'

'You arrogant bastard,' I say, finally shoving him away, but before I can make it to the door he's standing in front of me, blocking my way. He grabs me around the waist and pulls me close until we're chest to chest, hip to hip and, with the slightest tilt of my head upwards, face to face.

'Aren't you?' he whispers, his lips brushing mine.

I put my hands on his shoulders and I mean to push him away again, I swear I do, but somehow I end up turned around and I shove him against the wall instead. He drags me with him, his hands around my hips, but he doesn't cross the line. He makes sure that when my mouth slams into his, I'm the one who puts it there.

I kiss him, yet again, and I hate him for it.

There's no messing around this time, no pausing to test the water. When our lips meet, there is no resistance. Our mouths part easily for each other, and somehow the scent of our marks is already in the air. This isn't normal, and it's not – I can't help but compare – like kissing Tabitha. It's not measured or polite, it's vicious and selfish, and I can't seem to hold myself back.

'Oh god.' I moan against his mouth and his fingers dig into my hips in response.

His lips trail across my cheek. A moment later he's pushing my leather jacket down my arms and onto the floor, leaving me in my tank top. He holds the back of my head and kisses his way down my throat. It's the most beautiful torture: the softness of his mouth, the hard press of his teeth. Silver don't bite other Silver for sustenance, but they do bite for pleasure. It's supposed to be incredible, if a little deviant. I've never experienced it myself, but Killian makes me curious.

He scrapes a tooth down my jugular.

'You bastard,' I moan.

He teases me between kisses against my pulse.

'You.' Kiss. 'Like.' Kiss. 'It.' Kiss. 'Don't you?'

Then he pulls my legs up around his hips and carries me to his desk, clearing the top with one arm while he lowers me down with the other.

'Well?' he says.

'I should have guessed you'd be into biting.'

He lets his teeth press into my neck, not enough to break the skin, but enough to make me arch my back, pressing my body flush against his.

'I had guessed that *you* would be,' he says against my skin. 'Am I right?'

He kisses his way up my neck as he slips one hand under my shirt.

'Well?' he asks. 'Yes or no?'

He nips at my neck again and I can't suppress my moan.

'Yes,' I whisper, and I hate him for making me say it.

'That's a little fucked up, you know,' he teases. 'I wonder where that comes from?'

'Maybe it's to do with the fact that my ex turned me into a vampire by biting my neck. Or maybe now is not the time for psychoanalysis,' I say, letting my frustration show.

'Then ask me,' he says.

'What?'

'Ask me for what you want. Tell me.'

He's looking down at me, bracing his hands on the desk to either side of my shoulders. Somehow his shirt has come undone and my hands are on his bare chest.

He leans down and kisses me, hot and long and painfully seductive, then his lips are on my bare shoulder, making their way back up. I can't bear the slow progress for more than a few seconds. I'm impatient with imagining what it would feel like to have his teeth against the skin he's teasing. I want it, and it has to be him.

His kiss, his lips, his teeth.

'Do it,' I say.

He groans.

'Bite me.'

He sinks his teeth into my neck.

I scream then, but not because it hurts.

It's the most exquisite pain and the most intense pleasure I've ever felt, like drinking blood laced with heroin, only a hundred times more euphoric. With the scent of our marks swirling in the air around us, mingling the two of us together, it feels as though he has crept inside my skin and seeded pieces of himself through my body in little explosions of perfect ecstasy.

My hands are under his shirt, around his back, and my fingernails dig into his flesh as he sucks at my neck. I can tell I've broken the skin because I can smell his blood in the air with my own and it's like synthesis, as though we are breaking and merging and wounding and healing all in one.

I am out of my skin and there is nothing but the two of us in some ethereal realm of the senses. By the time he lifts his head, I'm so high I'm not sure I'll ever come back down.

'Valentine,' he says, whispering my name like a caress.

Then he kisses me and I can taste my blood in his mouth. There's something awful about that, something that should horrify me, but instead of being revolted I want more. My legs tighten around him, pulling him closer as I tangle my fingers into his hair. I want every inch of him pressed up against me. I want his skin against mine.

I want to bite him back.

'Killian...' I murmur against his lips.

He pulls away to look at me, but instead of pleasure, there's shock in his eyes.

'What?' I ask.

'You've never called me by my name before.'

It's a mistake that terrifies me. First I slip up when I'm talking to Tabitha about him and now to Killian himself.

Drake. Not Killian, *Drake*.

We stare at each other.

Something breaks in those long seconds and reality comes flooding back. As it does, the two of us fracture apart. We are no longer just Jack and Drake, adversaries who cooperate only so far as is strictly necessary. Instead, we are also Killian and Valentine, whoever the hell they are.

The only thing I know for sure is that these strange new versions of us have marked each other, again.

And done worse besides.

'Don't,' he says, grabbing my hand as I push him away and hop off his desk.

But I shake off his grip. I want to shout at him, to berate him for whatever he did that got us into this situation, but I can't think of a single piece of blame to throw. It was me. It was all me. I want to scream, or cry, or both, but I don't want to do either of those things in front of him, so I grab my leather jacket from the floor and make for the exit.

'Valentine,' he says. 'Don't go.'

I laugh bitterly. 'How did you think this was going to end?'

I turn up the collar of my jacket to hide the bite. It'll heal over in the next hour or so, but until then I'll have the imprint of his teeth in my skin. I want to find that fact repulsive, but it sends the same kick of pleasure through me that I got from the bite in the first place, that I get now from the scent of his mark.

It's all over me and I crave it, even through my despair.

He takes a step towards me and I back towards the door.

'This isn't over,' he says.

'It bloody well is. And if you fuck with my personal life again, if you say *anything* to Dr Ross about this, I will make you regret it. Do you understand me, *Drake*?'

He crosses his arms over his naked chest. His hair is in disarray from where my fingers have pulled at it. It suits him, that dissolute edge, but I hate that I'm the one who created it.

'Alright, Valentine,' he says. 'Whatever you say. I suppose you're going to storm out again now?'

'You suppose right.'

I lift my chin and do exactly that.

When I stomp back into the college, I pass Naia and Cam in the lodge.

'Shut up,' I say, before either of them can comment on the renewed mark and before they can notice the bite. Then I stomp off back to my office to finish working on Grant's phone records.

I've barely started when my phone buzzes with a text message.

So, are you free tonight?

It's from Tabitha.

I could scream. For the second time now, I'm prevented from seeing her by Drake's mark. What would she say if she found out that I let it happen again? How could I possibly explain that away?

I can barely explain it to myself. I certainly can't excuse it.

I can't do tonight, I text back. *I have to work, sorry. How about tomorrow?*

I tap my fingers on the desk while I wait for *Tabitha is typing...* to resolve into a message, but the tapping isn't doing it for me so instead I thunk my forehead repeatedly into the wood.

Stupid. Stupid. Stupid.

My phone buzzes.

New body arriving tomorrow. Fun might have to wait until Friday. Say 8pm, in Oxford? Dinner and dancing?

My stomach flips guiltily with recollections of dancing on Sunday night in Drake's arms, but I push the feeling away and try to think of something else.

Then I remember the other night of the Massacres, when Tabitha and I danced the night away in the college bar. Some of it's still a blank, but I remember how it felt to wrap my hand around her waist and spin her out for a twirl, the way she laughed, and the way her smile was so wide it seemed like it could be the only thing in the world. I want that back. I want to erase the last week and wake up with her hair spread across my pillow, pencils lost and forgotten.

Sounds good, I reply. *I'll book somewhere nice.*

Grand. Thanks, hen. Speak soon.

I love it when she calls me *hen*. I can hear her voice in the words, wrapping around the endearment hopefully, as though she's wishing it might stick. And I want it to. I really do.

Which means I'm going to have to confess to her.

My phone buzzes again.

So, are you free tonight?

For a moment I think that I'm seeing a glitch, that Tabitha's earlier message has been delivered twice, but then I realise it's not from her. It's from Drake.

I block his number and turn off my phone.

23

ON THURSDAY, THE captain comes into my office and drops an evidence bag onto my desk. Inside it is the latest model of iPhone.

'David Grant's?' I ask her.

'The police finally released it. Have at it, Valentine.'

I rip open the bag and power up the phone, but of course it's locked with a passcode. That doesn't surprise me, but it's frustrating nonetheless. There has to be something in it that will help us make sense of the mess that was Grant's life, and I want to get my hands on it.

I have no idea how to crack a mobile phone, but thankfully I don't need to. We have Frank the Hacker for that. I pick up my desk phone and give him a call. He knocks on the door five minutes later.

'Morning, Jack,' he says. 'Up bright and early today.'

'I know,' I groan.

It's the fucking mark. It had me jumping out of bed at six this morning, all smiles and bluebirds and sparkly sunshine. I resent that it's reduced me to a Disney stereotype, even if I do feel better than I have in my entire life.

'Can you crack this for me?' I ask, sliding the phone over to Frank.

He picks it up and turns it over thoughtfully in his neat hands. He's a little guy, about five inches shorter than me, with curly red hair that doesn't do what it's told. Before we met, I expected our resident hacker to be a renegade outlaw with tattoos and piercings, or a grey-haired bore in a short-sleeved shirt. I didn't expect him to be cheerful and charming, or quite so pretty. He reminds me of Peter Pan.

'It'll take a while, I'm afraid,' he says, in the tone of voice generally employed by mechanics when your car's failed its MOT, so I'm surprised when he adds, 'Could be as much as half an hour.'

I let out a relieved breath.

'That'll be fine, Frank. Thanks.'

'I'll bring it back to you when it's done.' He gives me a jaunty salute, then goes back to his server-filled lair.

I like Frank. Quite apart from anything else, he's the first person who hasn't commented on the mark I'm wearing. For that alone, he will always have a special place in my heart.

Cam arrives at the office at about ten o'clock, with a cup of coffee in each hand. By that time, Frank has already returned with the unlocked phone and I'm scrolling through its contents.

'Is it safe to come in, yet?' Cam asks, holding out a cup like a peace offering. I take it.

'I don't know what you mean.'

He scents the air pointedly.

'Yes,' I say, 'I'm marked. Again. It should wear off soon. No, I don't want to talk about it. Can we move on?'

'I don't know,' he says as he takes a seat at his desk. 'You don't seem to be able to. That's all I'm saying. Maybe you should talk about it. It might help. I'll just sit and listen, no judgement.'

'Frank cracked Grant's phone for me,' I say, holding it up.

'Seamless subject change,' Cam laughs. 'Good work. Anything on it?'

'Not so far. He hasn't got any files linked, nothing in the cloud, but I'm going through his photos and messages.'

'Have you checked the phone calls?'

'Not yet.'

Cam brings his chair around to my side of the desk so he can see the screen too. We're looking for the unknown number that called Grant fifteen times in April.

'Okay,' I say, scrolling through the call history. 'When was the first call?'

'Fifteenth April.'

I identify the number, but I have to double-take it, because it's labelled, 'Work'.

'Work?' Cam says. 'What do you think that means?'

I access Grant's text messages, but there are none between him and the number. Only one thing for it. I call 'Work', on Grant's phone.

I think it's going to go straight to voicemail again, like it did when Cam and I tried calling from our own phones, but after three rings the call connects.

'Mr Grant,' says a female voice on the other end. 'What can I do for you? Do you need your office for the day?'

I lay the phone down on my desk and put it on speaker.

'Who is this, please?' I ask.

There's a pause on the other end of the line.

'Can I ask with whom I am speaking?' says the woman. She clearly doesn't want to reveal her identity, but what could be confidential about an office?

'I'm afraid Mr Grant is dead,' I say, cutting to the chase. 'We're investigating his murder.'

'What?'

'He was killed in the early hours of May first.'

'Oh my god.' She sounds breathless.

'Could you identify yourself, please?' I ask again.

'Of course,' she says when she's collected herself. She probably assumes we're the police; most people do. 'I'm Priya Bhasin. I'm the concierge at OfficeBox. We provide co-working office space off the Botley Road.'

'Are you there now?'

'Yes.'

'Then stay put. We'll come to you.'

OfficeBox sounds like a respectable establishment, and it certainly looks that way from their website (no phone number listed), but when we get to the address Ms Bhasin gave us there's nothing but a warren of garages and locked storage spaces. After wandering around for quarter of an hour, we find a solid metal door with a buzzer set into the wall under a small plaque that reads 'OB'.

'I guess this is the place,' Cam says.

'It doesn't look like any office I've ever seen.' I press the bell.

'Hello?' a tinny voice asks through the speaker.

'This is Jack Valentine,' I say. 'We're here to see Priya Bhasin.'

There's a buzz and the door swings open with an ominous creak. Cam and I both hesitate. After a moment, he raises his eyebrows and ushers me inside.

'Coward,' I say, pushing through the door.

He laughs. The sound echoes into the space beyond.

It's dark inside. When the door slams shut behind us, there's nothing but a feeble exit light above our heads to illuminate the corridor. The walls are bare concrete and slightly damp to the touch. It feels more like the entrance to an underground rave than to a co-working space.

We've almost exhausted the reach of the light when a door opens at the other end of the tunnel, casting a wedge of brightness into the dark. It's enough to make me squint.

'Detective Valentine?' I don't correct her. 'I'm Priya. Please, come in. Sorry about the entrance; we're having the main frontage redecorated.'

It sounds like a lie – we explored the area thoroughly and didn't find any alternative entrance, or any evidence of redecoration – but I let it slide. I want to see how this plays out, so for now I'll act the plod.

'No problem,' I say. 'We just have a few questions.'

'Of course.'

She steps aside to let us into the main reception of OfficeBox. Or whatever this place really is. The desk is rosewood inlaid with mother-of-pearl, the pile of the carpet is so deep I can feel it compressing beneath my feet, and the chairs are all leather and mahogany. There's a bar on one side of the room and an enormous television on the other, the screen blank at the moment.

Priya watches us take in the incongruity of the space with no sense of embarrassment. She's tall and svelte with strong features and brown skin that looks as though it's been dusted with gold. Her clothes are as decadent as the setting: a red pencil dress with black and gold accents, paired with treacherously high heels. She smiles welcomingly and offers us a drink.

'You said this was a co-working space?' Cam says. He looks around pointedly.

'That's right.' She's going to brazen this out. 'We have exclusive clientele.'

Apparently exclusive enough to demand the luxury of this reception space, but not so exclusive that they mind wading through a puddled bunker to get here. Either there's something here that they want enough to make it worth their while, or they're not so exclusive after all. Knowing what I do about David Grant, either could be true.

'We'd like to see Mr Grant's office,' I say.

'Of course.' Priya directs us to a side door. She gives the impression of being accommodating, but there's something going on behind her shiny veneer. While her expression is composed and still, her eyes move in jerky stutters, like a panicked deer's.

We follow her down a short hall, passing a couple of doors before we reach one at the end.

'This was Mr Grant's office,' she says, pulling a key from a lanyard at her waist. 'Some of the other spaces are shared, but this one was his alone.'

The door swings open to reveal a richly-furnished room beyond. It doesn't look like any office I've ever seen. There's a leather sofa against one wall, a television against another, a daybed against the third and a small kitchen against the one through which we enter. When I open the fridge, I find it full of chopped cocktail fruit and chilled alcohol.

'What exactly did Mr Grant use this space for?' I ask.

'Mostly business meetings, I believe,' Priya replies, but her gaze won't settle on my face.

Cam opens the blinds on the opposite wall. They look out into the grungy alley that leads back to the main road. He beckons me over, so I close the fridge and come to stand at his shoulder. As I look through the office window, everything becomes clear.

There's a door directly across the alley with a small sign at the side of it. It says, *Staff Entrance*, underneath a picture of a pink cat. Or, perhaps, a pussycat.

'Business meetings,' I say. 'Sure.'

Priya doesn't react. Instead, she is all professionalism as she says, 'Let me know when you're done. I'll be waiting in reception.'

'Thank you, Ms Bhasin,' Cam says.

She goes, but leaves the door open.

'There's nothing here, is there?' I sigh.

Cam is rifling through a few papers in the bin. 'I doubt it. Nothing useful, anyway.'

'Except the fact that David Grant was a world-class sleaze. I wonder what this room would look like under a UV light.'

Cam looks over his shoulder at me and grimaces. He has one hand jammed under the sofa cushions. 'I really wish you hadn't just said that.'

'I have hand sanitiser in the car.'

'Hurry up, then.'

We frisk the 'office' quickly and thoroughly, turning up nothing except a hoard of condoms and a collection of sex toys I could have done without seeing. When we get back out to the reception area, Priya is waiting.

I want to ask her why she does this job, why she smiles and schmoozes for creeps like David Grant, but it's clear she's not here because she enjoys it. I wonder what drove her to this.

'If you think of anything else,' I say, pulling my card from my pocket and handing it to her, 'or if you need help, you can call me.'

She turns the card in her fingers for a moment before sliding it onto the reception desk behind her. Her manner is dismissive. I know then that I'll never hear from her; she's the type who likes to think they can manage everything alone. I can recognise my own.

'I'm sorry I couldn't be more helpful,' she says, her jaw set. We'll get nothing out of her.

Cam must have come to the same conclusion, because he says, 'Goodbye, Ms Bhasin.'

I follow him out of the door. Priya watches us go, standing at the end of the concrete corridor, silhouetted in the warm light of the reception room. We're halfway to the exit when she calls to us.

'Did you find his notebook?'

'Not yet,' I call back.

I had let it slip my mind. It was still written on the whiteboard in the conference room as a lead to follow up, but once we discovered the Silver connection and Windsor's racket, the ins and outs of Grant's daily life paled into insignificance. With the embezzlement and his desire to turn Silver, a few scribbles seemed comparatively trivial.

'You should.' Her tone makes it clear that it's important. She knows something, but when I try to press her on it, she refuses to say more.

'Just find it,' she says. 'He never let it out of his sight. It won't be far away.'

Then she steps back into the light and closes the door, leaving us in the dark.

We call Boyd from the car. He and Naia are going back to Magdalen to look for the notebook. It starts to rain and I have a moment of spiteful joy at the fact that I'll be going back to my nice, warm office to flick through Grant's phone while they're out searching in the cold.

* * *

By the time mid-afternoon rolls around, I'm shifting in my seat. The mark is wearing off again and it's making me impatient. A small and undeniable part of me wants to go back up to Summertown and into Drake's arms, but the rest of me is desperate to speak to Tabitha and confess everything. I'm going to have to do it sooner or later, and the longer I wait, the worse I feel about it.

I want to call her up, to tell her right away, but is that just being selfish, demanding to confess on my own schedule to make myself feel better? Or is it worse to wait until I see her, to put her to the effort of coming out on a date that she might want to leave the moment she hears the truth? Should I drive out to her place and see her there, or would that make her feel as though she has nowhere to retreat to?

'Why don't you go for a walk?' Cam says from his side of the desk. 'You're twitching.'

'I think that might be a bad idea. You know what happened last time I went for a walk.'

He gives me a frank look. 'You don't have to go to his place, you know. Other walking destinations exist. There's a whole city out there, full of buildings that don't contain Baron Drake.'

'Ugh. Please don't say his name.'

'You're going to have to come to terms with this thing, you know. The longer you keep denying it, the worse it's going to get. You can't control a problem if you don't even acknowledge it exists.'

He's right, as usual.

'Fine,' I say, spinning myself out of my chair to stand up. 'Then I'll face it. Apparently, I have a crush on Killian Drake. God, I hate saying that out loud. It sounds so... sordid.'

'Because it is. You fancy the pants off him. So what are you going to do about it?'

'Well, obviously he's the worst person in the world, so I want to forget about it and move on.'

'And can you do that?'

I drop back down into my chair. 'I don't know.'

'Recent experience suggests not.'

'But... Tabitha.'

'You can't just decide not to like someone,' Cam says sadly. I know he's talking about himself as much as he is about me. 'I wish you could, but it doesn't work like that, particularly not when you're Silver. The pheromones will get you, one way or another. The best you can do is be honest and hope that your feelings will wear off over time.'

'I know,' I say, taking my phone off the desk and turning it in my hands. 'I just don't know how to tell her.'

'Jack,' Cam says, wheeling his desk chair over to mine. He takes my hands in his. 'Tabitha is painfully intelligent. The woman has about fifteen degrees. She *knows*, and you know she knows. So just talk to her about it, okay?'

'Okay.'

He kisses me on the forehead, then stands up and makes for the door. 'I'll give you a minute. You want anything from the canteen?'

'Blood? I think I might need it after this,' I say, hefting my phone in my hand.

'Sure. I'll take a break and be back in half an hour.'

'Thanks, Cam.'

He smiles at me and says, 'Chin up,' then closes the door behind himself.

The call takes six rings to connect. I sit and swivel in my chair as I wait. I'm about to chicken out when Tabitha picks up.

'Dr Ross,' she says.

'Tabitha, hey. It's Jack.'

'Hey, Jack.' I can hear the smile in her voice. 'How are you getting on, hen?'

'I need to talk to you about something. Have you got a minute? Or maybe I could come out to see you?'

There's a rustling in the background. 'I've got Mrs Alvarez on the slab at the moment, but I can leave her for a few minutes if you want to talk on the phone.'

That's one decision made, at least.

'Okay, well…' I take a deep breath, then I completely botch it. 'Something happened,' I say, 'and I wish it hadn't, but I need to be honest with you. I like you a lot, but I fucked up.'

'This is about Baron Drake, isn't it?'

'Yes.'

There's a pause on the other end of the line.

'Why don't you just tell me what happened?' she says eventually.

So I do. I tell her that I went to give him an earful about Monday's meeting and that things didn't go quite the way I'd expected.

'So you marked each other? Again?' she asks. Her voice comes out in a monotone, so I know she's having to control it.

'Yes.'

I'm certain that she's going to hang up on me then, but I can still hear her breathing down the line.

'I'm sorry,' I say. 'You don't deserve this.'

'No,' she says, 'I don't. But we didn't make any promises to each other.'

'I want to. Or at least, I want to be able to, but at the moment I can't. I don't know what else to say. I'd ask you if we can be friends, but that's not what I want either.'

'You don't know what you want, Jack, but it's not my job to help you find out.'

'I know that. I'm sorry.'

There's another long pause.

'Okay,' she says. 'This is what we're going to do. We're going to go out tomorrow night and go dancing, because I bought a new dress and I think we need several drinks to have this conversation properly. All right?'

'All right.' I was expecting a flat rejection, so right now I'll do whatever she wants if it means I might be able to salvage something from this mess.

'You're making the drinks,' she says.

'I'm not sure that Massacres are—'

'I said, you're making the drinks.' There's no arguing with that tone of voice.

'Sure. Whatever you want. Meet you in Jericho at eight?'

'See you then,' she says. 'Don't be late.'

'I wouldn't dare. And Tabitha?'

'Yes?'

'Thank you.'

'Don't thank me yet. I'm still deciding whether or not you're going to end up on my autopsy table.'

I'm not entirely sure it's a joke. She hangs up before I can reply.

24

BOYD AND NAIA finally straggle back to the college while I'm packing up my desk for the day.

'Any luck?' I call into the hallway as Boyd walks past on his way to their office.

'No notebook, no clues,' he calls back. 'Just dead ends, the stench of unwashed teenagers, and too many bloody geese.'

Naia is close behind him. She pokes her head into my office on her way past.

'One of them shat on his shoe,' she whispers. She's very obviously trying not to laugh. 'Then he slipped on the shit, which somehow defeated his Silver reflexes, and he ended up in the river.'

She gives up the struggle and snorts with laughter before collapsing into hysterics. By the time she gets herself back under control, there are tears in her eyes.

Boyd comes up behind her and I finally get a good look at him. There's weed in his hair, goose shit on his trousers, and dirty river water sticking his clothes to his skin. He's trying to carry himself with his usual dignity, but he squelches as he walks and he smells like wet dog.

I bite my lips together to stop myself from going the way of Naia, whose face is turning pink with the effort of suppressing another fit of the giggles.

'Suffice it to say that if the notebook was ever at Magdalen,' Boyd says, 'it's either hidden out of sight or it's been taken elsewhere.'

I clear my throat. 'So what do you suggest?'

'Maybe a shower?' Naia says, then she's off laughing again. I guess you had to be there.

While Boyd squelches off to get changed, I pick up the phone. I've had an idea.

'Mrs Grant?' I say when she picks up. 'This is Jack Valentine. I'm one of the investigators working on your husband's case. We met last week.'

I can tell she remembers me from the audible sound of her teeth grinding.

'Are you home right now? I have a favour to ask.'

It's getting dark by the time Naia and I pull up at the house, but there are no lights on inside.

'Jesus,' Naia says, grimacing at the architecture as she gets out of the car. 'What kind of brutalist nightmare is this?'

'The deputy could probably tell you. All I can tell you is that it's ugly as sin.'

We look up at the house. It rises into the twilight like an overgrown fish tank. The huge windows are all dark.

'She said she'd be home?' Naia asks.

I have to admit that the place doesn't look inhabited. It reminds me of a zoo exhibit that's been closed for refurbishment.

'Maybe she's watching the sunset,' I suggest.

'Or maybe she's done a runner.'

'She's got no reason to run. She's not Silver. We know she didn't do this.'

'No,' Naia corrects me. 'All we know is that she didn't do this alone.'

But Mrs Grant isn't running. She answers the door to our first knock, as though she's been waiting for us on the other side.

'Mrs Grant,' I say by way of greeting.

'Ms Valentine.'

She's barefoot, wearing a scruffy shirt and old jeans that sag from her hips. She looks as though she's aged about twenty years since Cam and I were here last. She's unsteady, absent all of her former composure.

I don't realise I'm staring until she clears her throat.

'You had a favour to ask, I believe?' she says, opening the door to invite us inside.

I don't bother to introduce Naia, and Mrs Grant doesn't ask her name. Once I get a look at the inside of the house, I understand why. The place is virtually empty, filled with voids where furniture once stood. Boxes are piled in every corner, spilling out bubblewrap and ornaments. It's clear that Mrs Grant has other things on her mind right now.

'You're moving?' I ask her.

'I don't have much of a choice.' She reaches behind one of the boxes and picks up a hefty glass of wine, then takes a swig. I'm betting it's not her first. 'They're taking everything.' She takes another swig. 'The house, the car, the holiday home in Penzance, the furniture, my jewellery. Thank Christ I prepaid the kids' university tuition.' Swig swig. 'The bastard even cashed in our pensions.'

Naia gives me a panicked look. We weren't expecting to have to deal with a tipsy widow.

'So where's the money?' I ask Mrs Grant.

'You tell me,' she says, draining her glass. 'He mortgaged everything then cleaned out our bank accounts – cash withdrawals – but I haven't seen one penny of it. It's not in the house, it's not in his office–'

'Did you know that your husband rented a space off the Botley Road?' I ask.

Mrs Grant looks at me and snorts. 'You mean *OfficeBox*?' She imbues her words with scorn. 'Whatever other faults I might have, I'm not quite as stupid as he thought I was. I saw the charge on the bank statement when I was packing up this lot and did some digging. Lo and behold, I discovered that it's right next door to the strip club. Between that and the awful pun – I mean, *OfficeBox*? – it didn't take a genius to work out what he needed a second office for. I imagine you've searched the place.'

'We have.'

'Did you find my money?'

'I'm afraid not.'

She slumps down onto a nearby box. 'Too much to hope for, I suppose. Was that why you wanted to talk to me?'

'Actually, I wanted to ask about his notebook.'

'His notebook?' she squints up at me, which forces me to conclude that firstly, she is much drunker than she seems, and secondly, it's already darker in here than it was when we arrived.

'Do you mind if I put the lights on, Mrs Grant?' I ask.

'Can't,' she says, filling up her glass from a bottle on the floor behind her. There isn't much left in it. 'Turns out David hadn't been paying the bills either. Try that one.' She points a wavering finger across the room to a box that has *Random Bollocks* scrawled on the side in gold pen. It's incongruously festive.

Naia roots around in the box for a few seconds, then pulls out a couple of candles and a lighter. We both sit on the floor as she sets them down between us and Mrs Grant. When they're lit, it's like we're all kids at a séance, or the world's creepiest sleepover.

'About your husband's notebook?' I ask.

'Huh?' Mrs Grant looks vaguely in my direction, but her gaze is wandering all over the place. 'His notebook? What about it?'

'Do you have any idea where it might be?'

She scrunches up her face in confusion. 'He didn't have it?'

'No.'

'He always had it. Always had a notebook.'

'There was more than one?' Naia asks.

'One at a time, but over time, more than one. Old ones. No idea where they are. Haven't found them in the house. Looked bloody everywhere, I can tell you that much. For the money.'

This was getting us nowhere. Time to change tack.

'Do you have a piece of clothing with his scent on?' I ask. 'Or maybe a hairbrush?'

'What? Why?'

'We have, erm–' I glance sideways at Naia. '–sniffer dogs. If they can pick up his scent, then maybe they can track down the notebook.'

'Really? They're that good?'

'They're very clever dogs. We have one bitch in particular–'

Naia shoots me a dirty look.

'Well, sure,' says Mrs Grant, oblivious. 'There's a coat by the door. Black wool, red lining. Take it. You may as well. If you don't, the bailiffs will.'

Naia goes to fetch it. She gives it a sniff, then nods at me. It'll do.

As Naia returns to the candlelight, Mrs Grant lets out a world-weary sigh.

'Men are shits, you know?' she warbles. 'You give them your best years, then you pump out their offspring and watch as your tits head south along with the rest of you, and then they leave you at home to cook their meals while they swan around town as though they're still twenty-one. Why?' She looks at each of us in turn, her expression pleading. 'Why are they like that?'

There's nothing I can say that will help, so I stay quiet.

'I just wish I knew why he needed all that money. Gambling? Prostitutes? Something worse? And the kids. I mean, Jesus, the kids. How do you live with someone for twenty years and not, I mean... Isn't it?'

She drifts off into incoherence, her eyes unfocused as she stares off over my shoulder. I wave a hand in front of her face, but she's gone.

'We can't leave her here,' I whisper to Naia.

'Why not?'

'I mean, look at her.' We turn to watch as Mrs Grant slides gracefully off her cardboard perch and onto the floor. She knocks over her wine glass on the way, but that's not much of a problem since it's already empty.

'Don't suppose you brought any wine with you?' she slurs. 'They've cleared out the cellar, too, the bloody wankers.'

'Is there anyone you can call?' I ask her. 'Anyone you can stay with tonight?'

'I'm fine,' she says. 'I don't need anyone. I'll be fine on my own.'

Naia smirks at me. 'Sounds familiar.'

'Oh, shut up,' I say, then I sigh and help Mrs Grant to her feet. 'Come on,' I say. 'Let's pack up your things.'

'What things?' She laughs. 'None of this is mine anymore.'

Then she's suddenly crying, sobbing into my arms. It takes half an hour to calm her down, by which time Naia has gathered together a bag of essentials and helped our not-so-merry widow into a pair of shoes.

'Where are we going?' Mrs Grant asks.

'Somewhere safe,' I say.

So, with limited options, we bundle her into the back of the car and drive her back to Solomon College to sleep it off.

'What's this about?' Boyd says as he meets us at the lodge. Naia called him from the car.

I'm cradling Mrs Grant in my arms. She's sleeping like a baby, by which I mean she's snotty and loud. It's already ten o'clock and I've had more than enough for the day.

'Here,' Naia says, tossing the coat to Boyd. 'It's Grant's scent.'

'So we'll go out looking again tomorrow morning?' he suggests.

'Yup.' Naia sighs. 'Back to Magdalen. Again.'

'I'll meet you here at half nine. In the meantime, I'll leave you to deal with whatever's going on here.' He waves a hand vaguely over the unconscious form of Mrs Grant, then retreats back into the college. Thus, like the antisocial creature he is, Boyd leaves me and Naia to deal with our slumbering witness. Except that in the small amount of time it took me to check my pigeon hole for post, Naia seems to have disappeared.

'Hey!' I yell into the quad. 'Get back here!'

'Shhhhh!' she yells from the far side. 'You'll wake her up. See you tomorrow, sucker.'

Resigned, I turn to the window where the porter sits. He's trying not to laugh.

'Can I have the key to one of the guest rooms, please?' I ask in my sweetest tone of voice. It never hurts to be on the porter's good side. 'We have a visitor.'

'I can see that.' He smiles. 'But I'm afraid there are none spare at the moment.'

'What?'

'Our visitors from London,' he says. 'They've taken them all.'

'All of them?' The volume of my voice wakes up Mrs Grant, who starts laughing and asking for more booze.

The porter shrugs. 'They don't pay me to ask why. I just do what the captain says.' Then he slides the counter window firmly shut to block out Mrs Grant's rambling.

I try to take her to the college sick bay, but the nurse tells me in no uncertain terms that her level of inebriation does not constitute a medical emergency, and that if I get my friends so wankered that they start singing show tunes relentlessly at top volume, then it's my job to sit up through the night with them, not his.

Which leaves me with just one option.

'Cam!' I yell, hammering on the door to his room. 'If you're asleep then wake up, and if you're not asleep then what's taking you so long?'

'I'm not asleep,' he says, rubbing his eyes as he opens the door. At first I think he's lying, but then I see that his cheeks are damp and realise his eyes aren't red from sleep.

'What happened?' I ask, but he just wipes his face with his palms and shakes his head.

'Never mind me. What happened here? I thought you were just going to ask her some questions. Did you have to knock her out?' Mrs Grant has settled down again and is now snoring in my arms.

'She knocked herself out,' I say, 'with a couple of bottles of Malbec. Just help me get her inside.' I try to push past him, but he blocks my way.

'Oh, no. She's not staying with me. You brought the drunk woman home, so she stays in your room. Those are the rules.'

'Cameron…' I whine.

'Out!' he says, but he follows me to my own room and helps me get Mrs Grant settled on my bed. In the recovery position, just in case. While we work, I tell him what we learned.

'So we're looking for multiple notebooks?' he asks.

'It sounds like it.'

'But we can't even find one.'

'Are we sure we've looked everywhere?' I say, thinking out loud as I put the bin under Mrs Grant's head. If she throws up in her sleep, I'd rather it wasn't on my duvet.

'We've checked his actual office, his fake office and his home,' Cam says. 'He didn't have a safe deposit box–'

'At least none that we can find.'

'–and there's no storage unit either. Where else could they be?'

I shake my head; we just don't know.

Mrs Grant stirs, muttering something.

'What's she saying?' Cam asks.

'Is she going to be sick?'

Then I finally make out the word she's repeating. Apparently she's not as out of it as I thought.

'Who's Jim?' Cam asks.

'Not Jim, *gym*. As in, the gym,' I say. 'I think she's trying to tell us he had a gym locker. Did Boyd and Naia check that?'

'Not as far as I know. We can confirm it when Sleeping Beauty wakes up tomorrow.'

'Okay,' I agree, but I don't need to confirm it.

I'm certain it's the answer. If I were a philandering, bankrupt, wannabe vampire then I'd want somewhere neutral and secure to store all my secrets, somewhere I knew neither my wife nor my business partners were likely to find them. A gym locker is the perfect place.

But for the moment, we're stuck here babysitting our pet drunkard, so we put on the television and settle in for the long haul. After half an hour of reruns that neither of us is really watching, I lean my head on Cam's shoulder.

'Are you really okay?' I ask.

There's a long pause before he answers. The laughter and light from the television spill over us.

'I don't know,' he says eventually. 'It's difficult. Some days I'm fine, but other days it just hits me harder. Then I think about what I've lost and wonder if I'll ever find it again.' He tries to smile. 'I'm sorry. That's maudlin.'

'I'm not judging. Be as maudlin as you like.'

'I'd rather not. It doesn't change anything. Let's not talk about it, okay? Let's talk about you and your exciting new romance.'

I groan.

'Did I say something wrong?' he asks.

'No. Yes. I don't know. I keep fucking up. I don't have to tell you that. You know.'

'I think the whole college knows.'

I hit him with a cushion.

'I'm not trying to be a bitch,' he says, holding his hands up defensively. 'But yeah, I can see how being marked by someone else might put a dampener on things with Tabitha.'

I flop back onto the sofa and cover my face with the cushion. I want to scream into it, but I also don't want to wake Mrs Grant, so I just let the frustration build until it spills over into nothing. When I drop the cushion again, I can feel the residual heat in my cheeks.

'It was messy,' I sigh. 'It was really, really messy. I'm not sure it's salvageable.'

'If it's meant to be, then it'll all work out.'

I laugh. 'My god, you're so corny.'

'No,' Cam insists, 'I really believe that. If you're the right match, then nothing will stand in your way, but if you're not, then nothing would have kept you together anyway. I have to believe that right now.'

I can understand why. I can see the tightness around his lips and the desperation in his eyes. If he can't believe that what happened with Ed wasn't his fault, then I'm not sure he'll be able to hold himself together.

'I like it,' I say, then I kiss his cheek and pull him into my arms. Hell, if we're going to be delusional then we may as well do it together. 'Let's both believe that everything will turn out the way it ought to be.'

'You're just humouring me,' he says, but he's smiling.

'And you're annoying me. Shut up and watch TV.'

I expect him to stay, because he usually would, but when I wake up on the sofa in the middle of the night, the television's off, Mrs Grant's snoring, and Cam is gone. I know he's only next door, but it feels as though he's a million miles away.

25

THE NEXT DAY is Friday. Date day. Grovelling day.

I need to pick out something to wear that isn't stained or full of holes, but first I need to get through my working day, and before that I need to get the snoring monster that is Mrs Grant out of my room and back where she belongs. Wherever that is.

I knock on Cam's door.

'Hey,' he says sleepily. It's still early, I realise. 'What's wrong? Is your sofa on fire? Why are you awake?'

'Just anxious, I guess. Are you okay?'

'I'm fine,' he says, pasting on a smile. 'I was a bit blue last night, but I'm fine now. Completely fine. Never felt more fine, honestly.'

'You're such a bad liar.'

'I know.' He rubs his eyes with the back of his hand. 'What's up?'

'Are you ready to get going? I want to take Mrs Grant back to the house and see if we can get anything else out of her before Boyd and Naia go out on their notebook search.'

'Well, since I'm already up…' he says pointedly.

'I know. I'm sorry.' I look at the time on my phone and see it's only six in the morning. 'Oh, shit. I really am sorry.'

'It's fine.'

'Of course it is. Everything's fine with you this morning, right?'

He chuckles. 'Give me ten minutes to shower. I'll swing by yours.'

Between the two of us, we manage to steer a shaky Mrs Grant out of the college by way of the canteen. She has some orange juice, dry toast and a cup of tea. I'm praying that she can keep it all down on the drive. It's so bright outside that she squints and hisses at the sky like a fairytale vampire, but Cam tracks down some sunglasses from the lost property box in the lodge and that's enough to get her into the car.

'Thank you,' she says. She settles in the back seat and raises a shaking hand to her forehead. 'I'm not entirely clear on what happened last night, but thank you for looking after me. I can't tell you how embarrassed I am.'

It's the most she's said all morning.

'It's all right, Mrs Grant. Do you have somewhere to go once you've picked up your things from the house?'

'I can call my sister,' she says, though her tone is reluctant. 'I just couldn't bear it last night. She never liked David. I'm sure she'll be cackling like a witch at the prospect of putting me in my place. She loves to say *I told you so*.' Mrs Grant sighs. 'And she did. She told me over and over, and I didn't listen. What a fool I've been.'

She doesn't speak for the rest of the journey. I need to ask her some more questions, but they can wait until we've delivered her back home. For the moment, I use the time to think.

The injection site on Grant's arm. The lipstick on his mouth. DNA matching the London cases. Purple and green

256

under a dark coat. A pound of flesh missing from Grant's organs. Embezzled money. OfficeBox. Grant's notebook. Felton's drugs. Black Mary. Turning Silver.

I ponder it all on the drive, trying to make everything come together in a way that makes sense, but it won't cohere. There are too many pieces, and not enough gaps. Either that, or there's still something we're missing.

'I smell burning,' Cam says when we pull up at the house. 'Shall I pour water in your ear?'

I shake my head. 'I dunno, Cam. This case.'

We help Mrs Grant out of the car and through her front door.

'Thank you both, again,' she says, rubbing at her head. I don't envy her the hangover she's fighting today.

'There was one more thing, Mrs Grant,' I say, 'if you don't mind?'

'Yes?'

'You mentioned something last night about a gym. Did your husband have a gym locker?'

'That's right. At the leisure centre on the business park.'

'Do you have the key?'

She starts to shake her head, then thinks better of it and steadies herself against the doorframe. She looks like she might be sick.

Eventually, she says, 'It's a combination lock.'

Damn.

'Okay. Well, you look after yourself, Mrs Grant.'

'You too, Ms Valentine.'

With that, she closes the door behind her, locking herself inside the empty house. I guess she's on her own from here.

'Time to call Faizan,' I say to Cam as we walk back to the car.

We generally have a good relationship with the police. They might think we're nothing more than glorified campus security, but there are enough Silver high up in the force that we can usually get what we need from them without exerting too much pressure. But for some jobs, there's no replacement for boots on the ground. That's where our friend Faizan comes in. He's Silver, but he started as a lowly plod and worked his way up until he earned the rank he holds today: detective chief inspector. When we need doors opened and scenes held, he's the person we call.

'Faiz!' I say when he picks up the phone. 'How are you doing?'

'Oh, god,' he replies. 'Why are you being so friendly? Why are you calling so early? What do you want?'

Cam stifles a laugh. I'm calling on the car speakerphone, so he can hear every word.

'It's nothing big,' I say, 'I promise.'

'That's what you told me last time, then you made me shut down the botanical gardens to plough up the flower beds for body parts. Then there was the time you had me call off college bumps to dredge the river. And the time before that when—'

'It's nothing like that,' I interrupt. 'Today I just need you to open a locker at the gym on the Cowley business park.'

There's silence on the other end of the line.

'That's it?' Faizan says after a moment. 'You don't want me to demolish anything at all?'

'Nope. Well, you might need a warrant and some bolt cutters. There's a padlock with a combination that we don't know.'

'Bolt cutters,' he repeats. 'A call from Jack Valentine, and all I need is bolt cutters. I'll be honest, I'm very nearly disappointed.'

'Sorry, Faiz. Maybe next time.'

'No, thank you. Bolt cutters is my comfortable limit. Send through the details and I'll call you when it's done.'

I email Faizan while Cam drives us back to the college. He's already replied by the time we pull up at the lodge: *No problem. Warrant on the way.*

When we walk through the quad, Boyd and Naia are on their way out.

'Off to Magdalen,' Naia says, hefting David Grant's overcoat.

'Good luck!' Cam says with a smile.

Boyd scowls back. 'If this is the right coat, then we won't need luck.'

He's obviously still sore from yesterday. This would not be a good time to antagonise him. If I rub him up the wrong way, he'll have me doing the shit jobs for the rest of the month. I'll be clearing up blood bags by the end of the day.

'Try not to fall in the river!' I yell after him.

I have poor impulse control. This time, I get away with it.

Cam and I are spinning our wheels for the rest of the morning, because there's nothing we can do now except keep going over the information we already have, looking for something we've missed while we wait for the police to get their warrant. We're discussing the possibility of speaking to Windsor again when my phone rings.

'Yeah?' I say.

'Call off the search,' says Naia.

'What?'

'We've found his notebook.'

'What is it?' Cam whispers to me. I wave him into silence and put the phone on speaker.

'They found the notebook,' I say to him, before talking into the phone again. 'Where?'

'In the room he was tossed from. It had fallen down between the wall and the back of the radiator, right under the window. I'm guessing the killer missed it. We nearly did.'

'And?' Cam asks. 'What's in it?'

'It's, er... Difficult to describe.' It's not like Naia to be lost for words. That's when I know that whatever's in that notebook, I'm not going to like it. 'Better that you see it for yourselves. We'll be back in ten.'

We reconvene in Boyd and Naia's office.

Naia's expression is grim as she hands the black moleskin to me. It's a small thing, A6, and it has to be held closed with a rubber band because the pages are so crinkled with use that they want to spread. It looks inoffensive, which makes the contents that much more horrifying. I don't expect it to hold such awful secrets.

The first page is simply a list of names, all women, in well-worn ink. Here and there a drop of water has dissipated the names into blue chromatography. It takes me a moment to work out that it's a table of contents.

I flick through, stopping at the last page. The double spread is beautifully composed. A detailed ink drawing of a woman's face and shoulders covers the centre of the space, with a full-length portrait off to one side. It's a study of her form, an attempt to capture not just her likeness, but the way she moves, the way she takes up space. I can tell that it's been successful because I recognise the woman: she's the soprano Cam and I met the first time we went to the Playhouse.

If I look only at the sketches, then this notebook is a gorgeous artefact. Even though they've just been drawn in biro, the pictures are haunting and perfectly-executed, delicate to the point of reverence. But I can't divorce the pictures from the words that sit alongside. They weave in and around the images like vines, trapping them and pinning them down.

Alicia, twenty-one, rubbish lay, but she cried prettily all the way through.

Around a leg, *Bruises like a peach, pinch pinch pinch.*

Around her stomach and hips, *Ugly stretch marks.*

The empty parts of the page are filled with a list of their encounters, all dated.

Went backstage and drew her picture. She watched me doing it, thought I didn't notice.

Followed her back to the hotel, stayed out of sight. She didn't close the curtains when she stripped for her bath.

If I choke her, how many seconds will she take to stop breathing?

Every double spread is like this: beautiful drawings of beautiful girls, made ugly by the words that sit alongside them.

This is what David Grant was doing when he crowded the actors in their dressing room. He was picking targets, sizing them up, measuring their virtues and failings. His notes are like Felton's marionette displays, only somehow worse, because Felton was only preying on his victims for the blood that he needs to survive, whereas Grant wanted to take them apart, piece by piece, and play with what was left. You could argue that there is some vestige of compassion in what Felton does, but the dissection in Grant's notebook displays none at all. It is pure psychopathy.

I feel sick.

'Fuck,' I say, flicking through the pages. 'How many of them are there?'

'Maybe twenty,' says Boyd. 'The book's not full. There were probably others, because this one only seems to go back a few months.'

I look up at him. He's keeping his cool admirably well, but I can see his anger in the tension of his jaw. For all his annoying habits, Boyd is a singularly decent guy. I complain about how uptight he is, but that's only because he likes things done right. The notebook horrifies him because it's evidence of the world being wrong in a way he simply can't understand. Boyd is good at this job because he can spot that wrongness in people. I'm good because I can understand it.

I can imagine why someone would draw pictures like this, why they'd create a little Creep Box of their own, and suddenly I have very little interest in bringing David Grant's killer to justice.

'What are we thinking?' I ask.

'We're thinking we need to be careful.' He takes the notebook from my hands then opens it to the last page. There, facing the inner back cover, is a familiar symbol.

'Shit,' I breathe.

It's an 'S' topped with a radiate crown. An 'I' is slashed down its centre, pointed like a dagger. It's the mark of Solomon, the Primus, and the symbol of the Solis Invicti.

I look at Cam with one eyebrow raised, giving him my best I-told-you-so expression.

He sighs.

'*Drew's an okay guy*, you said. *Give him a chance.*' I parrot his own words back to him. 'Look how that turned out.'

'Come off it, Jack,' he replies, nudging me sideways. 'As if you had any idea this was coming. As if any of us did.'

The enormity of it hits me all at once. The contents of the rest of the notebook was bad enough on its own, but this final page is the one that pulls the rug out from underneath our feet. It's bad enough that no one wants to be the first to say the words out loud, but we all know what this means for the integrity of the investigation.

'So,' Boyd says, 'we keep this to ourselves for now?'

'Agreed,' Cam and I say.

We look at Naia. She's wavering, but finally she nods.

Boyd carefully tears the offending page from the back of the book, close to the seam. He is neat. You wouldn't notice it was missing unless you were looking for it. He's about to fold it into his pocket when Cam stops him, holding his wrist.

'What's that?' he asks, pointing at a tiny line of text that had been hidden by the seam. Boyd turns the page this way and that, then holds it out to show us.

It's a single name in a miniature version of Grant's handwriting: Benedict.

'Benedict,' says Boyd, shaking his head.

'You know the name?' I ask.

'He's the Tertius,' says Cam.

'Next in line after the Primus and the Secundus,' Boyd adds.

'Yes, thank you, Deputy,' I say. 'I might not have gone to public school and learned Latin, but I've been Silver long enough to know what the Tertius is.' I'm shaken and I'm taking it out on Boyd, but thankfully he's worked with me long enough that he doesn't take it personally.

'What do you think it means?' Cam asks.

'Well,' Naia says, looking around at us, 'I don't think we can be in any doubt that the Solis Invicti are involved here. Can we?'

'And the Tertius?'

'Hang on,' Boyd spreads his hands in a placating gesture. 'Let's not jump to conclusions here. This doesn't mean anything. It could just be aspirational. Maybe Grant heard about the Solis Invicti and decided he wanted to be one of them. Maybe he saw the symbol and drew it because of that wish. Maybe Benedict's name is only there because Grant found out he was the Tertius and decided to reach out to him. On its own, this means nothing. And let's not forget that neither Meyer nor the Secundus stopped me from looking at CGC's records. I can't believe that they're in on whatever this is.'

We're not convinced, but he's right: there's not enough here to start drawing conclusions. There's certainly not enough here for us to start accusing the Primus's elite guards of murder, or conspiracy, or worse.

So we make an agreement: We won't tell the Secundus. We won't tell Meyer. We won't even tell the captain.

We won't tell a soul.

26

WE TRY TO carry on as though there's nothing wrong. We take the rest of the notebook to the captain, not mentioning the now-missing page.

'The Solis Invicti will want to see this,' she says, flicking through the pages. 'Gods. This is... Well, I wouldn't expect this from a human.'

It's strange that we have higher moral expectations from humanity than we do of our own kind, but there it is. I suppose long lives give perversions time to grow and find company.

'Deputy,' she says, 'what's your plan?'

'We have a lead on a gym locker Grant used,' Boyd says.

'Faizan's dealing with it now,' Cam adds.

'And there's this.' Boyd takes the notebook and flicks back to the most recent drawing. 'This woman is one of the opera singers from the show Grant saw the night before he died. Jacqueline and Cam identified her from the first visit to the Playhouse. I thought we'd track her down and ask her some questions.'

The captain's gaze is fixed on the pages Boyd has spread open in front of her.

'All right, then. But don't show her this,' she says, her voice practically a whisper. 'She doesn't need to see the inside of that man's head.' She closes the notebook decisively then rises from her chair. 'This needs to go to the Invicti.'

My stomach drops second by second as she leads us to the conference room. Cam and I exchange a glance behind her back. The last thing I want to do is talk to the Invicti about our latest leads.

The Secundus is waiting there, barking out orders as his colleague types on a laptop, but this time it's not Meyer who's with him. Instead, he's accompanied by a huge guy who looks as though he's the result of some genetic experiment to crossbreed a human with bull. There isn't a single part of him that's not heavily-muscled, and yet he moves as though he weighs nothing at all. He reminds me of a boxer, deceptively light on his feet.

The Secundus introduces him as Benedict, no last name. Just Benedict, like he's the pope or something. So this is the Tertius.

I don't like the way he looks at me.

I'm skittish anyway after this morning's discovery. The questions are flying around in my head as I try to understand Grant's connection to the Solis Invicti. I'm looking at Benedict, probing his face as though I'll be able to see the truth written there. From the way he's looking back at me, it's almost as though he can see what I'm thinking.

Then it hits me: I've seen him recently. Very recently, in a context that made him hard to place, because he was wearing a suit.

He was at Windsor's party. He was the man in the upstairs room.

He's the one behind the Silver racket.

Shit.

'What's this?' the Secundus asks as Captain Langford hands him the notebook.

'Grant's notebook,' she says. 'We tracked it down.'

He flips through the pages, his eyes going wide, then passes it to Benedict. It might just be my imagination, but I'd swear that the contents of the book are no surprise to him. He turns the pages in a way that's almost perfunctory, as though they hold nothing he hasn't seen before.

'I'm not sure this takes us any further forward,' he says, tossing the notebook onto the table. 'We know we're not looking for a personal connection. The killer is the same scab that was active in London – we know that from the DNA – so looking into this man's life any further seems pointless.'

The Secundus gives him a look. I'm not sure exactly what he's trying to communicate to Benedict, but to me it reads like, *We have to give the locals something to do to keep them from getting under our feet.* Whatever the message, it seems to placate Benedict. He settles back into his chair and listens as the Secundus updates us on the latest news from London.

Apparently they've found the blood bar where the scab must have been drinking, a high-class place in Knightsbridge. I gather that they've yet to identify the individual, but I'm barely paying attention. I'm fixating on Benedict, watching the way his hands move across the keyboard of his laptop, the way his eyes keep flicking in my direction. He knows I'm watching him and it doesn't seem to bother him. Is that because he knows what I know, or because he doesn't? I don't have any clue how to read him.

'Well,' the Secundus says eventually, 'we'll let you get back to your investigation. Let us know if you find anything else.'

It's clearly a dismissal, so we all file out of the room. The captain lingers for a moment, as though she's not sure whether to stay or go, but then the Secundus says, 'Thank you, Captain Langford.'

They don't want her there either.

I wait until we're in the canteen with our lunch trays in front of us before I break the news to the rest of my team.

'It's Benedict,' I whisper.

Naia looks at me quizzically. 'Yes, we know. We had that whole conversation this morning when we found his name in the notebook.'

'No, I mean it's worse than that. You remember I told you about the guys who were pretending to turn people Silver at Windsor's party?'

'Yeah?'

'And there was the one guy running the whole show, the guy who looked so familiar but I couldn't place? Him. He was Benedict.'

Cam's eyes widen. He opens his mouth to reply, but then Ellie and Quentin walk into the canteen. They're from one of the other Seeker teams that are based here at the college, but we weren't expecting them back from Derbyshire until next week. They're more like rivals than friends to me, but Cam is a little more outgoing than I am and I don't know how he's going to handle this, so I kick him under the table and hiss, 'Not a word.'

'Hey, guys,' Ellie says with a cheery wave.

She's blonde and freckled and shows all her teeth when she smiles. She has the kind of jolly, get-things-done demeanour that suggests she had horses and large dogs when she was a girl, which would make sense since she was raised in a large Edwardian family. I bet Austen could have written her childhood. Quentin, on the other hand, is sulky and taciturn. I can't blame him for his name – he was born in the nineteenth century, after all – but I will blame him for his mohawk. That stupid pink hairstyle was adopted by choice.

'Hello,' Boyd says shiftily.

He's one of the worst actors I've ever met. I'm sure Ellie guesses that something's up, but if she does then she pretends not to notice.

'Hey, Deputy,' she twinkles at him.

It's hard to tell, but I think he's blushing.

'You're back early,' Naia says. 'What went wrong?'

'Nothing went wrong,' says Quentin.

Ellie puts an arm around him. 'It's all right, Quent. No one blames you.'

'I didn't *do* anything,' he insists, then he shakes off Ellie's arm and stomps away to join the lunch queue.

'There was a little snafu with the evidence,' she whispers to us. 'The Invicti got involved and then, well... Long story short, we're off the case.'

Cam and I exchange glances. Could it just be a coincidence?

Before we can ask for the details, Ellie says, 'Excuse me. I'd better go after him. I'll see you guys later.'

I need to make sure that I do see her later. Something tells me we want to hear the whole story.

I wait until she's out of earshot before I start talking again.

'Benedict is the one behind this,' I whisper. 'Which means the Invicti are deeper in this than we thought. It's not just a name in Grant's notebook, it's the Tertius being in charge of an unsanctioned Casting.'

'Or a sanctioned one,' says Boyd.

I'm not sure which would be worse.

Naia looks around at each of us.

'Then we're fucked, aren't we?' she says. 'If the Solis Invicti are the ones who killed Grant, then we need to keep our mouths shut. Maybe we should start thinking about finding a scapegoat.'

'What the hell are you talking about?' I say.

'You want to accuse the Tertius of this?'

'If we find the evidence, then of course.'

'Why?' she says, but she says it as though it's a rhetorical question. 'Where does our authority come from?'

I pause, because I don't like the answer.

'That's right,' she goes on. 'It comes from the Primus. So if the Primus ordered Grant's death, then that's case closed, accidental death recorded. You get that, right?'

'I get it,' I say.

'Good.' Naia starts shovelling food into her mouth, then points at me with her empty fork. 'Because David Grant was a scumbag,' she says through her mouthful. 'You do remember that, don't you?'

'Yes,' I look away to spare my eyes.

'He deserved to die. Who cares who killed him?'

Thankfully, I'm rescued from the spectacle of Naia's further mastication by the buzz of my phone in my pocket.

It's Faizan.

'Hey, Valentine,' he says.

'Hey. Do you have an update for me? Did you get to break out the explosives, or were bolt cutters enough?'

'Ha ha,' he says, with no trace of amusement. 'We've located his locker – the bolt cutters were plenty good enough, thank you – but it's empty. No books. The only good news is that the whole building is covered in video cameras. I'm requesting the footage now. I'll send it over as soon as I've had copies made.'

'Shit. Well, thanks anyway.'

'No worries. Shouldn't be long before the files come through – check your email in about an hour.'

'Will do. Thanks, Faiz.'

I hang up, then relate the conversation to the rest of the team.

Naia groans.

'Didn't we just agree that it doesn't matter who killed him?' she says. 'I don't want to spend the rest of the day watching video surveillance of sweaty old men who think they look great in lycra.'

'Tough,' says Boyd, 'because that's exactly what you're doing. We're not giving up on this before it's over.'

27

THAT AFTERNOON, THE four of us watch hour after hour of video showing gym bunnies of every size and shape walking past David Grant's locker. Time passes slowly.

It gives me a chance to start dreading my date with Tabitha this evening.

I was already feeling ambivalent about the whole thing, because on the one hand I was desperate to see her, but on the other I was worried about how the conversation was going to go. Now that I've had the whole afternoon to work myself up into a state about it, I'm feeling nervous. Once I've finally left the office to get changed, my hands shake as I button myself into my least-scruffy shirt.

As it turns out, I needn't have worried. When I get to the restaurant – a Lebanese place in Jericho – she's already sitting at the table, looking stunning in her new turquoise dress. She smiles as I walk in. It's not the same smile I've been seeing recently, either, the one of forbearance under trying circumstances. No, this is her genuine smile, the addictive one that I can't help reciprocating.

She kisses my cheek when I reach the table and says, 'I've missed you, hen.'

It feels like a benediction.

We don't dally over dinner. We're only here to line our stomachs for the night ahead, not for a gastronomic experience. While we eat, she tells me about her day – report writing, microscopic analysis of something or other, amusing anecdote about mass spectrometry that goes right over my head – and I start to feel nervous again. For the first time, I realise that there's more keeping us apart than this stupid chemistry I have with Drake.

Tabitha is clever. I mean, crazy clever. Her blue eyes and tumbling auburn curls might be what drew me to her in the first place, but the thing that keeps me coming back is her mind. She has a wicked sense of humour and the intelligence to match, and as I sit across the table from her and listen to her Scottish accent dancing across the syllables of technical language I don't understand, I'm intimidated.

How is this going to work if I'm too stupid to follow what she says? Will she feel unappreciated? Will she get bored and leave me for someone who can keep up?

That worry is what cements it in my mind: Drake's wrong. This isn't just a fling.

I want to keep her.

'Tabitha,' I say.

She stops mid-sentence and looks at me.

'I really like you,' I say. My heart is in my throat, but I suddenly need to say this out loud, so I rush on before I can think too hard about it. 'I know we haven't known each other that long, and I know I keep fucking up, but I really want this to work. Everything with Drake, it's done. It was never meant to happen in the first place and I wish it hadn't happened at all. I don't even know why you're still here, but I really want you to stay. You're clever, you're funny, you're beautiful, and you're so fucking sexy–'

She grabs my hand and leans over the table to lay one perfect, chaste kiss on my lips.

'Let's get out of here,' she says, pulling a few notes from her purse and leaving them on the table. 'I want a stronger drink.'

She leads me out of the restaurant and back across town. When we hit Broad Street, I know where she's taking me.

There aren't many places in Oxford where the Silver can be themselves openly. One of those places is Solomon College, and then there are smaller enclaves in private residences, like Drake's mansion and Windsor's country pad. But if you know where to look and if you're discreet enough to earn an invitation, there is one other option. I'm not the discreet type, so I haven't been to the club on Holywell Street since I was human. Winta brought me here, just once, and after the scene I made they never invited me back when I turned. I didn't blame them for that at the time, but I wonder now whether they'll shut the door in my face.

I wish Tabitha had picked a different venue, but I'm hardly in a position to complain.

She knocks on the street door in a jaunty rhythm and it swings open quickly.

'Dr Ross!' says the bouncer on the other side. 'Good to see you.'

She's tall with black hair and mid-brown skin, and she's wearing a smart trouser suit. It doesn't escape my notice that she's handsome, with strong features and a square face, nor do I fail to notice the warmth in her eyes as she looks at Tabitha. I take a step closer to my date, wrapping my arm around her waist, which draws the bouncer's gaze to me.

'Oh, hell no,' she says, looking me up and down. 'No Seekers, no brawlers,' she says, counting off my sins on her fingertips, 'and definitely no Jack Valentines.'

'Come on, Marina,' Tabitha wheedles, pulling me close to her. 'I'll make sure she behaves.'

The bouncer raises an eyebrow, unconvinced. 'You think you can civilise *her*?'

There's a ruckus from behind the bouncer, then a familiar figure appears at her side.

'Ms Valentine! I thought I heard your voice.' It's Gabriella De Palma, complete with teetering heels and perfect coiffure.

'Hello, Ms De Palma.'

'It's Gabriella, please,' she says, then she kisses me on both cheeks. I'm surprised by the overture, but I guess she's probably been drinking for a while and is in a friendly mood. I'm also a little uncomfortable, because until very recently she was a suspect in our murder case. Her alibi for the London murders is rock solid – there's no way she's our killer – but still. 'And where is your delectable partner this evening?'

'Not here,' I tell her. 'And also, gay.'

'The beautiful ones always are, darling.'

I look at Tabitha and smile. The adage certainly holds true for her.

Gabriella turns to the bouncer. 'Well? Why are you keeping them standing out there in the cold? Let them in.'

'But the rules–'

'Oh, bugger the rules.'

Which is how we end up drinking at the bar with Gabriella and a performance artist she introduces as L'Escalier, who turns out to be exactly as ridiculous as she sounds. Fortunately, she's also conscious enough of her own ridiculousness that she's good company. She's dressed in an outfit that's almost steampunk, with a black and white chequered shirt that makes my eyes ache and a top hat whose peak is circled by a tiny lacquered staircase.

I don't ask how she got her name. In fact, I have no idea what to say to her, but Tabitha seems right at home.

'I love your hat!' she says, grinning up at it. 'So much fun. Can I touch it?'

'You can try it on if you like,' L'Escalier says, grinning back at her as she removes the construction from her head. Underneath, her hair is a messy crop of platinum blond.

'Look,' Tabitha says to me, putting on the hat, 'now I'm as tall as you are!'

The other women laugh, because she's still a good few inches shy, but I'm distracted by the fall of her hair against her neck, the colour rich against the shoulders of her turquoise dress. The lighting in here is dark, but the yellow lamps pick out the glints of gold and red in her curls and I want to see them all, unbound by the ridiculous objet d'art.

I take the hat from her head and pull her close, kissing her cheek before bringing my lips to her ear.

'I like you just as you are,' I whisper.

She pushes me away a little, but she's pink-cheeked and smiling. I let her return to a more civilised distance and vow to control myself until it's late enough in the evening that no one will care about PDAs.

'Darlings,' Gabriella says to us, 'you are simply gorgeous together. Such contrast. Look at you, Tabby, with all the colour and the joy and the exuberance, next to you, Jackie, with the leather and the shadows and the clouds.'

'Please don't call me Jackie,' I say through gritted teeth.

'So fierce,' Gabriella says, curving her fingers into a claw and pawing at the air. 'Like a panther. Ah!' she exclaims, clapping her hands. 'The panther and the tabby cat! How perfect.'

I turn back to the bar. It's definitely time for a Massacre.

* * *

We drink. We dance. We drink some more.

L'Escalier performs her trademark mime-and-music routine, to the hilarity of the entire bar, then entertains us all with stories of her travels around the continent. Inevitably, it turns into a game where we take a drink every time she mentions a European city. I'm pretty sure she notices us playing after only a few minutes and increases the name-drops, which might explain why we're all smashed by ten o'clock.

It turns out that drunken Gabriella dances like an angel and tells jokes bawdy enough for a brothel. Maybe it's unprofessional for me to be partying with her, but it's pleasantly surprising to discover that we share a lot of common ground. The Gabriella I met at the Randolph had far too much refinement to sully herself with my company, but this version of her is someone I'd like to call a friend.

We continue the dancing. And the singing. And, after a while, the screaming lyrics in each other's faces.

Eventually, I manage to drag Tabitha away from our new friends and out into the courtyard garden, which is deserted at the moment since it's just started to drizzle. It's so hot inside that neither of us minds the rain. The tiny drops dust Tabitha's skin in flecks of crystal that glimmer in the lamplight.

'Did you want to talk?' I ask her, because that's what the Massacres were originally for. We're supposed to be talking about this mess I've got us into with Drake and the mark. I should probably tell her about him biting me, too.

'Do *you* want to talk?' she replies.

'God, no.'

'Then shall we just... not? Can we just go from here and forget everything else, hen? If you meant what you said, then why do we need to talk about it?'

'I meant every word.'

'Well, then.'

She smiles up at me. We are resolved: we will both forget about Killian Drake.

'I like the new dress,' I say, running my fingertip along the sweetheart neckline.

'You do?'

'I like it a lot.'

'So you're having a good time, hen?' she asks me.

'I'm having a better time now.'

She looks up at me, tossing her hair back from her face. 'Oh?'

I can't stop looking at her lips, her eyes. When her fingers find my belt loops and she pulls my hips against hers, I don't need any further convincing.

I lean down and kiss her, properly this time. My hand is stroking her hair back from her face, clutching the rich weight of it in my fist as my other hand wraps around her waist. Much as I like the dress, I wish she was wearing separates instead so I could touch her waist, skin to skin.

'Jack,' she whispers against my lips, but I'm not in the mood for conversation. I kiss her again, pushing her back against the wall next to the bar door, trapping her in the spread of my arms. I'd let her go if that were what she wanted, but I can tell from the way she's grasping at my shirt that she doesn't want me to stop either. Her skin is soft on mine, but her movements are urgent and sharp. When her fingertips come to rest on the bare skin of my stomach, the pleasant shock of her touch makes me groan. Before I know what I'm doing, I'm kissing my way down her neck.

I want this. I want her. I know both of these things to a certainty. Yet when I press my lips back against hers and coax her mouth open under mine, there is no scent surrounding us except the smoke of the guttering candle lanterns and the damp freshness of the rain.

I'm not marking her and I don't understand why. But then, she's not marking me either.

I kiss her more fiercely, because suddenly I feel like I have something to prove. Why can't I do this? Why will the mark not come out of me now when it was so immediate with Drake, when I didn't even want him? Why won't my body do what I want it to do?

I don't want to stop. I want to keep trying. I want to put this right. It's only the way Tabitha stills that calls me to a halt before I start undressing her right there in the courtyard.

'Jack,' she says again. She catches my hands and weaves her fingers through mine. 'It's too soon.'

'I know,' I say, taking a tiny step back. 'I know it is.'

She doesn't have to explain why. After everything I've done, every misstep with Drake, I can't expect her to trust me with her feelings. She isn't ready to let go of her reservations and I'm not going to push her. I'm only glad she hasn't given up on me already.

'Shall we go back inside?' she says brightly. 'I bet we can get them to put on some cheesy music if you want to have a proper dance.'

The smile she gives me is so devilish that I laugh despite my disappointment and let her drag me back into the bar.

I hail her a taxi at about midnight. I want to take her back to mine, but she has to be in London early tomorrow so she needs her sleep. It's the right call. I don't want to mess this up by rushing forward.

'Call you tomorrow?' she says.

'Yes, please.'

She brushes a quick kiss across my lips – too quick – then she's gone, carried away into the night, leaving me drunk and alone at the taxi rank under Carfax clock tower.

At least, I think I'm alone. I've walked halfway back to the college before I'm certain that someone is following me. I can hear their steps in the echo of my own.

I decide to do the old ambush trick by jumping up onto the roof of a nearby building, waiting for my pursuer to walk by, then jumping down to surprise them. Unfortunately, the Massacres have affected my balance and the execution of my brilliant plan leaves something to be desired. Instead of jumping up cleanly, I stumble into a dustbin and end up sitting on its lid. Whoever's following me must have heard the racket, but they keep coming nonetheless. Either they weren't really following me after all, or they're looking for a confrontation.

I sit and wait, blinking heavily as I try to clear my head. Perhaps it's just the Massacres slowing my reflexes, but I'm not surprised when Benedict rounds the corner.

'Waiting for me, Jack?' The use of my first name feels shockingly intimate.

'You're following me?'

'You're drunk.'

'I was thirsty.'

'And I was curious,' he says with a shrug. 'I have a friend who mentioned your name.'

'What friend would that be?' I ask, but I know.

I know because of Felton's threats and Windsor's party, but mostly I know because the Benedict I'm meeting tonight isn't the one I saw in the conference room at the college. He still gives the impression of being a coiled spring, a threat loaded and primed, but now his mask of respectability has slipped. Instead of being a weapon of the Solis Invicti, he's an undirected bundle of masculine swagger, a human leer.

He's Matthew Felton's friend. If Benedict wanted to dope up David Grant and drain his blood before chucking the body off Magdalen tower, then he'd know exactly who to call.

He winks at me, then he turns around and walks back the way he came, disappearing into the city.

Benedict – the Tertius – wants me scared.

Well, he got his wish. No more Massacres for me.

28

WHEN I DRAG myself into the office the next morning, the place is a hive of activity. There's a load of people I've never seen before flitting in and out, carrying equipment and papers between the captain's office and the conference room.

Boyd is not happy. He's standing by the wall outside, glowering at the interlopers with his arms crossed over his chest.

'What's going on?' I ask him.

'Someone called in a tip about the Boat Race murder. This lot came down from London this morning. Apparently we're completely superfluous now.'

We flatten ourselves against the wall as a man walks out of the captain's office carrying her printer.

'Fucking hell,' I say. 'It looks as though they're looting the place. Is she in there?'

'Nope. She's in the conference room with the rest of them.'

'Shouldn't we be in there too?'

Boyd's expression turns stormy. 'Apparently not.'

Uh oh.

By the time Cam and Naia join us, the Invicti and the captain are ensconced in the conference room with the door shut.

'Where's the captain?' Naia asks.

Boyd nods towards the conference room door. When Naia reaches for the handle, he holds her back.

'Not allowed,' he says. 'Captain's orders. Invicti only.'

Naia pouts and mirrors Boyd's stance, crossing her tattooed arms.

'Well, that sucks,' says Cam.

Boyd makes a harrumphing sound, as though he has plenty of his own thoughts on the matter, but he keeps them to himself.

'Any idea what it's about?' Cam asks.

'The Boat Race,' Boyd replies. 'They've had a tip-off. Someone called it in here, I guess because they knew the Secundus was in town.'

'Which means it couldn't have been a human,' I say.

'Exactly.'

We work carefully with the police to make sure that scab cases have minimal media impact. This current spate of murders has been challenging the limits of our imagination, but so far the four murders have gone unconnected by the general public. The New Year's Day Parade was written off as a random suicide, the Palm Sunday Procession ascribed to terrorism, and so far the police have managed to cast the May Morning incident as the result of an alcohol-fuelled dare. It's not so hard to believe when you consider that the entirety of Magdalen Bridge was filled with drunken students when it happened.

The Boat Race was actually the easiest death to explain away. As far as the spectators were aware, it was just an accidental drowning that got in the way of the race. That's why the tipoff is significant. Not only has it come from someone who knows the Boat Race death was a murder, but that person also knows that the four murders are being investigated together, by the Invicti. Only a Silver could know all of that, which means the tip has to be treated seriously.

No wonder there's been such a hubbub.

'Do you know what they said?' Cam asks.

'Something about Trooping the Colour,' says Boyd.

'They're planning to disrupt the Queen's birthday celebrations?'

'That's all I heard. Then they slammed the door in my face, and here we all are.'

We try to listen in, but the conference room was built with supernatural hearing in mind. I can just about hear that people are talking, but that's all. I can't make out the words.

When the Invicti finally come out of the conference room, my team is lined up in the corridor like a bunch of naughty schoolchildren waiting outside the headmaster's office. The interlopers all rush off on duties that must already have been assigned, leaving us behind with the captain.

'Well?' Boyd asks her.

'They're going back to London,' she says.

'All of them?'

I don't think I'm imagining the relief I see on Boyd's face. He's used to being second-in-command here and he's found it difficult to have his authority belittled by the presence of the Primus's supreme guard.

'All but one,' the captain says. Boyd's enthusiasm dampens a little. 'The Secundus is leaving Benedict behind to follow up on the investigation here.'

Of course he is.

'But everyone else is going back to London,' the captain is saying. 'Their main focus will be the three London murders from this point on.'

'And making sure there isn't another next month,' Cam says.

The captain raises her eyebrow and looks at Boyd. I resist the urge to wince, just barely.

'Someone's been telling tales out of school,' she says. 'But yes, there is some concern that there may be further incidents. We've always known that was a risk. For now, we just need to focus on solving our own murder, and let the Invicti worry about theirs.'

'I have a feeling it's going to be more complicated than that,' I say, looking at each of my team in turn. 'Captain, we need to talk. Privately.'

We give it an hour or so, so the Invicti have time to leave, then we congregate in the captain's office.

'All right,' she says. 'What's this about?'

I tell her about Benedict's performance at Windsor's party. I tell her about Felton's threats. Then I finish with what happened last night.

'Are you sure?' she asks when I've finished. 'Benedict's behaviour doesn't sound particularly hostile to me. In fact, it sounds like he was just taking your measure.'

'That's exactly what he was doing. He wanted to let me know he was watching me.'

'Which is normal behaviour for the Tertius, especially when he's sizing up the Seekers who are dealing with an important case. Surely you can see that, Jack.'

'Then what about the party at Windsor's? What about the men they killed?'

She leans forward to rest her elbows on her desk, then fists her hands under her chin.

'Let me ask you this,' she says, 'has there been a sudden spate of men reported missing? In fact, have you heard of any rich and influential humans – which, by your account, these men were – going missing at all?'

'No, but–'

'No,' she interrupts. 'Neither have I, and I assure you that I would have received such reports if there were any. I've been looking into it, as I said I would, but I can't find any evidence of a leak. I understand that you're rattled – we all are – and no one likes having the Solis Invicti here stepping on our toes, but who knows what the Primus is working on behind the scenes? There could be any number of reasons he might ask his Tertius to stage a scene like the one you saw in Aston, and not all of the explanations are sinister. Perhaps it was a sting, designed especially to draw out Grant's murderer. Perhaps Benedict was at that party for the same reason you were: to look for clues. Did you think of that?'

'But, Captain–' I protest.

I want to explain this to her in a way that will make her understand the threat in Benedict's words, in his body language and tone. I want to show her what I see in my head when I remember last night. I want to explain the rich freshness of the blood I smelled at Windsor's party, the way the scents matched the victims, and the certainty I have in my gut that the men who walked into that back room never walked out again.

I want to explain all of these things, but she interrupts me again.

'Now, where are we on the gym locker and the opera singer?'

'The locker was empty,' Boyd says. 'We've watched all the footage the gym has, but although we can see the moment Grant deposits his case in there, we haven't found any explanation for how it got out. At the moment, we're working on the basis that either there's footage missing, or someone got into the locker another way.'

'Another way?' the captain asks.

'Through the back, or through one of the other lockers maybe.'

She nods. 'Cam, Jack: look at the tapes again.'

We both groan.

'I don't want to hear it,' she says, glaring at me before turning back to Boyd. 'And the singer?'

'We're tracking her down this afternoon.'

'Good. Report back here afterwards.'

Boyd salutes, then we're all dismissed. Outside the captain's office, it looks as though a tornado has blown through. There are sheets of paper strewn along the corridor together with bits of cardboard and plastic that once contained the supplies the Solis Invicti have pillaged on their way out.

'Messy bastards, aren't they?' Naia says.

'I'm just glad they're gone,' says Boyd.

'You didn't show her the sheet you tore out of the back of the notebook,' I say to him, my tone accusing. 'She didn't believe me about Benedict. If you'd shown her the page so she could see that his name was right there, so she could have seen how mixed up Grant was with the Solis Invicti–'

'Jacqueline, stop.' Boyd looks me in the eye. I stop. 'I don't think she wanted to see it. Do you? Even if I'd shown it to her, she would have written it off as something to do with the Primus's plans, which are way above her pay grade. You know she can't go against them.'

We all stand there for a moment in silence. He's right, but it still hurts that the captain doesn't trust my judgement.

'Come on,' Cam says to us all, smiling that grin of his that says, *Buck up, chaps!* 'Let's go to the canteen. I'm guessing we could all do with some cake.'

Boyd and Naia are right behind him, so I give up and trail after them.

At least I still have my team. The captain may not be on board, but I know they believe me, even if they have no interest in pursuing the Invicti.

If I'm going to tie this case to Benedict, I'm going to have to do it on my own.

29

AFTER SOME DISCUSSION, we decide that Naia and I should be the ones to go and question the soprano, Alicia Tresor. I'd rather take Cam, because he's actually capable of questioning people delicately – a skill that sometimes eludes Naia – but in the end her extra X chromosome wins out.

I'm not sure where to find Tresor, so I give Gabriella a call. She put her number in my phone the other night when we were out at the club on Holywell Street.

'Valentina!' she trills down the phone. Apparently I've acquired a new nickname. 'What can I do for you, darling?'

'Hi, Gabriella. I was wondering if you could do me a favour. I wanted to speak to Alicia Tresor, the soprano, but we don't have an address for her. I wondered if you knew where she was staying at the moment.'

'Why would you need to speak to poor Alicia?'

This is why we generally try not to get too friendly with our witnesses. It gets complicated when they expect to be included in your investigation.

'It's nothing serious,' I lie. 'We're just tying up loose ends.'

'All right, then,' she says, rattling off the address. Apparently Ms Tresor is moving up in the world: the house is just off South Parade. 'But please, Valentina, be gentle with her. She's not been well and she's my best soprano. Will you promise me, *cara*?'

'I promise,' I say, lying again. 'Speak soon, Gabriella.'

'I hope so! You must come for dinner before the opera leaves town. I insist.'

It takes me a while to wrap up the conversation because Gabriella is effusive with her invitations to this gallery opening and that evening soirée, but eventually I manage to extricate myself so we can hit the road.

Tresor's home is fancier than I was expecting. A lot of the houses in this area are little Victorian terraces that have been converted with extension after extension, but this place was clearly always grand. It's Edwardian in period, with huge sash windows and limestone facing. The doorbell isn't a button you push, it's a handle you pull.

'I don't know why we're bothering with this,' Naia says as she rings it. 'It's going to get us precisely nowhere. I could be back at the college watching Drag Race right now, but oh no, I have to drive halfway around Oxford—'

The door opens behind her, revealing the frail shape of Alicia Tresor.

'Hello?' she says.

When we first met, she gave the impression of being cold and distant, but hard with it, using her beautiful features as a knife rather than a shield. Now, she seems like a hollow shell. She's painted her face with care and attention, but her eyes are dull. She is more broken than I realised, but at least now I understand why.

'Ms Tresor?' I say. 'I'm not sure if you remember me. My name's Jack Valentine. We met at the Playhouse.'

'Of course,' she smiles. 'You're the Baron's friend.'

That catches me off guard. Drake hadn't been there when Cam and I had met Tresor.

'Er, you know Baron Drake?' I say.

Tresor smiles sadly. 'He's been kind to us.'

'I bet,' Naia says under her breath.

I elbow her in the ribs. Whatever problems I might have with Drake, I'm not going to begrudge Alicia Tresor for thinking he's been kind to her, not when her alternative benefactor was David Grant. Speaking of which, it's time I cut to the chase.

'We've got a few questions about Mr Grant's murder, if you can spare us some time.'

'Oh.' Her face falls. 'Would you like to come in?' she offers, but suddenly she doesn't seem so friendly.

'Thank you.'

We follow her through the grand house to a room in the back that can only be called a parlour. There are side tables dotted around the space, embroidered cushions on every seat, and antique furniture with pretty curls carved in the wood. Gabriella De Palma would look perfectly at home here.

'Alicia?' comes a voice from a room off to one side. 'Who was that? Is everything all right?'

Iain Halberd, the stage manager we met at the Playhouse, walks into the room. He pulls up short when he sees us, stumbling a little as he recognises my face, but he recovers quickly.

'You're the detective, aren't you?' he says. 'Let me bring a tray.'

He's as brisk and efficient as I remember, bustling into the kitchen to fix tea and biscuits as though he belongs here. It occurs to me that perhaps he does. He might be twenty years older than Tresor and a fraction as good looking, but I've seen stranger couples in my time.

We all sit quietly while we wait for the tea. Tresor doesn't say a word until Halberd returns.

'What can we do for you?' he asks.

He serves us genuine teacups full of tea poured from a genuine teapot. I wonder if they're Wedgwood. Unlike Boyd, I can't tell from sight, but I've seen enough Antiques Roadshow to know that they wouldn't have come cheap.

'Settling in Oxford, are you?' I say, looking around the room. 'I thought you'd carry on touring with the opera.'

'Oh, we will,' says Halberd, 'but Alicia thought it was time to put down roots somewhere. Maybe after this tour is over, she might make it permanent. There's good work to be found here and Oxford's close enough to London if local work runs short.'

'I see.' I look at Tresor, who is apparently happy to let Halberd speak for her. 'Could we speak to Ms Tresor alone, Mr Halberd?'

Tresor looks at Halberd in a panic. She clearly doesn't want him to leave.

'No,' he says. 'I'm sorry, but no. I don't think I can agree to that.'

'For fuck's sake, she's an adult, isn't she?' says Naia. 'We only want to talk to her. You don't need to defend her damn honour.'

'Naia,' I say, trying very hard to keep my cool. Cam would be proud of me. 'Maybe you could go to the kitchen with Mr Halberd and help him make us some more tea.'

She rolls her eyes at me, but she goes, practically dragging poor Iain Halberd after her.

'Sorry about that,' I say when they've gone.

'I've got nothing to tell you,' Tresor says defensively.

'Ms Tresor, I know this is uncomfortable, but we've come across some information that suggests you had a... relationship with Mr Grant.'

'What information?' she demands. She's getting aggressive now, sitting absolutely still with her eyes narrowed and her gaze fixed.

I'm not going to tell her about the notebook. I can't tell her about that. If it were me and I knew that my body had been dissected like that... No. The captain's right. Better not.

'Anonymous source,' I say. 'Is it true?'

'No,' she says immediately.

'No?'

'No. I never had any kind of relationship with that man.' She practically spits the words.

'You don't seem to like him very much.'

'I didn't feel anything for him,' she says with a shrug that's belied by her obvious dismay. 'He was just a benefactor. I barely knew him.'

'Our information suggests otherwise.'

She leans forward and looks me in the eye.

'I barely knew him,' she repeats.

'Here we are,' Halberd says, bustling back into the room with another tray. 'More tea.' I haven't even touched my first cup.

Naia traipses in behind him. She clearly hasn't tried very hard to keep him out of the way, but I can't get too worked up about it. It's clear that Alicia Tresor isn't going to tell us a thing.

'Well,' I say, getting to my feet, 'I guess we've taken up enough of your time.'

'We're going?' Naia asks.

'We're going.'

* * *

Cam's at his desk when I get back to our office.

'How did it go?' he asks.

'Badly,' I say. 'Alicia Tresor was not in a talkative mood. She denied everything, but she obviously hated Grant. I can't blame her for not wanting to talk about it. If it were me, I'd want to put the whole thing behind me and move on as well. I don't think it's relevant anyway; we already knew Grant was a monster. I didn't need her to tell me that. But maybe she would have said more without Halberd there.'

'The stage manager?'

'He made us tea. Twice. Mostly, I think he was there to look after Tresor. She seems fragile. Angry as hell, but fragile.'

Cam shrugs. 'That's divas for you.'

'No,' I say, thinking about the way she'd snapped at me like a cornered cat. 'This was something else. Gabriella said she'd been ill.'

'You spoke to Gabriella?' he says it with censure.

'What? We've already ruled her out. I had to call her for the address.'

'Close bunch, these opera people, aren't they?' he says. 'I'm not sure you'd come over to make me tea if I were sick.'

'I would. Maybe. If you had alcohol in your fridge. And blood,' I say, eyeing the half-drunk bottle on his desk.

'Yeah, sure you would,' he says, passing me the bottle. 'By the way, I spoke to Ellie.'

'Yeah?'

I'd completely forgotten about our Seeker colleagues. I'd meant to follow up with Ellie myself to find out how her team managed to get kicked off the Derbyshire case by the Solis Invicti.

'Guess what their evidence "snafu" was.'

I drain the rest of the bottle then ask, 'What?'

'Apparently there was some kind of break in the chain of custody, which Ellie said was absolutely not Quentin's fault, but in a way that made me think it absolutely was. Anyway, basically some evidence went missing.'

'What kind of evidence?'

'Blood samples. And get this: they were investigating the disappearance of an affluent white man in his mid-forties who emptied his bank accounts before he went missing. The police were assuming he'd left his wife and taken the cash with him, but a local Silver scented the violence mark in his front garden and called it in.'

'Holy shit,' I breathe.

'Holy shit is right, but with the evidence gone, there's nothing to investigate.'

'The Invicti closed the case?'

'They did. So we're back to the official line: the guy left his wife.'

'Shit. I wonder how many other men have been doing that recently.'

'I'm guessing quite a few. At least as many as you saw at Percy's party.'

We sit quietly for a moment, considering the ramifications of that.

'Have you told the others?' I ask.

'No.' He runs his fingers back through his hair in a gesture of frustration. 'They don't like this, Jack. Hell, I don't like it. You know how I feel about the Solis Invicti. I respect them. I want to be one of them. And I know you're going to roll your eyes at me, but Drew really is a good guy. I can't believe that he'd go around killing people without good reason.'

'Then how do you explain this?'

'I don't know.' He looks troubled. 'Maybe Benedict's acting alone. After all, he's the common element. But honestly, when you take a look at the kind of guys who are going missing... Is it such a big loss? Aren't they doing the world a favour? Now that you've spoken to Alicia Tresor, now that you've seen the sick shit in Grant's notebook, wouldn't you have wanted him dead too?'

'Look,' I said, rolling my chair over to his desk. 'I'm not saying that David Grant didn't deserve to die. I think we all know what kind of man he was.'

Cam nods, at least partly placated.

'But the way they're doing this, Cam. It's shady. I don't think they're doing it out of some kind of moral imperative. I think they're doing it for the money. The only reason they're targeting men like Grant is that they're the perfect victims. They're greedy men. They want what isn't theirs and they're prepared to do whatever it takes to get it. If you had to find a group of people to gather a large amount of money together as quickly as possible, aren't they exactly the kind of lackeys you'd pick to get it for you? They embezzle and clean out their accounts, then when they disappear, there's an easy explanation: they ran off with a mistress. They're the type for it, anyway.'

'But money for what?' says Cam. 'If they're collecting this huge fortune, then where has it gone?'

Which is precisely the problem: I don't know. We can't exactly requisition the Invicti's bank records. For now, all of the cash seems to have evaporated into thin air, including David Grant's.

I think hard.

'There's only one place in this entire case where we've found more money than we were expecting, rather than less.'

'Yeah?' Cam says. 'Where?'

'The accounts of the companies Grant was using to skim the funds he embezzled. The ones with the suspicious names. You know, Solis Invicti Holdings and the others. The deputy was expecting them to be dummy companies, wasn't he? No cash. But they weren't.'

'You think that's where it all went?' he asks. 'You think the Invicti are collecting the buy-in money through those companies?'

'Right now, it's as good a theory as any.'

And there's absolutely nothing we can do to follow up on it. Boyd has already mined the financial records for all they're worth, but whoever is really running those companies is covering their tracks well.

For now, all we can do is go back to the surveillance videos.

30

I'M HALFWAY THROUGH watching my current video file when my computer screen flickers and goes black.

'What the–'

'Problem?' Cam asks.

'Fucking desktop died.'

I press the power button several times. Nothing. I try holding it down. Still nothing. Eventually, I crawl under the desk to check the power cable and find that it's been thoroughly nibbled. I don't want to contemplate what variety of creatures we might be sharing this office with, but the messy, rotten hole in the skirting board gives me a pretty good idea which one caused this disaster.

'Rats,' I say with a shudder.

'You're kidding,' says Cam.

I hold up the mangled cord. 'Nope.'

'Gotta go,' he says, jumping up and grabbing his coat from the back of his chair. 'I just remembered I have a thing to do.'

'Hey! It's just a couple of rats. You must have had loads when you were living in London back in the day. Weren't those houses infested with the things?'

'Yes, they were, and I didn't like them then either. Do you know how many diseases they carry?'

'We've got antibiotics these days, you know. It's not the Black Death. And anyway, you're Silver. You're not going to catch anything.'

He stares at me for a moment. 'The Black Death was in the fourteenth century. Exactly how old do you think I am?'

'Old enough to know better.'

'I do. That's why I'm leaving. Bye.'

He heads for the door.

'Go on then, you coward,' I say. 'I'll call maintenance. I'll fix the computer. I'll do everything around here, as usual.'

'I'm not going to dignify that with a response. But if you like, I'll bring you back a latte and a salted caramel brownie.'

I stick out my hand. 'Deal.'

Angie from maintenance is beyond excited when she gets to our office. She's a pleasant woman in her forties with thick brown hair that she keeps trimmed short. She has no idea that she works for a college full of immortal vampires, but then she doesn't pay attention to much that happens around here unless it needs fixing. I've rarely met anyone who takes such delight in their work, and I know the guy who owns the local ice-cream chain.

'I've been wanting to catch these little buggers for months,' she says. 'I keep hearing them in the walls, taunting me. So here's the plan: I'll put down some traps, then we'll all go away and wait for them to come out and get squished.'

I grimace at her glee. 'And how long is that going to take?'

'A few hours,' she says. 'Maybe a few days. A week at most.'

'No. Definitely not.'

'Jack, I'm not sure you understand: these rats are my nemeses.'

'And I'm not sure you understand, Angie: I can't work like this. I'm in the middle of some research that can't wait and I need my office back, rodent-free. Can't you just plug the hole and replace the skirting board so I can get back to work?'

With a little grumbling, Angie eventually agrees. I leave her to it while I go to search out a new power cord. I've got my head stuffed into a box of assorted wires in our stationery storeroom when the door slams shut behind me. When I look over my shoulder to work out what's happened, I see that I'm no longer alone.

'Hello, Jack,' Benedict says.

I straighten up quickly. 'Tertius.'

'Oh, call me Ben.'

He leans back against the closed door, giving the impression that this is just a casual conversation. That might have worked, except he's blocking the only exit, he's the size of a house and, now that I look at it closely, I can see that he's locked the door behind us. I didn't even realise it had a key.

'I thought it was time for us to have a little chat,' he says.

'Oh?'

'Yes. Have you ever thought about joining the Solis Invicti?' he asks. A coy smile plays around the corners of his mouth. 'You must have. Don't all the Seekers? It's the dream, am I right?'

'I like what I do,' I say warily.

'And you're good at it, from what I hear. For the most part. Tenacious, they say. Determined. Stubborn.' He says that last one as though it's not a compliment at all. 'You have potential.'

I don't know how to reply, because I have no idea what this is. If he were genuinely looking to recruit me, why would we be having this conversation in a storeroom? Why the secrecy? I can only conclude that this is either a bribe or a threat, and I'm not interested in either.

'I'm not sure I'm ready for the Invicti,' I say eventually.

'You surprise me,' he says with a laugh. 'You give the impression that you're ready for anything, but then you might be right. You still have a lot to learn about the Silver. How old are you now? Twenty? Thirty?'

'Eighteen years human, twenty years Silver.'

'Ah, so young. That explains it. You still have some growing to do.' He rests one hand back on the door and taps his fingers against it. 'But after a decade or so of training under my tutelage, you might come good.'

Ten years in the proximity of this monster? I can't think of anything worse. I never had any intention of leaving Oxford to join the Solis Invicti, but now I'm even more resolved. His tone is so grating, so condescending, as though he assumes I can think of no greater honour than being offered his patronage. It makes me angry, which makes me want to provoke him. I have a powerful need to wipe the sly smile off his face.

'I saw you, you know,' I say, my tone casual. 'At Windsor's party.'

There's a fraction of a second, a fraction so short that I would have missed it if I wasn't Silver, when I see his smile slip. The expression underneath is ugly.

'Did you, now?' he says. 'You know, I'd never have believed the Baron was shacking up with you if I hadn't seen you together that night. Everyone remarked on how besotted you seemed with him. I hope you didn't take it too hard when he ditched you so quickly. But then, you can't have expected him to hang around for long.'

'I was the one who ditched him, actually,' I say, pretending nonchalance.

Benedict's mouth twitches into a smile, and too late I realise that I shouldn't have engaged with the comment at all. He knows now that his barb has struck its mark.

'Well,' he says, 'for me, the party was more business than pleasure.'

'Really?' I ask. 'Were you not just seeing old friends?' The subtext hangs in the silence after my words: *Friends like Matthew Felton.*

He smiles indulgently. 'We don't all have as much leisure time as you do, Jack. The Solis Invicti are spoken for every moment of every day. That's how we work. Whatever we do, we do for the Primus. You can take my word for that.'

There's almost a threat there. I won't let it stand.

'Well, that's not how the Seekers work,' I say. 'I don't take people's word for anything. I follow the evidence.'

He laughs, his voice a low chuckle that creeps its way up my spine.

'Of course you do. It's sweet, really. Naïve. It's almost charming, how you think you can ignore our history and our hierarchy, all in pursuit of your version of the truth, a version that has no relevance at all. I'm sure the Invicti could find a suitable position for a determined young Seeker who likes to "follow the evidence". In fact, I think I know exactly what I'd do with you.'

This time, it's definitely a threat. His jaw is clenched and I can see his fingernails digging into the wood of the door.

'I'm happy where I am, thank you,' I say curtly. I'm trying not to let him see my fear, but it's pointless to pretend; he'll be able to smell it all over me.

He smiles, a genuine smile now, as though he's flicked a switch behind his eyes to bring out the sunshine. If someone walked in without having heard the rest of our conversation, they'd think he was truly being friendly.

'It's good to know where you stand,' he says. 'I'll bear it in mind. But do consider the Solis Invicti. The benefits of being on our team are significant, especially when compared with the alternative. Think about it.'

'I will,' I say with a dry mouth.

He unlocks the door then and slips out into the corridor, walking so lightly that he's practically dancing.

I'm letting out a relieved breath when he pokes his head back around the door and startles me.

'Just watch where you go digging, won't you, Jack?' he says. 'You never know what you might disturb.'

Then he's gone for good. I wait a full minute before moving, counting his footsteps away along the corridor, just to make sure.

I'm still shaking when Cam gets back to the office with my coffee. Angie is long gone, having effected a quick fix to block the rat hole, and I've replaced my power cable, but I can't concentrate on the videos on my screen. My mind keeps flashing back to the closeness of the storeroom and the scent of violence on Benedict's skin.

What is wrong with me?

I can climb a fifty-storey building without being scared of the height. I can throw myself into a gunfight without worrying that I might not come out alive. I can even go toe-to-toe with Drake every day of the week and still not feel the least bit frightened.

And yet.

Something about the Tertius makes me want to crush myself into a ball and disappear. The truth is that, for all my fighting words about the Invicti, he terrifies me.

'Are you all right?' Cam asks as he hands over my drink and brownie. Then he picks up on my fear – he must be able to scent it as clearly as Benedict could – and looks around the room in a panic. 'The rat's gone, right? Please tell me the rat's gone.'

'It's gone. Angie blocked the hole and she'll replace the skirting board overnight. There's nothing to worry about.'

'If that's true, then why are you worried?'

I take a deep breath, trying to calm myself.

'Benedict cornered me in the storeroom,' I whisper.

Cam glances out into the corridor, then asks, 'What did he say?'

'He asked me if I wanted to join the Solis Invicti.'

Cam's mouth drops open.

'No,' I go on, 'not like that. It wasn't an invitation. It was more like, *Are you with us, or do I have to kill you*?'

'Shit.'

'Shit, indeed.'

'Okay,' Cam says after a moment, 'so what are we going to do about it?'

'Erm, nothing? What are you suggesting we do about it?'

He opens his mouth, then closes it. Then he opens it again and lifts a finger into the air, before slumping back into his chair without saying a word. Eventually, he says, 'We could tell the captain.'

'Yeah, right. I'll tell her that the Tertius offered me a job. I'm sure she'll take that as a serious threat, just like she did when I told her Benedict was at Windsor's party holding an illicit Casting ceremony.'

'Okay, then how about...' He trails off.

'How about what?'

'I'm thinking,' he says eventually. 'Just eat your brownie, will you?'

It takes another half hour before my hands stop shaking, and in that time we still haven't come up with a solution. All we can do is keep investigating the case and hope we come across something that will help.

The problem is that I can barely concentrate on my work. I've watched the same half-hour of video three times now, because I keep having to rewind it when I realise I've allowed my mind to drift off and my eyes to glaze over. Eventually, I sigh and load the next video. If there was anything interesting on the previous one, I'm sure it would have pulled me out of my reverie.

Maybe.

Who cares, anyway? We're not going to find the answers to our questions on these videos. The answers we want are locked up inside Benedict's head where we'll never get to them.

But, I realise, that's not the only place we could find them.

'What do you think would happen if we went to question Felton again?' I ask Cam.

'That depends,' he replies, leaning around his screen to meet my eye. 'Were you planning on going with fire this time, or without?'

'I could go either way.'

'As usual,' he says. 'Badum-tish.' He even does the dorky drums mime.

'You have a puerile mind, Cameron Sawyer. But seriously, do you think it's worth a shot?'

'Okay,' he says, leaning over his desk, 'let me ask you a question. Do you want to go and question Felton because you think you might be able to extract valuable information from him, or do you just want to poke the bear because Benedict frightens you?'

'Huh?' I'm not following him.

'I mean, it's like prodding a bad tooth, isn't it? Much as I love you, Jack, you're self-destructive. If something scares you, your first instinct is to run right at it without thinking so you can get the scary part out of the way. I'm just suggesting that maybe that's what you're trying to do here. Maybe you only want to go and question Felton because you want to provoke Benedict into doing his worst.'

I think about it for a moment.

'You might be right–' I say eventually.

'Good.'

'–but I still want to do it.'

Cam thunks his forehead against the desk.

'Fine,' he says, looking up at me. 'But I'm bringing him in. You're staying here and staying away from the Tertius.'

'Guide's promise,' I say, holding up my right hand.

'If you were a girl guide,' he says, 'then I was a jolly London chimney sweep with an Australian accent. Swear on something you actually believe in. Like gin. Swear on gin.'

I duly swear and, true to his word, Cam goes off to collect our suspect.

31

CAM USHERS FELTON into the meeting room with a waft of cigarette smoke and chemicals.

'Oh, no,' Felton says when he sees me sitting at the table.

'Hello, Matthew,' I smile at him sweetly. At least, I try to, but it's possible that my smile has a few too many teeth in it to be described as sweet. There's only so much sugar I can muster up for a pervert like Felton.

'I'm not talking to her,' he says, trying to back out of the room. 'No way in hell.'

'Mr Felton,' Cam says, 'there's a camera in this room.' He points to the black dot in the ceiling. 'Nothing is going to happen to you as long as you're here.'

'Of course we can't make any promises for after you've left–'

'Jack, you're not helping. Mr Felton, please, sit down.'

He does so eventually, eyeing me warily all the time.

'You know I don't have to be here?' he says to Cam. 'I'm here as a favour, to help with your enquiries, like the human police say. It's like I told her last time,' he points at me with a stabbing gesture, 'I've done nothing wrong.'

'I think we have different definitions of the word "wrong",' I say.

'Fine, then I've done nothing illegal.'

'I think we have different definitions of the word–'

'I didn't break Silver law!' Felton yells, exasperated. 'Everything I do is cool with the Primus – hell, sometimes he even uses my services – so who gives a fuck?'

'Mr Felton–' Cam says.

'Do you know how much blood I had to drink to heal those burns?' Felton says to me. 'You and your crazy friend nearly fried me. The doc said if the fire had been any hotter, I would have been charcoal. It would've taken months for me to come back – months! – if I managed it at all.'

'Next time I'll bring petrol,' I say dismissively, as though I'm not utterly serious.

'Mr Felton,' Cam says, raising his voice. 'We didn't ask you here to talk about your blood-drinking habits.'

'Nothing wrong with them,' he mumbles.

'We asked you here to talk about the murder of David Grant.'

'I told the Invicti where I was,' Felton says, on the defensive again. 'You know I couldn't have done those London murders. I didn't kill the man. I barely even knew him.'

'But you'd seen him around?' Cam asks. 'Maybe at one of Sir Percival's parties?'

'Why aren't you asking her?' Felton gestures at me with his thumb. 'She's the one who loves crashing them.'

'I was invited, thank you very much,' I say indignantly.

'Because you're boning the Baron. I guess his tastes aren't as refined as he likes to think they are.'

I'm about to lunge for Felton, but Cam jumps up from his seat and puts a hand on each of our chests, pushing us back down.

'Oh-kay,' he says. 'Let's all just calm down, shall we? Jack, why don't you move over there–' He points to a chair in the corner. '–and let me ask the questions from now on.'

We have a brief, silent exchange, but I do as he asks. After all, it's clear that I'm not going to be the one who gets Felton to talk.

'Okay, then,' Cam says, settling back into his seat. 'Mr Felton. Tell us about David Grant.'

Felton shrugs. 'He was just a guy. One of the humans that sometimes turned up to Percy's gatherings.'

'And he knew about the existence of the Silver?'

Felton gives Cam a sly look. 'Is that what this is about?' he asks. 'You think I've been going around telling people that vampires are fucking real?' He laughs as though this is the funniest thing he's ever heard.

'Everyone in Aston seemed pretty relaxed about it,' I say from my corner. 'In fact, they seemed to think there was some kind of selection process going on, that humans were able to buy their way into turning Silver.'

'Is that what you think?' He chuckles. 'Well, I guess you can just go on thinking that if you want, but you'd be wrong.'

'I was there, Felton. I saw it all.'

'Then what are you going to do about it?'

He's got me there. He knows as well as I do that there's precisely nothing to be done. My irritation is building, but Cam jumps in before I can do anything ill-advised.

'About David Grant,' he says. 'What did you know about him?'

'He was all right,' Felton says, turning to look at Cam. 'We had some things in common.'

'I bet you did,' I mutter under my breath, but Felton carries on as though I haven't spoken.

'I met him a few times, through a mutual friend.' Felton smirks at me, and I know exactly who he's talking about. Interesting that Benedict made the introductions, rather than the other way around. 'I didn't have any business with Grant, but we knew each other well enough to say hi. That's about it.'

'And who *do* you have business with?' Cam asks.

'No one, these days,' Felton huffs. 'You guys took away all my equipment.'

'You can take that up with the captain when we're done here. What exactly is the nature of your business, Mr Felton?'

He shifts in his seat. 'I provide products to certain associates of mine.'

'What kind of products?'

'Products they might not be able to make on their own.'

'Do you mean drugs?' Cam says wearily. 'We're not working with the police on this, Mr Felton. We're the Seekers. We don't care about the drugs.'

'Then why are you asking about them?' Felton yells, suddenly aggressive.

Yup, it's about the drugs all right.

'We're trying to work out if other people might have used your drugs to incapacitate Mr Grant. That's all.'

'What is this shit?' Felton's glance is darting between me and Cam at light speed. He's definitely on something right now. 'I told her. I told her – just before she tried to burn down my house with me in it, by the way – that I don't use roofies. Who uses roofies anymore? There's more market for chloroform than for fucking roofies.'

'So if we went and searched your place right now,' Cam says, 'you're saying we wouldn't find any rohypnol. None at all.'

'Well, no, I mean, yeah, I've got some. I mean, I have it, but no one uses it. Why would they? The stuff is crap and it tastes like crap. I told her that. I told her it tastes like crap.'

Felton's face is turning a strange, shiny red. It's fascinating because the Silver don't usually suffer from flushing sweats under any circumstances. We can blush, but we don't usually have the blood to spare for this kind of firework display. Either Felton's been drinking a ridiculous amount of blood or he's using himself as a guinea pig for his own pharmaceuticals.

I'm about to ask about Felton's other concoctions and the people who buy them, but then the door to the meeting room opens abruptly and Benedict walks in. He doesn't look happy.

'What's this about, Mr Sawyer?' he asks, but he's looking at me.

'They just dragged me in here, Ben,' says Felton. 'Started implying I had something to do with a load of humans finding out about the Silver–'

'Shut up, Matthew,' he interrupts. 'My god, you look like shit. Get out of here and go clean yourself up.'

'But I need to get my things back from–'

'Leave!' Benedict says, looking at Felton so fiercely that for a moment I think his shirt is going to start smoking under the glare.

When Felton has scurried out, Benedict turns to Cam.

'I believe there's surveillance footage for you to be working on, Mr Sawyer.' It sounds like a dismissal.

'Er, yes,' Cam says. He gives me a worried look, but at my nod he leaves the room.

Then it's just me and Benedict. He leans against the wall and crosses his sizeable arms over his chest.

'You're not very good at taking a hint, are you, Jack?'

I will my hands not to start shaking again.

'I don't know what you're talking about,' I say, playing the innocent because I know there's a camera in this room. If I can just get him to admit to something, anything…

But just as the thought crystallises in my mind, his eyes flick up to the lens in the ceiling. He smiles at me. He's no fool.

'I'm sorry if I didn't make myself clear when we spoke earlier,' he says, his tone conciliatory. He's playing it for the audience. 'Here's my advice: you can't focus all your efforts on one individual when there isn't a shred of evidence to back up your accusations against them. It just looks like bias, or worse, harassment. That won't make you very popular. Do you understand, Jack?'

I don't say anything, because I can hear the subtext of his words and inside I'm seething with frustration. He knows I'm going after the Solis Invicti, he knows that's what this interview was about, and he's going to chase me every step of the way.

Our battle lines have been drawn.

'You need to be careful,' he says in an avuncular tone that makes my skin crawl. 'I'd hate for you to throw away such a promising future.'

'What do you mean?' I say. It's a weak effort to get him to say something incriminating, but it's all I can think of in the pressure of the moment.

He just smiles and says, 'Don't worry, Jack. Next time I'll be sure that I make myself crystal clear. Now, don't you have work to do?'

'Shit,' I say as I close the door of the office behind me. My heart is pounding in my chest. By Silver standards, anyway.

'Are you okay?' Cam asks, getting up from his chair. 'What did he say?'

'Oh, you know, thinly-veiled threats and intimidation. The usual.' I laugh shakily.

'This is my fault. I never should have brought Felton in.'

'Stop that,' I say. I nudge him back down into his seat then take my own chair. 'Who asked you to fetch him? I practically bullied you into it.'

'So much for staying away from the Tertius,' he says.

Cam is about as angry as he gets right now, but I know his anger isn't directed at me. He's scared of what Benedict might do.

'He didn't hurt me,' I say.

'Yet.'

'Cam, I'm fine.'

But I'm not, not really. I'm scared and conflicted and I have no idea what to do next. At this point, I'm ninety-nine percent certain that Benedict was behind Grant's death, but even if I can prove it, there's no point. It seems like the more I chase the truth, the more shit I'm bringing down on me and my team from the Solis Invicti.

The whole thing is futile.

'I hate this case,' I say.

'Preach.'

But there's nothing else for us to do, so we both turn back to our computers.

'How much video have you got left to watch?' I ask.

'Erm…' Cam clicks his mouse a few times. 'About three hours.'

I groan. 'How are you getting through it so fast?'

'Because I'm actually doing my work,' he says, his eyes fixed on the screen now, 'instead of spending half my time antagonising the Invicti and the other half complaining.'

'Fine,' I say, bringing up the remaining files on my own screen. 'I'll get on with it. But I want you to know that I hate you.'

He smiles. 'I know, sweetie. I hate you too.'

We're trying to pretend otherwise, but we're both still rattled. It takes me a while to settle down, but soon my eyes are glazing over while I watch the screen.

I stifle a yawn and fish through my desk drawer to see if I've got any chocolate stashed in there, but I come up empty. I always do. I'm not sure what deluded part of my brain thinks that I would ever buy chocolate without eating it instantly. It's not as though I understand the concept of impulse control.

I turn back to my monitor. I've left it running for a good minute or so while I wasn't watching, so I only catch the tail end of a figure walking offscreen, but something about it makes me stop and rewind.

I watch the section through from the beginning.

When I'm done, I flip it back thirty seconds and watch it again. And again. Only when I'm a hundred percent sure do I turn to Cam and say, 'Look.'

'What?' he asks, absent-mindedly chewing on the end of his pen.

'Come here and look.'

He gets up from his chair and comes around my desk to look over my shoulder. I press play.

There, on the monitor, a figure comes into view. He walks towards the lockers wearing long tracksuit bottoms and a sweatshirt that looks as though it hasn't seen daylight since the nineties. When he reaches the locker next to Grant's, he stands in front of the combination lock, blocking the movement of his hands from the camera. A few seconds later he swings the locker door open and reaches deep inside it, so deep that his head and shoulders disappear into the steel casing. After a bit of rooting around, he emerges with a black duffle bag, clicks the combination lock back in place, then starts to walk away. As he turns, the camera finally gets a clear look at his face.

It's Iain Halberd.

'Well, that's unexpected,' says Cam.

'Tell me about it.'

'You think he got into Grant's locker somehow?'

'If anyone could, it would be him. He's handy, right?'

'He certainly seemed that way when we visited the theatre. But let's not jump to conclusions. It could be perfectly innocent.'

'Really? What other reason could he have for going to that leisure centre?'

We check the rest of the camera angles we have around that time and confirm our suspicions: Halberd never used the gym, he just walked to the lockers, collected the bag and walked back out.

'One of us needs to go and speak to him,' Cam says.

'I'll do it,' I volunteer. I know where he'll be and I really need to get out of the office. Benedict will be in the conference room, which he's set up as his own office, and I can almost feel the menace seeping through the walls. The sooner I can get out of his way, the better.

'You go tell the others,' I say. 'I won't be long.'

I throw on my jacket.

'What are you expecting to find?' Cam asks as I make for the door.

'I don't know. He can't be the killer, because he's not Silver.'

'No.'

'But if he's in a relationship with Alicia Tresor, then he has one hell of a motive.'

32

WHEN I WALK out of the college, Drake is waiting in the lodge.

'What are you doing here?' I ask, brushing past him on my way out.

He follows. His posture is loose, hands in his pockets, but there's visible tension in his shoulders. He is not as calm as he's pretending to be.

'You didn't reply to my messages,' he says.

'I blocked your number.'

'Then I'll have to get another.' He says it like a joke, but it sounds like a threat.

'I'll block that one, too.'

'Valentine, wait.' He grabs me by the arm, pulling me to a stop. 'Will you not even talk to me?'

'I don't see that we've got much to say to each other.'

He looks away for a moment, exasperated.

'Are we back to this, already?' he says. 'You're just going to carry on as though nothing happened? You can't ignore this thing between us.'

He's right, but not in the way he thinks. I still feel the same, still feel every thread of desire that's pulling me towards him, but the sensation doesn't surprise me. I'm expecting the scent of his skin to make me want to draw him close, in the same way that I expect my body to incline towards his, but because I'm expecting it, I can control it.

Cam was right again: ignoring my feelings did no good, but acknowledging them lets me choose not to act on them.

But with Drake's hand wrapped around my arm, his face inches from mine, so close I can scent his skin, it's hard. I'm not one to deny myself, so pushing him away is possibly the hardest thing I've done in my life.

But I do it anyway.

'I'm not ignoring it,' I say, removing his hand from my arm finger by finger. 'I've acknowledged it, I've examined it, and I've decided I don't want it. So I'm making an effort to avoid getting into situations where it might become an issue. Situations like this one.'

'Avoid, ignore, it doesn't matter what word you use. It's not going to just go away.'

'Yes, it is. It'll fade over time. Everything does.'

He laughs. It is not a mirthful sound. It cracks and splinters. 'You'd think so, wouldn't you? But as it turns out, you're wrong. Let me ask you this: how do you feel about Winta these days?'

The words hit me like a punch in the gut.

'Any closer to getting over her, are you?' he says. The words are spiteful.

This isn't like him. Yes, I've always thought he was a bastard and yes, I may have called him evil on occasion, but he isn't really. Not like this. Whatever else Killian Drake has been to me, he has always been measured and in control. But this... He is not himself tonight.

'This isn't about Winta,' I say, walking away from him. 'I've made my decision. I'm not going to change my mind. I don't *want* you, Drake.'

'Don't you?'

He grabs me again, his fingers clamping around my wrist.

'Let go of me.' I squirm, but I can't get free. He won't let go.

He drags me into a nearby alley that is less an actual alley than it is a crack between the buildings on either side of it. It's only four feet across and when he slams me up against one of its walls, his body seems to take up the rest of the space.

I'm expecting something like this from Benedict, or even from Felton, but not from Drake. I never would have pegged him for that type of predator. He takes me by surprise.

Here's the problem: yes, I'm superhuman, yes, I'm combat-trained, and yes, I can take down most other Silver without breaking a sweat. But Drake isn't *most other Silver*. He's trained too, he's older than me, and he's stronger too. I might be quicker, but I wasn't expecting him to come at me and now that he has both of my wrists pinned up over my head in a single hand, I am royally fucked. All I can do is kick at him, which he knows, so he traps my legs with his own, and now that's off the cards too.

'That's not how it works,' he whispers, leaning in. 'You don't just move on without finishing what you've started.'

The fear hits me in the bottom of my gut. Drake might normally be dangerous in his own way, but I've never thought he would actually hurt me, not until right now. There's something determined in his eyes as he stares at me, his irises so dark in the shadows that I can't distinguish them from his pupils. It makes him seem even more inhuman than I know he is.

And yet.

Beneath the fear, beneath my body's desperation to get away from him and hide somewhere safe, there is a part of me that thrills at the way his scent surrounds me. A primal part of me still wants this, and I hate it.

'What are you doing, Drake?' I say.

'That's not what you called me on Wednesday.' His free hand is at my face now, coaxing strands of my hair loose from its ponytail. He looks at each one in turn as though it fascinates him, before dropping it to select another. 'I thought we were past that. I thought you'd accepted the inevitable.'

His fingers trail down my neck, following the loose hair down to my throat.

'Stop fighting, Valentine.'

I do exactly the opposite, lunging away from the wall as I make a futile attempt to break free. In response, he backhands me across the face, snapping my head against the wall. I might be able to take more of a beating than a human can, but he can deal superhuman damage. If he hits me that hard again then I might pass out.

'You can't fight it,' he says, leaning in.

'What is wrong with you?' I spit out. My mouth is full of blood.

'You're in denial.'

I'm seeing stars.

I meet his eyes in a last, desperate effort to get through to him.

'Killian…'

He flashes his silver, his eyes suddenly dilating, as though something has snapped in his brain. He jerks away, dropping his hands as he backs up against the opposite wall.

'The blood,' he says.

He wipes his forehead and I realise that he's sweating.

'What?' I ask, rubbing at the bruises rising on my neck. He doesn't look well.

'The blood. I drank your blood. I'd heard...'

He stops, cocking his head as he looks off into the distance. I hear it a fraction of a second after he does: a soft buzzing sound, like the brushing of fabric against fabric, or the beating of a moth's wings. He steps in front of me, moving so quickly that his movement strobes, then the noise stops in a soft thunk. There's a dart with a glass vial attached to it sticking out of the side of his neck. If he hadn't moved when he did, it would have ended up in my chest.

'Drake?'

He staggers a little, putting one hand against the passage wall to prop himself up while the other pulls the dart from his neck. Then he's falling, spinning as he goes down to the ground, so insensible that his face smashes right into the cobbles.

For a moment, I just look at him. I'm half tempted to leave him where he is and make my escape, but he did just take a bullet for me, of sorts. I pick up the dart and slip it into my pocket.

He doesn't even bat an eyelid when I prod him with my foot.

'Shit.'

I crouch at his side, then slap his face to try to bring him round. At least, that's the reason I give myself. After what he just put me through, it's payback. Maybe I slap him a few times more than is strictly necessary, but who's going to know?

He has a pulse, but it's slow.

When I hear the buzzing sound again, I realise I made a basic error in assuming that there would only be one dart. I manage to dodge the second, which tinkles somewhere in the alley behind me, then scoop Drake up into my arms. Thankfully, we're not far from the college. I sling his unconscious body over my shoulder and run for sick bay.

The nurse is on duty, but other than helping me get Drake into the bed and taking some basic vitals, he has no idea how to help him, or if he's going to be okay. In fact, he looks terrified to be treating him at all.

'I'm going to call the duty doctor,' he says, reaching for the phone.

'Confidentially,' I remind him. The last thing we need is word getting around that the Baron of Oxford is incapacitated.

Cam strides into the room while the nurse is on the phone.

'I thought I saw you come back in. Christ, Jack, what did you do to him?'

'It wasn't me. It was this,' I say, holding up the dart.

'Someone shot him?'

'Seems that way. Can you take this to Ed? We need someone to analyse whatever the hell it is and tell us what we're dealing with.'

He clears his throat uncomfortably, but he takes the dart.

'I'd better wake up the captain too,' he says. 'I'll be back as soon as I can.'

'Thanks.'

As I turn back to the bed, my hair shifts around my face and Cam sees the bruises Drake's hand left on my cheek. They haven't had time to heal yet. He stops dead.

'He did that to you?' Cam says, his voice dangerously quiet.

'He wasn't himself.'

'Yeah, sure.'

'Seriously, he wasn't himself. I don't know what got into him tonight, but he wasn't well, even before the dart.' I'm starting to panic, because Cam is as loyal as they come and I know he won't let this go, but I can hear Drake's pulse slowing with every second Cam stands there, not taking the dart to Ed.

I don't want Drake to die.

I can't let him die.

'Please,' I say to Cam. 'I need him to survive this.'

'All right. I'm going,' he points a finger at me, 'but we're talking about this later.'

When the doctor arrives, I have to stifle a groan.

It's Tabitha. Of course it is.

She looks between me and Drake's unconscious body for a moment, then snaps on her gloves and gets to work.

'What have we got?' she asks the nurse.

'He was shot with some kind of dart. They're testing it now.' The nurse pushes back the collar of Drake's shirt to show the puncture wound to Tabitha. When I first brought him in here it was barely visible, but now it looks black and angry.

'Fuck,' I mutter. 'What is it?'

'Some kind of poison, I'd guess,' Tabitha says, pulling a pencil from her hair to prod at the surrounding flesh. It looks rock hard. 'Maybe a new drug. Something synthetic.'

'There's a drug that can take down the Silver?'

'Not one I've ever heard of,' Tabitha says, 'but apparently, yes. Unless it was reacting with something already in his system. You were there when it happened?'

The question isn't loaded, because this is Tabitha in her efficient professional mode, but it feels awkward nonetheless.

'We were outside the college, just at the end of the street.'

'What was he like before it happened?' I can feel her eyes on the bruises around my neck. They must be fading by now, but they tell a story all on their own.

'He was acting strange.'

'Strange how?' she asks as she opens his eyes one by one and shines a torch across them.

'Aggressive.' I swallow. 'Demanding.'

The professional front slips a little. 'You're all right, hen?' she says softly, her gaze flicking to my cheek.

'I'm fine. Honestly.' But I'm not. I feel as though I'm coming apart at the seams and I don't know whether it's because Drake attacked me, or because he's in danger, or because Tabitha's here and I really don't want to tell her the thing I need to say next. We agreed that we would put all of this behind us and start fresh and I want to do that so much, but...

'Jack?'

'He said something, right before it happened.' The words are a whispered confession. 'I asked him what was wrong, and he said it was the blood.'

'The blood?'

I take a deep breath and let it out in a rush. 'He drank my blood.'

'He bit you?' She looks at my neck, searching for the wound.

'No, Tabitha. I mean... not tonight.'

I can almost see the shutters slamming down behind her eyes.

'Oh,' she says, and it's the *Oh* that I hate, the one that deflates her like a leaking balloon. 'You mean Wednesday.'

'Yes. Wednesday.'

Wednesday. The day I fucked everything up. The day when I betrayed Tabitha and let Drake bite me, which might be the cause of whatever's happening to him now. If I could rip Wednesday into pieces, scrunch it into a ball and set it on fire, then I would.

'Well,' Tabitha says, gathering herself together on a breath, 'I suppose Silver blood might have an effect. We can work that out once we know what was in the vial. I'll bear it in mind.'

She turns back to her patient and I know I'm being dismissed, but I can't just leave, so I hang around in the anteroom instead.

When Drake is finally stable, Tabitha leaves to join Ed in the lab and I move to Drake's bedside. For the first half hour I just sit there, watching and listening as the machines beep. There are several strapped to his body, machines the Silver don't normally need, but I guess these aren't normal circumstances. In amongst the wires, he looks almost human.

I remember the scent of Drake's skin, obscured now by the clinical odour of detergent. I remember the whistle of the dart through the air. I remember him stepping in front of me and I don't understand at all.

'What the hell were you doing?' I murmur to his unconscious body.

Unsurprisingly, he doesn't respond. Surprisingly, his continued silence makes me angry. Maybe it's just that the whole situation makes me feel tired and helpless, but now that I've started, I find I can't stop.

'You should have run. Or you could have just pushed me out of the way. You didn't have to take it in the neck like some kind of fucking hero. You're not a hero, Drake, that's clear enough, so why the fuck would you even pretend?'

I'm on my feet now, pacing around the bed without realising it. I drop back down into the chair and take his hand in mine. His skin is so cold.

'I don't know, Killian,' I whisper. 'It's all just pretend.'

'Jack?'

I drop Drake's hand like it's electric and look up to see Cam poking his head around the door.

'We got the results,' he says.

When I hurry back out into the anteroom, Ed is waiting there with Tabitha.

'There won't be any change tonight,' she says to me, 'but he'll be fine.'

I nod mutely.

'I promise you,' she says, taking my hand in hers. 'When you wake up tomorrow, he'll be back to his old self again.'

'That's a shame,' I reply.

I'm trying to joke like I would normally, but no one's buying it. They're all looking at me with sympathy, as though Drake means more to me than he does, than he should. I want to tell them that they're wrong, that he's just a pain in my arse – that he just attacked me, for fuck's sake – but right now I can't find the words.

'I need to switch out his drip,' Tabitha says, hurrying back into Drake's room.

'Did you see this?' Cam whispers to me once she's out of earshot.

He pulls the dart out of his pocket and tips it up to the light. The markings are faint, but when he holds it at just the right angle I can see what he wants me to see: the logo of the Solis Invicti, engraved into the glass.

'New weaponry?' I ask.

'That's what I'm thinking. Ed?'

'It's something new, all right,' he says. 'The drug was complicated, but there were some common components I recognise from other tests I've run recently. It's so distinctive that it's practically a signature.'

He doesn't have to say the name out loud, because I'm already thinking it. There's only one Silver I know who likes messing around with sedatives and whose products have been in Ed's lab recently.

'Shit,' I say.

'This was a warning, wasn't it?' Cam says. 'That dart was meant for you, Jack.'

There's only one conclusion I can reach: Benedict wants me to stay away from Felton, and he's willing to make the Baron of Oxford collateral damage to get the job done.

33

I CAN'T SLEEP, so I sneak back down to sick bay in the early hours of the morning. Tabitha has gone for the night, and the nurse has been replaced by someone else, but Drake seems to be improving. His hand is less cold, at least.

I sit down next to the bed and watch him breathe, slowly, in and out. In and out.

The next thing I know, I'm blinking awake with a crick in my neck and the warmth of someone else's skin against my cheek.

'Morning, Valentine.'

I jerk away from Drake's hand so sharply that I nearly fall out of my chair.

'Don't touch me,' I say, pointing a finger at him. 'Don't ever touch me.'

'Valentine, I–'

He's interrupted by a noise from the anteroom.

I hurry out, not wanting to be caught in Drake's room, but Tabitha is already waiting by the nurse's station.

I stop dead.

'I was just–'

'You were worried,' she says, 'I know. It's okay, Jack. You don't have to explain. You're allowed to care.'

'I don't care.'

She gives me a look.

'Okay, I care a bit, but about last night: I was trying to avoid him. I don't want to see him. I've made my choice.'

She looks away. 'You talk about it as though the choice is yours.'

'Isn't it?'

'He's the Baron, Jack,' she says, hopelessly. 'If he tells me to leave you alone–'

'He won't.' I take her hands in mine, trying to reassure her. 'You're only worried because you think he cares about me, but you're wrong. You saw what he did last night.'

She puts her hand to the side of my face, warm and comforting. The bruises have gone now, but the memory of last night is lingering unpleasantly.

'You could argue that what he did last night is the very definition of caring about you, hen,' she says. 'It might not be a healthy way to do it, but I don't think apathy inspires that kind of aggression. He's dangerous, Jack, and I don't mean just because of what happened. You don't say no to a man that powerful.'

'I bloody well do.'

'But I don't.' She takes her hand away. 'He knows that. He told me as much this morning, while you were still asleep. I'm not like you. I'm not a fighter.'

Her words make my stomach drop.

'What exactly did he say to you?'

'I've got to get back to my regular patients,' she says, shrugging out of her doctor's coat. 'You know, the dead ones.'

'Tabitha, what did he say to you?'

But she doesn't answer. She just turns away from me to collect her bag from the nurse's station. She's halfway out of the door when I catch her arm and draw her back.

'Tabs, please. Stop. Wait. Let me talk to him.'

She looks at me, and the look she gives me is so helpless that I drop her arm. I think she'll run, but she doesn't.

'You should know,' she says, lowering her voice to the slightest whisper. 'It's a form of psychosis.'

'What is?'

'The...' She pauses. When she speaks again, it's as though she's pulled on her Dr Ross persona. 'Silver blood can induce it in certain circumstances. It's why we don't encourage people to drink from each other. The Massacres are bad enough, but when you combine the blood with the emotional charge from a possessive scent mark, you get something completely different.' There's censure in her tone, but I can't blame her for it. After what I did on Wednesday, she has a right to be angry.

'I'm sorry,' I whisper.

She sighs. 'He's the Baron, Jack. If he thinks you're his, then what can I do about that? I can't make that decision. You likely can't make it either, but you need to know that what happened last night... He may not have been in control.' She takes a deep breath. 'If it was out of character, then you can put it down to the psychosis.'

I can tell that the words cost her. The last thing she wants is to be his defender. It's the last thing I want, too. I'm left wondering whether his behaviour really was out of character. I'm not so sure I didn't just see a glimpse of the real Drake.

'Are you going to forgive him?' she asks. Her voice is strained and small.

'Forgive him? He hit me. Which was not only painful, but also annoying, because I've wanted to slap him across the face him for years. If he were a gentleman then he would have let me go first.'

She looks at me incredulously.

'You're joking about this?'

'Of course I am. I joke about everything.'

She looks horrified.

'Tabitha, please. Just wait. Please. Promise me you'll wait.'

She looks at her watch then says, 'I can't.' Her voice is so quiet that I barely hear it. 'But call me.'

'Thank you,' I say. 'I will. As soon as I leave here.'

I've never felt relief like it in my life.

She leaves me behind with only Drake and the nurse for company.

I take a few moments to compose myself before storming back into his room.

'You didn't have to stay, Valentine,' he says from his sick bed. He's smirking. I wonder if he overheard my conversation with Tabitha.

'Apparently I did, because here I am. What the hell did you say to her?'

'Nothing she didn't know already.'

'What did you say, Drake?'

He looks at me for a long moment. 'You want her.'

'I do,' I say, more sure of it than ever. 'Are you going to get in my way?'

'Should I?'

I could scream.

'Why are you so infuriating?' I yell, pacing the room. 'I don't know why you think you have the right to dictate my choices, but you don't. I don't give a shit that you're the Baron. I don't give a shit what you want me to do. Just because I kissed you a couple of times when I was suffering from temporary, mark-induced insanity, that doesn't mean you own me.'

'That's exactly what the mark means, actually.'

I thought it wasn't possible for me to get any more angry. I was wrong.

'Don't you dare *actually* me! Am I wearing your mark now? No. Maybe you think you've earned my gratitude because you took that dart for me, but since you'd been beating me up a few moments earlier, I think those two things cancel each other out. Don't you? You have no claim to me, Killian, and you never will.'

'Valentine.'

I whirl on him. 'What?'

'I'm sorry,' he says. I have to double-take, because I'm not sure I've ever heard those words from his mouth before. 'For last night. Not for what I said to Tabitha, which was only the truth, after all. But I won't interfere.'

'You'd better not,' I say, dropping down into the chair at his bedside. 'You're an insufferable bastard. You know that?'

'So you say.'

His voice is cocky, but he won't meet my eye. That scares me more than he did last night, more than the thought of him dying, more even than the thought of losing Tabitha, because Killian Drake looks everyone in the eye. He's never humble, never submissive, and never ashamed.

Until now.

Tabitha promised me he would be back to his old self this morning. Well, she was wrong.

'They analysed the contents of the dart,' I say, trying to push past the awkwardness. 'It's something new. But you can relax; it was definitely me they were aiming for.'

He sits up straighter at that. 'How can you be so sure?'

'You don't want to know the details.'

'I think you should tell me anyway.'

I imagine what Drake would do if he knew that the dart had been inscribed with the logo of the Solis Invicti, if he knew that it was the Tertius himself who was after me. Then I remember Drake's alibi for David Grant's murder: he was in London with the Primus. I remember that he calls the Secundus 'Drew'.

Maybe he already knows exactly what's going on. Maybe he's in on the whole thing. But if he is, then why would Benedict shoot him?

Whatever the truth of the matter, I don't trust Drake enough to share the details with him.

'I can deal with it,' I say.

'How much trouble are you in?'

'No more than usual.'

'Oh, great,' he says sarcastically. 'That's really reassuring.'

'It's not your problem.'

'What if I want it to be?'

'You don't get to decide that, Drake,' I say, getting angry again. 'I do.'

'If it happens in Oxford, it's my problem. I'm the Baron.'

'And you're also the guy who attacked me last night, or have you already forgotten that?'

I don't realise I've been yelling until I hear the faint echo of my voice bouncing off the walls of the bare room.

'You don't trust me,' he says softly.

'Drake...'

This isn't what I wanted at all. I hate this strange, contrite version of him. He should be yelling back at me, telling me how stupid and reckless I am for getting mixed up in this.

Instead, he says, 'You don't have to stay.'

I have no intention of staying, or of forgiving him, but he needs to know the truth before I go. Despite everything, I need to tell him.

'About last night,' I say. 'Apparently it's something to do with the blood, combined with the scent mark. Tabitha said it's a kind of psychosis.'

'Is it?' he says scornfully, dismissing the diagnosis. 'How can it be when everything I felt – the greed, the lust, the jealousy – was as familiar to me as this shirt, as the back of my own hand?' He finally looks me in the eye. 'As familiar as your face, your scent. You unbalance me in ways I can't explain. Maybe it is psychosis, or maybe I shouldn't absolve myself so easily.' Then his gaze is trailing away from mine again, settling in the distance over my shoulder. 'I told you I wasn't a good man, Valentine. I meant it.'

I don't know what to say to that, so for a few minutes we just sit together in silence. It's uncomfortable. I'm usually riled up around him, angry and antagonistic even when he's unconscious, but there's something growing in the empty space between us now. There's a hopeless chaos to it, beyond both my control and his. I have no idea which way it will go.

I'm not sure I want to know.

'Well, this has been fun,' he says eventually, 'but isn't it about time you stormed out?'

I get to my feet.

'See you, Drake.'

He looks up at me with empty eyes. 'Goodbye, Valentine.'

I call Tabitha the moment I leave sick bay. I'm worried that she still won't be convinced, but when I tell her Drake agreed not to interfere, I can hear her smiling down the phone. She's going to try to swing by tonight, if she can get away.

That leaves me a lot of hours to occupy, so I go to the office. The others are waiting for me there.

'Cam told us what happened,' Naia says, looking at my neck as though she expects the bruises to be there still. 'Are you okay?'

'I'm Silver. Of course I'm okay.' I'm about as un-okay as I could be, but thankfully I'm damn good at pretending. 'Any more news on the dart?'

'It looks like the Solis Invicti are experimenting with new toys,' Cam says. 'According to the Secundus, these ones haven't been put into commission yet. They're still testing.'

'You called the *Secundus*?' I ask, incredulous.

'Actually,' Boyd says, 'he called us. Apparently he received a report about the dart.'

'From?'

'I don't know. He didn't say.'

'Didn't you ask?'

'No, I didn't,' Boyd says irritably. 'He's the Secundus. If you think you can get more out of him than I did, then why don't you call him back?'

We both know there's no point in that. If the Secundus had wanted us to know, then he would have told us.

'Okay,' I hold my hands up in surrender. 'Fine. He received an anonymous report. That's not suspicious at all.'

'I know,' Boyd says on a sigh. 'I'll be honest, Jacqueline. I'm worried.'

'You think they're all in on this?' Naia asks. 'Not just Benedict, but the Secundus too? The *Primus*?'

'But what is *this*?' Cam asks. 'What are they trying to do? Why have a fake turning ceremony at Windsor's? Why try to warn off Jack? Why shoot her with one of their darts and give us the evidence we need to link it to Felton?'

'Maybe the captain's right,' he says. 'Maybe it's all innocent and we're just not seeing the bigger picture.'

'You would say that,' Naia scoffs.

'Money and weapons,' I say, putting the pieces together as best I can. 'They get the money from the human buy-ins. Then they get the poison they need from Felton. That's why they're protecting him. That's why they're trying to scare me off.'

'But why do they need money and weapons?' Cam asks. 'They're the Solis Invicti. They already run the country.'

'Maybe that's not enough,' says Naia. 'Maybe they want more.'

'Or maybe there's something coming for them,' says Boyd, 'for all of us, and we have no idea it even exists.'

'But why wouldn't they tell us?' Naia asks.

Boyd has no answer for her.

'Defence or offence,' Cam says. 'Neither sounds good.'

We all ponder that for a moment.

'There's something else you should know, too,' Boyd says to me. 'Good news, I think. Benedict left this morning.'

'What? Why?'

'They found the London scab.'

'You're kidding me.'

'A guy called Charles Legrange. They had taken samples from all the blood bars in London and compared them against the DNA profile Ed found under Grant's fingernails, the one that matched the latest two London bodies. Eventually, they found the bar that served the correct mix of DNA. That's when the Secundus and the other Invicti left Oxford. They were staking it out when another tip came in, which told them exactly who they were looking for. They nabbed him last night.'

'Shit,' I say, because this guy hadn't even been on our radar. 'Well, who is he?'

Boyd shrugs. 'Just some Silver. He's not in the Creep Box. I guess he's been around a while because he wasn't hurting for money, but no one suspected him before the tip.'

'So, what?' I ask. 'He just got bored and decided to cause a spectacle?'

'Seems that way.'

I look at each of my team in turn, but they have no other explanation for me. Apparently it really is that straightforward.

'I don't get it,' I say.

'It gets weirder,' says Cam. 'He was at a meeting in London when Grant went missing, so he can't have been the one who killed him.'

'A meeting?'

'With the Secundus, the Tertius and a load of other London Silver.'

I narrow my eyes. 'What kind of meeting?'

'Social, apparently. Nothing sinister.'

'Or so they say.'

Boyd nods reluctantly. He knows as well as I do that we can't trust anything we hear from the Invicti at the moment.

'At least they're out of here,' Cam says. 'That's a bonus, right?'

'But we're no closer to solving the case,' says Naia. 'And suddenly all the alibis we have are less than worthless. We cleared a load of suspects on the basis of their alibis for the London murders, but now we know they're not connected. The only thing that matters is where they were when Grant died. We're going to have to look at them all over again.'

'Which will be pointless,' I say, 'since our theory is that the Invicti are the ones behind it anyway.'

'*Your* theory,' Boyd says.

'Whatever. David Grant died at the hands of a Silver just after he cleaned out his bank accounts. What if the Invicti killed him and took it, just like they killed all the men at Windsor's party?'

'Now, Jacqueline…' Boyd says.

He's going to tell me that we have no proof those men are even dead. He's going to remind me what the captain said, I know, but I can't stand to hear him being reasonable right now.

'No, Deputy. Just consider it. Please.'

'All right,' says Naia. 'But how are you going to prove it? And even if you do, who'll care?'

'*I* care!' I say, my hands curling into fists at my sides. It's the gesture of a frustrated toddler, but that's how I feel right now. I am utterly powerless.

'Jack,' Cam says gently, 'We need to be realistic. It might be time to throw in the towel on this one.'

I think of Felton's marionettes, then of Alicia Tresor and all the other women whom David Grant reduced to their broken parts in his notebook.

I don't want to let this go.

I'd be lying if I said I gave a toss about David Grant or any of the men whose deaths Benedict likely sanctioned in his Silver racket, but I do care about stopping the men who are enabled by their boys' club. Most of all, I care about the fall-out they created along the way, the women they tried to break.

'No,' I say.

'Look, I can probably give you until the end of the week,' Boyd says. 'Let me talk to the captain. Take the rest of the day off and get some sleep, everyone. Tomorrow we'll review what we have and try to find a way forward. All right?'

'I was supposed to be interviewing Halberd. That's what I was doing when I left last night, when–'

'I think that can wait until tomorrow,' Boyd says, which just goes to show how little faith he has that we'll be able to solve this one. He'd never normally leave a lead hanging.

I grind my teeth, but I say, 'All right.'

If it makes him happy, I'll pretend to comply. I'll wait a day, but I have no intention of letting this lie.

In the end, Tabitha can't get away for the evening, so I'm alone. I wait until everyone else has gone to bed before I creep back down to sick bay. I'm not sure what I was hoping to find, but Drake's bed is empty now, the covers changed and made ready for the next emergency.

My hand trails along the sheets, unwillingly recalling the touch of his fingers against mine, the brush of his lips against my throat. His teeth.

'He left this afternoon,' Cam says from the doorway, startling me.

'I thought you were asleep.'

'I know. I followed you down here.' He smiles. 'I had a hunch this was where you'd be going.'

'Ugh.' I sit down on the bed with my head in my hands. 'I don't know why I can't shake him.'

Cam sits down beside me.

'Yes, you do,' he says. 'He got under your skin, even before this haemapsychosis. He's been there for years. It's going to take time for you to get past this, if that's what you want.'

I look at him, surprised he'd even suggest there was another option. I expected he'd be baying for Drake's blood after last night, but apparently not.

'Of course I want to,' I say. 'After everything that's happened, after everything he's done, Cam, how could I do anything else?'

The words are like a refrain in my head: *He's one of them.*

Cam shrugs. 'You can make your own decisions, is all I'm saying. Whether anyone else thinks it's right or wrong, it's really none of their business. You don't have to justify your choices to me. You get to decide what's good for you.'

'I think we can agree that he isn't.'

Cam shrugs again and I groan.

'If you're looking for someone to tell you what to do,' he says, 'then you're talking to the wrong person. I'm done giving advice. You'll have to work it out for yourself.'

'You are so unhelpful.'

'I know.' He grins. For the first time in a while, the smile seems genuine.

'You're in a good mood,' I say.

'I wouldn't say *good. Better*, maybe. Ed and I talked.'

'Oh?' Thinking back to last night, they did seem as though they were on better terms. More relaxed around each other. Easier.

'Things didn't go the way I wanted them to,' he says, 'so I thought this was the end. But we've known each other for centuries. You don't just forget about a friendship like that, or blink it out of existence because you each want different things. I guess I hadn't been thinking about it in those terms. So, I don't know. We're not back to where we were, but we'll work it out. We love each other. That hasn't changed just because he wants to be with someone else.'

'Shit, Cam,' I murmur. It's all very sensible and mature of him, but to me the whole situation just sounds bleak as hell. 'I'm sorry.'

'You can't control how other people feel, any more than you can control how you feel yourself. It's not his fault. No one's to blame.'

'That's really how you feel?'

'Yes. No.' He laughs bitterly. 'I really want to destroy things, but my head knows it won't help even if my heart doesn't. I'm not cutting and running. It's worth salvaging something from what we had, but I can't do that if I'm too proud to try.'

He smiles. It's a dig at me, I can tell from the glint in his eye.

'What exactly are you getting at?' I ask.

'Uh-uh. No more advice, remember?'

'You're not fooling anyone,' I say. 'Your advice is just becoming more cryptic. It's too late for puzzles.'

'Come on, Jack,' he says, pulling me into a hug. 'You never listen to anyone's advice anyway, so what does it matter?'

'It doesn't,' I say, 'because I've already made my decision.'

'All right, then.' He stands and pulls me to my feet. 'Then here's another decision for you: ice cream. Chocolate chip cookie dough, or mint choc chip?'

We swing by the canteen then bundle into Cam's bed with our ice cream. Finally, after a couple of hours of binging Netflix, we fall into a restless, sugar-coma sleep.

34

I WAKE UP alone in Cam's bed with a post-it stuck on my forehead. It says, *Pancakes for breakfast. Meet you in the canteen.*

I drag myself through his shower, liberally helping myself to his Lush shower gel, then pull on yesterday's clothes and traipse downstairs. Yes, I could have gone next door to get clean clothes and yes, I could have used my own shower, but Cam's is nicer and I couldn't be arsed. Sometimes – not often, but sometimes – I miss the early-morning spring in my step that came along with Drake's mark.

I feel guilty for that thought the moment I check my phone and see a message from Tabitha.

Sorry I missed you yesterday. Dinner tonight?

I text back, *Definitely. Shall I cook for a change?*

Her reply comes instantly: *That sounds dangerous.*

I'd be insulted, but you're not wrong. Let's go out.

Looking forward to it, hen x

I'm smiling at my phone as I walk into the canteen. I continue smiling as I notice the absurd plate of pancakes Cam has set out for me at our table, but then I see the faces

342

of the rest of my team surrounding it and I realise these are consolation pancakes, not celebration pancakes.

There's bad news.

'What is it?' I say as I take my seat.

'I got a message from Ed,' Cam says. 'The poison dart? It's missing from his lab, together with all the reports and digital files relating to it.'

'What?'

'It gets worse.' He looks to Boyd.

'We've had orders from the captain,' Boyd says. 'There was no poison dart. The Baron was never hurt. He was never in sick bay. As far as we're concerned, Saturday night was incident-free.'

I gape at him.

'And Drake's all right with that?' I ask.

Boyd pushes away his plate, pancakes half-eaten. 'Apparently.'

'So there'll be no repercussions for what happened the night before last. None at all.'

'What did you expect?' Naia says with a bark of laughter. 'Did you think it would be fair?'

'He's the Baron!'

'And they're the Invicti. You're thinking like a human. That's not how we work, Jack. It's not about what's right or wrong. The Silver never had anything to do with justice. It's all about power, influence and how much you can get away with. I thought you liked that about us.'

'I preferred it when it wasn't aimed at me.'

'Yeah, well,' she shrugs. 'I advise you not to go throwing yourself into the crosshairs. You'll live longer.'

I can't help but hear the resemblance between her words and Benedict's. They sound like a threat. I'm still trying to unpick her meaning when Boyd looks up from his phone and starts handing out tasks.

'Here's the plan for the day,' he says. 'Cam and Jacqueline are going to interview Halberd, while Naia and I finish working through the financials.'

Naia groans. 'I thought we were done with those.'

'We were, but I managed to scrape a few more reports from CGC's systems yesterday.'

'Why? It's not like we're going to find anything new.'

'No, but we have to tie up all the loose ends before we close the case.'

'Close the case? You've solved it?' I ask through a mouthful of pancake. I want to feel guilty for flashing my half-chewed food at Naia, but I'm not happy with her right now and part of me hopes she might take the sight as a lesson. She doesn't even notice.

'No,' Boyd says. 'We haven't solved it. That's the point. We're not going to solve it.'

'Why?'

'You know why,' Naia says.

I seethe.

'Because the Invicti told us not to.' I want to shout, but I whisper it instead. We're not alone here. 'Did this come from the captain? I thought you were going to talk to her.'

'I tried, Jacqueline, but she's just doing what she's told,' Boyd says. 'Like we all should once in a while. This one's over. They've got Legrange. They don't care about Grant. We're to finish our assignments, review the evidence, then write up our reports.'

'Reports?' Naia groans again. 'Since when do we have to write reports?'

'The Invicti have asked for one.'

'I bet,' I say darkly. They'll want to know exactly how much we discovered so they can cover their arses.

'Be back by eleven,' Boyd says as he and Naia stand to clear their trays. 'We only have until the end of the day and we'll need time to get this right.'

From the tone of his voice, I know what he really means.

We need to get our stories straight.

When Cam and I knock on Tresor's door, it's Halberd who opens it. He clearly spends a lot of time "visiting" here.

'Mr Halberd,' I say. 'We have some more questions.'

He looks over his shoulder and into the house. 'I'm afraid Alicia isn't feeling well at the–'

'Not for Ms Tresor, Mr Halberd. Our questions are for you.'

There's a brief flicker of panic in his eyes before he stands aside so we can pass.

There's tea again. Lots of tea, which he serves in the beautiful tea service. And biscuits, those pink wafer things that taste like sugary cardboard. I decline.

'Are you a member of a gym at all?' I ask him once he stops buzzing around us and sits down.

'A gym?' He looks startled by the question, then he smiles as though he's trying to make us forget his first reaction. 'What use would I have for a gym? We're on tour half of the year and I get enough exercise running around backstage.'

'I only ask because of this.' I pull the video up on my phone and show it to him. 'This footage was taken last week at David Grant's gym, a number of days after he died. And this is you, isn't it?'

I pause the video at the moment when we see his face. The picture's a little fuzzy, but it's unmistakably him.

I'm watching him closely, so I know when he decides to fold.

'Okay,' he says under his breath. 'Okay. There are some things you need to know about David Grant.'

Cam and I exchange a glance, but we keep quiet. I'm not expecting Halberd to tell us anything we don't know already, but if we give him enough rope then he might just use it to hang himself.

'He wasn't a nice guy,' Halberd says softly. His eyes are on the corridor that leads upstairs, so I'm guessing he doesn't want Tresor to hear this. 'He was one of our biggest benefactors. When you've got someone who's pouring that much money into a company like ours, you don't say no to them. You might try to put them off from engaging with the company socially, or avoid them in indirect ways, but you don't just turn them away. We should have, though.' He looks down at his hands. 'That was my fault.'

'What happened, Mr Halberd?' Cam prompts.

'Nothing,' he says. 'And everything, I suppose. From what I can gather, David told Alicia he liked her and Alicia, she was angry. Really angry. She wanted us to cut him off, stop taking his donations, but we couldn't, not when he was bringing in new benefactors all the time. Then things changed. One day everything was fine, but the next we could barely get her to sing. It went on for weeks. She didn't want to perform anymore, not when he was there, and eventually she just wouldn't go on stage. We had to put in her understudy for the last performance he came to.'

Interesting.

'Finally,' he goes on, 'when she found out he was dead, she told me he'd been following her around, drawing her in his notebook.' He twists his mouth. 'Writing things. I just wanted to make sure the notebooks never got out. She was

346

so worried. So when she told me where he kept them, I decided to make sure they never saw the light of day. She had nothing to do with it. She didn't even know I was going to do it until it was already done.'

'How did you pull it off?' asks Cam.

He shrugs. 'Any job is easy when you have the right tools. I borrowed a gym pass then dismantled the locker next to Grant's from the inside. They're really not as secure as you'd think.'

'And the books?'

Halberd wets his lips nervously. 'I burned them. I didn't want her to see. She didn't need that. She's already been struggling…'

'Gabriella said she'd been ill,' I say.

'It's been a difficult few months, but she'll get on top again. She just needs a chance to put all this behind her and move on. I'm trying to help her with that. Please, you don't have to involve her, do you? If you need to charge me for theft or whatever then I'll come with you now, I won't make a fuss, but please don't get her mixed up in this.'

'We don't need to do that,' Cam says, making the decision for both of us. 'I doubt anyone would bother over some missing notebooks.'

Halberd lets out a breath, his eyes fixed on the floor as though he's trying to compose himself. When he looks up again, his eyes are shining with the ghost of tears.

'Thank you,' he says.

We finish our tea quickly, then he sees us to the door.

'If the contents of Grant's notebook are true,' Cam says as we walk back to the car, 'then Halberd doesn't know a fraction of what that man did to Alicia.'

'I know,' I say. 'And I believe every word he wrote. Don't you?'

'I do.' He sighs sadly. 'And that got us nowhere. Halberd's an opportunist, but he's not a murderer.'

'We knew that going in,' I say. 'Besides, we did learn one thing. We can guess where all Grant's money went: buying him access to Alicia Tresor.'

'Yeah,' Cam says, but he doesn't look convinced.

'What?'

'We know he donated a lot to the opera company, but it can't have been *that* much. Not so much that he utterly bankrupted himself *and* CGC. That was a separate pile of money, a fortune by all accounts, one he was gathering to pay off Benedict and turn Silver. So what happened to it?'

'You know what I'm going to say, Cam.'

'He gave it to Benedict?'

'He gave it to Benedict. Then Benedict killed him.'

'You're probably right,' he says, 'but you know it doesn't matter. We can't say that in the report. We're no further forward. This is over, Jack.'

'I know.' The words fracture in my throat.

I feel utterly powerless.

We spend the rest of the morning reviewing the evidence in my and Cam's office, trying to make sense of it all at the same time as we're deciding what to put in the report. It's anticlimactic, to say the least, because the only conclusions we can draw are exactly the ones we have to leave out.

Boyd crosses his arms over his chest and says, 'What do we know?'

'Grant was a creep,' says Naia. 'He cheated on his wife and stalked women from the opera, from the theatre, from the street–'

'All of them human, though,' Cam says. 'The murderer was Silver.'

'And we know Grant was trying to turn Silver himself,' I say. 'We know he was buddying up with Windsor's boys' club to do it, which means he must have been on Benedict's radar, because he was trying to stump up the cash buy-in.'

'That doesn't go in the report,' Naia chimes in.

'But we do need to mention that he was embezzling from CGC,' says Boyd. 'We identified nineteen different companies with names connected to the Silver or the Solis Invicti. Grant invested his clients' funds in those companies, or pretended to, then recorded them as loss-making and skimmed a chunk of cash off the top for himself. Cash that's now missing. As far as we can tell, none of the investors were Silver, so the embezzlement can't have been the motive.'

'But the "pound of flesh" must have some significance,' says Naia.

'Or it's just a coincidence,' says Cam. 'A weird fetish. Some killers like trophies.'

'I'm sticking with Shylock,' says Naia. 'Maybe someone else lent Grant money. Maybe he had a gambling problem. Can we get away with giving that as a possible motive, without even mentioning the company names?'

Boyd hums and hahs. 'They're a matter of record,' he says eventually.

'Then maybe we can say that Grant worked out the existence of the Silver and someone killed him to keep him quiet,' Naia says, getting creative. 'Maybe someone thought he was becoming a liability. I mean, it's not exactly subtle to name a company *Solis Invicti Holdings*, is it?'

'You want to pin this murder on the Seekers?' I ask incredulously. 'Exactly whose side are you on?'

'It doesn't have to be a Seeker,' Naia says.

'Then who?'

'In reality,' says Cam, 'it was probably someone involved in Windsor's racket.'

'Which means Benedict,' I say, 'which means the Solis Invicti are involved.'

'Or one of them is, at least.'

'None of which is going in the report,' says Boyd, but I've hit my stride now and I want to play it out.

'We know they could have got Felton to drug Grant for them,' I rush on. 'There's a connection there, even if he won't admit it. And if the murderer is one of the Solis Invicti, it makes sense that they would copycat the London killer. After all, they were the ones with the details of each incident. They even had access to the DNA. All they had to do was plant their existing DNA samples at the scene under David Grant's fingernails and they had an instant connection. It was just bad luck that Charles Legrange's alibi came out of the woodwork.'

'Jacqueline, stop,' says Boyd.

'It all fits together,' I protest.

'Look, I'm not denying that, but you know it doesn't matter. We have to focus on finishing the job we've been given.'

'Covering up for the Solis Invicti, you mean,' I say, bitterly.

'For chrissake,' Naia interrupts, 'covering up for the Silver is our entire job. How is this any different, Jack? Why have you suddenly got your knickers in a twist about the morals of what we do?'

'Why haven't you?' I say. 'Doesn't it piss you off that men like Grant, Felton and Windsor are being enabled by what we do?'

'Of course it does!' She sighs and sits down on the edge of the desk next to me, then says more gently, 'Of course it does, but you don't fight people like that by going headfirst at the Solis Invicti. That's not how you win. We have to play the game.'

She might be right, but I'm not sure I like it.

'I don't want to get so caught up that I forget we're only playing along,' I say.

'I get that. But you have to stop thinking in human terms. You don't fight a Silver battle over days or weeks or months. You fight it over years, decades, centuries even. It's not a sprint, Jack. If you try to rush it, or make too much of a nuisance of yourself before you have any power behind you, then you'll just get chewed up and spat out. Look what just happened with Benedict.'

I can tell that she's choosing her words carefully to avoid saying the words we can all hear regardless: *Look what happened to the Baron because you picked a fight with the Tertius. That's your fault.*

'I know,' I say.

'Let's focus on the embezzlement,' Boyd says. 'Take another look at the companies.'

'What's happening to them now?' Cam asks. 'Is someone shutting them down? If Grant was killed to bury the names, then it would make sense that someone would tidy that loose end away. They'd want to extract the money, wouldn't they? Maybe we can explain it that way.' He sounds tired, resigned.

'I remember seeing something in the records...' Boyd says.

Cam moves the papers around on his desk. 'Do you have them?'

'I think they're in my office,' says Boyd, heading across the hall to get them. Cam follows him out.

While they're gone, Naia and I sit in silence. We don't have much more to say to each other. After a while, Naia starts to fiddle with the detritus that has accumulated in my desk tidy. Well, it's not so much a desk tidy as an empty cardboard box that sits on my desk, but it's where I throw everything that has no immediate use.

She picks something up and squints at it.

'Is this the ticket from the opera you guys went to see? The one at the Playhouse?'

I check. 'Yeah. Same one Grant went to see the night before he died.'

'But it's not,' Naia says. 'You went to see La Traviata, right?'

'Sure,' I say, although I have no idea what the damned thing was called. I was too busy trying to ignore Killian Drake to concentrate on the show. Plus, it was all in Italian.

'That's not what was written on David Grant's ticket,' Naia says. 'I'm sure.'

I take her word for it, because Naia might be flaky and mercurial, but she's never wrong when it comes to the facts. I grab my laptop off my desk – my desktop power cord has been sacrificed to the rat gods once again – and fire up the browser, then search through the theatre listings for the previous week.

'You're right,' I say. 'It wasn't La Whatsit. It was something called Tosca.' I keep reading. 'Passion and jealousy... Blah blah... Tosca tries to save her lover from the police... Blah blah blah... She evades the police and ends up throwing herself from a parapet.'

Naia and I stare at each other.

'She what?'

I reread it, just to be sure. 'She kills the police guy then kills herself by jumping from a tower.'

'Holy shit.'

'It could just be a coincidence,' I say. 'It's not a perfect fit for what happened to Grant.'

But she's got her teeth into this anomaly and, truth be told, so have I. This is our last-ditch effort to solve the case before we have to write a fictional report and consign it to eternity.

'Can you find any more information about the show?' she asks. 'Maybe a programme? Is there anything to indicate whether this was a spur-of-the-moment change or not?'

I scroll through the Playhouse's website, clicking on the most recent listings, then I come across a cache of photos from the opera's dress rehearsals.

'Oh my god,' I say, clicking on a photo to enlarge it.

Naia leans over my shoulder. 'What?'

No.

My heart sinks. I don't want this to be the way our investigation ends, but the evidence is right there on the screen in front of me. Now that I think about it, it makes sense. The drawings in Grant's notebook, the lipstick on his mouth, and the way the opera company members are all so close.

I can finally put the pieces together. Even though the picture they make isn't one I want to see, there's no other way to arrange them.

I turn the laptop to face Naia. The photo on the screen is a wide-angle shot, showing the whole stage. The cast are standing upstage, while Gabriella stands at the front with her back to the camera, her arms flung out widely as she demonstrates some direction she wants followed. But I'm not looking at her arms. I'm looking at her long green skirt – some designer concoction of patterned satin – and the purple flowers that creep along its bottom edge.

The photo is dated April thirtieth, the day before the murder.

By the time Naia sees what I see, I've shoved the laptop into her hands and run out of the door.

35

I BRING CAM, because he charmed the pants off her last time and I know I can count on him to do it again.

'Gabriella,' he says, smiling when she opens the door.

We're at the Randolph again. The room behind her is a mess. There are clothes strewn everywhere, piled on the bed and draped over chairs. The opera is over and they're about to move on.

'Cameron, darling,' she says, throwing out her arms then kissing him on both cheeks. Her welcome is so exuberant that it's almost as though she's been expecting us. 'And darling Valentina.' She kisses me too. 'Come in, come in, do.'

She rushes into the room ahead of us, clearing the seating area so we can all sit down. Even though she's alone and clearly in the middle of packing, she's wearing full makeup and heels. It's so foreign to me that I feel like the two of us are from different species.

Then I remember why we're here and I think we might not be so different after all.

'So,' she says, settling into a chair opposite us. 'Can I get you some tea? Coffee?'

'No, thank you, Gabriella,' I say.

'Sorry about the mess. If you think this is bad, you should see the theatre. It's pandemonium.' She laughs.

We don't join in. That's when she understands why we've come.

She drops the smile. There's no point in pretending cheerfulness anymore.

'I suppose I shouldn't be surprised that you worked it out,' she says.

'Maybe not,' says Cam. 'After all, there are only so many Silver in Oxford, and only one with such a good reason to kill David Grant. You're protective of your company.'

She nods, slumping in her seat. It's the first time I've ever seen her discomposed.

'Does it matter that he deserved it?' she asks.

'It matters that you made it so public.'

'I know,' she sighs. 'It had to be.'

'You were sending a message.'

'There are plenty more men like David Grant, Silver and human. I suppose you found his notebook?'

'We did,' I say. 'We saw his last drawing.'

'He was a fool. He thought he could take whatever he liked. The worst thing about it is that he wasn't even wrong. He almost got away with it. There's a reason men like him prey on the young ones, the girls who don't feel powerful. They never told me, you know. I asked them. I asked, but they never said. Alicia never said. They thought I would protect him over them. Can you imagine?'

She curls in on herself as she speaks, leaning forward with her elbows on her knees, all bunched together as though she can shield herself from what has already happened.

'I didn't know,' she says. 'Even with all my senses, I was blind. Then I started catching his scent in places it didn't belong: around the stage door, at the hotel, on her clothes. And the bruises.'

She sits back and looks at her hands, turning her rings. They are loose on her fingers, hanging between the knuckles.

'Someone had to stop him.'

I couldn't agree more. No wonder I felt such commonality with her. If the decision were mine alone, then I would turn around and walk away from this case. We have our answer, and the answer is that justice caught up with David Grant.

But the decision isn't mine. The Seekers have been involved. The Invicti have been involved. David Grant's influential friends will exact their retribution if we don't do it for them. Ours will be kinder.

'Some men expect to receive everything they want,' Gabriella goes on, 'and David Grant was one of those men, but worse: when he had finally taken what he wanted, he balked at the consequences.'

Cam glances at me, then back to Gabriella. 'Consequences?'

'The kind you don't have to worry about, darling.' She smiles and reaches over to squeeze Cam's arm, but it's a sad smile, on the verge of cracking into tears. 'She was pregnant. When she refused to *take care of it*, as he said, he beat her until she lost the baby anyway. That's when I found her. The blood, you know. So I thought: an eye for an eye, as it were. Or a pound of flesh, to be specific.'

The comparison is crude enough to make me wince. Gabriella misinterprets it.

'He deserved everything he got, and more,' she says.

'I'm sure,' says Cam, 'but this isn't the same story Iain Halberd told us.'

'Well,' she looks down at her hands and fiddles with a ruby ring on her middle finger. 'Iain's a nice boy, but he's not very worldly. It's hard for him to think beyond his own experience. He'd never hurt Alicia, so while he knows something happened with David, he'd never imagine it had gone as far as it did. He has that kind of innocence. It's a good thing for Alicia. It's what she needs, for now.'

'But he's seen the books,' Cam says.

'Yes. That reminds me: you might as well have these now.'

She pulls a stack of moleskin notebooks from a box under a nearby chair. They're well-worn and familiar, held shut with bands and ribbons, as though they're precious keepsakes instead of the records of David Grant's abuse.

Cam takes them from her. 'We've been looking for these.'

'Well, now you've found them.'

'Halberd told us he'd burned them,' I say.

'I told him I had. Perhaps you should.'

Cam opens one up and flicks through the pages, just to make sure. From the way his brow furrows, I know they contain more of the same drawings we've already seen.

'How did you find out where they were, Gabriella?'

She tips her head from side to side, apparently deciding how much she should tell us.

'An acquaintance of mine uses the same gym,' she says finally. Then she looks at me and says, 'A mutual acquaintance,' and I know she means Drake. 'That acquaintance told me that David sometimes kept precious items in his locker. I had a suspicion that the books would be among them.'

'And what other precious items were in there before you cleaned it out?' I ask.

Gabriella looks me dead in the eye and I know my own suspicions are correct.

'We took only the notebooks,' she says firmly, then adds, 'and what was owed to Alicia.'

So that's what had happened to Grant's fortune. It never made its way into Benedict's pockets. It was stolen from his locker and invested in a grand house with large sash windows off South Parade.

Mystery solved.

We don't have to subdue Gabriella. Usually, we drain our Silver prisoners into compliance and lock them up until the Baron is ready to pass judgement on them, but Gabriella doesn't fight us. She climbs into the back of the car without protest and lets us drive her up to Summertown.

Her submission makes me feel even worse than I already do.

I drive while Cam calls Drake – I still have his number blocked and I don't want to give him ideas – but there's no avoiding him when we pull up to the house. He's waiting on his doorstep with one goon on either side of him, but he soon dismisses them when he realises that Gabriella hasn't been restrained.

Cam helps Gabriella out of the car while I go to meet Drake.

'Jack,' he greets me quietly.

'Drake.'

We look at each other for a few beats.

'So,' he says, 'this is how it ends?'

I have a feeling he's not just talking about the investigation.

'I guess it is.'

His eyes search mine for a moment that seems to stretch into eternity, then he stands aside to usher us all inside. Cam and Gabriella have caught up with us.

Her trial is quick.

She admits everything.

When we take her into the basement to enact her punishment, she walks to it willingly, with her head held high.

'What's the news?' says Naia when we return to the college.

She and Boyd are hanging out in the common room. Surprisingly, Ed is with them. Even more surprisingly, he and Cam smile when they see each other and exchange a fist-bump that makes them both look like dweebs. Things are starting to get back to normal, then.

Naia is lying along one of the sofas with her ankles crossed over its arm, while Boyd sits in an armchair and sips from a bottle of blood. It's clear that for them, this case is done and dusted.

'Did they lock her up?' Naia asks.

'He boxed her,' says Cam. 'One year.'

It's about the worst punishment we have. The Silver is drained of every drop of their blood, then sealed in a crate that's locked away underground until their sentence is up. Some people say it's the origin of the whole vampires-sleeping-in-coffins myth, but the difference is that the entombed Silver isn't at rest. Instead, they're suspended in a half-dead state, in pain all the time, but too weak to do anything to free themselves. Some of the Silver come out completely mad. Some don't come out at all.

'Fuuuuck,' says Naia.

'She'll get through it,' I say, because I have to believe that. I remember how regally she walked into the crate and I tell myself she'll walk out in exactly the same way. I can't imagine anything else.

'Well, at least it's over, and it was nothing to do with the Invicti,' Naia says triumphantly.

'Wasn't it?' I ask.

I think of all the loose ends still unresolved: Benedict at Windsor's party, apparently killing humans for their money; the missing man in Derbyshire, whose case was taken from Ellie and Quentin by the Invicti; the money in the suspiciously-named companies; and, finally, the dart in Drake's neck, meant for me.

Perhaps those things had nothing to do with David Grant's death, but one way or another our investigation brought them out into the light when the Invicti would have preferred they remained hidden. Benedict is up to something, with or without the Primus's approval. I still mean to find out what that is.

'You need to get past this, Jacqueline,' Boyd says, taking a swig from his bottle. 'It was all a misunderstanding, like the captain said. She spoke to the Primus.'

'The Primus?' I'm surprised, because although the captain is undoubtedly a high-ranking member of our society, the idea of her speaking directly to the Primus is a little overwhelming. He usually deals with the Seekers through the Secundus.

'Special audience, apparently,' Naia says. 'Big to-do.'

'The captain told us when we went to update her about Gabriella,' Boyd says. 'You can stop worrying about Benedict. The scene you saw at Windsor's party was exactly what she suggested it was: a sting.'

'Really,' I say flatly.

'Really. Someone – they're not sure who – blabbed to a human about Windsor's party. A whole group of them turned up and then it was too late. The cat was out of the bag. The Invicti were able to convince some of the humans that it was a fake coven, a role-playing game, but for the others there was no choice. The Invicti had to dispose of them. But it was only a few locals. The Invicti were able to make it look natural.'

'Nice of them to do our jobs for us,' Naia says.

Cam and I exchange glances, and I know he's remembering the missing man from Derbyshire. He wasn't a last-minute party crasher. He was someone who'd been planning and saving for a long time. So, for that matter, was David Grant. Trying to turn Silver wasn't what killed him in the end, but I'm sure it would have eventually if Gabriella hadn't got to him first.

But that's not the only reason the story doesn't fit the facts. I'm remembering the night of Windsor's party too, specifically what Mainwaring and Harrison said to Drake: *They're all expected to buy their entrance. Can't let just anyone become immortal.* As though Windsor's boys' club is the gatekeeper. Whatever Benedict did with the candidates afterwards – and I'm pretty certain now that he killed every single one – the other Silver at the party genuinely believed the humans were going to be turned.

There's no way to fit that into the narrative we're being told now.

'And check this out,' Naia says, breaking into my thoughts. She passes me an envelope. It's addressed to me, but it's already been opened.

'Seriously?' I ask her, flourishing the ripped seal.

She shrugs. 'No secrets amongst Seekers.'

The paper stock is heavy and layered, and there's an embossed watermark on the back of the envelope. It's the Solis Invicti symbol, the symbol of Solomon.

'It's from him?' I ask, pulling out the paper inside.

'Read it,' says Naia. 'Out loud.'

'*Dear Ms Valentine,*' I read. '*Please accept my personal apology for the incidents of Saturday night. I am informed by my guard that they were conducting an impromptu weapons test and, inadvertently, there was an error in the trajectory that resulted in your endangerment.*' I snort derisively. 'Error, my arse.'

'Read the rest,' Ed says.

'*I have written to Baron Drake separately to apologise for the harm that he suffered and to tender appropriate compensation for his inconvenience. Your continued efforts for the Seekers are appreciated. Yours sincerely,* then there's a squiggle that I guess is his signature, because it says *Primus* underneath.'

'That's pretty cool,' Cam says.

'What?' I ask. 'This incredibly dry excuse for an apology? He sounds like a robot that was born in the eighteenth century.'

'B.C., maybe,' Boyd says.

'You've had a letter from the Primus,' Cam says. 'How are you not excited about that? He actually knows who you are. He said he appreciated your efforts. I'd give anything for that. You're basically a shoe-in for the Invicti with that kind of praise from the Primus.'

I smile, trying to react how the others expect me to, but I'm fixating on the precise words of the letter.

I am informed by my guard.

I have a pretty good idea whom he means by that: Benedict. The Primus is taking his word for what happened that night, which is worth nothing as far as I'm concerned. But it does suggest that the Primus himself isn't complicit. If he was, would he really ask for an explanation from Benedict? Would he bother to write me a letter like this? I don't know.

The only thing I'm certain of is that, for me at least, this isn't over.

36

'SO IT WAS Gabriella all along?' Tabitha asks at dinner that night.

She seems even more upset about it than I am. We both liked Gabriella, but it was Tabitha who'd really bonded with her. I wonder now whether that whole evening with L'Escalier was just a ploy to keep her above my suspicion. If so, it worked, right up until the end.

'She was clever,' I say as I remember. 'She played us like a violin.'

Tabitha smiles at me indulgently. 'Surely not.'

'You want to hear it?'

'Tell me.'

We're back at the Italian where we had our first date. Tabitha suggested it, saying it would be symbolic, like a fresh start. Secretly, I think she was just craving pasta, but I don't mind. It's quiet tonight. Quiet enough that I can tell Tabitha the truth without worrying about being overheard.

'Gabriella invited him for a drink after the performance. Backstage, intimate, because that was what he liked. Unfortunately, that invitation didn't stop him from paying one last visit to Alicia on his way, hence the lipstick.

Gabriella was able to stop it at a kiss, but I guess that put the fire in her veins for what came next. She roofied him and hooked him up to a drip so he'd stay out, but alive, while she secured her alibi.'

'The Baron, right?' Tabitha says.

She knows some of this already from the files she had access to while she was performing the post mortem, but this is the question I was hoping she wouldn't ask. We've avoided Drake's name so carefully all evening that I'm loathe to drop it into the middle of the table now, just when things are going so well.

'That's right,' I say, moving past it. 'The only problem was, he didn't show. So her alibi wasn't quite as water-tight as she wanted it to be. Not that it mattered, because after Grant's embezzlement and his connection to the Silver came out, we never looked at her again. There were too many other suspects, all of whom were much less likeable.'

Tabitha sighs. 'I wish it hadn't been her.'

'She had good reason for what she did. I can understand it.'

'Me too, hen.' Tabitha takes a gulp of her wine. 'Me too. Anyway, go on.'

'So, once she'd sat in the dining room at the Randolph for a bit, making sure she was seen on her own, she crept out of her hotel window and went back to the Playhouse to work on his body.'

'I guess she drained the blood so she wouldn't make a mess when she came to extract his organs. Did you ever find them, by the way?'

'His organs?' I ask, putting down the mouthful of lasagne I had carefully loaded onto my fork.

'Yes. Did they ever show up?'

'Not yet.'

'Hmm,' Tabitha says, twirling her spaghetti. The look on her face is worrying me.

'What?' I ask.

'I don't know. It's just, well. If it were me, and I were that angry...'

'Do I want to know how you're going to finish this sentence?'

'Well,' she says reasonably, 'it's not unknown for people to eat the organs of their vanquished foes. It's a way of taking their power into yourself, or of expressing your disdain for their humanity. You know, in the fifth century in Italy–'

'Do we have to talk about this while we're eating Italian?'

She grins devilishly and turns back to her food. 'I had no idea you were so squeamish.'

'And I had no idea you were so twisted.'

'Yes, you did.'

'Okay, fine, I did.' It's one of the things I like most about her. Even if I find it a tiny bit disturbing. 'But anyway, after she'd done whatever she did with the pound of David Grant's flesh, she waited for the choir to begin singing, then chucked his body off the tower. Which is where we were unlucky: firstly, because his notebook slipped down the back of the radiator just before he fell, and secondly, because Gabriella is ridiculously quick on her feet, even for the Silver. She was gone without a trace before we'd even started looking for her. If Black Mary hadn't happened to see the flash of her skirt and if I hadn't happened to see the photo of her wearing that skirt on the Playhouse website, then we might never have found the truth.'

'There's just one thing I don't understand,' Tabitha says.

'What's that?'

'If all this is true – and I'm not saying it isn't, much though I might wish things were otherwise – then how do you explain the DNA results? How did the DNA from under Grant's fingernails match up with the London profiles?'

'She's clever, Tabs.' I sigh and take a long drink. 'She worked out who the London scab was weeks ago, long before the Invicti were anywhere near solving the case. I guess she has contacts they don't. She wouldn't give us the details, but someone mentioned Legrange to her, and she followed it up.'

'But why?'

'She found out about Alicia while they were still in London preparing for the opera tour, and she saw an opportunity. If she could find the scab, then she could make an example of Grant and frame the scab for his murder. She planned it all beautifully. She wanted to use the London murders to do some good.'

'As she saw it.'

'Right,' I say, pretending I don't agree with what Gabriella did. I don't know why I bother; I'm sure Tabitha sees right through me. I don't think she minds.

'Gabriella knew she'd need something to link Legrange to Grant's death,' I go on, 'so she followed Legrange to his favourite blood bar and visited the same people he drank from. On the night before the murder, she drank the blood she'd saved from them so that when Grant scratched her skin, it was loaded with the donors' DNA, the same donors who'd fed Legrange.'

'And the anonymous tip was her.'

'Yes. Both of them were. It turns out that she didn't just tell the Invicti what event he was targeting next, she told them his name and where to find him. Apparently she didn't have much faith that they'd manage to put it together on their own. I can't say I blame her for that.'

'Jack...'

This time, her disapproval is real. She'll agree that Gabriella might have done the right thing, but she won't hear me say a word against the Invicti. Either it's because she works for them and doesn't think they're that bad, or she thinks it's dangerous for me to voice criticisms against them. I wish I knew which.

I haven't told Tabitha about the case I'm building against Benedict. I can't, not when I'm unsure of her loyalties. It wouldn't be fair to her or safe for me, so she's having the official version of the story, minus Benedict and the Solis Invicti.

'Well, anyway,' I say, 'the only thing she couldn't anticipate was that Legrange would have an alibi, and a solid one at that.'

'Bad luck,' she says.

'Bad luck,' I agree.

'And *Tosca*? You mentioned they changed the opera.'

'She was making a statement,' I say. 'She saw it as a monument of sorts. His last performance, in tribute to Alicia.'

We finish our meal in silence, each lost in our own thoughts until the waiter comes and asks if we'd like another bottle of wine. I'm tempted to say yes – I generally do when it comes to alcohol – but Tabitha refuses. She has to be back in London in the morning to help tie up the loose ends on the Legrange reports. The Invicti really do care a lot about their records.

'What'll happen to Gabriella now?' Tabitha asks.

'She was sentenced this afternoon,' I say. 'Boxed, one year.'

The colour drains from Tabitha's face.

'Boxed?' she says.

'I know it seems harsh,' I say, 'but it should have been a decade. You know that. Legrange is getting half a century.'

Tabitha looks as though her heart is breaking.

'A whole year?' she asks me. 'But she didn't do anything wrong. Not really.'

I wish she were right, but we both know that's not how the Seekers work.

'She broke the cardinal rule, Tabs. She risked exposing us by killing Grant in such a flamboyant way.'

'But there was no harm done. And it's Gabriella. The Primus is her friend, isn't he? And the Baron. How could he do that to her?'

'You know he had to.'

'So you're taking his side? Couldn't you have tried to talk him round?'

'Tabitha, please,' I say, reaching across the table for her hand. 'I don't have that kind of power over him.'

'Don't you?'

I look her dead in the eye. 'No.'

Her face falls, then she squeezes my hand. 'I'm sorry. It's just that if I were in her position, if David Grant had done that to someone I loved...' She lets out a long breath. 'I think I'd do the same.'

'I know you would. You threatened to autopsy me, and I'm your girlfriend.'

'You deserved it.'

'I did,' I agree.

Then she looks up at me through her eyelashes and says, 'You're my girlfriend?'

I realise that we've never discussed it, not once. 'I'm sorry,' I say. 'Is it too soon? Do you not want me to be?'

'No,' she says, smiling to herself. 'It suits me down to the ground, as long as I'm yours too.'

'Yes, please,' I smile back at her.

'All right, then.'

I try not to grin, because it feels inappropriate when we were only just talking about Gabriella being boxed, but I'm struggling to tamp down my happiness.

'We're really going to try it?' I ask. 'You're sure?'

She leans over the table and takes my hand. 'If you want to, then I'm with you, hen.'

When it's time for her to go home, I kiss her goodnight at the crossroads under Carfax Tower. This time I don't have to reach for it; the mark is already waiting. We mark each other right there, in the centre of Oxford, as the bells toll above us.

I'm ready for bed when I get back to my rooms, but I wake up quickly when I find that an envelope has been slipped under my door. It's small and inoffensive, but I'm on my guard because I can smell the familiar scent on it and I know whose fingers touched it last.

Drake.

Normally, letters for me would be left at the lodge in my pigeon hole, but apparently that wasn't good enough for him. He's been here, right outside my room. He knows exactly where I live.

Is this a threat?

I close the door behind me before I open the envelope. It's heavy for its size and about quarter of an inch thick. Inside is a stack of photos; proper, old-school photos, printed on real photograph paper. It takes me a while to realise what the photos are showing me, but when I do, I have to sit down.

The first has been taken through one of the college windows. It's dark outside, but the light from inside streams out from a wide gap in the curtains. It frames Benedict, who's facing the camera, and the back of a woman in a suit. In the next photo, she's side-on, and in the third I can see her whole face.

It's Captain Langford. She's laughing.

The next series of photos has been taken in the daytime, in University Parks. Benedict and the captain walk side by side, their heads close together as they talk. In one photo, their hands almost touch, as though they're passing something between them. The final photo is a close up of their hands. I can just see the glint of a glass tube, the flecks of engraving between the captain's fingers.

It's one of the poison darts.

'Fuck!' I scream out loud, throwing the photos on the floor. 'Fuck, fuck, fuck.'

The captain's in on it. Whatever it is that Benedict is trying to do in London with the Solis Invicti, or here in Oxford with Felton, or out in Aston with Windsor, the captain is part of the plan. Why else would she have one of the darts? Why else would she be sneaking off for secret meetings with Benedict?

I revisit every moment in this case where I raised my concerns about the Invicti, remembering how she brushed them aside, how she suggested that everything Benedict had done at Windsor's was part of some elaborate sting operation, and how it had been the captain who eventually confirmed that to my team.

Had she even spoken to the Primus? Had he even been the author of the letter I received, or had she made the whole thing up?

I feel sick.

I drop my head down between my knees, trying to stop the rolling in my stomach and the flashing darkness behind my eyelids.

If I can't trust the captain, then who can I trust? Boyd? Naia? Cam? Or even Tabitha?

As I blink away my spotty vision, my gaze falls on the photos on the floor and I notice something I missed. The photos weren't the only thing in the envelope. Behind the last one is a note, written on a slip of cream card in perfect cursive.

Tell no one, it says.
Burn these.
And be careful. Please.
I'm with you.
Killian

37

A COUPLE OF days later, I go to see Naia with a can of petrol in my hand. It's the first thing she looks at when she answers the door, and she knows exactly why I'm carrying it. It's four in the morning, which probably gives her a clue.

'Are you coming?' I ask her, shaking the can so she can hear the fluid sloshing around inside.

She rubs the sleep from her eyes. Someone is stirring in the bed behind her.

'Are you insane?' she whispers.

'Nope, just highly motivated. Are you coming or not?'

She's going to say no. Despite everything we saw in that attic room, despite everything we've learned during the course of this investigation, she's going to say no. She's going to choose the Solis Invicti over all the girls Felton has yet to assault.

She says, 'No.'

I knew it was coming, but I'm still surprised. And angry. Extremely fucking angry. She was the one who led the charge last time. She was the one who kicked his head in and set him on fire. She knows he's a creep, but she's going to let him carry on regardless, all because of a promotion she might never even get. Or maybe she's been working with the Invicti all along.

She has always been a hypocrite.

But I don't say any of this. Instead, I just turn and walk away down the dimly-lit corridor. I hear Naia's door shut behind me as I reach the stairs. She's locked herself back inside. It feels like a betrayal, because we both know this is necessary. Someone has to stop Felton, but she knows I'll take care of it with or without her. She's happy to keep her hands clean.

I, on the other hand, have nothing to lose. This might not be the sensible thing to do. It might not be the careful thing to do, particularly with the threat of Benedict looming at the back of my mind, but that won't stop me.

I will do what needs to be done.

It doesn't take long to get to Iffley Road. I could have walked the distance, but the petrol can would have made me conspicuous. Instead, I take one of the Seeker cars and park it on a side street.

It's quiet. This is about the only time of day you would find Oxford sleeping, in the lull between late-night drinkers and early-morning runners. I've seen them cross each other's paths more than once during my decades in this city, but it's a cold Tuesday morning and my only company is the birds.

I wouldn't have thought it possible in such a short period of time, but the drifts of fag ends in the front garden are discernibly deeper than they were on my last visit to this tumbledown chemistry lab. The post piled up behind the front door is deeper too, though this time the house is not open. I have to smash the doorjamb to get in.

It's not enough to wake Felton.

Creeping my way up to the attic room, I find him in his usual spot beneath the eaves, curled up asleep on his grubby mattress. Either that, or he's passed out under the influence of one of his concoctions. A video plays on the iPad that rests forgotten in his lap. It's one of his own, a puppet show. He must have resorted to reliving old memories, because there's no one else in the attic now but the two of us. I don't think he'd keep his captives anywhere else, but I search the rest of the house anyway, just to make sure. When I come back up to the attic, I spill the petrol behind me as I go. The smell of it makes me feel alive.

I had planned to do this more subtly. I had planned to tamper with Felton's drugs. That way, one of his victims would have remembered being abducted and we could have caught Felton in a legitimate scab violation. He would have been found guilty of exposing the existence of the Silver to a human. Punishment would have followed and justice would have been served. One human's trauma seemed like a small price to pay to save countless others.

But how can I trust the system, with all that I know now? Benedict would have got Felton out of the charges somehow. Nothing would have changed. Felton would have carried on making marionettes. The only thing that will change his behaviour is a threat he can't ignore.

This is personal.

I soak the boards at the foot of Felton's mattress and leave the jerrycan there. Then I pull the box of matches from my pocket and strike one to life with a satisfying rasp of sandpaper.

This is the point at which I make a choice. This is when I decide whether I'll follow the current or race against it instead. I can do what Naia suggests and just stick with the status quo, or I can try to get to the bottom of this conspiracy and put it to bed.

It's an easy decision to make. I've never been one to take the easy way out.

I toss the match.

I will never absolve Windsor's boys' club. I will never kowtow to Benedict's threats. I will never be one of the Solis Invicti.

I would rather watch them burn.

Thank you so much for reading this book. I really hope you enjoyed it, and I appreciate you taking a chance on an indie author. If you'd like to read more from me, then I have suggestions!

***

Join my Readers' Club and receive a FREE short story!

www.josiejaffrey.com/subscribe

You'll also receive my monthly newsletter, including exclusive news, giveaways and offers.

***

If you enjoyed *May Day*, why not read *Killian's Dead*? It's the short story prequel to the *Seekers* series, following Jack as she first discovers the Silver.

***

Support me on Patreon!

My patrons receive draft chapters and a new short story every month, together with other exciting perks for higher-level patrons.

www.patreon.com/josiejaffrey

***

Please leave a review!

If you enjoyed *May Day*, I'd be so grateful if you would please review it. Book reviews can make a huge difference to the success of a novel, particularly those of self-published authors like me. If you have time to leave a review, even if it's just a sentence or two, then I'd really appreciate it.

***

Get in touch!

I love hearing from readers! If you'd like to contact me, you can do that through my website, Twitter, Facebook or Instagram.

Acknowledgements

Thanks to Vicky for beta-reading, moral support and everything else she does behind the scenes as my publicist.

Thanks to Asha for proof-reading and beta-reading everything, and for all the admin she does as my author assistant, with endless positivity and cat photos.

Thanks to my Patreon supporters Caine, Careta, Dee, Justine and Oz, without whose support I might never have collected the motivation to finish this novel.

And above all, thanks to Max, as always.

CONTENT WARNINGS

General warning for violence/murder.

General warning for blood/gore, including blood drinking, description of injuries, dead bodies, forensic investigation, autopsy.

Brief mention of suicide.

Blood drinking as sexual/pleasurable behaviour.

Some swearing (up to and including 'fuck').

Use of 'date rape' drugs including rohypnol, in non-sexual context.

Predatory sexual behaviour discussed on-page but not seen, including stalking, sexual assault and rape, physical abuse of women for sexual pleasure. Use/abuse of prostitutes mentioned.

Misogyny from side characters.

Brief mention of miscarriage.

Milton Keynes UK
Ingram Content Group UK Ltd.
UKHW041907091023
430255UK00003B/163